STRONG AS STEEL

OTHER BOOKS BY JON LAND

*Published by Forge Books

Strong
as
Steel

A CAITLIN STRONG NOVEL

Jon Land

A Tom Doherty Associates Book
New York

This is a work of fiction. All of the characters, organizations, and events portrayed in this novel are either products of the author's imagination or are used fictitiously.

A Forge Book
Published by Tom Doherty Associates
175 Fifth Avenue
New York, NY 10010

www.tor-forge.com

Forge® is a registered trademark of Macmillan Publishing Group, LLC.

Library of Congress Cataloging-in-Publication Data

Names: Land, Jon, author. | Land, Jon. Caitlin Strong novel.
Title: Strong as steel / Jon Land.
Description: First Edition. | New York : Forge Book, 2019. | Series: Caitlin
    Strong novel | "A Tom Doherty Associates Book."
Identifiers: LCCN 2018048355| ISBN 9780765384676 (hardcover) | ISBN
    9780765384690 (ebook)
Subjects: LCSH: Texas Rangers—Fiction. | GSAFD: Suspense fiction. | Suspense
    fiction.
Classification: LCC PS3562.A469 S75 2019 | DDC 813/.54—dc23
LC record available at https://lccn.loc.gov/2018048355

Our books may be purchased in bulk for promotional, educational, or business use. Please contact your local bookseller or the Macmillan Corporate and Premium Sales Department at 1-800-221-7945, extension 5442, or by email at MacmillanSpecialMarkets@macmillan.com.

First Edition: April 2019

Printed in the United States of America

0 9 8 7 6 5 4 3 2 1

For the production managers, copyeditors, editorial assistants, delivery drivers, jobbers, wholesalers, stockroom workers, printers, cover designers, warehouse staffers, interns, mailroom personnel, and more.

The unsung heroes of the publishing business.

A strong woman is a woman determined to do something
others are determined not be done.

—MARGE PIERCY

Strong as Steel

PROLOGUE

O God, whose end is justice,
Whose strength is all our stay,
Be near and bless my mission
As I go forth today.

Let wisdom guide my actions,
Let courage fill my heart,
And help me, Lord, in every hour
To do a Ranger's part.

Protect when danger threatens,
Sustain when trails are rough,
Help me to keep my standard high
And smile at each rebuff.

When night comes down upon me,
I pray thee, Lord, be nigh,
Whither on lonely scout
Or camped under the Texas sky.

Keep me, O God, in life
And when my days shall end,
Forgive my sins and take me in,
For Jesus' sake, Amen.

—*Texas Ranger's Prayer*
Captain Pierre Bernard Hill
Chaplin of the Texas Rangers

PORT OF ORDU, TURKEY; 1959

The *liman reisi* of the Port of Ordu watched the freighter crest the currents, alerted to its presence by the captain of a passing ship who reported it seemed to be floundering and he couldn't see anyone at their posts on the bridge. As far as the *liman risi* could tell, the freighter was gaining speed instead of reducing it as the ship approached its apportioned pier. He stopped short of sounding the alarm because he recognized her as the *Dolunay*, captained by Aykan Talu, one of the most experienced in the region. No doubt Talu had yet to slow his engines to better negotiate the unusually stiff currents a larger freighter would have sliced through in effortless fashion.

When he was still picking up speed a quarter mile out, though, the harbormaster blew the klaxon three times, paused, and then blew it three more. Within seconds, a pair of Turkish Coastal Patrol boats were speeding into this channel of the Black Sea, drawing close enough to the *Dolunay* to signal her to hold back and throttle down. Not exactly routine, but not necessarily cause for alarm, either, with an experienced captain like Talu at the helm.

Until the first patrol boat to reach the *Dolunay* tried to hail the ship.

"She's not responding," the captain reported, struggling not to sound panicked. "Repeat, she's not responding. No sight of crew members on deck, no evidence of—"

The captain's voice cut off so abruptly that the harbormaster thought it must be some kind of malfunction.

"Coastal Patrol," he said into his walkie-talkie, held now in a hand that had gone clammy, "please repeat. I say again, Coastal Patrol, please repeat."

But there was nothing to repeat. What the *liman reisi* of the Port of Ordu heard next from the captain were words spoken for the first time.

"I see bodies! The deck is littered with them!"

The harbormaster wanted to ask Coastal Patrol to repeat that, but there was no need. He'd heard the words clearly enough, and there was no mistaking their portent.

"She's not responding, not slowing! They must all be dead, the entire crew. We need a tug! We need a tug fast!"

But Coastal Patrol knew as well as the harbormaster that no tug could reach the *Dolunay* in time to turn her, not when she was this close to port and, actually, was gaining speed.

"Do you copy?" the captain demanded through the walkie-talkie's speaker. "Repeat, do you copy?"

The *liman reisi* of the Port of Ordu did, but he had never felt more helpless, enduring the next agonizing moments before the freighter and all her tonnage slammed into the pier that had been evacuated by his advance warning. The old floating wood system folded up like playing cards, spewing shards and splinters in all directions. Momentum swung the *Dolunay* to starboard, obliterating rows of smaller fishing vessels that had just returned from the sea and showering the docks with their catch.

The repeated impacts seemed on the verge of toppling the freighter over, but she had maintained ballast to keep her upright. The harbormaster watched with breath held as something else pitched over the *Dolunay*'s decks to join the dead fish: bodies, at least a dozen of them, dropping like anchors into the sea and shoved toward land by the ship's forward momentum.

The *liman reisi* had heard of such seafaring legends before, ghost ships roaming the seas and somehow finding themselves back to some port. But this was no legend, no ghost ship.

The *Dolunay* barreled on, its nose plowing through both the cushioned and the concrete safety barriers before claiming the land for its own.

"*The entire crew is dead!*" the harbormaster heard in his head, unsure whether it was through the walkie-talkie or the product of his own terrified thoughts. "*They're all dead!*"

MEXICO CITY, MEXICO; 1964

It sounded like firecrackers.

Halfway up the church aisle, beneath the dim spill of light, that's what the little girl thought.

Firecrackers...

It was a wedding, after all, her own parents' wedding. A time to celebrate, and people celebrated with firecrackers all the time. The little girl kept right on walking, holding tight to the cushion bearing the ring that her father would place over her mother's finger, just as they'd rehearsed. He imagined this was the way it was for all parents who didn't get married until they had a child, so that child could tote the ring up the aisle.

The little girl clung to the small cushion with all her strength to avoid dropping it; her father would be very disappointed if she dropped it, and Alejandro Diaz was a very scary man when he was angry. But she had the sense that many of the men who worked for her father were scared of him all the time, not knowing Alejandro Diaz as the man still fond of singing his daughter to sleep at night.

So, even when the well-dressed lot on both sides of the center aisle began to scream and run, even when some of them began to fall and the firecrackers continued to sound, the little girl kept trudging up the aisle, her face squeezed tight in determination.

Look at me, Papa! Look at me!

But Alejandro Diaz couldn't look at her, because he was looking at her mother, who was clutched in his arms, something they hadn't rehearsed. Her mother's brilliant white dress was speckled with red.

Blood. Leaking out of her right there on the church altar, beneath Jesus Himself suspended from a cross.

The little girl knew Jesus was a good man, the son of God Himself, so how could He let something like this happen?

She was still tightly clutching the cushion, a fluffy white pillow really, when the next crackle of firecrackers blew red, chalky mist out of her father's ear. Alejandro Diaz jerked to that side, as if yanked by a rope. Then his head snapped sideways at the next crackle, which blew him backward through a funnel of his own blood.

The little girl thought she'd dropped the cushion and let the ring fall, but when she looked down she was still holding it before her, as people she didn't know rushed up and down the aisle screaming.

Crack, crack, crack!

Their motions seemed to reflect the sound, almost like they were dancing to its staccato music. They had rehearsed the dancing part, too, with the little girl's shiny shoes perched atop her father's boots. But she wasn't going to be dancing with him now.

She wasn't going to be dancing with him ever.

The firecrackers continued to *pop, pop, pop*. The wedding guests continued to run and scream and bleed, a few coughing blood from their mouths, while others were doubled over in the pews, looking like they were sleeping. The little girl stood suspended amid the carnage, as if she weren't there at all.

Her mother wasn't moving.

Her father wasn't moving.

The little girl thought he was looking at her, and she wanted to hold up the cushion for him to see that she hadn't dropped the ring. But his eyes stayed open, didn't close, just beneath the feet of the man named Jesus Christ, son of God, who looked down upon the scene with despair stretched over His features.

The little girl wanted to scream, wanted to run, wanted to cry. But instead she stood in the aisle beneath the altar, with her gaze fastened on those sad eyes of Jesus Christ, who looked as weak and helpless as she was.

Jim Strong climbed out of his truck, next to the open freight car that had been secured by local sheriff's deputies, his Texas Ranger badge gleaming in the spill of the full moon.

"Never seen nothing like this, Ranger," Sheriff Arthur "Dabs" Dabney said over the wind whistling through the West Texas scrub brush, as he approached Jim. "Not now, not ever."

Jim had once heard that Dabney's stomach could block out the moon, and the longtime Pecos County sheriff liked to boast that he'd lost five hundred pounds—fifty pounds, ten different times. From the looks of things, Dabney had abandoned even the pretext of that effort. His gait was more a lumber as he strode across a parched patch of land toward Jim.

"Whole crew, is it?"

Dabney took off his hat and put it right back on. "All five. Conductor, engineer, two brakemen, and a fireman. All murdered and dumped off the train like they were bags of laundry. I got what's left of 'em covered up on the other side of the train, along with a pair of bonus bodies."

"What's that mean?"

"A couple of men we can't identify. Mexicans, by all accounts—cartel, from their scars and tats. Both wearing guns they never got to use."

"Show me."

• • •

Dabney's assessment was pretty much spot-on, at least in stating the obvious. And he was just smart enough to let his evaluation stop there.

Jim circled around the bodies, letting his mind ponder the rest. Whoever had killed the crew had been lying in wait and had made sure to position the bodies so they'd be out of view of anyone passing by the station. "Professional" was the word that came to mind next. The way the bodies of the train crew had fallen, it looked to Jim as if they'd been lined up before being summarily executed. As for the Mexicans, packing shiny pearl-handled .45-caliber pistols, their gravel-streaked clothes indicated they'd likely been shot elsewhere and dragged here to join the others.

"How many shooters you reckon we're looking at, Ranger?" Dabney asked him.

"One."

"Come again?"

"Wounds on the crew members are identical, two shots each, both to the head from behind. Angle of the wounds on these last two tell me they'd started to turn, after the first three had been shot."

"And the Mexicans?"

"Both shot twice in the face. He must've come up on them fast, before they had a chance to go for their guns."

"One guy," Dabney repeated, shaking his head and scratching at his scalp at the same time. "I can't wait to see what you make of what I need to show you next, Ranger."

Jim fell into step behind the Pecos County sheriff, moving toward the one freight car with its sliding door open. Beyond the train and the tracks, the Fort Stockton station comprised a dozen bays outfitted with doors that slid upward like those in garages. Set close to the tracks behind the great steel behemoth to allow for easy loading or unloading. The recent signing of the North American Free Trade Agreement, better known as NAFTA, had proven a boon for freight depots like this, the surge in activity leading to a need for additional operating hours and the workers to man them.

Jim had been informed that this particular train had originated somewhere up north and was supposed to terminate in Chihuahua, Mexico. The manifest listed nothing to load or off-load here in Fort Stockton, no stop at the depot even scheduled.

"You wanna tell me what's waiting for us in that car?"

"Three more bodies, Ranger," Dabney told him. "But damned if I can fig-ure out what killed them."

Jim Strong peeled back the tarpaulins the deputies had used to cover the bodies inside the open freight car. The faces looked uniformly flat and even, no pain or emotion showing anywhere. Nor were there any wounds Jim could find—knife, gun, or anything else. Their skulls were all intact, meaning nobody had taken them out with a baseball bat, club, or two-by-four, either. Finding a single dead body in such a state would've left Jim curious; finding three left him mystified. And they weren't Mexicans, suggesting a connec-tion with whomever had killed the train's crew and two Mexicans.

"You found them like this?" he asked Dabney. "None of your men touched nothing?"

"No, sir. We're not all yokels in these parts, you know. All we did was make sure they'd gone to the great beyond is all, so we'd know whether to call for an ambulance or coroner."

"He on the way?"

"Tied up at a traffic accident on the interstate."

"No matter. We got us a medical examiner in San Antonio who's as good as any. We can arrange to get all ten bodies to him."

Dabney ran his gaze over the three clustered about the empty freight car floor. "You got any initial notions, Ranger?"

Jim followed the sheriff's gaze back to the bodies. "Looks like they all dropped to the floor of their own volition to take a nap."

Needing some air, Jim poked his head out the open freight car door. The train beyond, property of the Kansas City, Mexico, and Orient Railroad, stretched as far as Jim could see to the south and almost that far to the north.

"You get ahold of the actual freight manifest while I was driving here, Dabs?"

"What for? The car's empty. Believe we're looking at those murderous hobos been killing up a storm. That's what we're looking at, if you ask me. Shot up the five members of the crew and then moved on to the Mexicans and these boys."

Jim knew Dabney was referring to the Freight Train Riders of America, a loose assemblage of generally nomadic criminals reputed to be responsible for a spate of murders from coast to coast.

"What did they use to kill them?" Jim asked, glancing toward the trio of bodies again. "Harsh language? Why not shoot them, like the others?"

Dabney's only answer was a shrug. Jim moved back to the nearest body and got his mini Maglite out to give it a closer look. Not Mexican, for sure, and, in Jim's mind, not from Texas, either. The bodies had a strangely uniform look to them, virtual carbon copies. All three of them were dressed in black, wearing tactical pants that were popular among trained professionals with or without military service on their résumés. A few years back, Jim had been called to a bar that had been busted up by some mercenaries he proceeded to bust himself. That was as close as he could come to figuring how to describe these three men. The fact that they weren't armed suggested otherwise, though, especially given the seven bodies stacked on the other side of the train.

"I don't think you answered my question, Dabs," Jim said, looking up from his closer inspection of the nearest body.

"What question was that, Ranger?"

"The one about the shipping manifest."

Dabney puckered his lips, then blew some breath out through them. "I even put my evidence gloves on before I started flipping pages. Followed official procedure and all that."

"Welcome to the twentieth century, Sheriff. Now tell me what you found on those pages."

"This is car one-thirty-eight. Empty, as in no cargo."

Jim weighed the ramifications of that. He didn't like being this far from his normal jurisdiction around San Antonio, because it was too far away from his daughter, Caitlin, to suit his taste. She was closing in on fourteen now, too much of her own mind, and growing up so fast that Jim had gotten to wondering when the day would come that he'd blink and she'd be gone. He didn't want to lose a single minute with her, and he considered himself blessed for all the years he'd been able to leave her in the care of his own father. The legendary Earl Strong had liked nothing better than to regale her with tales of his own days as a Texas Ranger, never sparing a single detail, even when it came soaked in blood. His father was four years gone now, having slipped away during an afternoon nap while Caitlin, fortunately, was at school.

"Empty, eh?" Jim said to Dabney, and swept the beam of his Maglite across the freight car's floor. "Tell me what you see, Sheriff."

"Goddamn nothing."

"How about the fact that the planks look discolored in these three rectangular patches?"

Dabney squinted to better follow the beam. "Discolored?"

"In comparison to the spots left open by what this train hauled here from up north. I'm thinking the freight must've piled through some weather on the way up here, and this car seems to have a leaky roof. So the discoloration you see here is actually dry patches where the floor was covered up by cargo."

Jim ran his beam around the perimeter of one of the lighter patches, drawing a perfect rectangle maybe four feet by six, give or take a few inches.

"Three shipping crates, by the looks of things," he resumed. "Maybe more, if they were piled atop one another. Then there's these marks."

"What marks?"

Jim angled the beam downward on a straight path to the freight car's door. "Scratches in the wood where whoever off-loaded these crates must've dragged them across the floor." He ran his thumbnail along the line of one of the scratches. "Depth tells me whatever was in those crates was plenty heavy, a few hundred pounds at the very least."

Dabney tried to smirk, but came up short. "That thumb of yours a new Ranger investigative tool?"

"There was a time when I rode a horse more than a pickup. I learned to make do."

"I ever tell you I once worked with your daddy?"

"Pretty much every lawman in Texas worked with Earl Strong at one point or another."

"I miss him, even though I didn't know the man all that well."

"I miss him too, Dabs."

"What about these two dead Mexicans, Ranger? Where do they fit into this picture you're drawing?"

"I think they were guarding whatever was loaded inside this car," Jim Strong answered, surprised by his own honesty.

Dabney's bulbous face puckered, an indication that he was deep in what passed for thought. "You figure these boys were killed by whoever stole those shipping crates, Ranger?"

"I think they were here to steal the shipping crates. But the fact that they got themselves killed didn't stop whoever accompanied them from finishing the job."

Dabney started to scratch at his scalp again, forgetting he'd put his hat back on. "Not a goddamn mark on them, not a single one, like they got struck by lightning bolts or something."

"You ever see what a body looks like that's been struck by lightning, Sheriff?" Jim asked, picturing the two occasions in his career he'd come upon just that. "Because, believe me, we'd know it."

"Well, jeez, Ranger, I was only making a point."

Jim Strong left it there, wanted to give Dabney something to hang his hat on. "You check the bodies for IDs?"

"Yes, sir, and they weren't carrying a thing that could help us identify them, even with all those pockets in their pants."

Jim nodded, pretending he was impressed by something he'd already figured out himself. What he couldn't figure was the precise chronology and whether the single shooter had somehow managed to drive off with the stolen crates all by himself, a job better fit for King Kong.

He turned his flashlight beam back on those dry patches of wood, three of them lined up in a neat row like coffins.

"We don't know shit, do we, Ranger?" Dabney asked, suddenly by Jim's side.

"All we know, Dabs," he said, "is that whatever was inside those crates was worth ten men dying over."

Part One

In the 1830s, Rangers were paid $1.25 a day, and had to furnish their own arms, mounts, and other equipment. They elected their own officers. Until more formal organization of Ranger forces occurred after the Civil War, Rangers existed primarily as volunteer companies, which were raised when the need arose and disbanded when their work was done. Because of this, many famous Rangers of the Republic of Texas period and the early years of statehood were men whose "formal" Ranger service may have lasted only a brief time. But because of their very active lives during these formative years, these men are remembered as Rangers, and their tradition of bravery and spirit of adventure became part of the Ranger tradition and legend.

—"Lone on the Range:
Texas Lawmen" by Jesse Sublett, *Texas Monthly*, December 31, 1969

I

DALLAS, TEXAS

"You want to tell me what I'm doing here again?" Caitlin Strong said to Captain Bub McNelly of the Texas Criminal Investigations Division.

McNelly, who favored string ties and shiny cowboy boots, turned to the quartet of figures in equally shiny windbreakers, milling behind him in the makeshift staging area. Caitlin had heard he was a descendant of the famed Texas Ranger captain Leander McNelly, a man who'd once told the whole of the U.S. government to go to hell, but wasn't too keen on the freedom with which Rangers still operated today.

"Special Response Teams hang their hat on being multijurisdictional," McNelly told her. "Consider yourself the representative Ranger."

"Since when does an SRT look more comfortable holding briefcases than firearms?"

"I need to tell you that computers are the real weapons these days?" McNelly asked her. "And those boys accompanying us are forensic experts who know how to fire back."

"Just two guns, yours and mine, backing them up," Caitlin noted.

"I don't need a computer to do the math, Ranger," McNelly said, while the four techs wearing windbreakers hovered behind them in front of the elevator. "You and I serve the warrant on the geek squad upstairs and let the experts do their thing with brains instead of bullets. How hard can it be?"

They were about to serve a search warrant on an information technology firm on the forty-second floor of the Bank of America Plaza, the city's tallest building. Caitlin had served plenty of more "traditional" search warrants in her time, on the likes of biker gangs, drug dealers, and various other suspects. The kind of service that found her backed up by guns, and plenty of them, instead of briefcases and backpacks.

A chime sounded ahead of the elevator door sliding open.

"In my experience," Caitlin said, stepping in first to position herself so the door didn't close again before the SRT computer forensics techs were inside, "it pays to have brains *and* bullets."

McNelly smiled thinly. "That's why you're here, Ranger. You were specifically requested for the job."

"By who?"

"I don't know. Orders came from the top down."

The cab began its ascent. If this were a Ranger operation, as opposed to CID, Caitlin would have insisted on securing the space in question prior to bringing up the civilians. Because that was clearly what these personnel in ill-fitting windbreakers pulled from a rack were. Civilians.

"Get your warrant ready, Captain," she told McNelly, as the cab whisked past the floors between L and 42.

He flapped the trifolded document in the air between them. "Got it right here."

"What's CTP stand for again?" Caitlin asked, referring to the acronym of the company on which they were about to serve the warrant.

"Communications Technology Providers. I thought I told you that."

"Maybe you did, but you never told me what the company did to get on the Criminal Investigations Division's radar. I'm guessing that's because somebody ordered you to take me along for the ride. All well and good, in this political world we live in, until something goes bad."

McNelly flashed Caitlin a smirk, as a chime sounded to indicate the elevator had reached its desired floor. "I can tell you this much, Ranger. The suspects we're after here don't know a gun from their own assholes. Worst thing they can do is infect us with a computer virus."

He led the way through the open door, without waiting for Caitlin to respond. She exited next, followed in a tight bunch by those four computer techs in their windbreakers, which made it look like they'd stuck their arms through Hefty bags.

The doors along the hall were uniformly glass, sleek and modern, some frosted. According to the building layout Caitlin had studied, Communications Technology Providers occupied a pair of adjoining office suites adding up to nearly five thousand square feet in total. One was a corner office, meaning at least a portion of those suites would enjoy wraparound windows and plenty of natural light.

Caitlin had just reflexively shoved her jacket back behind the holster housing her SIG Sauer P-226 nine-millimeter pistol, when the glass double-door entrance to Communications Technology Providers ruptured behind a fusillade of gunfire.

2

CARACAS, VENEZUELA

"Do you have anything to say before sentence is carried out, Colonel?" General Santa Anna Vargas asked Guillermo Paz.

"I was wondering about your name," Paz said from atop the gallows in the military prison yard outside Venezuela's capital city. "Were you named after Antonio López de Santa Anna, the Mexican general who lost Texas?"

Vargas's expression turned quizzical. He looked about at the officer cadre poised with him atop the platform, as if to exchange smiles at the doomed man's flippant remark. But they had heard too much about Guillermo Paz and the reputation he'd earned as a colonel with the Directorate of Intelligence and Prevention Services, better known as the Venezuelan secret police, to find any amusement in anything the man said.

Paz figured that God's tolerance for his murderous actions could only get him so far, the fact being that, while he'd long ago lost track of the number of people he'd killed, the Almighty certainly hadn't. So maybe it had finally caught up with him. He'd come back "home" for his mother's funeral, unable to deny himself the fulfillment of an obligation and duty he saw as sacrosanct to the mission his life had become. What kind of man didn't come home to attend his mother's funeral? Guillermo Paz, all seven feet and three hundred rock-hard pounds of him, wasn't about to risk squandering all the moral progress he'd made by shirking such a duty.

He felt a soldier position a stool behind him, to facilitate the task of looping the rope noose around his neck. He could feel the man's trembling hands struggling to complete the simple task, and might have offered to help if his hands weren't bound behind his back. Three additional soldiers, not part of the execution squad, stood farther back, assault rifles trained on Paz in case those bonds didn't hold. Two of them had made the mistake of positioning themselves so the sun blazing down out of a cloudless sky shined straight into their eyes. Not that it should have mattered to a doomed man. It was just something Paz couldn't help but notice amid the humidity that made the air feel like someone was wringing moisture out of a sponge.

"You haven't answered my question," he said to Vargas. "You can't kill me until you do."

"Yes," Vargas relented, "I was named for the great man and general."

"Too bad your parents forgot the Antonio López part. Not much of a first name they gave you. I'm wondering if people think you may have been named after Santa Claus instead."

Vargas took a step backward and signaled a priest holding an open Bible to come forward. "I understand you found religion."

"More accurately, you might say it found me."

"Our esteemed president insisted on extending you this courtesy. Do you have a favorite prayer?"

Paz felt the soldier on the stool behind him tighten the noose. His eyes swam about the ground below, the military prison yard filled with soldiers from the Venezuelan army, standing at attention, called to witness the price of Paz's indiscretion and perceived treason. Paz couldn't even begin to count them all. He wondered if they were really here as a warning or, perhaps, to further discourage any attempt at escape.

Paz aimed his gaze back at Vargas. "Is your mother still alive?"

"She is."

"I hope you make time to visit her often. I wish I had visited mine more. I wish I hadn't waited until her funeral."

"Do you have a prayer you'd like the padre to read or not?" Vargas snapped, impatient to have this over with.

Paz responded with his gaze on the priest, who was clutching his Bible in a grip so tight he'd squeezed the blood from his fingers. "I remember another priest who steered me down the proper course in life, to choose good over evil. He was murdered by the gangs because of his efforts. I was ten years old when I found him bleeding to death from a knife wound suffered for no more than trying to help the local impoverished lot the gangs sought to control. I held his head in my lap, my own tears falling onto his robes, as my first priest took his last breath. I closed his eyes and crossed myself the way my priest had taught me, silently swearing to avenge him. Then I went about collecting the bread and vegetables the man had died for, that had spilled out of the grocery bags when he fell."

His impatience growing, Vargas signaled the priest to start reading, without waiting for Paz to make his selection.

"*Padre nuestro, que estás en el cielo,*" the priest started, reciting the Lord's Prayer in Spanish. "*Santificado sea tu nombre.*"

"I found my mother crying when I returned to the tiny clapboard house with a tin roof I shared with my four brothers and sisters," Paz said, interrupting the priest's train of thought and causing him to lose his place. "She'd been struck by one of her visions she called *desfallecimientos,* which was Spanish for 'spells.'"

A gust of wind flipped the pages of the Bible about, the priest quickly struggling to find the one he'd lost, which contained the Lord's Prayer.

"You see, my mother was a *bruja,* a witch," Paz continued to Vargas. "The people of the hillside slum where we lived, in Caracas, stayed away from her as a result, even the most hardened criminal element afraid to cross her, lest they risk a spell being cast against them.

"'I didn't steal it,' I told her, laying out our small share of the food the priest would've allotted us. 'I didn't take anything that wasn't mine.'"

The priest relocated the page he'd been reading from and resumed. "*Venga tu reino. Hágase tu voluntad en la tierra cmo en el cielo.*"

"'But you're going to take plenty in the years to come,' my mother told me. 'You're going to take more lives than I can see. Your fate was sealed today, and now I see why, just as I see the blood staining your clothes.'"

"'I didn't hurt anyone, Madre,' I insisted."

"'But you will. You will hurt many, more than you or I can count.'"

"'I'll find another priest,' I pleaded. 'I'll pray!'"

"'It won't matter,' my mother said. 'The smell of blood will be forever strong on you, Guillermo.'"

"*Danos hoy nuestro pan de cada día,*" the priest resumed, his voice quickening to be done with his reading of the prayer as quickly as possible. "*Perdona nuestras ofensas, como también nosotros perdonamos a los que nos ofenden.*"

"And, true to my mother's word, it has been—even stronger than she could've possibly foreseen," Paz continued, still ignoring the prayer and aiming his next words straight at General Vargas. "But I'm not that man anymore. I haven't been since the day I first crossed paths with my Texas Ranger."

Paz could have elaborated further but chose not to. He'd been retained to kill that Texas Ranger, a woman, of all things, a fact that bothered Paz not in the least, until their eyes met in the midst of a gunfight and he saw what had been missing in his own. He'd never returned to Venezuela after that, calling Texas and America home now, thanks to an arrangement with Homeland Security that kept him inoculated from prosecution. All he needed was to do the bidding of a shadowy subdivision of Homeland, under the leadership of an equally shadowy man.

"Don't get me wrong," Paz continued, "I've spilled plenty of blood since, but the smell of it no longer clings to me the same way. It's important to me that you know that, because I'm about to spill a whole lot more and I want to confess that in advance." He moved his eyes back on the priest. "So, Padre, will you hear my confession? Can you absolve me of the sins I'm about to commit?"

Vargas stepped over to the wooden lever that would release the trapdoor beneath Paz's feet and send him plunging to his death.

"*No nos dejes caer en tentación y líbranos del mal,*" the priest said, taking that as his cue to resume. He tried to meet Paz's gaze, but couldn't. "*Amén.*"

"*Lo siento,*" Paz said to him, as Vargas's grasp tightened on the lever. "I'm sorry."

And that's when the first shots sounded.

3

DALLAS, TEXAS

The glass blew outward like ice crystals, showering the air, pinging to the floor in oddly melodic fashion.

"Get clear!" Caitlin ordered the four techs wearing windbreakers, her pistol already palmed, adding "Take cover!" when they failed to budge.

Then she was in motion, pressed against the near wall, with McNelly pinned close enough that she could smell the lavender-scented soap he must've showered with that morning. He was using a walkie-talkie feature on his cell phone to call for backup, and, in that moment, how Caitlin wished he was indeed a descendant of the legendary Texas Ranger captain Leander McNelly and just as good with a gun.

She could hear the soft *rat-tat-tat* clacking of silenced automatic fire, overcome in splotches by the desperate cries and screams of those at which that fire was aimed. Going in guns blazing to any situation was hard enough without having a clue about the number and placement of the opposition, much less with a partner Caitlin figured hardly knew his way around a gunfight. McNelly had his own nine-millimeter in hand by then, his hold on it anything but steady.

"Stay here and wait for the backup," she rasped to him, her tone just above a whisper. "I don't need you in my way. Only way you use that Glock is if somebody with a gun comes out ahead of me."

Caitlin's boots crunched over the first shards of glass, fifteen, maybe twenty feet from the shattered entrance of Communications Technology Providers. That much force concentrated behind that many bullets had its own way of rewriting the rules of physics.

The screaming intensified when she neared the door and caught the first glimpse of movement, as shadows or reflections off the jagged remnants of the glass double doors. Movement was what Caitlin had learned to key on from her grandfather, the great Earl Strong, from the time she was seven.

"Little girl," he would say, "if you wait to see the whites of a man's eyes, they'll be the last sight you ever see."

Inside the suite of offices, shadows swept across walls, seeming to merge into one another, as the acrid stench of gun smoke and muzzle powder pushed into Caitlin's nostrils.

Three shooters, four at most. . . .

Just short of the shattered entrance to CTP, she managed to identify three separate fire streams, along with a potential fourth. Caitlin reached the entrance to find a gunman in black fatigues wearing a ski mask, angling what looked like an assault rifle she didn't recognize over a desk, before firing a three-shot burst into whomever had taken cover there.

She sidestepped through the steel frame that had supported the shattered glass, snaring her jacket on a jagged shard stubbornly clinging to a corner. She felt the fabric tear as she added a second hand to her SIG and put two bullets in the back of the gunman's skull. Impact snapped his head backward, then violently back to the front, doubling the gunman over and slamming him face-first into the same desk behind which his final victim had taken cover.

Caitlin cursed herself for not better familiarizing herself with the layout of Communications Technology Providers, gleaning now that it featured an L-shaped open floor plan dominated by floor-to-ceiling glass that splashed sunlight in all directions. She felt a breeze and realized that bullets had stitched a splotchy pattern of holes across the entire far wall. The stench of blood stung her nostrils. Too much was happening too fast to record the multitude of downed bodies and impressionistic blood patterns dripping down the sleek glass forming the walls.

A second masked gunman spun out from the back side of the sprawling floor's L-shaped design, alerted no doubt by the heavy boom of Caitlin's SIG. She'd already trained her gun that way, and she fired five more shots the instant his dark shape flashed before her. Caitlin thought she recorded three hits, one and maybe two in the throat and the other dead center in the face, coughing bone, cartilage, skin, and blood into the air, nothing left recognizable where they had been.

She hit the floor next, close enough to an automatic burst fired by the third gunman to feel the heat of the bullets sizzling over her. She landed with her legs straddling one body and her torso perched on another, ready with her SIG the instant she heard *click*.

Even polished gunmen often forgot how quickly a magazine gets drained when firing on full auto. The third gunman had ejected the spent mag and was jamming home a replacement when Caitlin got him low, bullets in both ankles, enough to yank the world out from under him. He hit the floor, already draining his fresh mag, fibers of the drop ceiling showering the air.

He managed to right his fire on Caitlin, just as she rolled off the two bodies that had cushioned her drop. No angle on him from where she found herself. The downed gunman was plenty the worse for wear, but his aim was still on mark. So she sighted in on a fire extinguisher bracketed to the wall, put two bullets into it, and heard the instant hiss of white, noxious gas escaping. Enough to force the third gunman to roll straight into her line of sight again.

Caitlin was sighting in on him when a fresh stitch of fire chewed up floor tile and Lucite desk chips all around her—fired, it seemed, from nowhere at all.

Four gunmen, indeed, not three.

But Caitlin couldn't find him. No choice but to roll and keep rolling. The loosed chemical from the punctured fire extinguisher had clouded the air in thick white patches, and she aimed her roll for the thickest one. The gunman she'd shot in both legs trailed her with his fire the whole way, draining his second magazine. Caitlin heard the distinctive *thwack* of yet another being shoved home. She emptied the rest of her mag in his general direction, slowing her roll enough to snap a fresh one into place and rack the slide to chamber a round.

She tried to right her aim, but a burst of fire from origins she couldn't identify—the fourth gunman again—chased her back down before she even got off a shot. Caitlin finally pinpointed his position as being behind a toppled desk with a black granite top that had cracked when it spilled over. She couldn't see the unfamiliar assault rifle's barrel, and she imagined its sleek, black, burning shape morphing with the granite and poking its way through. Perfect camouflage, under the circumstances, and Caitlin realized she was effectively pinned down between a pair of gunmen who knew their way around a gunfight. She was calculating her options when a dual stitch of fire blew the ceiling out and sent husks of its particleboard raining down upon her.

4

Caracas, Venezuela

Those first shots were mere spits, the heavy rounds muffled by silencers. General Vargas was hit first, dead center in the forehead, which forced his hands to snap reflexively upward off the lever that had been about to send Paz to his death.

Paz, for his part, had stalled the whole process long enough to allow him to weaken the rope binding his wrists together behind him to at last tear his hands free. He stripped the noose off next, even as the next rounds of sniper fire tore the feet out from beneath more of the soldiers atop the platform.

By then, Paz had yanked a Kalashnikov assault rifle from the grasp of a still-twitching soldier and angled it downward on a phalanx of soldiers charging for the ladder, at ground level. The fact that they could only climb single file made it the easiest shooting he'd ever done. Paz heard a rattle and spun around. A wounded soldier was feeling for his trigger in a trembling hand, certain to fire a burst before Paz could steady his Kalashnikov, when another pair of sniper shots showered the soldier's blood, bone, and brain matter into the air.

Cort Wesley Masters cursed himself for not putting the man down in the first place. From his perch, camouflaged in a tree that looked down over the stockade yard from three hundred yards away, he'd let his attention stray briefly to the chaos erupting on the ground, redirecting his vision just in time.

He owed the colonel this much for all the scrapes they'd gotten into to-gether, along with Caitlin Strong. All the times they'd fought battles on Texas soil with so much at stake. One part of Cort Wesley believed Paz's theory that the Lone Star State lay at some moral or metaphysical epicenter where all manner of evil gathered. Another part of him, though, figured Texas was simply so goddamn flat that all the shit running downhill naturally collected there.

Either way, when Cort Wesley got the call about Paz's plight, from their mutual benefactor at Homeland Security, he only asked how soon the travel arrangements could get made. Caracas felt like pretty much every other god-forsaken place where he'd fought in an earlier phase of his life, starting with Iraq. Several other Special Forces tours had followed, until Cort Wesley ran afoul of an officer who got dropped into a hot zone with cold feet. More accu-rately, that officer had run afoul of Cort Wesley, who ended up leaving the service with what would have been a dishonorable discharge if any record of his actual exploits had existed.

He returned home to San Antonio to become an enforcer for the Branca crime family, which paid him more than enough to ensure a good life for his former girlfriend, Maura Torres, and the two sons he hadn't met. He might never have met them if the very Guillermo Paz, whose life he'd just saved, hadn't been responsible for ending Maura's. But that was another time, a thousand years ago, it seemed, and Paz had saved both his and Caitlin's lives a dozen times over in the years since. A changed man, to say the least, cer-tainly worthy of the considerable effort expended to rescue him from his own decision to risk returning home to Caracas for his mother's funeral.

So now Cort Wesley found himself up a tree in the steaming heat, racking a fresh magazine into his MK12 Special Purpose Rifle, a modified variant of the M16 family of weapons. The SPR grew out of a requirement of the Navy SEALs and Army Special Forces for a compact, light sniper weapon. To fulfill that need, the SPR had been fitted with a threaded-muzzle, match-grade, free-floating stainless steel heavy barrel. It fired the MK 262 Mod 1 open-tipped match round, specifically developed for this gun, a semiautomatic fed from a twenty- or thirty-round STANAG magazine.

Cort Wesley preferred the SPR for its modular design, which allowed it to be configured with a range of butt stocks, optics, and other accessories. The perfect sniper system, in other words, for engagements such as this, when speed and accuracy were more important than shot length and round weight. He felt right at home with the 5.56-millimeter rounds that had already dropped a pile of bodies onto the gallows platform.

All because Guillermo Paz had to come home for his mother's funeral.

Good thing I didn't come alone, Cort Wesley thought, as fresh fire erupted at ground level amid bodies rushing, fleeing, and falling in all directions.

He started to resteady the rifle, settling himself anew with a series of deep breaths, when his right arm cramped up. Cort Wesley tried to stretch the life back into it, but the arm had locked solid and refused to bend. It felt as if air had flooded his veins all the way down from the shoulder, spreading numbness from his fingers to the socket itself.

Damn, he thought, coming to grips, in that moment, with why not many army types past their midforties were out running around like Rambo. He should take this as a lesson, ease back on the throttle a bit.

Not yet, though. Cort Wesley needed to finish what he'd started here, so he shifted the grasp on the sniper rifle to his left arm. Using his cramped-up right to balance the stock, he pressed his left eye against the sight and curled his left index finger over the trigger.

The gun in his grasp, the cold steel growing warm, made Guillermo Paz feel right at home. The irony of what his blessed mother might think of the bullets pouring downward toward the troops struggling to right their weapons was not lost on Paz. As he discarded a spent rifle in favor of a fresh one, he could hear her imagined voice in his head—or maybe it wasn't so imagined, after all.

"*I warned you, Guillermo. This is what I saw in my vision that day you came home with blood drying on your clothes.*"

Paz wondered if his mother's vision had included the seven men he called his own, disguised in their original form as Venezuelan military, catch the soldiers utterly by surprise in their cross fire. Almost instantly, resistance gave way to retreat. His home country's poorly paid protectors were hardly about to risk their lives to lay siege to the man whose exploits had become the product of legend.

"*You can't escape your nature any more than you can stop breathing, Guillermo. But a nature doesn't define a person's soul. Your penchant for killing is no different than my visions and my being born a witch. That defines what we are, not who we are.*"

His mother's voice continued to sound in Paz's head, battling the heavy cacophony of gunfire while somehow rising above it.

"*I know you have tried, Guillermo, and that you continue to try. I am proud of your efforts to awaken the good in your soul. I never mentioned the Texas Ranger to you, but I saw her in that original vision, how she would be your savior, just as you would be hers. Even now your Texas Ranger finds herself swallowed by the blood she has spent her years shedding. The two of you have needed each other since the first time your eyes met, Guillermo. But you are about to need each other more than ever."*

Paz heard his mother say this as he flung his second Kalashnikov aside and picked up a third in its place.

And his mother was never wrong.

5

DALLAS, TEXAS

The clearly coordinated move threw Caitlin off, with both its bold nature and its effectiveness. She knew the man behind the toppled desk would be rushing her, even before she heard the thud of his steps. Just as she knew that using the next moments to push the ruptured ceiling tiles off of her was just what the gunman expected and wanted her to do.

So Caitlin didn't do it.

She trained her ears instead of her eyes, focusing on the clamor of his footsteps, military-grade boots squeaking across the polished tile. Her pistol poked up and through the debris coating her, firing blindly on a slight arc from left to right and back again. She used up the whole mag, a wild spray of gunfire sounding just before the crash of the gunman's body going down.

Shedding the ceiling debris from her, feeling the chalky residue it left on her skin and clothes, Caitlin reclaimed her feet amid the warm soak of blood pooling around her. There had to be at least a dozen bodies on this side of the L-shaped floor alone.

A fresh burst of fire from the man spilling blood from both his legs was waiting when Caitlin popped up over desk level. The advantage, strangely, belonged to him, thanks to the cover provided by the angle at which he'd fallen. Caitlin dropped back down behind the desk, not about to expose herself in a way that tempted his superior fire to find a next-to-impossible shot. This being her final magazine, she had to play it safe and smart. She regrouped behind a sleek and heavy black desk, with two more toppled ones separating her from the downed man.

Bang! Bang! Bang!

Caitlin recognized the sound of fresh nine-millimeter fire that wasn't her own.

"Drop it! Drop it now!" she heard Bub McNelly of the Texas Criminal Investigations Division screech from the general area of the shattered entrance. "I said, drop it—"

The rest of his words were swallowed by a burst of silenced gunfire from the automatic weapon that had been trained on her. She cursed McNelly, keenly aware that the man's first-ever gunfight had pitted him against professionals packing special operations–grade ordnance.

And his last.

She heard his cries and screams, as she burst upward to find the 5.56-millimeter fire twisting him one way and then the other. The gunman she'd shot in both legs had managed to prop himself up on a desk and lean against a chair. Caitlin fired, and kept firing, the bullets left in the magazine draining as quickly as she could pull the trigger.

The next image she recorded was the desk chair rolling across the floor as the final gunman toppled off the desk with his head lopped to the side at a strange angle from two bullets that had found his neck.

Caitlin heard a clicking noise, thought it was coming from him, until she realized she had continued to pull her SIG Sauer's trigger after the slide had locked open. She made herself stop and rushed to Bub McNelly, clinging to the hope that he'd managed to survive the brutal barrage that had turned him into a pincushion.

But his eyes were fixed sightlessly on the ceiling, seeming to stare through it, toward something bigger and better beyond.

6

Caracas, Venezuela

The MK12 SPR resisted Cort Wesley's every move, defying his efforts to find the same fluidity with the untrained left as had been the case with the right. It felt like learning the whole sniper process again from scratch, what he'd once heard a shooter far more expert than himself say was akin to trying to ride a bike backward. His first shots with his left eye calling the action and his left hand on the trigger missed badly. He quickly found his aim again, but at the expense of speed. Everything felt different, and the cramping in his right arm was showing no signs of letting up.

I'm too old for this shit....

Just moments ago, wielding the MK12 SPR from such a safe distance had left him feeling invincible, godlike in the sense that he could take down anything his crosshairs painted, without the targets knowing where the fire had come from. Now, the slowing of his motions and inconsistency of his aim left him feeling vulnerable. He was barely managing to drop the machine gunners in the guard towers and the Venezuelan snipers placed squarely in the open atop the roofs of those buildings in the stockade complex that looked down over the gallows tower.

Now that tower belonged squarely to Guillermo Paz, the colonel weaving his way about the spilled bodies in nimble, dance-like fashion. Cort Wesley realized Paz was wielding two Kalashnikovs now, firing them in opposite directions as if his aim were the result of divine intervention, neither of his arms cramping up in the least.

Even from this distance, Cort Wesley suddenly discerned through all the tumult the sound of breaking glass and swung his MK12 SPR back up and around, toward the buildings and the muzzle bores he knew he'd find protruding through the jagged shards left in the window glass.

He rotated from one to the other, not even the length of a breath separating his shots, at last finding the rhythm with his left side that had been eluding him. The shots came so quickly as to seem the result of firing on full auto, his left index finger pulling so fast and hard on the trigger that he feared it too might seize up solid on him.

Cort Wesley was still firing when a brisk wind like that kicked up by an approaching storm shook the heavy branch on which he was perched. The next moment revealed a familiar sound that deafened his hearing to all else, drowning out the remnants of gunfire, at the same time that a big, dark shadow crossed overhead.

Paz saw the Black Hawk coming, staged from a Venezuelan military airfield overseen by an officer who was desperate to flee the country with his family. It seemed to slice the air more than fly through it, twin M60 machine guns offering discouraging fire downward to keep its path forward clear.

Paz was ready when a black rope ladder dropped down out of the hold, dangling for the platform. He shouldered one of the remaining Kalashnikovs and grabbed hold of the lowest rung as soon as it came within range. He felt himself swooped up and away, soaring weightlessly through the air and wondering if this might be what dropping through the trapdoor of the gallows platform would've felt like.

Almost killed by one rope, only to be saved by another.

Cort Wesley clambered down the big araguaney tree, dropping out of its protective canopy for the thinner brush on the ground fifty feet below. He knew this to be the country's national tree, known for its resilience and lush appearance, especially after the annual rainy season. They normally didn't grow to be this tall, and his original recon of the area had counted its presence as a fine omen.

Climbing to his planned perch had been smooth and easy. The descent, on the other hand, made with his right arm stiff and numb, became a harrowing exercise that again brought him face-to-face with his age and mortality. Anyone who has used a sniper rifle in combat, forced to endure long stretches deployed in a single position, is no stranger to cramping. But that cramping had never lasted this long before, his right arm dangling heavy and useless when he finally reached the ground.

Rifle slung over his shoulder and right arm stiff by his side, Cort Wesley found the wooded trail that led to the pickup point. He heard the rattle of big truck engines tearing forward, reinforcements called in by desperate reports emanating from the stockade grounds. He couldn't yet see them through the foliage, but listening to their engines become louder left him backpedaling with a digital detonator in hand, working his left thumb, instead of his right, over a digital red button on the screen and touching it the same way he would to enter a digit on his cell phone. A moment's hesitation followed and then...

Boom!

...as the explosives he'd laid at strategic intervals just under the dirt roadbed erupted, one after the other, to disable the convoy. The rendezvous point where the Black Hawk would be waiting lay in a clearing a quarter mile away, an easy trek from here, with pursuit cut off from the rear.

Cort Wesley brought his right arm across his body with his left and propped his right hand against his belt, letting himself think of getting back home to his sons.

PART TWO

Desperately seeking to interest a hide-bound ordnance department in his revolving pistol, Samuel Colt approached [Samuel] Walker for an endorsement. Responding enthusiastically, the captain described how a handful of Rangers armed with the Paterson Colt had bested five times their number of Comanches at Walker Creek in 1844.... "With improvements," Walker asserted, "I think they can be rendered the most perfect weapon in the World for light mounted troops."

—Robert M. Utley, *Lone Star Justice:*
The First Century of the Texas Rangers
Oxford University Press, 2002

7

"How's your day going, Ranger?" Captain D. W. Tepper asked Caitlin, closing behind him the door to the empty office suite in which she'd been placed.

"About the same as yours, I imagine," she said, rising from the rolling desk chair that was the suite's lone piece of furniture. "Better than Bub McNelly's, in any event," she added sadly.

"Any relation?"

"He sure acted like it in the end. He saved my life, Captain."

"Well," Tepper said, taking off his Stetson to rub at the bare patches of scalp with the tips of his fingers, which were stained by cigarettes, "I'd like to know how a simple warrant service ended in a shooting war."

"This one wasn't on me, Captain. Wrong place at the wrong time."

"And now we got thirteen civilians and one police officer dead. You figure McNelly knew something he kept from you?"

Caitlin shook her head. "If he had any reason to suspect violence, he would've wanted more than a single Texas Ranger as backup."

Tepper pulled a fresh pack of Marlboro Reds from an inside jacket pocket and peeled back the plastic. He looked back toward Caitlin before tapping the first cigarette out.

"This is neutral territory," said the commander of Texas Ranger Company G, "so don't even think of trying to stop me."

"The building has a no-smoking policy, Captain."

"That they do," Tepper nodded, "but they also have a no-killing-civilians-on-the-premises policy. So I guess it's a day for breaking the rules."

Four hours after the shooting had ended, Caitlin was still at the now completely evacuated Bank of America Plaza. A combination of federal and local authorities, their names and agencies lost in a blur, had stuck her in this stray desk chair in an empty office suite on a separate floor, where she'd answered the same questions repeatedly. Reciting over and over again the events that had followed the first shots fired inside Communications Technology Providers made them no easier to bear, given the fate of Captain Bub McNelly.

He'd been pronounced dead on the scene, his body chewed up and spit out by the assault rifle fire that had poured into him. His legendary ancestral namesake had probably been in more than a hundred gunfights and had survived them all, while Captain Bub had perished in his very first, likely saving Caitlin's life in the process.

Caitlin knew military training when she saw it, and the four men she'd killed in the CTP offices upstairs clearly qualified there, meaning somebody had hired them to wipe out the workers of an information technology company. That seemed like going after a mosquito with a Magnum, which made no sense, until she considered the possibility that the timing, given the pending warrant service, was no coincidence.

"You want to tell me what the Criminal Investigations Division was going after CTP for?"

"Would if I could, Ranger," Tepper said, readying a lighter he flashed before Caitlin. "Just bought this, too, so it's still got a flint."

"For now," said Caitlin, a light glimmer flashing in her eyes.

"You wanna tell me who sends four gunmen straight out of central casting to take out a bunch of nerds who live on pizza and Red Bull?"

"Been asking myself that for the past four hours. It would help if we took a closer look at that warrant and then spoke to McNelly's superiors at CID."

"Already did that," Tepper told her, through the smoke wafting between them. "They told me to eat shit. Figure of speech." Tepper looked down, then up again. "I've known Bub McNelly since before I was a Ranger. Man had no business in a gunfight."

"So I told him. He didn't want people to know he was descended from a famous man-killing Texas Ranger. Didn't want his bar set that high."

"Or low, depending on your perspective."

Caitlin met his gaze. "He saved my life, D.W. We have to make sure that comes to something. What are the chances of Young Roger getting a look at whatever's on all those computers?" Caitlin asked, referring to the genius who was the Rangers' go-to guy on all things technology.

"Since it was Rangers serving the warrant, I was thinking of taking possession of all the machines for safekeeping."

"That's sure to piss off whoever was behind getting it written, Captain."

"That would be me," said a voice from the doorway.

8

DALLAS, TEXAS

"That's no way to treat an old friend," said the man Caitlin knew only as "Jones," who stopped just short of the light pouring through the windows, more comfortable in the shadows.

"I should have figured," she said, shaking her head. "Makes clear why I was asked to come along for the ride."

"Serve a simple search warrant," Jones acknowledged, nodding.

"If it were that simple, you wouldn't have needed me."

"I wanted to make sure it got done right."

"And look how that turned out. What was this Communications Technology Providers up to that left you playing me as a card, Jones?"

"Long story."

"It always is." Caitlin turned her attention back to D. W. Tepper. "Hey, Captain, do I have your permission to shoot this asshole?"

"Looking to break your own daily shooting record, Ranger?" Jones smirked.

"With you, it'd be a mercy killing."

Caitlin looked toward Tepper again and noticed that his attention was riveted on either an email or a text message that had just come in on his phone, announced with a typically annoying chime. She'd taught him to silence the sound, but he'd switched it back on after missing too many important messages.

"Captain?"

"What?" he asked absently, without looking up.

"Something important there?"

He lifted his eyes from the screen. "It may come as a surprise to you, Ranger, but life does go on in Texas, even when you're not the center of it."

"Is it something about Cort Wesley?" she asked, suddenly fearing the worst about his sudden trip to Venezuela at the request of none other than Jones.

"He's good to go," Jones said, when Tepper's attention was claimed anew by whatever his cell phone was displaying. "Paz, too. Heading back home as we speak."

His mind still elsewhere, Tepper started for the door, as if the deaths of thirteen IT specialists and their four killers paled by comparison with something else.

"Captain?"

He swung back toward her, just short of the door. "Life goes on in Texas, even when you're not the center of it."

"You already said that."

"Maybe I figured you weren't listening, like always."

Caitlin could tell Tepper wasn't just distracted but also suddenly anxious, even unsettled—rare for him, when it wasn't her doing the unsettling. He stopped even with Jones on his way to the door.

"Since this is your show, I don't believe I'm needed here." Tepper worked the knob but stopped short of exiting. "I'd leave the door open, if I were you, so somebody'll hear your screams if things go bad."

"They already did," Jones said to Tepper, waiting for him to take his leave. Then he closed the door and looked back at Caitlin.

"I had no idea anything like this was going to happen, Ranger."

"You never do, Jones, but it always does. And what are you doing here, anyway? What's Homeland's stake in this? Or is that classified?"

"Everything I do is classified. But let me put it this way: I'm here because CTP worked for me. Those poor bastards who got massacred upstairs were on my payroll."

9

DALLAS, TEXAS

Caitlin couldn't say exactly what Jones did for Homeland Security, especially these days, and she doubted that anybody else could, either. He operated in the muck, among the dregs of society who were plotting to harm the country from the inside. Caitlin doubted he'd ever written a report or detailed the specifics of his operations in any way. He lived in the dark, calling on the likes of Guillermo Paz and the colonel's henchmen to deal with matters always out of view of the light. When those matters brought him to Texas, which seemed to be every other day, he'd seek out Caitlin the way he might a former classmate.

She'd first met him when his name was still Smith and he was attached to the American embassy in Bahrain. Enough of a relationship formed for the two of them to have remained in contact and to have actually worked together on several more occasions. Sometimes Jones surprised her, but mostly he could be relied on to live down to Caitlin's expectations.

The empty office suite's dull lighting kept Jones's face cloaked in the shadows where he was most comfortable. Caitlin tried to remember the color of his eyes but couldn't, as if he'd been trained to never look at anyone long enough for anything to register. He was wearing a sport jacket over a button-down shirt and pressed trousers, making him seem like a high school teacher. He'd even let his hair grow out a bit, no longer fancying the tightly cropped, military-style haircut that had been one of his signatures for as long as she'd known him.

Caitlin couldn't say she was surprised that Communications Technology Providers was a Homeland-slash-Jones contractor. He operated so far beneath the radar as to sometimes need a backhoe to dig back to the surface.

"You mean Homeland's payroll," she said to him.

"So to speak," Jones acknowledged, grudgingly.

"Why do I think communications technologies has little to do with CTP's actual job description?"

"Because it's got *nothing* to do with it. CTP is a private intelligence-gathering outfit."

Caitlin ran that through her mind. "You want to tell me what that means exactly, Jones?"

"You think governments are the only ones who need a daily dose of intel? You know how many proxy wars American mercenaries are fighting right now around the world? You have any idea how many conglomerates need to know the threat levels where they're building or expanding operations? When an oil company wants to do some digging, or some pharmaceutical outfit wants to build a new plant in a Third World country where they can pay workers pennies, who are they going to call to find out who's who and what's what?"

"I'm guessing not Ghostbusters."

Jones nodded, as if he actually appreciated her quip. "You're not too far off.

CTP was the kind of company where you went to help stage zero-footprint operations."

"I'd ask you to repeat that term, but I know I still wouldn't understand it."

"Pretty much means what it says, Ranger. 'Zero footprint' means no trace back, allows for plausible deniability if things don't go as planned or there's a mission breach somewhere along the way."

Caitlin felt herself nodding. "So CTP was providing the intel for work like the kind Paz and his men do for you."

Jones flashed that trademark smirk that made Caitlin want to take a hammer to his mouth. "What work would that be?"

"I get the point. What I don't get is why you wanted a warrant served on this private intel firm giving you that zero footprint, and why you arranged for me to serve it."

"Isn't it obvious?"

"Not to me."

"CTP was up to something."

Now it was Caitlin who couldn't confine her smirk. "Of course they were; they worked for you."

"I'm talking something else, something under my radar, which comes as close as can be to enemy action."

"You think bad guys hired them for some nefarious purpose?"

Jones started to smirk again, but seemed to catch himself. "Nice word—'nefarious.'"

"Guess you inspire my vocabulary, Jones."

"And, yes, I think bad guys hired Communications Technology Providers for the kind of money that made it worth keeping quiet. I know this may come as a shock to you, Ranger, but I'm discreet about who I choose to do business with. Homeland giving me a free hand means not getting it chopped off. And if things went bad at CTP on my watch, they'd go bad for me, too."

"So the warrant was about learning what it was they were hiding from you."

Jones nodded. "And whether it might somehow be connected to any intelligence they'd assembled for Homeland. If that were the case, I figured they might put up the kind of fuss you, better than anyone, could diffuse."

"I'm going to take that as a compliment, even though you dropped me into a meat grinder."

"But not the meat grinder I was expecting."

Caitlin let the air settle between them. She thought she felt a breeze, but no windows were open. Then she tried to get a fix on Jones's shifty eyes, but they kept avoiding her gaze.

"You can see what I'm getting at here, Ranger."

"Not really."

"Whatever CTP was doing on the down low is what got them all killed."

"You thinking whoever sent those shooters got wind of the warrant?"

"Makes this their unlucky day—perpetrating a mass murder at the same time America's greatest gunfighter happened to be in the building."

"And who would that be?"

Jones let that question hang in the air between them. "This is my operation now, Ranger. My people are en route to confiscate every hard drive, soft drive, thumb drive, and flash drive from CTP's office. And that warrant you were about to serve gives us permission to work the Cloud as well."

"How do you serve a warrant on the Cloud, Jones?" Caitlin asked him, wondering if the Ranger forensics teams could grab the computers before Jones's team arrived.

"Good question. I'll let you know when somebody explains the answer to me. In the meantime, you're free to go."

"There's a line of officials still waiting to talk to me."

"Not anymore. Like I said, it's my show now. That means I don't need to hear any more from you at this point than I already know. Hope you don't mind me keeping mention of your name out of this?"

"You can do that?"

"I'm Homeland Security, Ranger. That gives me license to take any names I want, kick any ass I want, part the seas, raise the dead, and stop the clocks."

"You forgot 'walk on water,'" Caitlin told him.

Jones glanced toward the now closed door through which D. W. Tepper had exited without explanation a few minutes before. "Since when does your captain leave an active crime scene?"

"I'm guessing since he had somewhere more important he needed to be."

"Any idea where?" Jones asked her, a typical ring of suspicion lacing his voice.

"No, but I intend to find out."

IO

Caitlin steered her SUV toward the portable construction lights illuminating a parched, desert-like swath of land about a two-hour drive from San Antonio, just off the 110 freeway. D. W. Tepper wasn't answering his cell phone, so she had called Ranger Company G headquarters to find where he'd gone in such a rush from the aftermath of the multiple shooting in Dallas.

"I'm not supposed to tell anyone where he is," reported a retired Ranger named Revins, who served as dispatcher on a part-time basis. "He told me that especially meant you."

"I'll never tell," she promised.

"Only reason why you should know where to find him is I was around when he and your dad had a case that took them to these parts."

"My dad?"

"You didn't hear it from me, Ranger, but it sure looks like what's surfaced in the desert has brought back some bad memories."

Around Caitlin, thick creosote bushes dominated the landscape, painting the otherwise parched soil a lavish green. The landscape reminded Caitlin more of the Chihuahuan Desert to the west than the western portions of Texas Hill Country in which the town of Sonora lay. Thunderstorms were common during spring and fall months, but at this time of year the area was starved of precipitation, accounting for the desert-like appearance of the rolling land in which Caitlin found herself. The lit-up area looked to be perched on the edge of a mesa, where all flora gave way to thin sloped hills formed of a sandy soil bed inlaid with rocks and boulders. She'd heard of the Caverns of Sonora, a national landmark located a few miles to the west, while the small town itself, the seat of Sutton County, sat five or so miles to the east.

Drawing closer, Caitlin spotted a combination of light and heavy construction equipment mixed in among the police cars, the coroner's wagon, and the pickup truck belonging to D. W. Tepper.

"We found another, Captain!" she heard a voice yell, as she climbed out of her SUV.

All the digging around a swimming pool–size swath of ground, oval in shape, had clouded the air illuminated by the heavy lights. She spotted D. W.

Tepper standing on the lip of the freshly dug hole, cigarette smoke fluttering about the dust and dirt cloud.

Caitlin approached and came right up next to him without saying a word, noticing a professionally dug rectangular trench maybe a dozen feet beneath them. Everyone else, meanwhile, was focused either on the third skeleton, which was being lifted out of a shallower section of dug-out earth, atop a tarpaulin, or the two already resting on the flat ground set back from the trench.

"Dog found a bone its owner had the good sense to realize was human," Tepper said, without acknowledging her. "We're up to four bodies now."

"As in skeletal remains."

Tepper turned his head toward her, looking annoyed before sucking a fresh drag out of the dwindling Marlboro. "Instead of getting me to quit, maybe you should take up smoking, instead."

"And why's that?"

"Because everyone needs a vice. It's good for the soul. Keeps a person more moderated."

"Some might say my vice is shooting people."

Tepper turned back to the trench before him. "That's my point. Maybe swap one for another. I figured you'd still be in Dallas, maybe for the next month or so, given the shape of things when I left."

"Jones dismissed me. Said my presence was no longer required."

"Do I smell a cover-up coming?"

"It's Jones, Captain. The murdered techies were mostly in his employ, providing intel for what he called zero-footprint operations."

"Is there such a thing?"

"Jones's world is dominated by them."

"You said 'mostly,'" Tepper reflected.

"Apparently, Communications Technology Providers was doing some freelancing on the side for a party or parties unknown."

"And Jones thinks one of those parties was behind those shooters you gunned down," Tepper concluded.

Caitlin nodded. "As near as I can figure." She gazed about, listening to the generator's lawnmower-like engine sounds, which cut through the otherwise stark silence of the night. "Nice place to escape to."

"No blood, sight or smell, to deal with."

"That's the thing about skeletons. Any idea how old they are, Captain?"

"I could venture a guess."

"But you don't have to guess, do you?" Caitlin said, recalling the words of the retired Ranger dispatcher.

Tepper swung from the trench again and, this time, held his gaze upon Caitlin. "How'd you know that?"

"You told me."

"When?"

"The way you're standing, the way you're taking it all in. You're not surprised at what was recovered here."

Tepper cast his gaze back into the empty rectangular trench. "I'm more surprised by what wasn't."

Caitlin joined his gaze. "So somebody dug out whatever used to be down there and disturbed the bones buried with it just enough to grab that dog's attention."

"Lucky dog."

"He didn't get to keep the bone, I'm guessing."

Tepper gestured toward the areas of the flat, arid ground that crime scene techs had denoted with yellow flags wedged into the ground in irregular, splotchy patterns. "See those? Crime scene techs have managed to identify a whole bunch of tire impressions from a backhoe. We should know the manufacturer and model number by tomorrow."

"Explaining how this ditch got dug out."

"I had the techs scour the surrounding area, see if they found them anywhere else."

"To determine whether somebody was jabbing blindly at the ground or knew exactly what they were doing."

"Could you just let me finish?"

"Sorry if I took the words right out of your mouth, Captain."

Tepper smacked his lips together and gazed about, as if looking for a water bottle he'd set down somewhere. "Techs found other tracks in the nearby area, indicative of the flatbed that hauled the backhoe here."

"I don't suppose there are any security cameras in the area."

"Not for a couple hundred miles in every direction. Maybe you can get your friend Jones to see if any reconnaissance satellites were over the area at the time."

"He's got plenty on his mind already right now."

The Marlboro burned down close enough to singe Tepper's fingertips. He shed the cigarette and stamped it out with a force indicating he was trying to snuff out more than just a flickering flame.

"Funny, Ranger, how you know all the tales of your granddad's exploits, because Earl Strong told you himself, but almost nothing of your dad's exploits."

"Like this?" said Caitlin, her expression gesturing toward the trench, as she again recalled the dispatcher Revins's words.

"For sure," Tepper told her. "For sure."

11

San Antonio, Texas; 1994

"That's all you can tell me, Doc?" Jim Strong said to Frank Dean Whatley, one of six medical examiners on staff at the Bexar County Medical Examiner's Office, but the one he had the most faith in.

"You only brought the bodies in last night, Ranger," Whatley said, referring specifically to the corpses found in the freight car without a mark on them.

"And I imagine they're in the same condition now as they were then. Question being how they got that way."

"Near as I can tell, they died of respiratory arrest and heart failure."

"Both?"

"Take your pick."

"Why don't you pick for me, Doc?"

Whatley checked his watch, as if he had somewhere else to be, with the day winding down. His wife had recently been hospitalized, having drunk herself into a stupor following their teenage son's murder at the hands of a Latino gang. Every Ranger who was part of Company F attended the funeral but, in spite of their best efforts, they'd yet to arrest the perpetrators, which frustrated Jim Strong as much as it did Whatley himself. Just last year, the medical examiner's office had moved from its dedicated facility at 600 North Leona to a new 52,000-square-foot facility on the campus of the University of Texas Health Science Center at San Antonio, which it shared with the Bexar County Criminal Investigation Laboratory.

"You need to go visit your wife?" Jim asked him.

"She's had a particularly bad day. Getting her off the booze seems even worse than leaving her on it."

"I've had my own battles with the bottle, Doc. Won my share, but lost plenty of them along the way. It's a process."

"Which makes me feel helpless."

"I still go to meetings from time to time. Maybe she could go down that route. I'd be happy to introduce her to the right folks, help find her the right sponsor."

Whatley was clearly less than enamored by the prospects of that. "Not the right time for that, Ranger."

"One thing I can tell you about the right time: wait for it and odds are it'll never come. You want me to take a turn talking this out with her, I'd be happy to help."

Whatley frowned from behind his desk, one of three squeezed into an office. "Wish I could be more helpful about what killed the three men in that freight car. I sent everything I've been able to gather so far to the Centers for Disease Control in Atlanta."

"The CDC? What the hell you want to get them involved for?"

"First off, it's procedure with deaths like this, so I didn't have a choice."

"Deaths like what?"

"That are deemed otherwise inexplicable."

"You said respiratory arrest and heart failure. I say that's explicable."

Whatley glanced at his watch again, then matched the time to the wall clock. "The *what*, maybe, but not the *how*, as in the cause of those two fatal factors."

"And you're thinking a germ, a virus, a bug—something like that?"

"I don't know what to think. Did you know the first toxicology test in the state of Texas was performed by this office in May of 1958?"

"No, I didn't," Jim admitted.

"I don't even know where we were located back then, but the test was for arsenic, of all things. And it sure wasn't arsenic that killed those three men in the train car. Truth be told, I don't know of a single bio-organism that can kill three men exactly the same way at what looks to be the same time, from your report."

"Which part of my report, Doc?"

"The part that described the placement of the bodies. None had time to even get out of that freight car before they were stricken. They went from showing symptoms to dead in a manner of seconds."

"How many seconds might that be?"

Whatley checked the notes scribbled on a pad in front of him before responding. "Well, based on the condition of the other organs, I'd say less than thirty, for sure, and maybe as few as half that."

"You're telling me whatever got taken out of that freight car might have killed them in fifteen seconds?"

Whatley rose from behind his desk, impatience flashing on his features. He was a man who badly wanted to be somewhere else, and Jim couldn't blame him, under the circumstances.

"I didn't tell you that at all, Ranger. All we know with reasonable certainty is that they died in the train car. I never said their deaths were caused by the car's contents. Could be they caught whatever killed them another place and time entirely but didn't have the bad luck to die until they were inside that car. And there's something else."

"I'm still listening, Doc."

"First responders on the scene found the car empty, which we can take to mean that somebody else removed whatever was inside. So why didn't they die too?"

"Good question. Got any notions on the subject?"

"Not a one." Whatley shrugged. "The forensic team did a detailed check of that car, in full hazmat gear, and their report didn't mention anything that gets us any closer to an answer." Whatley looked down at his notes again, flipping pages as if in search of something he couldn't find, before letting them flop down. "All we've got is your notion that there were three 'shipping crates' removed from the car. That's what you called them, shipping crates."

Jim Strong was trying to assemble a picture from all the pieces in his head, but he didn't have enough of them yet. "Near as I could tell from the marks they left behind, and the scratch marks on the floor where somebody had dragged them. Manifest listed the freight car in question as empty, so the only way to figure out what was stolen is to make the trip down to where the crates were headed. Chihuahua, Mexico."

"Suck it up, D.W. My truck is a no-smoking zone."

"We got a six-hour drive ahead of us, Jim," D. W. Tepper said to him from the passenger seat.

"We'll take a couple bathroom and water breaks along the way. You can light up then."

"Well, Ranger Strong, it'll give me more time to formulate my will."

"What makes you more likely to die today than any other, Ranger Tepper?"

"We're going to Mexico, where Rangers are still affectionately referred to as Texas Devils or something. Not exactly a prime vacation spot for anybody wearing a cinco pesos badge."

Jim responded with his eyes fixed straight ahead into an endless ribbon of light reflecting off the parched flatlands through which they were driving. "This train was headed to the Chihuahua railroad station, scheduled last stop. That means somebody was waiting for it to show up and is now missing whatever got clipped from that freight car in Fort Stockton. Could be we'll be providing them a service, more than enough reason not to go OK Corral on our asses."

"And these could be the same people who went through a whole lot of trouble to hide the existence of whatever it was they were bringing south of the border?"

"I suppose."

"Yeah," Tepper groused, and went back to studying the half-empty pack of Marlboro Reds, fighting off the urge to light one up. "So your plan is to head to Chihuahua to smoke out whoever was ready to take delivery of that cargo."

"In the hope they're willing to tell us what it was," Jim told him.

"Think I'll get to work on that will."

Once they had completed the six-hour drive to Chihuahua, made thirty minutes longer by D. W. Tepper's increasing tobacco urges, Jim steered his pickup toward the ornate train station that looked lifted from a different age. Located on the outskirts of the city itself, the station was nestled in the shadow of the mountains, amid the scrub brush from which Chihuahua, and much of Mexico, had been built.

"You figure we should stow our badges?" Tepper asked.

"No, sir. Better folks know who we are to start with than find out later, maybe after they've gone to guns. Besides, when was the last time a Texas Ranger got himself killed in Mexico, D.W.?"

"Hard to say, given that I don't know a single one in our ranks who ventures down here, unless it's to get lit up for a bachelor party or the like. And in that case, you wouldn't be seeing a badge."

"Then look at us as pioneers," Jim said, stretching the tightness spawned by the long drive through heat the open windows barely made a dent in.

He set off without further word, D. W. Tepper falling in behind him as he lit up a fresh Marlboro. "That's one good thing about being down here. They allow smoking everywhere."

"Yup, there's no shortage of ways to get yourself killed in Mexico."

A pair of freight trains, each toting a long line of cars, was stacked back to back at the station's loading dock. Sweat-soaked workers toiled in the blazing sun to fill the cars with their allotted goods, made possible by NAFTA. Goods had always flowed between Mexico and the United States. The signing of the free trade agreement, though, had increased the traffic tenfold. But Jim Strong suspected that whatever had been removed from that freight car the night before had nothing to do with that trend.

He started his questioning at the main desk inside the freight terminal, waiting in line like everybody else so as not to piss anyone off. He spoke damn good Spanish, although you wouldn't know that from the clerk's reaction, which was to pretend he didn't understand much, before he went to fetch his immediate superior. That process was repeated two more times, everyone professing to know nothing about a freight train that was still cordoned off in Fort Stockton, or the missing contents of one of its freight cars.

"They're stalling," Jim Strong said to Tepper.

"You mean, as opposed to just telling us shit?"

"You know who's based in Chihuahua?"

"I don't have anyone from these parts on my Rolodex, Ranger Strong."

"Luna Diaz Delgado."

"The late Hector Delgado's wife?"

Jim nodded. "Also known as 'la Viuda Roja.'"

"The Red Widow," Tepper translated.

"On account of all the blood she spilled avenging her husband's murder, a reputation that explains how she's been able to outlast all her rivals and counterparts these last few years. She didn't just kill the four heads of the cartels who conspired to murder her husband, D.W. She killed their whole families."

"That's right," Tepper recalled. He felt about his pockets for his Marlboros but couldn't find them anywhere. "Made each cartel boss watch as she personally slit the throats of their children to make her point, from what I learned."

"There's plenty of rumors of how exactly she earned her nickname to choose from. I've heard told the cartels don't dare make a move on her, that they missed their chance when they took out her husband."

Tepper was still feeling about his pockets. "Did you steal my cigarettes again?"

"Why would I do that?"

"Because every time you see me looking for them, you get that gleam in your eye."

"Maybe because it adds a few more days to your life."

"But it's *my* life, Jim Strong, and I have the right to wreck it any way I so choose."

"You need an intervention, D.W."

"What I need is my cigarettes."

A new face appeared behind the counter before them, some kind of yard supervisor, judging by the grease coating his jacket and the grime swept down his face with the sweat. Jim Strong was in the middle of posing his next question when the supervisor's eyes widened, an instant before he dropped down beneath the counter. Jim and D. W. Tepper swung in one fluid motion, whipping from their holsters the .45s each of them carried and holding them tight.

Before them, in what looked like a scene staged from an old gangster movie, were six brutish-looking men wielding either twelve-gauge shotguns or old-fashioned Thompson submachine guns. For someone who appreciated history as much as Jim, those Thompsons were a source of more pleasure than fear. Either painstakingly kept up or brilliantly restored, the magazine-fed (as opposed to drum-fed) tommy guns looked brand spanking new and as formidable as ever.

Neither Ranger said a word, their .45s steadied before them. Then the two gunmen in the center, set slightly back from the others, moved aside to create an opening for Luna Diaz Delgado, la Viuda Roja, to pass through.

Her high heels clacked against the depot's old wooden floor, everything about her bleeding elegance, from the perfect length of her stride to the way the designer dress hugged her shapely lines and how her hair, the color of a raven's feathers, tumbled past her shoulders.

"I think we should talk, Tejano," the Red Widow said to Jim Strong.

12

SONORA, TEXAS

"She still runs a good part of the show south of the border," Caitlin said, when Tepper halted his tale. "But I never knew my dad had a run-in with her."

"It was a hell of a lot more than that, Ranger, believe me."

"So why stop there, Captain?"

"Because, Ranger, Jim Strong had his reasons for never wanting you to hear this story, and I figure respecting his wishes is the best course to follow."

Caitlin turned back to the rectangular ditch dug out before them. "His reasons for that have anything to do with what somebody pulled out of this hole? Because I'm thinking that whatever got clipped from the freight train that night in 1994, before it reached Mexico, ended up getting buried here. And the reason you're all out of sorts is now somebody went and dug it up again."

"So, what, now you're my psychiatrist?"

"Maybe I just know the feeling of laying eyes on something I thought was gone forever."

"Right now, all we're laying eyes on is an empty hole."

"And you have no idea what used to be inside it?" Caitlin said.

"Not a clue."

"How about the identities of the men behind those skeletons?"

Tepper swung from the ditch and glared at Caitlin. "I look like a psychic to you, Ranger?"

"I'm not a psychic, either, and yet I've got a feeling ballistics just might find evidence that it was forty-five-caliber shells that killed the four men once attached to those skeletons." Caitlin knew she should have left things there, but she couldn't hold back. "I think you have reason to believe Jim Strong was the one who put them in the ground. So tell me, D.W., if we run any slugs we find through ballistics, will they match up with your forty-five, too?"

Caitlin expected that comment might raise Tepper's ire, but his expression remained flat and expressionless. Empty, the way a man's does when he's forgotten how to smile.

"Your dad and I worked the case together through most of it, until the investigation went south and I was dispatched to Huntsville, where a whole bunch of prison riots had broken out."

"Leaving the freight car investigation to my father."

"He was ordered to Huntsville, too, difference being he didn't go." Tepper took off his Stetson and scratched at his scalp again, then curled his fingers up before him as if to look for the Marlboro he'd already shed. "Guess it runs in the family."

"Disobeying orders?"

"Some would call that insubordination, Ranger. Grounds for dismissal."

"But just another day at the office for a Texas Ranger." Caitlin stopped, realized she was holding her breath along with her words. "And you didn't answer my question."

"Which question was that?"

"Whether it was my dad who planted these bodies in the ground like watermelon seeds."

Tepper's expression tightened anew, looking strained, as if he might've been in physical pain. "I wasn't around. Been reassigned, remember?"

"Sure, D.W., whatever you say."

"You don't want to believe me, that's your prerogative." He shook his head. "I think this kind of thing has been following the Strongs around ever since your great-great-granddad Steeldust Jack did his ranging." Tepper deliberately worked another Marlboro free of the pack, as if daring Caitlin to say something, then resumed when she didn't. "Luna Diaz Delgado's still one of the most powerful people in Mexico. Heads of the cartels don't lift a finger unless she blesses their ring. That means she'd make a worthy target for the winds of Hurricane Caitlin to topple over, and I don't want to go putting thoughts in your head."

"You think I don't already know everything there is to know about her?"

"Well, you didn't know your own dad mixed it up with her once."

"Define 'mixed it up,' Captain."

"A topic for another day," said Tepper, his spine seeming to stiffen.

"Midnight's not too far off. I can wait."

Tepper turned to face her head-on. Caitlin hadn't realized he'd lit up another cigarette until the smoke rose between them.

"Leave this one alone, Ranger. Will you trust me on that?"

"Not unless you tell me why, D.W."

"Because it's something Jim Strong wouldn't want you to know."

Caitlin felt a pressure in her chest, an overall heaviness settling over her. She swung away from Tepper to simmer down and avoid the argument that her stubbornness otherwise would have likely resulted in. She found herself gazing out into the darkest part of the desert, a vast black hole of nothing.

Except for a single dim flash of light. Caitlin wrote it off as the product of her imagination, until it flashed again, then a third time, when the wind picked up.

"Captain," Caitlin said, turning back around.

"I'm done arguing the point, Ranger. Getting in the ring with you means the bell never sounds."

Caitlin glanced back into the emptiness and caught the flicker again. "There's something out there we need to check out."

13

"Did you truly believe God would not punish you for your indiscretion?"

Enrico Molinari's towering shape swept through the residents gathered on the edge of the village's landscape of once fertile fields, now reduced to a decaying wasteland. The men tried not to recoil at the sight of his patchwork face, at the jagged scars where grafted skin had been sewed in place. The women mostly turned away or looked down in revulsion, while the children were brought to tears and cries.

He spoke English because that was the country's native language, left over from colonial times, although villages like Eziama Obiato had begun to fancy Hausa, from the precolonial days. That inclination was symbolic of another national tendency of late, that which had brought Molinari and his troops here to make an example of this village. It was not the only village to have fallen prey to a scourge that had drawn the attention of his superiors and had led to his being dispatched, just the one they'd decided to make an example of.

"You wish to know what has become of the firstborn sons of your village," Molinari said to those gathered before him like loyal subjects. "You cower at my feet and beg for a mercy you would never have needed had you not turned away from our Lord. Before you stands my legion of soldiers in His army sent here under His charge to fulfill a mission of His calling."

The legion Molinari spoke of formed a neat line of thirty well-armed commandos, not mercenaries but those whose faith was boundless and unquestioning. Men like him, for whom killing was a holy task, to be celebrated as a kind of Eucharist and ultimate duty before the Lord. His men stood shoulder to shoulder, blocking the sight in the field beyond, soon to be revealed to the villagers.

"There is only one God," Molinari continued, loud enough for all of them to hear. "And you have betrayed His word. You have sought solace among the false god of heathens and foolishly expected no recrimination for such a blasphemous transgression from His teachings.

"*For the wrath of God,*" Molinari continued, quoting Romans, "*is revealed from heaven against all ungodliness and unrighteousness of men, who by their unrighteousness suppress the truth.* And such a truth is the very word you have turned away from, and know that *He will punish those who do not know God and do not obey the gospel of our Lord Jesus*," Molinari said, finishing with a quote from Thessalonians.

As a child, he had dreamed of being a priest, but he enjoyed the company of women too much to survive the seminary. This bitterly disappointed his family, who were mollified only slightly by Molinari's decision to join the Italian army, where his physical stature and prowess allowed him to rise swiftly through the ranks, ultimately becoming a member of Italy's elite Special Forces group known as 9th Reggimento d'Assalto Paracadutisti, the 9th Paratroopers Assault Regiment, or *Col Moschin*. Because of his vast bulk and his height, which stretched to nearly seven feet, they had to design a special parachute for him.

Being part of the Italian version of the British Special Air Service paved the way for a career in law enforcement with the carabinieri. There, he earned the reputation as a crime-busting officer who was not afraid to mix it up with the most powerful elements of Italian organized crime. The stalwart, uncompromising giant stoked fear in the hearts of mob figures and provided a face for Italy's determined efforts to, at long last, rid this scourge from the country.

Until he walked into a trap, his men killed and Molinari captured. They forced him to kneel, his hands and feet bound with chains. Then they doused him with gasoline and, while a video camera whirred, set him on fire.

The agony that had followed had given birth to another man entirely, in mind and spirit as well as in body. A man freed from the bonds of laws and mores to serve justice on those who threatened the word of God and risked the integrity of His sacred house.

Eziama Obiato was a prime example of the scourge sweeping through Nigeria, the scourge of Islam, which was uprooting Christianity as the nation's dominant religion. The entire African subcontinent was in danger of being swept away, and all previous, more docile efforts at reconciliation undertaken by the Vatican fathers had failed. Molinari and his men had become the Church's last resort, called upon when all else had failed to dispel this vast threat to Christianity itself.

In service to the true army of God, a legion of those who believed in His word in an unfaltering manner and were willing to back up their beliefs with blood.

In service to the Order.

Molinari had not randomly chosen Eziama Obiato to serve as an example to the rest of the country, straying from faith. Instead, the village had been a strategic selection, thanks to the common boundaries it shared with four other government areas in the Nigerian state of Imo.

"This morning," Molinari continued, "you witnessed me burn your much-revered palm trees that bear three branches that symbolize unity, progress, and faith. But since you've lost your faith, you no longer deserve the other two. And your firstborn sons were taken so you might know the pain you have caused God by heeding the blasphemous words of Islam. Those words burn in your throat just as the leaves of your trees perished in a blaze. And now you will behold the punishment for the error of your ways and the sinful straying that led me here today."

With that, Molinari's men, all soldiers beholden to the Order, parted to reveal the firstborn sons of Eziama Obiato buried in the ground so only their heads rose above the soil. Dozens of them, arranged in neat, even rows, in the form of a spring planting, gagged to silence their screams. But their eyes swam with terror, pleading for help, for mercy, which disappeared with the appearance of the massive cultivator being driven by another of Molinari's men.

The villagers gasped, cried, screamed, dropped to their knees in the semblance of Christian prayer.

"It is too late for that now," Molinari told them, as the cultivator's razor-sharp tongs chewed through the ground. "You should have thought of your faith before you squandered it and became the enemies of God. *To whom shall I speak and give warning that they may hear? Behold, their ears are closed and they cannot listen. Behold, the word of the Lord has become a reproach to them; they have no delight in it.*"

The cultivator continued on, the land receding in its path, drawing straight in line with the exposed heads of the village's firstborn sons.

"This great machine was a gift of the very Church you forsake, though when you turned away from His name, you still continued to employ it for your own gains. So what has Islam done for you, besides bring His wrath upon you in my dispatch? *But I am full of the wrath of the Lord; I am weary with holding it in. So I will pour it out on the children in the street and in the gathering of young men to others.*"

The cultivator churned the ground in a blur, bringing to the top richer, deeper-colored soil from beneath the residue of crop life that had been laid to waste ahead of Molinari's coming.

"Watch!" he ordered those villagers who sought to close their eyes to the inevitable. "Behold His wrath being visited upon you!"

The cultivator rolled over the first rows, making a crackling, crunching sound not unlike the one it made when devouring stray branches, spraying blood, bone, brain matter to soak into the soil.

"*Their houses shall be turned over to others,*" Molinari said, his voice carrying over the crunching, as well as the cries of the villagers, "*their fields and their sons together. For I will stretch out My hand against the inhabitants of the land,* declares the Lord."

The cultivator ground to a halt, its work done. Molinari kept his gaze fastened that way, eyes feasting on the finished product.

"This is the price you pay for not keeping that hand in yours, when it was extended with love by the Father. This is the price you pay for betraying His word and besmirching His kingdom."

Molinari walked off toward the field, leaving his men with the still shrieking villagers. He stopped at the midpoint of the cultivator's work, his boots crunching over the refuse left in its wake.

"It is done, Your Eminence," he reported into his satellite phone.

"Good to hear," the prefect of the Order replied, "because your presence is required elsewhere, immediately. In America, Captain, the state of Texas."

14

Sonora, Texas

The headlights of Caitlin's SUV bounced off a rock formation spilling out from the nest of mesas that dipped and darted through the landscape. She ground the tires to a halt there and climbed out ahead of D. W. Tepper. Caitlin kept her pace slow so he could keep up with her across the uneven land laden with boulders that glowed red beneath the spill of their flashlights.

The source of the flickering light rested upon a flat nesting of scrub amid a natural rock formation. She helped Tepper atop it, fifteen feet above the wasteland beyond, in the shadow of the jagged mesas that sliced the greater landscape like scissors.

Tepper dropped his hands on his knees while Caitlin dropped her hand toward the remnants of a small fire that, when fueled by the wind, kicked up the flickering flames she'd spotted. The rock formation offered a view clear to the construction lights set up over the dug-out trench from which something, in addition to those skeletons, had been removed.

"What do you make of this, Captain?" Caitlin said, kneeling by the remains of the fire enclosed by a nest of stones.

Tepper crouched alongside her and, still breathing hard, sifted his hand through some stray ash. "Whoever was here didn't leave too long ago."

Caitlin shined her flashlight about, but the smooth rock face wasn't conducive to holding footprints and there was nothing else in evidence that could tell her anything about who had been here.

"Someone was watching that site you're investigating, Captain," she said suddenly.

"Here we go again...."

"Hear me out on this. Hard to believe it was just coincidence, given the sight line straight to that hole in the ground."

Tepper started to rise, Caitlin needing to help him make it all the way back upright. "Where you going with this, Ranger?"

"Maybe whoever it was also happened to be around when that backhoe dug up the contents of that hole."

Tepper had the look of a man who wanted to be anywhere else in the world but here. "Or maybe they were roasting marshmallows and telling ghost stories around the campfire."

Caitlin ignored his comment and knelt back down, smoothing her hand through the cooling ash and feeling it pass over something smooth and white amid the char. She closed her fingers around what turned out to be a jagged, half-burned piece of paper, blackened at the edges. She shined her flashlight against it and stood up so Tepper could better regard it.

"Looks like some kind of receipt, Captain," she said, sliding an evidence pouch out of her pocket.

"You take those things into the shower with you?" He frowned.

"Only if I'm expecting to find something important in the drain."

Tepper squinted to give the piece of paper a closer look, as Caitlin fit it into the pouch. "Your dad and I used to use baggies. This was back in the Stone Age, when nobody knew what 'Ziploc' meant."

"I'm going to have this checked out," Caitlin said, sliding the evidence pouch into her pocket. "See if it leads anywhere."

Tepper cupped a hand against his ear. "Hear that, Ranger?"

"Hear what?"

"The winds of Hurricane Caitlin picking up, about to barrel down on the world." He lowered his hand and fought the wind to light a cigarette. "Yup, here we go again."

PART THREE

In 1878, the Rangers received a tip that the legendary train robber, Sam Bass, planned to knock over the bank in Round Rock. Bass was killed in a shoot-out with the Rangers. According to one account, the outlaw's last words were "Life is but a bubble, trouble wherever you go."

—"Lone on the Range:
Texas Lawmen" by Jesse Sublett, *Texas Monthly*, December 31, 1969

15

"I haven't been here in many years, muchachos, not since your great grandfather was murdered."

Luna Diaz Delgado held both her grandchildren's hands as she led them about the Zócalo, Mexico City's sprawling open air plaza reserved for only the most special of events.

Because today was turning out to be very special indeed. The sun burned hot, seeming to bake the concrete and turn the plaza into an oven, but the children didn't seem to mind, glad to have their grandmother all to themselves amid a smattering of both locals and tourists. Luna had men watching, on guard for the unexpected, but they kept their distance so as to allow for a measure of privacy and not unsettle her grandchildren.

"This was where your great-grandfather was assassinated," Luna told her oldest granddaughter and grandson. "A cowardly act, given it took all the cartels together to pull off, and then only barely."

"Were you sad?" wondered her nine-year-old grandson, Diego, taking Luna's hand.

"I was more angry than sad, and anger is a preferable emotion to grief any day. But you have to channel that anger. You have to learn patience."

Ten-year-old Isabella took the hand her brother had shed as quickly as he had grabbed it. "What does that mean?"

"In my case, it meant laying back for many, many years. I was one of the few survivors of the massacre that took my parents' life on the day of their wedding. I knew if I was patient, appeared weak and timid, I would have my revenge. It worked, because the cartels ignored me. They ignored me until the day I came for them, after they killed your grandfather, too."

"Abuela, you're hurting me," whined Isabella.

Luna Diaz Delgado looked down and realized how hard she was squeezing her granddaughter's hand. "*Lo siento,*" she apologized, letting it go and patting the girl's head.

"What did you do when you came for them?" Diego asked her.

"I made them watch as I killed their families, their wives and children, before I killed them last. I did it myself, because I needed the satisfaction. I needed to feel whole again."

Diego's mouth had dropped, his eyes moistening. "You killed their children?"

"But not their grandchildren," Luna comforted, which was true enough.

"Oh," the boy said, his tears forgotten before they began to fall.

"You know what they called me after that? 'La Viuda Roja.' Do you know what that means?"

"It's a spider." Diego nodded. "The red widow."

"Ah, the red widow isn't just any spider. They are the only species of spiders that hide their webs. They weave them in unopened palmetto leaves, making them almost impossible to spot. Their primary source of food are scarab beetles, which are much larger and stronger. The outlying stands of the web trap them, and when they struggle to pull free, they end up snared in the denser tangle of threads below, trapping them in the web for the red widow to eat slowly over time."

Diego's nose wrinkled in revulsion, but Isabella smiled.

"I'm glad you killed them, Abuela. I would have killed them too," she insisted. "They deserved it."

Luna ran her hand through her granddaughter's long, dark hair. "Yes, they did."

"La Viuda Roja," Isabella repeated. "I hope I have a name like that someday."

"But Abuela . . ." Diego started.

"Yes, muchacho?"

The boy's expression grew pained again. "I don't understand."

Isabella smirked, understanding all too well. Luna Diaz Delgado loved all her grandchildren equally, but Isabella, all ten years of her, was the apple of her eye, the first blood relative she believed capable of inheriting the family empire she had first maintained and then expanded, after the murder of her husband many years before.

"What was Abuelo like?" Isabella asked, as if reading her mind.

"My husband, your abuelo, was a very strong man whose lone weakness was he'd never give in to anyone."

"Why is that weak, Abuela?" Diego asked.

"Because true strength means keeping up appearances, letting people believe they own the upper hand, which fills them with a false sense of power. They aren't moved to action, because in their minds it is beneath them and their interests to do so. Abuelo did not believe in appearances and, as a result, the enemies he once thought were his friends killed him in this very plaza, where he'd come to meet them for a standard negotiation."

"I would have beaten them up," said Diego.

"I would have killed them, too," said Isabella, smiling tightly.

Luna couldn't help but smile. Yes, this little girl was the real thing, a spitting image of her grandmother in all the ways you couldn't see as well as the ways you could.

"Like Aunt Nola," Isabella added.

The smile slipped from Luna's face at the reference to the youngest of her four children. "Why do you say that?"

"Because she told me."

"Told you what?"

"That she kills people. It was when we were staying at your house and I was scared because I had a bad dream. Aunt Nola came into our room and told me I shouldn't be scared because if anyone tried to hurt me, she'd kill them, like she's killed lots of people. That's what she said."

"I don't remember," Diego interjected. "I was asleep."

"I never felt scared again after that," Isabella added.

Her resemblance to Nola was striking. And the truth was, Nola served Luna Diaz Delgado with her skills, just as Isabella would with hers, one day in the future.

"Your aunt Nola is very strong," Luna said, leaving it there.

"As strong as you, Abuela?" Isabella asked her, lovingly.

"Yes," Luna replied to her granddaughter, stroking her hair again, "but not as strong as you're going to be, *mi amor*."

"I'm tired," whined Diego. "Can we stop now?"

"Almost," she said, smoothing Isabella's hair. "There's one more thing we need to do first."

16

The Zócalo has been a gathering place for Mexicans all the way back to the Aztecs, serving as the prime location for major public ceremonies and military performances, anything with great pomp and circumstance. The plaza was enclosed by buildings on three sides and bracketed by towering flagpoles showcasing the Mexican flag billowing in the breeze.

Luna had watched many a swearing-in, issuance of a royal proclamation, military parade, and Holy Week ceremony from the rooftop Portal de Mercaderes restaurant looking east to the entire complex known as the Palacio Nacional. As a young girl, Luna recalled the Zócalo being little more than a decaying concrete block dotted with light poles and train tracks and a single flagpole rising from the center.

"I want to stop," Diego wheezed, grinding his sneakers into the pavement and stamping at it with his feet. "I want to go home."

"Soon," Luna said, doing her best to comfort him, while not letting the boy see the displeasure roosting in her eyes. "We're almost there."

They walked on, off the Zócalo. Down one side street and then another to an empty fountain with a statue of the Holy Mother in its center, set before a church that had been shuttered since Luna had bought the property. She had stationed plenty of men in the area to dissuade others from approaching today and, true to her instructions, none of them was in view.

The Holy Mother statue, and fountain itself, had been carved by a famed Mexican sculptor. Isabella stuck her hand forward, as if imagining she might catch some of the cool spray, and Luna watched a suddenly reanimated Diego mimic his sister's motion.

"What happened to the water, Abuela?" he asked her.

"I had it drained," she told her grandchildren. "This is an ugly place. There is no place for beauty here. Believe me, muchachos. Religion is meant for the weak. Your abuelo believed in God, never took a week off from church in his life, and look where that got him. I wish you had gotten the chance to know him. He would have loved you very much."

"He looks scary in his pictures," Diego noted.

"He *was* scary, all times except when he was around his family. And if he looked scary in the family pictures, it was because even then he was thinking of how to keep us all safe from his enemies, some of which he knew and some of which he didn't. He believed keeping his family safe was the best way he could serve the God to whom he believed he owed everything, all of his wealth and power. But where was that God when he was betrayed? Where was God when those who deceived and destroyed him deserved divine punishment? Where God had failed Abuelo, I succeeded."

"I'm hungry," whined Diego.

"You're always hungry," snickered Isabella.

"That is my life's mission," Luna told them both. "I will avenge your abuelo by making sure no others follow the false path their faith leads them down. I will show the world they are the victims of a sham perpetrated by those who need them to be weak and ineffectual. For the second time, fate has delivered the means to do this, to expose these purported men of faith for the charlatans they are. Soon it will be in my possession and the world will be forever changed."

"The ship!" Isabella beamed, recalling another part of her grandmother's story. "The ship with all the dead people you told us about. What you need was on board that!"

Luna nodded, impressed by her granddaughter's assumption. "Very good, muchacha. Your abuelo would be alive today if not for the sham places like this perpetuated on humanity. I want the two of you to think of that anytime you find yourself straying down that same path. Do you understand?"

Both her grandchildren nodded, even though it was clear that they didn't. Luna did not believe in letting children remain children for long. The longer they did so, the weaker they would be as adults. She had no problem imparting the rigors of reality to them to test their mettle, to see if they might be worthy of a place at a table far different from the one where they gathered as a family at the holidays.

Luna led her granddaughter by the hand toward the church steps, beckoning Diego to come along almost as an afterthought. She held her breath the whole way up the stairs and had to remind herself to breathe, once she'd pushed open the heavy wooden doors and stepped into the dust-ravaged church. It looked so much smaller than her memory showed her, tiny by some standards, to the point where she could not picture where all the bodies had fallen on her parents' wedding day, when she had served as a ring bearer who never got to deliver the ring. Standing there in the weak shroud of light radiating through the entrance, she recalled a similar light pushing through this same church's shadows just before that sound she'd taken as firecrackers began to ripple through the air.

Luna Diaz Delgado stood inside the church for the first time since that day, the sweet smell of incense replaced by mold and wood rot. She could've just let it crumble, as it would in time, but she was a patient woman and had waited a long time for the right day to complete the task she'd dreamed of for many years.

The cans of kerosene lay just where she'd ordered them left. Two of them—one for her and one for Isabella.

"Where's mine?" Diego asked, after she handed the second one to her granddaughter.

"Next time," Luna told him, turning to address Isabella. "I'm going to take this side. You take the other and just do everything you see me do, and be careful not to let any splash back upon you."

"*Si*, Abuela."

With that, the Red Widow twisted off the top of the can and began to pour out the kerosene, careful to soak portions of the pews as well as the floor. She glanced over at Isabella, ever so pleased to see the little girl mirroring her motions exactly. From this angle, amid the darkness barely broken by the spill of light pushing through the stained glass windows, Isabella didn't look like a little girl at all.

She looked like a woman.

They drained their cans within seconds of each other, then walked hand in hand back down the aisle toward the sulking Diego.

"Wait outside," Luna instructed.

"But, Abuela—"

"Do as I say," she ordered, no room for negotiation in her voice.

Diego fumed and stamped out of the church, leaving Luna alone with her granddaughter. She made sure Isabella saw the box of wooden matches she removed from her pocket.

"It would be nice if memories could be burned up as easily as wood. They can't be, so we must satisfy ourselves with burning their source."

"I don't like this place," Isabella said, behind a deep breath.

"The air still smells of blood, at least in my imagination, the blood of those I loved the most." She gestured toward the suspended figure of Christ in the midst of the Crucifixion. "That will be the last to catch, meaning He will have to bear witness to the burning of His house, just as I once did."

La Viuda Roja, the Red Widow, handed the box of matches to her granddaughter.

"But I want you to set the flame, my love. I want you to ignite the inferno that will consume this place people want to believe is holy. This is just the beginning, only the start."

Isabella slid open the box, removed a match, and ran the tip against the striker. The match flared to life.

"The flames you are about to set will soon consume every other building like this, so that false hope can be vanquished forever, so that people can no longer be played for fools."

Isabella tossed the match.

In the light of the catching flames, Luna Diaz Delgado thought she saw a tiny ring bearer wearing a white dress trudging up the aisle with a cushion clutched before her. Her father and mother staring lovingly toward her, their final smiles aimed Luna's way.

The surge of heat reached her before the crackle of firecrackers in memory. She took Isabella's hand and backed toward the door, suddenly reluctant to leave this place she hated, for the last time before it fell. Outside, she closed the big doors behind her, the glow of the flames already showing in the stained glass windows.

Diego, who'd been hopping around at the foot of the stone stairs, glimpsed the smoke starting to sift through the building.

"Abuela," he called out, "should we call el Departamento de Bomberos?"

"No, muchacho," Luna told him, unable to take her eyes from the building. "There are some fires that can't be stopped."

17

SHAVANO PARK, TEXAS

"What's wrong with your arm?"

Caitlin had just poured a cup of coffee when she heard footsteps outside on the front porch. She'd picked up her coffee, only after unsnapping the safety strap over her SIG Sauer, and peered through the living room blinds into the morning sun to find Cort Wesley Masters with a take-out cup of his own. He was seated on the front porch swing, sipping at the cup in his left hand while his right splayed next to him like deadweight.

"I can move it now," he said, flexing the fingers stiffly.

"You couldn't move it before?"

"Cramped up on me while I was leading the rescue of your friend Paz."

"He's your friend too," Caitlin said, not bothering to hide her concern. "And that was yesterday."

"Was it?" Cort Wesley asked, checking his watch. "I don't even know what day it is."

Caitlin touched his right arm, then pressed her fingers deeper, as if to push the life back into it, until he jerked it away.

"Do you have to do that?"

"Did that hurt?"

"I didn't feel a thing."

"Like, *nothing*?"

Cort Wesley flexed his fingers again, managing the task more easily. "See, it's getting better."

Caitlin backed off. "You get it checked out?"

"Why?"

"Because arms are supposed to move."

"It's a cramp, Ranger."

"You still haven't answered my question."

Cort Wesley sipped some more coffee. "The team medic checked me out on the flight home."

"What'd he say?"

"That it looked like a cramp."

"Looked like," Caitlin repeated.

"How about I get it checked out tomorrow and you leave me alone today?"

"Is that a proposition, Cort Wesley?"

He forced a smile. "As close as you're going to get to one, if you keep badgering me."

Cort Wesley nodded as he sifted through the steam to take a sip. "I need to tell you something."

"You trying to change the subject?"

Cort Wesley grabbed hold of Caitlin's left wrist and squeezed. "How's that feel?"

"Ouch."

He released his grasp. "See, I'm fine."

"What is it you want to tell me?"

Cort Wesley started balling his fingers into a fist, then opening them again, the motion growing smoother each time. "Down there, working that sniper rifle and watching the bodies drop like rag dolls, it felt strange and yet familiar. But I didn't realize why until I got back. I'm in the living room, looking at that flat screen the boys play their video games on, and I realize, that's it—gunning down those soldiers on the gallows platform didn't feel any different than getting my butt kicked by Luke and Dylan. Makes you wonder, doesn't it?"

Caitlin smiled thinly, reflectively. "I don't think you need to be worried about Dylan and Luke becoming desensitized to violence, not after all they've been through."

Dylan had just turned twenty-two and was still thinking about returning to Brown University to complete his junior year. Seventeen-year-old Luke, about to enter his senior year at Village Prep in Houston, was currently on a European tour organized by the school. It was hard, impossible even, to imagine how far they'd come and how much they'd grown since that day she'd watched their mother get gunned down, just steps away from this very swing.

"Jones wants to see me," Cort Wesley said suddenly.

"I saw him yesterday. Turns out the IT outfit that got wiped out was his go-to for private intelligence gathering. When did he call?"

"Message was waiting when my plane finally landed, a few hours back."

Caitlin started to raise her mug again, then changed her mind. "Wanna bet it's about Communications Technology Providers?"

"What's that?"

"The place that got hit." Caitlin had sketched out the broad strokes to Cort Wesley the night before, while he'd been flying home, but she had left out the details. "You know the one thing I can't get out of my mind?"

"I'm guessing there's a whole bunch of things, Ranger."

"One in particular, though. It's strange, but I didn't recognize the assault rifles the shooters were wielding."

"You not recognizing a firearm?"

"That's why it's stuck in my mind."

"European?"

"If so, that's where the shooters must have come from. Meaning they brought their guns with them."

"I see what you mean." Cort Wesley nodded, finishing his coffee and hoping Caitlin wouldn't say anything else about him holding the large take-out cup in his left hand instead of his right. "So what do you figure Jones needs me for?"

"My guess is trust is at a premium. He's circling the wagons."

"How's that involve me?"

"He trusts you."

"Well, I don't trust the son of a bitch as far as I can throw him."

"Not very far, with your arm like that, Cort Wesley. Anyway, in Jones's world, that passes for affection."

The two of them stood side by side against the front railing, looking out into the front yard.

"We never come out here in the day."

"It's August, Ranger. Forecast is for close to a hundred again."

"It's not always August, Cort Wesley."

"True enough. So maybe we don't want anyone to see us together."

"You think anyone's looking?"

Cort Wesley gazed out toward the neighborhood beyond. "They notice whenever a car backfires or somebody plays an action movie too loud with their windows open. Four of the houses we can see from where we're standing have renters in them now. I'm trying to make myself believe us turning the neighborhood into a war zone doesn't have anything to do with that, but somebody told me the homes on this street are worth a third less than comparable ones in Shavano Park."

"So we're bad for home values now?"

"I believe it's the occasional shoot-out that's the problem. Three of the homes where the owners still reside have installed bulletproof glass on their windows."

"Must've set them back a pretty penny."

"They haven't told me yet."

Caitlin squared her shoulders toward him. "You offered to pay?"

"Those kids from that neo-Nazi gang just missed a baby's crib with a five-point-five-six-millimeter from a fully auto M16. The bulletproof windows were my idea."

"Where you meeting Jones?"

"Bluebonnet Café in Marble Falls."

"That's our place, Jones and mine."

"You jealous, Ranger?"

"No, he's all yours. Just make sure you get that arm checked out on the way," Caitlin said, setting her coffee back down on the railing when her phone rang.

"How soon can you get down to headquarters?" Captain D. W. Tepper asked her when she answered it.

18

San Antonio, Texas

"Hey," Guillermo Paz announced to the five- and six-year-olds enjoying their morning snack, "who's ready for story time?"

The kids around him at Alamo Daycare cackled and hooted, rushing to claim the pillows littered across the floor.

"You've got to finish your milk first," Paz told them. "We're not going to start until everyone finishes their milk."

Paz felt a tugging on his leg and looked down to see a boy who barely came up to his knee, who was wiggling about with his legs pressed close together.

"Colonel Gee," he said, using the name they all called him. "I got to go wee-wee."

"So go."

"My mommy or daddy always takes me," responded the boy, whose name tag identified him as Marcus.

Paz knelt down, still well over a head taller than the boy, who was only at Alamo Daycare because citywide budget cuts had reduced the number of all-day kindergarten classes. "I just got back from my mommy's funeral."

The boy's shoulders sank, but his knees remained squeezed together to ward off an accident.

"When I was your age, we didn't have a bathroom in our house. We were supposed to use an outhouse behind the shack we called a home. But the smell in there was so bad, lots of times we just used the trench that ran behind our shack. We lived in a hillside slum, and the trench had been dug that way so the sewage could run downhill."

Marcus had curled his teeth over his lower lip. "I think I'll go to the bathroom myself."

"Good idea."

And it gave Paz one, too. He had been volunteering at Alamo Daycare for just over a month, before his imprisonment in his native Venezuela had forced him to take an unexpected sabbatical. This followed a stint volunteering at a soup kitchen he ended up leaving after mounting complaints from the homeless that he scared them. Paz shrugged the ignominy off, convinced it was more the life counsel he dispensed with their grilled cheese sandwiches at lunch and the religious services he forced the nighttime residents to attend after dinner that accounted for his dismissal.

After all, none of the five-year-olds who called him Colonel Gee seemed scared, and Paz found himself much more comfortable presiding over story hour than chapel hour.

"Who wants to hear about what I did while I was away?" Paz asked his young charges.

The tiny hands of the boys and girls shot up into the air, then went down, except for a girl whose name tag read "Lucy."

"Colonel Gee?"

"Yes, Lucy."

"Did you kill anyone while you were on your trip?"

"That's part of the story."

The kids got settled in, lounging comfortably atop their pillows and cushions, as he started.

"I wasn't supposed to go home anymore. They didn't like me there. I didn't have any friends, only enemies."

The kids uttered a collective sad sigh at that.

"All my friends were dead," he continued, "and I didn't have that many to start with. Who here loves their mother?"

All the hands shot up enthusiastically.

"I loved mine, too. But it had been a very long time since I'd seen her."

"Why's that?" Lucy asked him, raising her hand but not waiting for Paz to recognize her.

"I live in America now, in Texas. My life is here. And it would've been dangerous for my mother if I were anywhere near Caracas."

"What carcass?" asked a boy whose name tag was blocked from Paz's field of vision.

"Caracas," Paz corrected. "The city where I was born, where I lived when I was your age."

"Where you went wee-wee in a trench?" wondered the girl named Lucy.

"That's right. It's also where I killed my first man."

All the kids leaned forward now, hanging on his next words—even Marcus, who'd made a triumphant return from the boys' room.

"I was fifteen at the time," Paz continued.

"That's old," noted Marcus.

"Five years before, the man had stabbed my priest to death. I killed him with the same knife. I still have it. I'll bring it in for show-and-tell on Friday."

The children clapped.

"Why'd you wait so long?" asked Alex, which Paz knew was short for Alejandro.

"I waited until I was strong enough. Shakespeare wrote in *Hamlet*, 'This above all: to thine own self be true, and it must follow, as the night the day, thou canst not then be false to any man.' In other words, don't fool yourself, and if I had tried to kill the man who killed my priest when I was young and weak, I would have died too. So I waited until I grew bigger and stronger and until fate brought us together, and I knew it was a gift from God.

"My mother knew her time was coming, that she was going to die. She called me from the hospital and told me not to come home for her funeral. She told she'd be watching over me and that if I listened hard enough, I'd hear her words to me."

"And did you, Colonel Gee?" This from Buck.

Buck? Really? What kind of parent names their son Buck?

"Whenever I needed to hear them the most."

"But you went home anyway," Elena pointed out. "You did what your mommy told you not to."

"I had to go to her funeral because it was the right thing to do, even more so because I knew they'd be waiting for me. These were the same men who've been after me since I ran away, and I knew they wouldn't be able to resist witnessing my hanging."

"What's hanging?" asked Buck.

"They break your neck with a rope when you fall through a trapdoor."

"Does it hurt?"

"I don't know, because my friend killed all the bad men before they could open the door."

"I have friends," said Marcus.

"That's good."

"But they've never killed anyone."

"Maybe they will," Paz told the boy. "Maybe *you* will. But only if they do bad things, evil things. You only kill those who want to hurt you or others. Protecting the innocent, that's a good thing. Is anyone here a bully?"

No hands went up into the air.

"Who here hates bullies?"

All the hands shot up again.

"You could practice on them," Paz said to his young charges. "Not kill them, but hurt them after they hurt others. Let them know that kind of behavior won't be tolerated. Stop them in their tracks. Do you know what I'm getting at here?"

Blank, expressionless faces stared back at Paz.

"George Orwell," Paz continued, "wrote, 'People sleep peaceably in their beds at night only because rough men stand ready to do violence on their behalf.'"

"Are you a rough man, Colonel Gee?"

"Oh, yes, most definitely. I was born that way, just as my mother was born a bruja."

"A witch?" a girl named Paulina blurted out. "Your mother was a witch."

"That's what all the villagers thought, on account of the fact she got feelings about things, like visions," Paz related, thinking specifically of the one that had come up when he'd returned to their shack covered in blood after his priest died in his arms.

"You're going to take more lives than I can see. Your fate was sealed today, and now I see why, just as I see the blood staining your clothes. . . . The smell of blood will be forever strong on you, Guillermo."

Paz was about to tell the children how right she had turned out to be, when the day blackened outside. He turned back to his charges, wondering if they were seeing the same scene unfold out the window, but they were gone.

Replaced, to a child, with skeletons.

But the skeletons were moving, shifting about, just as the kids had been, and Paz even saw the mouths moving as he vaguely registered words aimed his way.

What's wrong, Colonel Gee?

We want to hear the rest of the story.

Yeah!

Did you kill all the bad guys?

It was impossible to kill all the bad guys, Paz wanted to tell the kids; there were just too many of them. Outside, beyond the windows, the darkness continued to thicken, and Paz was struck by a sense at once both familiar and unwelcome.

Something was coming.

Like his mother, he had the gift of visions. He lacked her talent for specifics, but he could see the big and bad well in advance of its coming. He knew, in that moment, that his Texas Ranger was going to get swept away in this, yet another maelstrom—the outlaw, too.

This was why God had brought him to Texas in the first place, why He had brought Caitlin Strong into his life. Turned out, the Almighty had had some pretty big plans for him, seeming to funnel a vast amount of the evil riddling the world straight to Texas. Like it was the epicenter of the immoral universe, the metaphysical low point to which so much of the world's shit sank.

"Colonel Gee?"

A girl's voice roused him and he realized he'd squeezed his eyes closed. When he opened them, the room was empty save for a man standing in the very back of the room, directly before him, a man as big as he was.

A man with no face, just a black void where it was supposed to be.

Paz held his eyes shut again, and this time, when he opened them, the sun was back and the skeletons were gone, the flesh-and-blood kids back in their places.

"Can we hear the rest of the story?" a boy asked.

"Everything but the ending," Paz told him, "because I don't know that part yet."

19

SAN ANTONIO, TEXAS

"You missed all the fun, Ranger," Young Roger greeted Caitlin, as soon as she entered Company G's conference room, which he had appropriated for the computer equipment confiscated from Communications Technology Providers the day before.

All of which was now gone.

"You lose something?"

"Somebody came and took it."

"Who?"

"They didn't say, not to me anyway. Captain Tepper brought them down here, looking none too happy about the prospects."

Jones, Caitlin thought, asserting his authority along with the fact that Homeland was taking point with this.

"Please tell me you got something."

"I got plenty, all of it tucked on a thumb drive I was ready to swallow, if it came to that."

"Good thing you won't have to pass it now," Caitlin told him.

Young Roger was in his midthirties but still didn't look much older than Dylan. Though a Ranger himself, the title was mostly honorary, provided in recognition of the technological expertise he brought to the table, which had helped the Rangers solve a number of Internet-based crimes, ranging from identity theft to credit card fraud to the busting of a major pedophile and kiddie porn ring. He worked out of all seven Ranger company offices on a rotating basis. Young Roger wore his hair too long and was never happier than when playing guitar for his band, the Rats, whose independent record label had just released their third CD, with a release party planned at Antone's, Austin's top club venue. Their alternative brand of music wasn't the kind she preferred, but it had grown on her, and hearing it live had given her a fresh perspective on the band's talent.

"You want to lay it out for me, Rog?" Caitlin picked up.

"I've got to sort through some more of the contents before I'm ready. You wouldn't believe some of the shit this Communications Technology Providers was into."

Caitlin recalled Jones explaining private intelligence firms and zero-footprint operations. "I wouldn't believe it if they weren't. Something else," she said, sliding the evidence pouch from the night before from her pocket. "I'd like to know what you make of this."

Young Roger inspected the charred piece of paper through the plastic. "Not much at first glance. Maybe not much more at second."

"I've got faith in you, Rog."

He looked at the contents of the pouch again, turning it upside down to check the other side. "It might be misplaced this time, Ranger."

"Just wave your magic wand and see what you can come up with."

"Abracadabra," Young Roger mocked, waving an imaginary wand through the air. "If only it were that easy."

"With you, it usually is."

He took another look at the front of the paper through the pouch's plastic. "You notice this thin smudge of red?"

"I thought it might be blood."

"Of course you did. But it looks symmetrical."

"Whatever that means."

"For me to find out."

"Anything more you can tell me about the men who came for the computers and servers, Rog?" Caitlin asked him.

"That's above my pay grade. You'll have to ask Captain Tepper."

"Meaning me," Tepper's voice chimed in from the conference room entrance.

20

SAN ANTONIO, TEXAS

They adjourned to Tepper's office on the third floor, Caitlin closing the door behind them after he took a seat behind his desk. This Texas Ranger company had been headquartered in San Antonio since before even her grandfather's time. A few years back, when Company F was relocated to Waco, Company G was established here as part of a long-awaited, modest Ranger expansion.

Since it was still morning, Tepper hadn't turned on the air-conditioning yet, and the summer heat was starting to push its way through the open window.

"Jones?" Caitlin started in, taking the chair set in front of Tepper's desk.

"Their IDs read Homeland, yup."

"Why the qualifier, Captain?"

Tepper stuck a Marlboro Red into his mouth and spoke with it dangling out the corner. "You want to give me back the lighter you just whisked off my desk?"

Caitlin tossed him the Bic she was still holding in her hand. "What happened to the one you kept chained to your desk with a computer lock?"

"That was an ashtray, and somebody sawed right through the cable and made off with it."

"You don't say."

"Wouldn't know anything about that, would you, Ranger?"

"Want to search me?"

"The ashtray disappeared a couple days ago. Wish I'd searched you then. Next time, I'm going to rig the thing to explode."

"Thanks for the warning, D.W. Now get back to Homeland. Jones didn't come himself?"

"Maybe he stayed in the car."

"That's not his style."

"Jones doesn't have any style, Ranger."

"Anyway," Caitlin said, leaning forward, "it turns out Young Roger had already transferred plenty of the data on those computers onto a thumb drive."

"That boy never ceases to amaze me."

"You should see his band."

Tepper lit up his Marlboro and chuckled. "You know the last concert I went to? Bruce Springsteen."

"The Boss? Now I'm impressed."

"Don't be. I don't think he was the Boss yet. It was 1974, at Liberty Hall up in Houston. Your dad and I were there on business."

"What would that be?"

Tepper yanked the cigarette from his mouth and held it before him, letting the smoke collect in the air between them. "Jesus Christ, that was over forty years ago. I can't even remember what I was doing going back four hours."

"Cort Wesley's on his way to meet up with Jones now. Sounds like it's connected to whatever he thinks led to the massacre yesterday."

"Five of the workers from that computer company, it turns out, are going to make it. Five lives saved, Ranger. All in all, not a bad day's work."

"Right place at the right time, Captain, but not soon enough to save the others, and I'm including Bub McNelly there."

"Anything else you want to know about the fate of those computers, you'll have to ask Jones."

"I can't wait. Meanwhile, Young Roger's going to sift through all the accumulated data in search of the reason why somebody ordered the deaths of all those techies."

Tepper started to flick the ashes into his ashtray, realizing just in time he'd yet to replace the one that had gone missing, and flicked them off into the trash can instead.

"Careful, D.W.," warned Caitlin. "Don't want to go starting fires, now."

"No worries, Ranger. Thanks to the winds of Hurricane Caitlin, I'm used to putting them out."

21

Marble Falls, Texas

"Sorry, cowboy," Jones greeted him, rising from the other side of the table, "we're way early for pie happy hour."

Cort Wesley pulled his chair out and settled down in it. "That's okay," he said, using his left hand to open a menu that had been set on the paper place mat listing the vast array of pie choices for later in the day, "you can buy me breakfast instead."

The Bluebonnet Café might've been famous for its daily buy one slice, get another slice free promotion, but all the food was good. Big portions served home style upon the same tables that had been there since the place opened a million years before. Their table was bare wood, neatly polished, with each chip, scratch, or mar bearing the story of someone who'd brought a piece of their life through the entrance.

"You up to speed on what happened in Dallas yesterday?" Jones asked, his voice lowered a few octaves.

Cort Wesley laid his right forearm on the table, feeling like he was lifting deadweight. "I thought you wanted to talk about Caracas."

"Caracas never happened, totally off the books. That's why I sent you. That also means no reports, in writing or otherwise."

"Plausible deniability in case the Venezuelan government issues a formal complaint?"

"They won't, and Washington wouldn't give them the time of day even if they did. I do have one question for you, before we drop the whole thing: What the hell was Paz thinking?"

"You're asking me?"

"It's a question only you or the Ranger can answer."

Cort Wesley didn't need to ponder the issue further. He worked his right hand into and out of a fist to assure himself that the cramping that had plagued him was continuing to improve. "I think it all played out exactly the way he wanted it to. I think leaving Venezuela the way he did left him feeling like he ran away, so he ran back and left them something they could remember him by."

"He couldn't have known I'd send in the cavalry, cowboy."

"Really? This is Paz we're talking about." Cort Wesley waited for a server to fill the big coffee mug placed in front of him. "And he's clearly not what you called me here to talk about."

"I'm putting you on yesterday's massacre, on behalf of Homeland."

"Texas Rangers already got it covered, Jones."

"Not their jurisdiction."

"Since when did that stop you-know-who?"

Jones nodded, grudgingly accepting Cort Wesley's point. "We'll let her work the boundaries while you work outside the lines, as in getting me a line on who was responsible. I'm more interested in that than what they were after. Take Paz along for the ride, if you want."

"That a suggestion or an order?" Cort Wesley asked him, settling on a veggie egg white omelet.

"Whoever it is you're after thought nothing of machine-gunning a whole bunch of civilians yesterday, cowboy. You tell me."

The server came and took Cort Wesley's order, Jones saying he was fine with just coffee.

"Can you get me a detailed ballistics report? And any crime scene photos that picture the guns the shooters came packing?"

"Sure, as soon as you tell me what you need them for."

"This morning Caitlin mentioned something about not recognizing the weapons the shooters were using. Since she's shot just about every gun on the planet, that raised a flag."

Jones shifted uncomfortably in his chair. "I've got grunts I can send off to chase bullets."

"They don't have my sources or my perspective. I've been at this awhile, Jones."

"In case you've forgotten, I'm no stranger to it, either. I didn't always drive a desk, cowboy."

"Since those were your people who got gunned down yesterday," Cort Wesley told him, "I hope your license isn't up for renewal anytime soon."

"The bodies are only part of my problem," Jones said, as if he were speaking of a lost dry cleaning order.

"Touching display of compassion."

Jones gave the place mat menu a fresh look, as if regretting that he hadn't ordered anything. "You talk to the Ranger this morning?"

"I don't even know what time it is. I haven't exactly gotten a lot of sleep lately."

"I'll take that as a yes, so let me give you the latest: all the computer equipment she removed from Communications Technology Providers without authorization was confiscated from Company G headquarters."

"I'd expect nothing less of you, given how much you enjoy marking your territory."

Jones leaned forward, close enough for Cort Wesley to smell the black coffee on his breath. "That's the problem, cowboy, because I had nothing to do with it. No one associated with Homeland or any part of the U.S. government did."

Cort Wesley held his stare, unsettled for the first time since he'd sat down. "What's that leave us with?"

"Exactly what I expect you to find out," Jones said, lowering his gaze. "After you get that arm checked out."

"You noticed?"

Jones shook his head.

"Caitlin?"

Jones nodded.

"I think I might shoot her."

"She told me you'd say that, cowboy. Told me to tell you only if you use your right hand."

22

SAN ANTONIO, TEXAS

"Got a few minutes, Doc?" Caitlin asked Bexar County Medical Examiner Frank Dean Whatley, fortunate enough to have caught him in his office instead of the lab.

"Not if it's about those skeletons Captain Tepper dug out of the desert last night. And if it's about those poor bastards left dead after that shoot-out in Dallas yesterday, you've come to the wrong city."

"I'm here about bodies, all right, just not either of those sets."

"Is there another gunfight you've been involved in lately that slipped my mind?"

"Not me, Doc, and not a gunfight, either."

Frank Dean Whatley had been the Bexar County medical examiner since the time Caitlin was in diapers. In recent years he'd grown a belly that hung out over his thin belt, seeming to force his spine to angle inward at the torso. Whatley's teenage son had been killed by Latino gangbangers when Caitlin was a mere kid herself. Ever since then, he'd harbored a virulent hatred for that particular race, from the bag boys at the local H-E-B supermarket to the politicians who professed to be peacemakers. With his wife lost first in life and then in death to alcoholism, he'd probably stayed in the job too long. But he had nothing to go home to, no real life outside the office, and remained exceptionally good at his job, which he approached with rare pathos and compassion for those who had the misfortune of ending up on one of his steel slabs. Caitlin had run into him at a Walmart once, pushing a cart full of linens. He had said he liked refreshing the supply, out of respect for those whose deaths he was charged with detailing.

The Bexar County Medical Examiner's Office and morgue was located just off the Loop 410, not far from the Babcock Road exit on Merton Mintor. It was a three-story beige building that also housed the county health department and the city offices for Medicaid. The office inevitably smelled of cleaning solvent, with a faint scent of menthol clinging to the walls like paint to disguise the odor of decaying flesh. The lighting was dull in the hallways and overly bright in offices like Whatley's. She'd had occasion to come here often over the years, but normally to discuss current investigations, as opposed to those undertaken twenty-five years ago.

Whatley looked up from the stack of papers he was sorting through on his desk, eyeing Caitlin with a frown nearly swallowed by his encroaching jowls. "You're talking about Fort Stockton, those bodies your dad came upon at the freight yard in 1994."

"I am indeed."

He looked back down. "Jim Strong worked that case with Captain Tepper. Ask him."

"I did. He sketched the broad details about the night in question, what was waiting for my dad in that freight car, and how it took them both to Chihuahua."

Whatley pondered that briefly. "He didn't tell you about the bodies, what became of them after I tried to figure out what killed them?"

"Tried?"

"Long story, Ranger."

"That's why I'm here, Doc."

Whatley gave her a long, hard gaze, as if looking for something he'd never seen before. "Where did D. W. Tepper leave off, exactly?"

"In Mexico, when he and my dad came face-to-face with the Red Widow."

"Then pull up a chair and strap yourself in, Ranger. It gets a little crazy from there...."

23

Chihuahua, Mexico; 1994

"So what do you say, Tejano?" the woman known as the Red Widow continued, from across the Chihuahua train depot. "Can we call a truce?"

"I don't have any bone to pick with you, señora," Jim Strong said, unsettled slightly by the tinny echo of his voice

"I was speaking of the history between Mexico and the Texas Rangers."

"Last time I checked, ma'am, that history doesn't include you and me. We got no history between us whatsoever. Isn't that right, D.W?" he added, looking toward Tepper.

"Not directly, anyway," the Red Widow said, with just enough of a smile to let Jim know they'd crossed paths in the past, at least peripherally.

"Well, if it turns out I killed any of yours, I hope you won't take it personally."

"Likewise, Tejano."

"I believe you have me confused with someone else, ma'am."

"And why would you believe that?"

"Because the term 'Tejano' refers to a Texan who's a Mexican American. That's not me."

"The term was also used to denote residents of your state who were descended from the original Spanish-speaking settlers, the true founders of Texas. So calling you that implies respect and honor, even if it's not technically accurate. Call it a colloquialism."

"Then I'll accept it in that spirit exactly, providing you have your men there lower those Thompsons."

Delgado waved a hand to signal them to do just that, and Jim watched the guns go down en masse. "Magnificent weapons, aren't they? Formidable and historic at the same time."

"I've never shot one myself, ma'am. Neither has my partner here. But my dad, Earl Strong, knew his way around a Thompson from both sides of the barrel," Jim said, picturing the fury of what a drum- or mag-fed burst of .45-caliber shells could do to a man.

"I appreciate your sense of history and its importance, Tejano. Something else we have in common."

"I wasn't aware we had anything in common."

Luna Diaz Delgado ignored his comment. "You're here about last night's train car robbery in Fort Stockton."

"There's also the matter of those three men found dead inside the empty car, not to mention a murdered train crew and two men identified from their photos as ex–Mexican Special Forces. They were killed without even getting to their guns. Means they faced formidable opposition, I'd say."

Luna Diaz Delgado wasn't a young woman, although Jim Strong couldn't have said exactly how old she was. Staring at her from across the old railway station, all he could see was her beauty. Like all Rangers, and Texas law enforcement in general, he'd heard all the stories about her. How Luna Diaz had been one of the few survivors of the massacre that had taken the lives of her parents. The massacre had been laid at the feet of rival drug cartels, and Luna had ended up being raised by working-class relatives of her mother, embarking on a much different future than being part of a family that eschewed power.

By her mid teens, that future left her as a waitress at a Mexican bar frequented by cartel honchos, which included one Hector Delgado. One night, while Delgado sat at his usual back corner table, Luna overheard a pair of men she'd already figured for gunmen talking about making their move. So she kept her eyes on the two men, until she spotted the sawed-off shotguns beneath the bulky coats they'd yet to shed.

Luna's intention had been to approach Hector Delgado to warn him. But that plan went bust when the two would-be assassins drew back their coats to go for their sawed-offs. The only thing Luna had time to do was grab the heavy top-shelf tequila bottle she'd pulled from the bar in case she needed it. The men were shoving their chairs aside when she slammed the bottle over the head of the nearest man, felt it shatter against his skull, spraying glass and alcohol through the air. All she had left was the neck of the bottle, finished in a jagged edge, which she promptly jammed into the second man's throat as he was yanking his sawed-off from some makeshift holster. A blood spurt erupted, showering her and pretty much everyone else within ten feet of its spray.

Hector Delgado didn't just thank Luna for saving his life, he married her at the tender age of what turned out to be sixteen—well, Jim corrected in his mind, seventeen by the day of their wedding. That was 1980, by his recollection, and Luna Diaz Delgado didn't look any less beautiful fourteen years later, at the age of thirty-one. She'd seamlessly taken over her husband's criminal enterprise after he was assassinated two years before, and according to what Mexican authorities knew but couldn't prove, she had proceeded to kill the three other cartel leaders thought to be complicit in Hector's murder, along with their families. In the years since, that story had been corrected to eliminate the conspiracy angle, Luna opting to kill all three drug titans because she didn't know which of them was behind her husband's death.

The legend of Luna Diaz Delgado had been born, and now Jim Strong found himself standing thirty feet away from the person behind it.

"The missing cargo is none of your concern, Tejano," Delgado asserted.

"Since we're having this discussion, ma'am, I'm going to guess that cargo belongs to you."

"Guessing and knowing are two entirely different things. This is no concern of yours, no concern of the Texas Rangers, your state, or your country."

Jim Strong took off his Stetson and held it by his hip. "Well, ma'am, there is the matter of the train crew. Their murders are surely of concern to their families—all based in Texas, which makes it my concern, too."

Delgado nodded, conceding Jim's point. Neither had moved to close the gap between them, but they hadn't widened that gap either.

Their positions were frozen in time and space, two predators sizing each other up and opting not to chance a fight that would likely lead to the death of both.

It was Jim Strong who broke the silence. "I've said what I came here to say, ma'am. Learning more about that cargo headed here would help me bring a killer to justice, a killer who's hurt people on both sides of the border. I mistakenly believed you might want to help me catch a killer so I could get you your cargo back."

"I'm sorry you misjudged the situation, Tejano. But leaving this case alone is for your own good, yours and your daughter, Caitlin's. Fourteen years old now—have I got that right?"

Jim Strong felt himself stiffen. "Let's leave family out of this, ma'am. Notice I haven't mentioned your sons, all three of them in school under false identities back in Texas for safekeeping. If you'd like, I can check in on them from time to time, just to make sure they're okay."

Delgado stood there like a statue before him. "You came into my world today, Tejano. You don't want me coming into yours."

The threat should have gotten a rise out of Jim, should have angered, if not enraged him. But somehow the woman known as the Red Widow didn't pack a lot of bite behind the comment, as if it were something she had to say. Jim had barely recorded the words, too busy staring at her to be either frightened or intimidated. She was like some devilish she-beast hypnotizing him with her looks and guile, a modern-day Medusa. He knew he needed to break her stare or risk turning to stone there and then.

"I believe Ranger Tepper and I will be going," he managed finally.

"I approve of your decision."

"I don't care one way or another about your approval, ma'am."

Luna Diaz Delgado's expression flirted with a smile. Jim Strong felt something melt inside him and couldn't take his eyes off her, whether he turned to stone or not.

"It's for the best, Ranger, believe me."

"What is?"

"For both of us," the Red Widow continued, as an afterthought.

"Care to explain yourself, señora?"

"I believe I already have. And I don't want to keep you any longer. It's a long drive home, after all."

Jim Strong's eyes fell on the thugs holding the freshly oiled and shiny Thompsons. "Ranger Tepper and me are gonna make our way out now, ma'am. We'll keep our hands in evidence and in return I expect you'll order your men to do the same and not raise those Thompsons again."

"They heard you, Tejano. My men all speak very good English."

Jim gave them a longer look, picturing these men, or others just like them, backing Luna Diaz Delgado's efforts to gain revenge for her husband's murder. Standing at the ready while she killed the family members of her rivals one at a time. It was impossible to visualize someone this beautiful being capable of acts so heinous and violent.

"I'll keep you informed on our progress recovering your cargo that cost ten men their lives, señora," Jim said, tipping his hat her way.

Something changed in Luna Diaz Delgado's expression, a mix of fear and vulnerability showing for a brief moment. "Trust me, Tejano, that's only the beginning if we don't get it back."

24

"I don't suppose you can tell me where things went from there," Caitlin said, when Doc Whatley stopped.

"There is one other thing, Ranger."

"More of the story?" Caitlin posed expectantly.

"Could be. I'm not sure."

"How's that, Doc?"

"I spent the morning examining the four skeletons Captain Tepper supervised being lifted out of the desert near Sonora last night. What you're about to hear didn't come from me, Ranger. I haven't gotten all that far yet, but I can tell you, based on the condition and general decomposition, that those bones have been in the ground for right around twenty-five years."

"Dating just about back to 1994," Caitlin surmised, recalling how anxious and on edge D. W. Tepper had been the night before.

"Like I said, you didn't hear it from me."

"Anything else you didn't tell me?"

Whatley's expression remained flat. "The owners of those skeletons had all been shot. Big bullets, too. I'd say forty-five caliber."

"My dad carried a forty-five. And now we've got something gone missing from a railroad car in 1994 and something somebody went to great pains to bury forever being yanked out of the ground. Makes you think, doesn't it?"

Whatley didn't respond, having gone as far as he could.

"Anything else, Ranger?"

"You mean, besides the rest of the story about Jim Strong getting mixed up with Luna Diaz Delgado?"

"She's still at it, you know, still among the most powerful and definitely the most feared in Mexico."

"I've heard of her," Caitlin told him, "like pretty much everybody else in Texas law enforcement has. But nothing's ever led us to cross paths."

"Now *that* would be a confrontation people would be willing to pay to see."

"If the occasion comes up, maybe we could sell tickets on pay-per-view. Now get back to those bodies, Doc, the ones my dad found in that train car."

Whatley frowned, then shrugged behind his desk. "There's not a lot to tell.

I couldn't make hide nor hair of what caused their deaths. I suppose a man's heart can just stop and his breathing can seize up without firm explanation in science. But three men at the very same time, after being exposed to the very same thing?"

"'Exposed,'" Caitlin repeated.

"It was a conclusion I came to on my own, having eliminated everything else. Captain Tepper told you the crime scene techs that removed the bodies wore hazmat gear, right?"

"He did."

"The problem being, whatever hazard there might've been was long gone by the time they got to the scene, and Jim Strong before them."

"D.W. mentioned my dad coming to the conclusion that something heavy had been removed from that freight car—three shipping crates of identical size, was the way Captain Tepper put it."

"So your next question is did Jim Strong ever find out what they contained?"

"You must be psychic, Doc."

"Don't have to be psychic to state the obvious. But I can't help you. I wish I could, but I can't. Maybe if the CDC hadn't removed the bodies from my possession, I'd be able to tell you more about how this worked out. But if you're trying to connect that freight car, the bodies, and Delgado's missing cargo to those bones and whatever else was in that big hole in the ground, you'll have to find the clues you need someplace else. If it was Jim Strong who buried the bodies with whatever it was that got dug up from that ditch, it's the first I'm hearing of it, and I don't know anyone else who's ever heard anything, either."

"Well, Doc, somebody knew where to dig. That same somebody made a connection that we can't, and whatever Jim Strong thought he'd buried forever is back in the world again."

Whatley looked like a man feeling for a wallet he feared had slipped from his pocket. "No proof at this point that it was those same three packing crates, something you'd be wise to keep in mind."

"Sure thing, but the possibility remains. It's out there."

Whatley hesitated before responding. "You still got your dad's old forty-five lying around?"

"You know I do."

"Bring it down and let me run it through ballistics. Let's find out one way or another if the slugs that killed those four bodies somebody buried in the desert came from that weapon."

"I'll go get the forty-five right now, Doc. I'm unofficially off duty until DPS clears me in yesterday's shooting."

"That never stopped you before, Ranger."

"And it's not stopping me now. You might say this case that might involve my father got dropped in my lap at just the right time."

Whatley scolded her with his gaze. "You'd be doing exactly what you're doing now, even if it were the wrong time."

"True enough."

A heaviness settled between them, Whatley holding his gaze on Caitlin in accusatory fashion, the way he might focus on a criminal from the witness box in court. "Don't do it, Ranger."

"Don't do what, Doc?"

"What you're thinking."

"What am I thinking?"

"That the best way to find out the connection between that night in Fort Stockton in 1994 and whatever got pulled out of the ground last night is to pay a visit to Luna Diaz Delgado."

"Know something about her I don't?"

Whatley squeezed his hands into fists. "Just the fact that the gangbangers who murdered my son worked for a cartel that was under her control. This woman's been like a human Venus flytrap ever since she took over for her husband."

"All the same, Delgado might be the only person who can tell me what killed those three men in the train car, maybe even who made their bodies disappear."

Whatley looked hardly impressed with the prospects of that. "If she didn't tell Jim Strong, what makes you think she'll tell you?"

"We don't know what she told my dad after their first meeting, do we?"

"No, Ranger, but we sure know Delgado's still around, almost twenty-five years later, while everyone who's crossed her is long gone."

"Sounds to me like she knows which fights to pick, Doc."

"So?"

"So she didn't pick one with the first Texas Ranger she met and she's not going to pick one with the second."

"You sure about that?" Whatley posed, in a voice that dragged out like a stuck record.

25

"You look like the greeter at Walmart, Gunny," Cort Wesley Masters said to the man behind the main counter of the Nardis Gun Club, the longer standing of two in the area, located at the intersection of the 410 and I-10. "All that's missing is the smock."

The grizzled man with close-cropped hair, angular face, and ridged cheekbones glanced down at the black polo shirt embroidered with the Nardis logo. "Way we go about our business here is more like Disney World. Goddamn Magic Kingdom of Magnums."

"How about the Tomorrowland of Tommy Guns?"

"I was thinking more like the Haunted Mansion of HKs."

"Works for me, Gunny."

"What can I do for you, sir? Need a lane? Just got in a few beauties you'd fall in love with at first sight."

"Another time, Gunny," Cort Wesley said, thinking of the right hand he'd tucked into his pocket so the man behind the counter wouldn't notice anything awry. "And how many times have I told you not to call me 'sir'?"

"I imagine quite a few, but I can't rightly remember the exact number...sir."

"I need your help with something."

"I'm all ears, or eyes if that's what you need."

"Eyes for starters. You been paying any attention to the gunfight in Dallas yesterday?"

"Whole lot of folks got plugged, bad guys and good. I heard it was your girlfriend who gunned down the bad."

"My girlfriend?"

"You got another term to describe her?"

Cort Wesley realized he didn't, though several options came to mind that he couldn't quite put a label on. Like the way she'd become as close a thing to a mother as his boys had had over the years. Maybe his resistance to Gunny's term was over the fact that his last girlfriend, and the mother of his boys, Maura Torres, had been gunned down on account of him. Such things tend to have lasting effects.

Gunny's full name was Sergeant Tom Baer. Their paths had first crossed during Operation Desert Storm, where Cort Wesley had served with the Special Forces—first men in, last men out, as they say. Baer had already enjoyed a full career up until then but had served anyway, and had even forced himself back into the army in some ill-defined capacity when Iraq heated up for a second time at the same time that Afghanistan got hot for the first. And Cort Wesley had no doubt that if things got hot somewhere else today, Gunnery Sergeant Tom Baer would be on the first plane out tomorrow.

The Nardis Gun Club, meanwhile, offered San Antonio's most polished shooting facility, if not the city's outright finest. It boasted a dozen firing lanes where club members could shoot numerous ammo loads at targets strung at various distances. In stark contrast to the days when teenagers learned to shoot in their backyards, this was where Cort Wesley had taken both Dylan and Luke. Dylan had taken to the process right from the get-go, a fact that now haunted Cort Wesley, given how often his oldest son had ended up on both sides of a gun barrel. Luke, on the other hand, was far from a natural and seemed to hate the whole atmosphere, as much as his brother loved it.

Go figure, right?

For somebody who'd grown up in a time of no-frills shooting ranges, the Nardis Gun Club felt more like a country club. From a lounge stuffed with leather couches to a snack bar to a training and service staff outfitted in those matching polo shirts, the club boasted a family-oriented atmosphere and featured a regular newsletter, a member-of-the-month board, regular shooting competitions, occasional guest speakers from the shooting or law enforcement communities, and instructors who looked more like golf pros. Cort Wesley figured that Gunny's presence as manager represented a compromise with the old school of doing things—a living, breathing, war-born symbol lifted from another age and world to be plopped right down amid the automatic air fresheners that pushed the scent of gun oil from the air.

"Well," Tom Baer started from behind the counter, "it's a quiet time of day, so you've got my full attention. How 'bout you show me what's tucked in that envelope there?"

26

Cort Wesley used his left hand to slide out from the envelope pictures of the assault rifles the shooters had used in Dallas the day before.

"Okay," Tom Baer said, lifting onto the bridge of his nose a pair of reading glasses that had been dangling from his neck, "what am I looking at?"

Cort Wesley was still looking at him, wearing a slight smirk on his face.

Tom Baer took his glasses off and put them on again. "You wanna check my driver's license, see if I'm old enough to wear them?"

"In my mind, Gunny, a man who walks on water doesn't have vision problems."

"Yeah? Well, check these out," he said to Cort Wesley, turning his head from one side to the other to reveal the pair of hearing aids curled around the cartilage. "Price I'm paying for teaching dumb lugs like you how to shoot straight."

"So turning sixty-five had nothing to do with it."

Tom Baer laid his beefy forearms on the glass gun display counter in a way that inflated the size of his ropy biceps ridged with veins. "I've been kicking ass for around sixty of those years and have no intention of stopping, in case you're keeping score."

"You were kicking ass when you were five?"

"Playgrounds have a pecking order, sir, and I wasn't about to let anyone beat me to the top of the jungle gym." He started to arrange the photos in neat rows before him. "Now, let's see what we got here...." Baer whistled. "Man oh man, that Ranger girlfriend of yours must be one hell of a shot to take out a hit team wielding these. How is it you've never brought the great Caitlin Strong around here for a go at our range?"

"I'm afraid you'd steal her from me, Gunny."

"Yup, my balls have the consistency of old-fashioned hardball rounds. Too bad they've shrunk to about the same size."

Cort Wesley was still smiling when Baer plopped a finger down on the assault rifles, all with perforated sound suppressors affixed to the ends of their squat barrels.

"That, my friend," Baer started, tapping at the picture, "is a PM-84 Glauberyt nine-millimeter Para submachine gun. Manufactured in three different plants and standard issue for divisions of the Polish military, as well as mostly special operations outfits in those Eastern European countries that separated from the Soviet Union. Now, a few years back, someone in ordnance for the Polish military filled out a requisition order with a typo that resulted in the government being the proud owner of ten thousand weapons they had no use for."

"Don't tell me, Gunny ... the Poles sold them as surplus."

"Okay, I won't tell you. But that doesn't change the fact it happened. They sold almost that entire batch of PM-84s to anyone who was offering anywhere near the asking price, the vast majority of orders coming through in bulk. End result: anybody tall enough to ride Space Mountain at Disney, like my grandkids, could buy a state-of-the-art killing machine for pennies on the dollar."

"What you're telling me is there might be no way to trace the weapons."

Tom Baer lifted the picture up and regarded it again before responding. "Sometimes, who you can rule out leaves you with the best candidates to rule in. Not a single NATO nation uses this weapon, and even less ever train with it. Need I tell you how important that is?"

"Refresh my memory."

"Professionals only work in real time with the weapons they train with. I really need to tell you that?"

"I just wanted to hear it from an expert, Gunny."

"Well, let me know when you find one. I'm gonna hazard a guess here: those four shooters your girlfriend plugged came with no IDs and nothing whatsoever to give you any notion of who they might be or where they might've come from."

Cort Wesley nodded. "I'm impressed."

"I do consult from time to time. And, in case you've forgotten, there was a time before glasses and hearing aids when I actually practiced what I preached."

"I seem to remember a time or two."

"Bottom line being that you're looking at Europeans here. And I'd start my search in Italy, Austria, or Latvia."

"Why?"

"Because," said Gunnery Sergeant Tom Baer, "those are the countries that bought the most PM-84s when Poland held that fire sale. If I'd been on the mailing list, I'd have ordered up a couple myself. Magnificent weapon. I never heard of a single one jamming in the field, and I don't have to tell you how rare that is for submachine guns."

Cort Wesley was about to direct Baer's attention to the photographs of a sleek, elegant semiautomatic pistol, when Baer snatched up one of them on his own.

"To further the case I'm making here," he started, eyes remaining fastened on the photo like a camera, "this is a Steyr M series semiauto pistol—the M9, my personal favorite of the line manufactured by the Austrian gun maker Steyr Mannlicher. Not so coincidentally, Austria and Italy again are among the two biggest buyers, and have been ever since 1999, when the M series first came out."

"Think you could narrow it down a bit more than that, Gunny?"

"As in . . ."

"As in what groups might be most likely to be operational with these weapons in those countries."

Tom Baer's forehead crinkled as he pondered Cort Wesley's question. "That's a pretty big pond to cast my line into. But I've got my share of sources among the gun-worshipping hordes over in Europe who might be able to narrow things down a bit." Gunny thought for a moment, Cort Wesley watching him fiddle with his matching hearing aids. "Gunmen traveling as light as these were must've had a staging ground where they stowed their passports, airline tickets. Out-of-the-way motel off the beaten path, most likely. You find that, you find them, and render me superfluous. And while you're at it, ask your girlfriend if she remembers anything about their stances, the way they held their weapons, the precision of their reload. Those kinds of answers can further narrow down their point of origin, get us closer to the source."

"But it's a safe bet we're looking at Europeans here," Cort Wesley said, still trying to make sense of that.

"They're sure as shit not Texans, and I don't know a single gunman in the entire US of A who'd use a PM-84 or a Steyr. They're more likely to use a Star Wars blaster or lightsaber, even though the Steyr compares favorably to the Glock, which has never been my weapon of choice, and is a distant cousin of the SIG Sauer line, like the one your girlfriend used up in Dallas yesterday. I'm surprised SIG hasn't come a-calling to make her their international spokesman."

"They did. The conversation didn't go well."

Baer chuckled, coming up just short of a laugh. "How could it? Gunfighters don't fancy giving endorsements. Might as well paint a target on their backs."

"Caitlin Strong doesn't need to endorse a gun line for that, Gunny. The target's already permanently in place."

"Texas Rangers wouldn't have it any other way, either. I've worked with enough of them, on this range and others, to appreciate their respect, even reverence, for the weapon they're holding. And I respect any man, or woman, who's part of an outfit that requires a certain shooting standard to get in and stay in. Where's the little lady shoot, by the way?"

"Old range without couches or smoothies, where her grandfather taught her."

Tom Baer nodded. "I think I know the place. We got an anniversary celebration coming up, and it just so happens I was looking for a special guest. Think you could ask your girlfriend?"

"Sure thing. Least I can do, Gunny."

Baer gazed about lethargically, as if totally unimpressed by his surroundings. "Not what she's used to, of course. At her range, they likely spray the air with gun oil to make people feel at home."

Cort Wesley sniffed at the air. "What was it I smelled when I first stepped through the door?"

"Something linen-scented from Glade, if you can believe that shit."

"Beats the smell of blood, Gunny."

Baer started to smile, then stopped, with a gleam holding in his eyes. "Not for my money, Captain Masters."

27

San Antonio, Texas

As a soldier in an army dedicated to eliminating any threats posed to the Catholic Church, the first thing Enrico Molinari did upon reaching San Antonio was to seek out a venue to properly pay reverence to those whom he served.

San Fernando Cathedral on West Main Plaza had been founded in March of 1731 by a group of fifteen families from the Canary Islands, at the invitation of King Philip V of Spain. It was the oldest continuously functioning religious community in the entire state, and also the oldest standing church building and cathedral sanctuary in the United States, adding to both its majesty and its holiness. Jim Bowie had been married here before dying at the Alamo at the hands of Santa Anna, who used the building as an observation post. The cathedral claimed that Bowie, along with Lieutenant Colonel William Travis and Davy Crockett himself, had been ceremonially buried in the church's graveyard as his official resting place.

Molinari was not enough of a student of Texas history to know if that was true, one way or another. Since the heroes' bodies had all been burned after the famous battle, he supposed anybody could claim anything they wanted to.

Only within a house of the Lord like this one could Molinari conjure the memories of his becoming, from that very moment the flames swallowed him in a single *poof*, the pain instantly indescribable, but somehow welcome. The heat first roasted and then stole his breath, left him praying for the moment darkness would replace the bright flames and he'd be on his way to someplace else.

Then Molinari felt a wash of air and something cold shoving its way through the heat. He pictured his body melting into nothing, sucked back into the ground from which it had once sprung. He realized the pain was back, a million times worse. He wanted to scream, but there was no air, and when the breath came, it felt like somebody else's being shoved into his lungs.

In a brief moment of clarity and consciousness, Molinari realized he'd been rescued, and he wanted to tell his fellow officers not to bother, to just let him die so he wouldn't feel the pain anymore. But he couldn't speak at all, much less those words, and instead of letting him die they did everything they could to make sure he lived. Of course, none of those efforts mattered, couldn't matter, because Molinari had been burned so badly. Just some more pain to endure, hopefully broken by pain medication, before death mercifully took him in its grasp. But then the most unexpected thing happened: he lived. Doctors proclaimed it a miracle.

For Molinari's part, that only lasted until he looked in the mirror at the monster he had become.

The miracle of his survival turned Molinari into a cause célèbre. Religious groups and movements claimed him as their own, racing to see which could pay his substantial medical bills first. But one group rose above the others by going beyond even that, by having him transferred to the world's premier burn clinic, where the costs of his treatment were virtually incalculable.

An endless series of skin grafts ensued, many of the procedures experimental and years away from approval in the United States. The pain they wrought was worse than anything, even those initial moments when the flames first consumed him. The process unfolded over what could have been months but was more likely years. Molinari's sense of time was lost to the haze of medications that cut through the agony while they sliced away his very being. He had the real sense that he was mired in the midst of a great becoming, a biblical teaching, even prophecy come to life.

But we all, with unveiled face, beholding as in a mirror the glory of the Lord, are being transformed into the same image, from glory to glory, just as from the Lord, the Spirit.

That passage from Second Corinthians came to define his life, both figuratively and literally. The months, and years, passed, with more surgeries to complete his remaking, his becoming. They even managed to repair his face, thanks to an experimental procedure that combined plasmapheresis with something called microtransplantation, where swaths of donated skin made him look like a poorly sewed scarecrow before the scars receded.

And He was transfigured before them; and His face shone like the sun, and His garments became as white as light.

Just as written in Matthew. The miracle complete, the old Molinari gone and a new man, quite literally, rising in his place.

Your beauty should not come from outward adornment, such as elaborate hairstyles and the wearing of gold jewelry or fine clothes. Rather, it should be that of your inner self, the unfading beauty of a gentle and quiet spirit, which is of great worth in God's sight.

From the Book of Peter, and Molinari took from it the concept not so much of hope but of purpose, what he might take to replace all he had lost. He found solace and meaning in his former life of killing, realizing it had been a training ground for his great becoming. Just as doctors had stitched various parts together to make his face whole, Molinari gathered the pieces of his life toward the same end.

He would be a warrior for God, upholding the missions of the mysterious forces that had brought him to the clinic and had wrought his becoming.

Mysterious forces that called themselves the Order, dedicated to preserving the word of God above all else. They were warriors in service to a fragile truth that had nonetheless endured for centuries. As guardians of the dogma upon which the cornerstone of Christianity had been laid, the Order's mission was to preserve the word of God by silencing those who dared to speak over it.

And now this holy mission had brought him to Texas.

Back to Texas.

Call it unfinished business, an opportunity to correct a great wrong, to turn failure into success. To serve God in the most meaningful way he ever had.

Texas had been his first assignment on behalf of the Order. And now God's mysterious ways had brought him back to bestow a miracle upon mankind: the means to vanquish the enemies of the Church forever.

He removed a small, folded slip of paper from his pocket, opening it as he exited the ornate cathedral. The contact number he'd been provided with was different from the one he'd dialed twenty-five years ago, but he recognized the voice on the other end of the line as the same.

"Greetings, brother," the voice said.

"I await your instructions," Molinari told him.

"I'll send them to this number. Memorize them immediately, since the message will disappear in seconds."

"I understand. You indicated the opportunity we thought lost twenty-five years ago has been regained."

"Yes," the familiar voice told him, "but circumstances have changed since my original report was issued. I'm afraid we've encountered a . . . problem."

28

AUSTIN, TEXAS

"You want to dance with me or just go find a room someplace?" the young woman said to Dylan Torres, laying her shot glass back on the bar at Antone's, Austin's most popular nightclub and, especially, music venue.

"Why don't we do another tequila shot to help us decide?" the oldest son of Cort Wesley Masters asked her.

"No more Cuervo, though. I'd rather eat the worm."

"Patrón?"

"Only if it's the silver. Top-shelf."

"Ouch. I look like I'm made of money to you?"

"I don't know what you look like, boy, but it suits me just fine."

Dylan slapped a twenty down on the bar, added a ten atop it, and ordered up a pair of Patrón Silver shots. "So what's your name?" he asked.

"Who's asking?"

"Dylan Torres," Dylan said, leaving it there.

"Are you famous or something?"

"Why?"

"You look familiar. Like from television or something."

"I've been hearing that since I was fourteen."

"Don't blame me 'cause you're pretty, boy."

"It takes one to know one," Dylan said, handing one of the just-poured shots to the raven-haired girl and keeping the second one for himself. "To beauty," he toasted.

"To beauty."

They drained their shots and grabbed matching slices of lime in mirror-like fashion, Dylan no longer caring about the friends who'd wandered off on him to get closer to the stage. He studied the girl in the mirror, pretending to play it cool. Her wavy black hair kept claiming his attention, and her eyes seemed to be the same color. Dylan had never met anyone with black eyes before—dark, dark blue maybe, but not black. Her skin was flawless and left Dylan imagining what might be under her blouse and her shiny, leather-like leggings, which were tucked into brown boots that climbed past her ankles. She smelled of jasmine, or lavender or something, just enough to hide the slight scent of tobacco that rode her clothes the way it did for people who prefer vaping.

"Selina," the girl said suddenly, "as in Kyle."

"Catwoman," Dylan followed, extending his hand. "Nice to officially meet you, Selina."

Selina looked at the hand but didn't take it. "That the best you can do?"

"I'm trying to be a gentleman here."

Selina leaned in and whispered in his ear, "Stop trying."

She was a pharmaceutical rep, age twenty-six, which made her four years or so his senior. He texted his friends to tell them they were on their own and then walked with Selina the short distance down a few blocks to the Hyatt Place, where she was staying.

"You bring guys back on all your business trips?" Dylan asked, stopping short of pulling her in close or even holding her hand.

Selina saved him further consideration of the dilemma by cupping his butt with her hand as they approached the Hyatt marquee. "This is my first one, at least without a trainer, so I'm kind of establishing a tradition."

"Well, I'm glad to be your first."

Selina laughed easily at that. "Yeah, not even close."

"What if you were mine?"

"Am I?"

"I asked you what if I was."

She stopped just short of the hotel entrance, sizing him up. "I'm guessing, with that look of yours, you've been with as many women as I have men. Unless you're gay. Then you would've been with even more men than me."

"My brother's gay."

Dylan's comment didn't throw Selina at all. "If he looks like you, I'm sure he's doing just fine."

"He's still in high school."

"Proving my point," she said, taking him by the hand and yanking him through the sliding doors.

Dylan didn't bother mentioning that it had been a while since he'd had sex, the whole process tarnished by a Native American girl who'd nearly broken him in two after he'd followed her from Brown University to her reservation back home. He didn't bother telling Selina that, because then he'd have to explain his obsession with the girl, and how she'd died in his arms. He'd taken a leave of absence from Brown, which pretty much meant dropping out, to chase the girl back to Texas, only to realize he was just another part of her plan. Talk about feeling like a loser, having his heart ripped out to the point where he'd lost his confidence—until tonight in Antone's, when Selina approached him.

Talk about being a buzzkill.

Instead, he tried his best to pick up where he'd left off over a year ago, only to find himself feeling fifteen again, the whole sex thing done practically before it started.

"Oops," Dylan said.

"Don't stop," Selina said from beneath him.

And they didn't stop, for hours, Dylan finding the process a lot like riding a bicycle, except for the spill he'd taken during their first ride. He'd been on peyote the last time he'd had sex, and it felt good not to be on anything stronger than tequila tonight, although he found himself hoping she sold Viagra or something so there might be some samples hanging around.

Selina was methodical, practiced, turning the night into forever, to the point where Dylan came to dread any peek of sunshine through the drawn blinds. His phone was somewhere, his clothes were somewhere, and he felt like he were somewhere other than here, anywhere he wanted to be, in the darkness, so long as Selina was with him and they didn't stop. A few times he thought he'd stopped breathing and wondered if he were dead, if Selina were some magical spirit meant to escort him into an afterlife consumed by pleasure.

Catwoman, indeed.

He didn't remember lying down, didn't remember finally passing out, only waking up to the sun streaming in through the open blinds, alone in the big bed. Selina's side was empty, not even an impression left in her wake. And her stuff was gone, too, including the scent that rode her body like a spring meadow.

Maybe I imagined the whole thing.

Then he looked up from the sink, with his face dripping water, to find something written in black Magic Marker on his forehead. Dylan knew a phone number when he saw one, but he had to position a handheld mirror in order to read this one.

Even after jotting the number down on a hotel memo pad and memorizing it, he didn't wash the marker off, just left the Hyatt with the numbers riding his forehead like a scar.

PART FOUR

A reporter did a human interest piece on the Texas Rangers. The reporter recognized the Colt Model 1911 the Ranger was carrying and asked him, "Why do you carry a .45?" The Ranger responded, "Because they don't make a .46."

—Texas Ranger legend

29

SAN ANTONIO, TEXAS

"Sorry I'm early, Colonel Gee," Caitlin Strong greeted Guillermo Paz, at the day care center where they'd arranged to meet.

She'd arrived just as his charges were leaving for the day, tiny backpacks slung in place and lunch boxes emblazoned with cartoon characters or superheroes in hand. She had come straight from Doc Whatley's office, where she'd delivered her father's .45. She got a kick out of how they referred to him as "Colonel Gee" and out of watching the biggest man she'd ever seen stoop to meet their hugs. The tallest in the group reached only as high as his waist, leaving Caitlin figuring she'd stumbled onto some twisted version of *Gulliver's Travels*, in which diminutive creatures known as Lilliputians took the title character hostage.

"Has a nice ring to it, don't you think?" he said, returning her grin.

"As a matter of fact, I do. And I think your priest would be proud of this latest stop on your Reconciling with God tour."

"Not exactly, Ranger, given that I was never close to Him until I met you, so there was nothing to reconcile. It's more like my Winning God Over tour."

"How's Father Boylston?" Caitlin asked him, referring to the priest from the famed San Fernando Cathedral who'd functioned as Paz's spiritual adviser until a stroke felled him.

"I'm heading over to the nursing home to feed him as soon as I get the place back in order," the big man said, an edge lacing his tone that was grim and sad at the same time. "He didn't eat much while I was away; I'm not sure he ate at all. But when I saw him again, yesterday, I'm almost certain he acknowledged my presence, maybe even cracked a little smile. I was worried he wasn't going to eat, that he's ready to cash in his chips."

"You can't really blame him."

"There is still strength in his eyes. I know it because I can see it there."

Caitlin looked at the man who'd saved her life more times than she could count, after initially being hired to take it, and saw him differently. Vulnerable, mournful, and clinging to false hope all at the same time. She knew Guillermo Paz for a lot of things, but clinging to hope wasn't one of them.

"I know what you're thinking," he said, staring at her with the familiar gleam back in his eyes. "But I can't help it. So much of who I am today rests with my priest. I'm worried that losing him means losing that part of myself. So I make myself believe there is hope for him, even though, as Tolkien has written, 'False hopes are more dangerous than fears.' But I've never been scared of anything before, from the time my first priest died in my arms until now."

"I think Francis Bacon had something to say on the subject, too."

Paz nodded, impressed by Caitlin's knowledge, thanks to a college class that had stuck in her head for some reason. "Specifically, that 'hope is a good breakfast, but it's a bad supper.' Meaning it's a fine thing so long as you don't cling to it too hard or long. Not too long ago, I told my priest I'd put him out of his misery if he asked me to. Now I realize I could never do that, for fear of the misery it might cause in me. That thought made me feel selfish, Ranger, and I think that's why I had to go home for my mother's funeral. To prove I was capable of something that wasn't selfish at all."

"Jones didn't tell me what was going on, until the rescue was already under way."

"You don't owe me any apologies."

"I wish I'd been there, all the same, Colonel. Least I could have done, given our history."

"The outlaw had everything under control, and Jones was able to sneak my men into the country so they could infiltrate the crowd. I'd never have forgiven myself if I hadn't gone, but I'm sure my mother will tell me how stupid I was for coming back for the funeral, when I see her in my dreams." Paz stopped, seeming to study her eyes. "Is there something you want to tell me about him?"

"Who?"

"The outlaw."

The night before, Caitlin had noticed Cort Wesley still favoring his right hand, the healing going much too slowly for her taste. She knew enough to know it hadn't been the product of a cramp at all, and she half wished he'd come home with that arm in a sling after some doctor had found a bullet lodged under the skin. As it was, the thought of the way he kept positioning his right arm to keep her from seeing it had kept her up much of the night worrying, because that's what she did whenever she found herself unable to do anything but think.

"I was going to ask you about his arm," Caitlin told Paz.

"He called it a cramp on the plane. My man who's a medic agreed."

"Agreed or diagnosed?"

"Fair question."

"And do you agree with the diagnosis, Colonel?"

"No, Ranger. The way he was carrying his arm, I thought he'd been shot."

Caitlin left things there and swung her gaze about the pastel-colored walls, over the toys, games, soft floor cushions, and libraries of both books and DVDs that were age appropriate.

"You said you needed to see me about something else, Ranger."

"It has to do with a case my father worked in 1994, and another that's surfaced today, the connection being none other than Luna Diaz Delgado."

"Your father worked a case involving la Viuda Roja?" Paz asked, genuinely interested.

"It wasn't long after her husband's assassination, a few years maybe. My dad was on the trail of whoever killed seven men, maybe even ten, to steal something off a freight train that made a fateful stop in Fort Stockton on its way to Chihuahua."

"Delgado's home base in Mexico."

"Exactly. And, as the story goes, she didn't deny that the cargo that never made it there was hers, but she did her best to warn him off."

Caitlin saw Paz's eyes flicker. "You mentioned both seven and ten victims. Which is it?"

"Hard to say. The entire five-man train crew and a couple ex–Mexican special operators serving as guards were shot to death. Three more bodies that were never identified were found inside the freight car in question, the cause of their deaths never positively determined."

"They weren't murdered like the others?"

Caitlin shook her head again. "They died of heart failure and respiratory arrest. The bodies were transferred to the Centers for Disease Control, but I haven't followed that up yet."

Paz sank into one of the beanbag chairs normally occupied by five-year-olds who weighed maybe a tenth of what he did. The chair wheezed in protest, and Caitlin thought she heard something pop as she plopped into the one next to his.

"That explains the past, Ranger. What happened to make it so relevant all of a sudden?"

"The skeletal remains of four bodies were found in the desert near Sonora. No IDs, obviously, but the preliminary tests date their killings back about, oh, twenty-five years."

"1994."

"I think you're getting the point. But there's more: those bodies had been buried in the middle of nowhere with something else that got pulled out of the ground by a backhoe."

"And you think it was the same thing that was stolen from that freight car, the property of Luna Diaz Delgado?"

Caitlin realized she was rocking back and forth, the contents of the beanbag chair crackling. "Just another of my crazy feelings probably. But it has a nice ring to it, doesn't it?"

Guillermo Paz's thick face, creased by light patches of scarring amid his naturally dark skin, tightened in concern. "How can I help?"

"What do you know about Delgado?"

"The Red Widow keeps to herself, outside of her business and political interests."

"Political?"

"She likes putting all that money she's making to good use by buying off as many Mexican politicians as possible. And the government considers itself in her debt, given that Delgado's effort at centralizing the drug trade has sharply cut back on internecine wars between the rival cartels that claim the lives of so many innocents." Paz stopped and looked at her closer, narrowing his gaze. "You want to pick up where your father left off with her. That's what you coming to me is about."

"And if I told you I intended to drive down there and have a little talk with her?"

"I'd tell you not to waste the gasoline, Ranger. If you don't know something already, you'll never hear it from the Red Widow." Paz leaned in toward her, his expression turning somber and serious. "Something you need to know. Yesterday, when I was telling my charges a story, I had one of my visions."

"Uh-oh."

"A new darkness is coming, Ranger. I don't know its source or purposes but

I know it means to consume us in its path. Now you come to me with this and it makes me think the darkness is beginning to reveal itself, that it somehow involves the Red Widow. And if that's the case, we know where this is going. Wherever la Viuda Roja goes, blood follows. The Red Widow has more than earned her nickname."

"So I've heard," Caitlin told Paz, "though not necessarily the specifics."

"A lot of victims, a lot of blood. Those are the only specifics you need in this case. And you'll be wasting your time. I doubt very much Delgado would see you and, if she did, you won't be able to get anything worthwhile from her."

"Worried that I've met my match, Colonel?"

"Have you ever seen two female tarantulas fight, Ranger?"

"Usually over a male during mating season, isn't it, Colonel?"

"And for his efforts, the male ends up being killed."

"Eaten as well, I seem to recall," Caitlin added.

She felt her phone buzz, drew it from her pocket, and saw a text message from Young Roger: NEED TO SEE YOU RIGHT AWAY, RANGER. IMPORTANT!!!!!!!!!

"If you're able to make the trip over the weekend, I could join you," Paz offered.

"Why just the weekend?" Caitlin asked, counting the exclamation points in Young Roger's message for some reason.

Paz swiped from the floor a stuffed bear left behind by one of the just-departed kids. "Because I have a story I promised my charges I'd finish on Monday."

30

SAN ANTONIO, TEXAS

Cort Wesley spooned the scrambled eggs he'd just made onto Dylan's plate.

"I think I'm gonna throw up," the boy said, pushing it away from him.

"It's called a hangover, son."

"I'm never drinking tequila again," Dylan moaned, face in his hands.

"I've said that a time or two myself. Don't eat until you're ready. Eggs warmed up in the microwave aren't as bad as they sound."

Cort Wesley took the plate from the table, covered it in plastic wrap, and slid it onto a shelf in the refrigerator.

"I'll bet you'll miss making me breakfast when I go back to school in a couple weeks."

"A couple weeks? Seems awfully early," Cort Wesley said, suddenly realizing how much he was going to miss having his oldest around.

"Football practice starts the third week in August."

"You back on the team?"

"Coach Estes hasn't decided yet."

"Is that a yes or a no?"

Cort Wesley thought Dylan was looking more through than at him. "Coach wants to talk to you, Dad."

"He want my permission?"

"That, and your opinion."

"About whether you should play or not?"

"About me in general. That's the impression I got."

"I'll call him today."

Dylan nodded, running his tongue around his mouth as if to make sure it was still there. "Just make sure to tell him what he wants to hear."

"And how am I supposed to know what that is?"

"Come on, you can bullshit with the best of them."

"I think you're confusing me with you, son."

"What is it they say about the apple and the tree?" Dylan started to smile, until a fresh throb struck him like a bell striker rattling about his skull. "Oh, man, I am never drinking again."

"Good idea."

"I'm sticking to drugs."

Cort Wesley waited for him to look back up again. "What's her name, son?"

"Who?"

"The girl."

"How'd you know?"

"'Cause you've got her phone number on your forehead."

The doorbell rang. Cort Wesley left Dylan and his hangover there in the kitchen and moved to answer it, yanking the door open to the sight of a beautiful dark-haired young woman, dressed to kill, with eyes that looked like eight balls shining out of her face.

"Hey, Mr. Torres, is Dylan around?"

"Name's Masters. I've got a notion of your phone number from Dylan's forehead, but not your name."

"It's Selina Escolante."

"Nice to meet you, Selina Escolante. Come right in," Cort Wesley offered, angling for the door himself. "Why don't I give the two of you some space."

Outside in his truck, Cort Wesley checked his phone to see if Tom Baer had called. But there was nothing there except a text from Caitlin that read simply, GOOD MORNING.

He hadn't been very good company since coming back from Venezuela, with his arm still bothering him and all, and he supposed this was her way of telling him to snap out of it. Cort Wesley was starting to wonder if this whole thing with his arm might be psychological in nature, conjured out of guilt by his subconscious—something like that. Maybe killing was like pouring water into a glass, the psyche only able to handle so much before it spilled over the top. And the response of his unconscious mind was to take his trigger hand away from him.

Made sense, when you thought about it that way.

Was he supposed to feel more guilt for all the lives he'd taken over the years? Was there a built-in obsolescence to a man's capacity to take the lives of others, perhaps at least partially explaining why combat was a young man's game? Maybe it was not for somebody pushing fifty, even if he was in the best shape of his life. Not that he regretted for even a moment agreeing to lead the mission to rescue Guillermo Paz. And, truth be told, he would have traded use of his arm for the colonel's life any day.

You hear that, subconscious?

He was going to drive over to the Nardis Gun Club to try forcing his right hand back into action by doing some shooting, but he ended up pulling over into a Valero parking lot instead, where he jogged his phone to the number of Brown University's head football coach, Phil Estes.

"Dylan told me you wanted to talk," Cort Wesley said, aiming his words toward his truck's Bluetooth speaker, "about him wanting to play football again."

"What do *you* want, Mr. Masters?" the coach asked him.

"For my son to be happy."

"Would he be happy not playing because he's way down the depth chart?"

"He's not the kind of kid you want to count out, Coach."

"I've witnessed that firsthand, but you really think calling him a kid is accurate?"

"What's that mean?" Cort Wesley wondered, closing the truck's windows and flipping on the air-conditioning.

"Sounds like he's had a pretty busy sabbatical."

"He told you?"

"Gave me the broad strokes."

"Coach," Cort Wesley started, finding his voice and his point, "those broad strokes are the whole point here. I think the main reason Dylan's got it in his head is that he wants to feel normal again, and being normal means getting back on the football field. You're right about what the last year's done to him, and from where I sit, I'm thinking he wants to pick up like that year never happened. I don't think he cares about playing; I think he cares about trying, competing. That's all he wants. He may not see the field except to practice, but that's enough to make new memories to replace the ones he can't chase out of his mind from the past few months. Make sense?"

"Plenty, Mr. Masters," Coach Estes said. "Tell Dylan to check his email for the preseason schedule."

31

San Antonio, Texas

Cort Wesley ended the call and drove to the walk-in Texas MedClinic located on North Loop 1604, also known as the Charles W. Anderson Loop. He'd passed the spot a million times without giving the sign a second thought. He checked in at the receptionist's desk, presented his insurance card, and filled out the required information while standing right there at the counter.

"You're here because of a cramp?" the receptionist said, after regarding the form.

Cort Wesley demonstrated the difficulty he had lifting and moving his right arm. "It's taking a long time to loosen up."

"How long?"

"Couple days now."

The receptionist added that notation to the form and looked back up at him. "Please take a seat."

Cort Wesley had barely sat down and begun fishing through the stale magazines when a nurse emerged through a door and called his name. Moments later he was sitting atop a cushioned exam table, his blood pressure deemed perfect and his heart, according to the nurse, strong enough to power a city bus.

A doctor replaced her in the room five minutes later.

"I'm Dr. Shazir. Let's take a look at that arm."

The doctor did more touching, prodding, and pushing than looking, then checked Cort Wesley's range of motion and the strength of his grasp and ran something that felt like a pencil up and down his arm while studying his reaction.

"You got that look, Doc," Cort Wesley said, because he had to say something.

Dr. Shazir glanced down at the form Cort Wesley had filled out, not finding what he was looking for. "When did the first symptoms appear?"

Cort Wesley worked the time backward. "Three days ago. Almost exactly."

"On a scale of one to ten, ten being normal and one being the onset of symptoms, where would you say you are now?"

"Five maybe?"

"Five?"

"Or six."

Dr. Shazir nodded, his expression still framed by concern not quite approaching worry. "Do you know what a transient ischemic attack is, Mr. Masters?"

"No."

"It's more commonly known as a TIA."

"The answer's still no, Doc."

Shazir nodded, as if preparing himself, instead of Cort Wesley, for what he was going to say next. "How about what's known as a 'warning stroke'?"

Cort Wesley felt his insides drop. "You think I had a stroke?"

"A *warning* stroke."

"What's the difference?"

"The fact that your arm is showing signs of improvement and there are no other apparent symptoms."

"And that's a good thing," Cort Wesley said, listening to his own words as if someone else had spoken them.

"Most certainly," Dr. Shazir told him, "although you'll need to get a complete medical workup, including a CT scan or MRI." He consulted the clipboard. "You don't list a primary physician here."

"That's because I don't have one. How about you?"

"I can order the labs and refer you to a neurologist."

"Neurologist?"

Shazir nodded. "To find out exactly what your risk factors are of suffering another episode, and for him to prescribe measures to prevent that, or a more serious stroke, from happening."

Cort Wesley again felt like somebody else was doing the talking for him. "And that's a possibility?"

"About a third of those who suffer a warning stroke suffer a more serious episode within the year."

"I don't like that math."

"That's why we need to get you to a neurologist as soon as possible. In the meantime, I'll prescribe blood thinners to reduce that likelihood substantially."

"So, Doc, I'm okay, but I may not be okay for long."

Shazir nodded patiently. "The blockage causing your TIA was likely broken up by natural clot dissolvers called anticoagulants, in the blood, so the blockage was likely centered in your arm and wasn't in place long enough to cause any lasting damage to the brain. Blood flow was restored quickly. The severity of any blockage-related stroke is determined by how long the tissue was without blood flow and the location of the injury in the brain. When an episode is diagnosed as a TIA, it's because there is evidence of a blockage but no lasting damage has happened yet."

Cort Wesley flexed his fingers. The motion felt sluggish, but he was able to tighten those fingers into a fist. Then he lifted the arm up and put it down again, repeating the process as if to prove the doctor wrong.

"Do you have a pharmacy you'd like us to call the prescription in to, Mr. Masters?" Shazir continued.

"No."

"I'll just write one out for you. Then you can fill it at your pharmacy of choice. And I can see if we've got any samples to get you started."

"I'd appreciate that, Doc," Cort Wesley said, still trying to make sense of all he'd heard.

"Have you been under an unusual level of stress lately?"

Cort Wesley didn't know how to answer that question, so he said, "Not particularly."

"Because you'll want to avoid stress as much as possible."

"And my arm?"

"I expect you to ultimately regain full motor function within the next week or so, in all likelihood, and you should continue to notice gradual improvement."

Cort Wesley found himself breathing easier. Literally.

"So I don't need to worry."

Dr. Shazir's gaze was noncommittal. "You're twice as likely to suffer a major stroke as the typical man your age."

"I don't like those odds."

"That's why we're going to do something about it, Mr. Masters. Would you like me to make an appointment for you with a neurologist?"

"I'd appreciate that, Doc. Anything else?"

"Just one thing, Mr. Masters: try not to worry—it's stressful."

"I'll do my best."

Cort Wesley bought a pair of original Hires Root Beers to go with the prescription he had filled at a pharmacy located near the walk-in clinic. Back outside, he popped both caps off with his thumb, under a round plastic table shaded by an umbrella, which technically belonged to the frozen yogurt shop next store. He was supposed to do a Skype call later, to talk with Luke in Europe, but the technical intricacies of getting the thing loaded escaped him, meaning he needed Dylan or Caitlin around to handle that chore.

Other than that, he had time to kill, nothing on the agenda besides waiting for Tom Baer to call him with whatever he'd been able to find out on surplus shipments of the nine-millimeter pistols and submachine guns that the killers Caitlin had gunned down had been toting.

He'd just swallowed two of the blood thinners with his initial gulp when he heard a voice that seemed to emanate from his own head.

"*What are we drinking to today, bubba?*" asked Leroy Epps.

32

SAN ANTONIO, TEXAS

"How about good health, champ?"

The ghost of the best friend Cort Wesley ever had in the world stopped just short of reaching for the other opened bottle of Hires, made with genuine sarsaparilla, but his eyes sparkled at the sight before growing grave.

"*Guess you're not so invincible after all,*" Leroy noted.

The spectral shape's lips were pale pink and crinkled with dryness, the morning sunlight casting his brown skin in a yellowish tint. The diabetes that had planted him in the ground had turned Leroy's eyes bloodshot and had numbed his limbs years before the sores and infections set in. As a boxer, he'd fought for the middleweight crown on three different occasions. He'd been knocked out once and had the belt stolen from him on paid-off judges' score-cards two other times. He'd been busted for killing a white man in self-defense and had died three years into Cort Wesley's four-year incarceration, but ever since, he always seemed to show up when Cort Wesley needed him the most. Cort Wesley had given up trying to figure out whether Leroy was a ghostly specter or a figment of his imagination. He just accepted the fact of Leroy's presence and was grateful that his old friend kept coming around to help him out of one scrape after another.

Prison officials had let Cort Wesley attend Leroy's funeral, which was held in a potter's field for inmates who didn't have any relatives left to claim the body. He'd been the only one standing at the graveside, besides the prison chaplain, when Mexican laborers had lowered the plank coffin into the ground. Cort Wesley tried to remember what he'd been thinking that day, but it was hard, since he'd done his best to erase those years not just from his memory but also from his very being.

One thing he did remember was that the service was the first time he'd smelled the talcum powder Leroy Epps had used to hide the stench of the fes-tering sores spawned by the diabetes. And in retrospect he realized that, for days after the funeral, Cort Wesley had been struck by the nagging feeling that Leroy wasn't gone at all. The scent of his talcum powder still hung heavy in the air inside his cell, and Cort Wesley woke up at least once every night, certain he saw Leroy standing there, watching over him, grinning, and sometimes even wink-ing, when the illusion held long enough.

"So, champ, am I gonna be joining you soon?" Cort Wesley asked him.

"*Not for me to say.*"

"'Cause you can't or won't?"

"*Little of both, I suppose, bubba.*"

"You hear what that doctor said?"

"*Didn't understand all of it, but I got the gist.*"

Cort Wesley massaged his bad arm. "Gist being I had a stroke."

Leroy shook his head. "*That's not what I heard.*"

"What'd you hear?"

"*TIA…*"

"Same thing."

"*Not from where I be. More like the difference between a cold and pneumonia, bubba.*"

Cort Wesley flexed his arm; the sluggishness was the same as it had been in the doctor's office. "What if it never comes back, champ? What if I have to spend the rest of my life treating my arm like it's a grocery bag?"

"*You trust me?*"

Cort Wesley nodded. "You, my boys, the Ranger, Paz, and that's about it."

"*Here's the way I see the world as it be.*"

"That the future you're looking at, champ?"

"*No, bubba, I'm looking at you, a man who's made plenty of mistakes in his time, but never the same one twice, on account of you learn not to trip in the same crack a second time. This TIA thing done tripped you up, but it didn't send you falling, and you'll get this worked out 'fore the next one does.*"

"What if my arm never works right again?"

"*You asked me that already. And that doctor said it would.*"

"He said *probably*."

"*Just like you're probably gonna take another breath in a few seconds.*"

"That's your answer?"

"*You want guarantees, go to Sears.*"

"They closed most of their stores."

"*No shit? Jeez, good thing I'm not in the market for a major appliance.*" Old Leroy's expression seemed to brighten, his eyes wet and wide. "*You fixing on telling the Ranger gal?*"

Cort Wesley shrugged, the idea that he was explaining himself to a ghost not bothering him in the least. "She's the one who got me to go to the clinic. Dylan's going back to school in a couple weeks. Telling him can wait."

"*You wanna tell me what's really bothering you?*"

"I'm scared, champ."

"*You never been scared of dying, in my recollection.*"

Cort Wesley swallowed some more Hires. "I'm scared of losing the only thing I'm good at."

"*Killing?*"

"Being able to shoot a gun, hold my own when I haven't got one. Hard to do either with only one arm that works right."

Leroy nodded knowingly. "*Like I said, killing.*"

"I don't want to look in the mirror and not recognize the man who looks back."

The ghost of his best friend seemed to be taking it all in, pondering. "*I ever tell you I played ball myself back in the day, just like your boy?*"

"No, champ. I only knew about the boxing."

"*Well, it's true. Plenty of sandlot when I was a boy growing up in Memphis, and then in high school for a time. Coulda gone on, played college ball, too.*"

"What happened?"

"*Well, bubba, it's like this. My daddy took sick and died, and there was nobody to put food on the table for my brothers and sisters. He and my mom liked kids so much they kept having them, and his passing left that responsibility with me. Guess you could say it altered my life path more than a little.*"

"Doesn't seem fair, does it?"

"*Since when is life fair? I shouldn't need to tell you that. That said, once in a while the good guys get to win, and I'm glad to hear your oldest is headed back to the field.*"

"Best thing in the world for him, champ."

"*You ever play?*"

"In high school, until too many personal foul penalties started piling up the suspensions."

"*Issues with your temper, I'm guessing, bubba.*"

"They call it 'anger management' these days. Add to that the fact that my dad needing me for jobs didn't take into account my practice or game schedule."

"*He never saw you play?*"

"Not even once."

"*Same with mine. He was the school janitor and he said he never came to games because he didn't want the kids to make fun of him. But it was really on account of him not wanting to embarrass me.*"

Cort Wesley thought he detected a slight crackling in Leroy's voice, the big, bloodshot eyes seeming to moisten. He reached down to collect his bottle of Hires again and noticed that the top third of the second bottle had been drained, as if it had evaporated into the air.

"*Anyway,*" the ghost was saying, "*he was one of the good guys, too. Hey, what say we head east and take in a game with your boy in uniform?*"

"I doubt he'll see much of the field."

"*Sidelines is close enough for me, bubba, though I don't suppose that makes much sense to you.*"

"How's that, champ?"

"*I can think of a lot of words to describe you, but 'spectator' sure ain't one of them. You gotta be carrying the ball all the time, even if there's no blocking in front of you and the defense is primed to tee off. Good work you done down in Venice-uela, by the way.*"

"Just another day at the office."

"*Well, don't get too comfortable in some cushy desk chair, 'cause more work's headed this way.*"

Cort Wesley felt a chill in the air, as if a cold front had passed right over the shaded picnic table at which he and Leroy were seated. "I thought you couldn't see that far ahead down the road."

"And that's the God's honest truth, bubba. But what's coming isn't that far down. In fact, it's near close enough to reach out and touch."

Cort Wesley drained the rest of his Hires and noticed that the second bottle was just about gone, too.

"Ah," from Leroy Epps, smacking his lips, which didn't looked parched anymore. *"Now* that *wet my whistle."*

Cort Wesley heard his cell phone ring and felt the thing vibrating in his pocket.

"That yours or mine, bubba?"

"Take a guess," Cort Wesley said, drawing the phone out and answering it.

"Good news," Tom Baer greeted him. "I got a line on those guns."

"You still know how to hit a target, Gunny."

"It gets better, Captain Masters. You don't have to go far to find them."

33

San Antonio, Texas

Young Roger had vacated the conference room for an empty side office on the second floor of Texas Ranger Company G headquarters. Caitlin had the sense that he was staring straight at the doorway in expectation of her arrival, the moment she glimpsed his form hunched over a laptop he wasn't regarding.

"It's about time," Young Roger said, his voice laced with uncharacteristic edge.

"Sounds like you found something."

"Is it true all great investigators don't believe in coincidence?"

"I don't know. Next time I run into one, I'll be sure to ask." Caitlin closed the door behind her. "I notice this particular office has a nice view of the street and building entrance."

"In case the men who came for those computers come back for me, Ranger."

Caitlin nodded, recalling Jones's insisting to Cort Wesley that whoever had confiscated them wasn't from Homeland or the U.S. government at all. "Any chance they were somebody else besides Homeland Security?"

"Now that you mention it, they spooked me so bad I never asked to see their IDs, just took them at their word, given that I was kind of expecting them to show up anyway."

"You remember anything that stands out?"

"They had badges dangling from their lanyards. Three words, the one being 'Criminal.' I think the second was 'Investigation' or something."

"Could the third have been 'Division'?"

"I suppose," Young Roger said. "Texas CID was the outfit you were serving that warrant for."

"But Homeland's been known to use locals to do their dirty work for them, so you weren't too far off. Pretty much on the money."

"Except Homeland claims they weren't involved."

"Taking their words at face value is like playing three-card monte against a man with four hands. I'll look into things further."

"Thanks, Ranger." He thought for a moment. "Speaking of which, Communications Technology Providers was a government-funded outfit, at least under the table, right?"

"Pretty much," Caitlin told him. "But, as a private intelligence outfit, they didn't rely on Jones and company for all their business."

Young Roger's eyes flashed, measuring Caitlin's words. "How much of a notion do you have of what a company like CTP does?"

"Besides the obvious, not much."

"What's the obvious?"

"I imagine the same thing you'd get from the CIA, on a smaller scale. Actionable intel on the movements of particular targets, electronic monitoring and surveillance, maybe analysis of material gathered in the field."

Young Roger nodded. "Go back to surveillance. You remember when the army was trying to find Osama bin Laden in the Tora Bora mountain range?"

"I remember they failed."

"And that failure ushered in a whole new technological age for geo-mapping. Taking technology developed by oil companies right here in Texas to find crude and adapting it to find human heat signatures, for movement detection, and especially to spot subterranean disruptions indicative of somebody digging in or digging out."

"Makes sense."

Young Roger nodded again. "That was CTP's specialty, their claim to fame, so to speak. Besides your friend Jones under the table, their primary business came from oil and gas exploration companies worldwide looking to hit veins with the same pinpoint accuracy as your phlebotomist when you have blood drawn."

"Okay, so..."

He swung all the way around in his desk chair to face his laptop, working some keys to bring up an elaborate graphic that made no sense to Caitlin. "So somebody hired Communications Technology Providers to do detailed geothermal scans of an area in South Texas roughly the size of Rhode Island."

"Okay, I'll bite," Caitlin said, recalling Jones's suspicion that CTP was moonlighting for someone he had reason to believe was unsavory. "Who?"

"I can't tell you that, but I can tell you where the company's search settled."

Young Roger hit a few more keys and his laptop screen divided into eight segments, each with a picture of an isolated segment of a Texas desert. He rolled his chair back, so she could come closer to the screen.

"Do any of these look familiar to you?" he asked Caitlin.

Caitlin approached and crouched slightly, running her eyes from one angle of the same patch to another. "Nope, not at all."

Young Roger's gaze cheated toward the window before he rolled his chair back in front of his laptop. Caitlin watched him click on an icon at the bottom of the screen, and an instant later four fresh pictures filled half the screen, pushing half the overhead shots off.

"How about now, Ranger?"

"Holy shit," was all Caitlin could say, her eyes narrowing to make sure she'd seen things right.

"That was my thought, too."

34

NEW BRAUNFELS, TEXAS

"*I got a bad feeling about this, bubba,*" Leroy Epps said from the passenger seat of Cort Wesley's truck.

Cort Wesley had finally given up trying to find the address Tom Baer had provided and had programmed it into his GPS. Frustrated, he'd tried to do it manually while driving, until the thing started talking to him in a voice that, for just a moment, he took to be a friend of Leroy's speaking from the backseat. But the voice simply prompted him to ask the right questions to get where he was going, and according to the navigation screen, he was just one mile and one turn away now.

"Why don't you reach into the glove compartment and hand me my Glock, champ?"

"*I ain't much for gripping things, in case you didn't notice. Kind of like you these days.*"

Cort Wesley shot the ghost a look. "Doesn't seem to be a problem when it comes to Hires."

"*Well now, I don't want your good money to go to waste, do I? And maybe it's you drinking both bottles and just imagining it's me.*"

"I think I'd know how much root beer I drank."

"*Like you know what your oldest is up to with his lady friend back at the house right now?*"

"You got something to say, just say it."

"*I thought I just did. Where I be, seeing 'round corners is like staring straight through this windshield. That girl's trouble, bubba, and remember you heard it here first.*"

"Yup, Dylan sure knows how to pick 'em, doesn't he?"

"According to the serial numbers on those PM-84 Glauberyt nine-millimeter Para submachine guns and Steyr pistols recovered from that gunfight," Tom Baer had told him over the phone, "they were part of a shipment delivered to Bane Sturgess."

"Who's Bane Sturgess, Gunny?"

"Nobody. It's a place, not a person. An international arms broker based in New Braunfels."

"Strange place to set up shop."

"That's the point. Arms brokers don't like to advertise their presence. Some of the big ones operate warehouses the size of a small town. Others are more like consolidators who operate out of a storefront. Bane Sturgess falls mostly into the latter category, although they do maintain several warehouses as way stations, all of them outside the U. S. to avoid the red tape and regulations."

"By 'consolidators,' you mean they move shipments from one place to another without ever actually coming into possession of the ordnance themselves."

"That's right, Captain. Some of these outfits move merchandise as big as tanks, choppers, and transport aircraft. Others stick to smaller armaments. Most never actually own a goddamn thing. They arrange shipment of the ordnance from one place to another and pocket their fee."

"Any idea where Bane Sturgess fits into that spectrum?"

"Definitely smaller scale, more boutique in that the company specializes in the kind of small arms surplus exactly like those dead gunmen in Dallas were carrying. I'd watch my back with them, though. I've heard they also dabble in the mercenary world, moving men the same way they move guns, and they fancy themselves special operators. The principals of the company, all former low-level military, are no strangers to the occasional bad deed themselves."

"In other words, Gunny, all this sounds right up their alley. Kind of men who like to play with their own merchandise."

"If there's money to be made, they go flag blind, if you know what I mean."

"I do."

"You mind if I ask you a question now?" Tom Baer asked, after a pause.

"Fire away, Gunny," Cort Wesley said, instantly regretting the lame attempt at humor.

"This Texas Ranger of yours, she took out four professional shooters armed to the teeth, on her lonesome. Have I got that right?"

"You do."

"Man," Baer continued, the amazement ringing in his voice, "she'd fit right in with our kind, wouldn't she? Step right in and hold her own."

"Besides the men you and I have spent much of our lives around, she's as good as it gets. If I didn't know better, I'd swear she was born in the middle of a gunfight."

"I'll go you one better, Captain. Uniforms like you and me do our shooting in battlefield environments. This Ranger does her shooting in the real world, where bystanders roam free and she's got maybe the length of a breath to think out her next move. No intelligence, no sit-reps, no drones, no surveillance. One minute she's driving to the shooting range and the next minute the shooting range is coming to her."

"Well put, Gunny," Cort Wesley told him.

"We could learn a thing or two from this gal, I'll tell you that much."

"I already have," Cort Wesley told him.

"Approaching your destination."

"Was that you or the other guy, champ?" Cort Wesley asked the fuzzy shape of Leroy Epps.

"Only destination I know is where I be now, and you most certainly haven't reached there yet, bubba. Wish I could say the same for..."

"Didn't catch the rest of that, champ," Cort Wesley said, figuring Leroy's comment had gotten lost somewhere in the celestial ether.

But the look on his face said otherwise, and then he was gone, as Cort Wesley pulled into a space directly in front of the address in question.

Cort Wesley's destination, the offices of Bane Sturgess, occupied a stand-alone building set right on the main road, near a strip mall and several office park–style buildings featuring individual offices that had all the originality of roadside motels. It was located on East Common Street, a few miles and maybe an age or two removed from the Gruene Historic District the city was known for.

The route his navigation machine had laid out had taken him down Seguin Avenue from one underpass to another and across ten blocks of San Antonio Street until he passed the Main Plaza with its old fountain, sculptures, music pavilion, and meticulously landscaped grounds. Cort Wesley thought he may have watched a parade or two from this vantage point as a boy, on a rare family outing, but he couldn't be sure.

"You have reached your destination."

He was glad the navigation device told him the trip was over, because he was tired of driving his truck with only a single hand. He'd forced the right one into position a few times, even managed to squeeze the wheel like normal. Each time, though, his hand ended up going numb, reminding Cort Wesley that he'd become a statistic, the latest in the one percent of men his age to suffer a stroke, or a "warning" stroke, as Dr. Shazir had called it.

He stepped out of his truck, closing the door to his pickup to trap the soft scent of Leroy Epps's talcum powder in his wake, still wondering what the ghost's unfinished comment may have been.

Cort Wesley didn't have to wonder long.

An embossed placard alongside a heavy entrance door read "Bane Sturgess," and nothing more. Could have been a law office or accounting firm, except those didn't come equipped with high-security entrances requiring all visitors to be buzzed in.

Before ringing the bell, Cort Wesley moved to a window, where he spotted a crack in the wooden slat blinds and peered inside. More than just his right hand went numb at what he saw.

35

The four new pictures Young Roger had brought up on his screen weren't overhead shots at all; they were wide-angle crime scene photos, taken at night—two nights ago, specifically—at the site in the desert on the outskirts of Sonora where Caitlin had found D. W. Tepper. It was the hole from which four bodies, and something else that remained unidentified, had been pulled from the ground.

To complete his point, Young Roger merged the photographs together, laying the night crime scene shots over the generic overheads taken during the day. The match was almost perfect.

"So," Caitlin started, "you're telling me Communications Technology Providers found this site for whoever dug that hole."

"That appears to be the case, yes." Young Roger nodded.

"And now the folks who worked there are all either dead or shot-up in San Antonio General. Any notion as to how this discovery relates to the time frame?"

"The project goes back quite a while. I haven't been able to access the time and date stamps for these reports, but it's pretty clear they were looking for what they ultimately found for several months at least."

"And when did they find it?"

Young Roger replied as he returned to the screen featuring CTP's original pictures of the find. "These were all in a file marked 'Current,' so your guess is as good as mine. But since that hole in the desert was dug sometime in the past seventy-two to ninety-six hours, I think that gives us a notion."

"But no notion as to what they pulled out of that hole," Caitlin said, eyeing the screen now, too.

"That's not entirely true," Young Roger said, bringing up a sheet containing data that made no sense to Caitlin. "CTP's seismic, geothermal, and geo-mapping studies revealed three separate objects."

Caitlin recalled that her father had surmised that three shipping crates had been removed from that freight car back in 1994. "My lucky number in this case."

"According to this report, the three objects were identical in size, three by four feet, approximately. They were heavy, too. CTP was able to measure the degradations in the ground to see how much they'd sunk after being buried. Amazing software, given that it actually takes into account the precise amount of rain the area got over twenty-five years, to provide the most accurate measurement possible."

"Which is..."

"Between two and three hundred pounds."

"Any idea what they were made of?"

Young Roger shook his head. "If they were able to figure that out, I haven't found the information yet."

"How about their contents?"

"I'm still working on that, but it's a long shot since CTP never actually examined the objects physically. Speaking of which..." Young Roger added, thinking of something else.

He eased out the evidence pouch containing the piece of paper that hadn't quite burned up amid the ash at the site in the desert overlooking the burial site.

"I don't have all the answers on this yet, Ranger, but I can tell you that red smudge isn't blood at all. Near as I and my equipment can figure, the smudge comes from a credit card machine."

"You mean that smudge up the side when the cash register paper roll's running down?"

"Exactly."

"So you're telling me it's a credit card receipt."

Young Roger nodded. "More to follow as soon as I can get to it."

Upstairs, Caitlin learned that Captain Tepper was currently at a Ranger company commanders' meeting in Austin. His longtime assistant, Flora, didn't know when he was due in, but she expected it to be soon.

"I'll wait in his office," Caitlin said.

"Er..."

"What is it?"

"The captain keeps his door locked now."

"You have the key?"

"Captain Tepper has the only key."

"Guess I'll wait for him somewhere else."

Caitlin was heading to the desk she worked from, downstairs, when a call came in, CORT WESLEY lighting up at the top.

"I'm in New Braunfels," he greeted her. "You need to get up here fast. And bring the cavalry."

36

SHAVANO PARK, TEXAS

"A Texas Ranger? You're kidding. And a woman?"

"Last time I checked."

"What is she, like, your mom?"

"Close as I've got, I guess," Dylan said, arms folded behind his head, fingers between his head and the pillow, on his twin bed.

It made for a tight squeeze, and he had to say, it was the best medicine for a hangover he'd ever experienced. The close quarters left Selina as much atop as alongside him, and he liked losing his hand in her thick, black hair.

"I want to meet her," she said, angling her frame to better regard him. "I want to meet Caitlin Strong. Think she'd like me?"

"If she doesn't, you'll be the first to know. She tends to get real protective about me and my brother."

"Your gay brother."

"You shouldn't say it that way."

Selina tightened her gaze. "All I'm saying is that if he looks anything like you, it's a waste, from a lady's perspective."

"So you're a lady now?"

"Last time I checked. You have an issue with that?"

"I was thinking you're still more like a girl."

"That's because you're still in college." Selina eased off him, and Dylan turned onto his side so they could face each other, the bed frame creaking under the weight and strain. "College *boys*, college *girls*, right?"

"Last time I checked."

"So tell me something."

"Okay."

Selina cupped her hand under her head, something mischievous flashing in her eyes. "Am I your first older woman?"

"Am I your first younger guy?"

"You mean boy?"

"Not a lot of difference between twenty-six and twenty-two," Dylan told her.

"No," Selina chided, stepping off the bed fully naked. "Not when it comes to a man and a woman, if you see my point."

What Dylan was seeing in the afternoon light sneaking in through the drawn blinds made his mouth gape. He swallowed hard and knew she'd caught him in the act, was glad when she swung toward his desk, which was empty save for the gun safe.

"What's the combination?" Selina asked, gliding toward it.

Dylan couldn't stop looking. He climbed out of bed after her, but not until pulling on his boxer briefs. "It's open. When my dad gave me the gun, he insisted I keep it in the box, but he didn't say I had to lock it."

Selina lifted the lockbox's lid. "Splitting hairs, aren't we?"

"What good's a gun if you can't get to it?"

"You can say that about a whole lot of things, boy."

"So you're a woman and I'm a boy."

"You wanna be a man and I'll be a girl?"

"I'd rather just be us," Dylan told her.

"That's no fun." Selina gingerly eased the Smith & Wesson nine-millimeter from the lockbox. "It's heavy."

"It's loaded," Dylan said, moving up close to her but stopping short of taking the gun from her grasp.

"Will you teach me how to shoot?"

"Doesn't look like you even know how to hold it."

"That's why I asked you to teach me. Come on, it'll be fun. I've got some sales calls later this afternoon, but I've got time tomorrow. Come on," Selina repeated, when Dylan hedged. "I taught you something, so now you teach me something."

"What'd you teach me?"

"What it's like to be with an older woman."

She aimed the Smith & Wesson at the mirror. Dylan was glad he never kept a round chambered, meaning Selina would have to rack the slide, something she clearly didn't know how to do. He knew he should stop her from treating a loaded gun like a toy, but something held him back. He was afraid she'd think less of him if he made a big deal about it.

Selina tried to hold the gun steady. "Maybe I should've been a Texas Ranger instead of a pharmaceutical rep."

"It's not in your blood."

"But it's in Caitlin's?"

Dylan nodded. "Going all the way back to her great-great-grandfather. It's kind of a family tradition."

"What about your dad? He seems tough."

"He is. Busted plenty of heads in his time."

"Bet he's shot some people, too."

"He was in the Gulf War, the real one," Dylan told her.

He could see her eyes gleam in the mirror. "I meant besides that."

"Er . . ."

Selina swung toward him. "How about you, boy? You ever shoot anyone?"

"Does it matter?"

"It's sexy."

"Then the answer's yes."

The gleam again. "Ever kill anyone?"

"Is that sexy too?"

"Even more so."

"I'm still taking the Fifth on that one," Dylan said, not in the mood to stoke unpleasant memories.

Selina returned the Smith to the lockbox, suddenly reluctant to meet his eyes. "I Googled you on my phone, came across some stuff about that shooting last year."

Dylan felt his shoulders stiffen. "So you asked me a question you already knew the answer to."

"It happened here," she continued, "right outside this house."

"Wasn't the first time."

"Huh?"

"That somebody got shot here."

Dylan backpedaled and sat down on the edge of his bed, realizing he'd taken the lockbox with him and laid it across his thighs.

"My mother."

Selina sat down next to him.

"I was here. I saw it. Caitlin Strong killed the man who did it. I saw that, too."

"How old were you?"

"Fourteen."

"A genuine boy."

She started to ease her arm around his shoulders but stopped midmotion when Dylan shifted slightly to the side.

"It was the first time I met her," he said. "Did I tell you she was the one who took me to visit Brown?"

"At least you were safe from gunfights there."

Dylan's expression toyed with a smile, recalling how his first trip to Providence, Rhode Island, had ended. "Yeah, about that..."

37

Chihuahua, Mexico

Luna Diaz Delgado drew her granddaughter, Isabella, closer to her in the courtyard of her palatial home.

"Today you learn a very important lesson, my love," she said, while keeping her gaze locked on the man kneeling on the ground before her, under the watchful eye of gunmen on either side of him. "You see, this man stole from us. His name is Vittorio Garcia, and he says he needed the money to pay for an operation for his oldest son and heir. Did I state that right, Vittorio?"

The man shuddering on the ground, bathed in dank sweat that stank of something like stale onions, nodded while keeping his gaze fixed downward at the pressed stone finish. "*Si*, jefa, it is true."

"Look at me, Vittorio."

He finally did, the reluctance clear in his gaze.

"And is it true," Delgado continued, "that you went to your superiors here to inform them of your plight?"

Garcia tried very hard not to regard the men poised on either side of him. "*Si*, jefa. They said there was nothing they could do."

"They tell me you were a good worker," Delgado said flatly, the emotion drained from her voice. "They tell me the men you supervise almost never fail to make their quotas, and on the few occasions they do, you make up for the shortfall from your own end. Is that accurate as well?"

"You'd have to ask them, jefa," Vittorio Garcia said, again fighting not to look up to either side.

"Oh, I have, and that's what they told me. You would beg me for mercy, Vittorio?"

"No, jefa."

"No?"

"I am guilty. After I betrayed the trust you showed in me, I am not worthy of your mercy."

"So you are prepared to die," Delgado stated, taking the big revolver from the man standing behind her.

"*Si*, jefa."

Delgado spun the cylinder, her small hand wielding the pistol with surprising dexterity. "Tell me one thing, Vittorio. Your son, he had the operation you paid for with the money you stole from me?"

Garcia nodded.

"And how is he doing?"

"He will live a long life now, jefa. I know I must pay for my crime, but I ask you to spare him."

Delgado held the gun poised low by her hip. "That is not necessary. He wasn't the one who stole from me. Your family is safe from the punishment you must bear alone, Vittorio."

"*Gracias,* jefa, *gracias,*" Garcia said, bowing his head reverently.

"I must do this to make an example of what happens when discretion is not exercised, when trust is broken. Because each man and woman under my command must act as I would, as my proxy. They must ask themselves, *Is this something our jefa would do?* or *How would our jefa respond?* It is the cost of leadership that a price must be paid for misjudgment that hurts my business. If I do not exact that price, how can I expect loyalty from the hundreds, thousands even, beholden to the cartel for their livelihood and the good of their families?"

Vittorio Garcia looked up, his expression resigned, even calm. "I did this for my family, jefa."

"And would you do it again, Vittorio?"

"I would," the man said, nodding, without hesitation.

"I am sorry I must make an example of you," Delgado said solemnly. "I am sorry for the action you have forced upon me."

The pistol came up in line with his face.

Garcia closed his eyes but did not lower his head.

Luna Diaz Delgado steadied her pistol, feeling Isabella squeeze tighter against her. She patted the girl's head with her free hand, turning her face away from the blouse she'd pressed her eyes against.

"Watch, my love."

With that, she turned the pistol to the right.

And fired.

Turned the pistol to the left and fired.

And fired.

The bodies of Vittorio Garcia's underboss and boss fell dead to the ground, one after the other.

Delgado waited for Garcia to open his eyes before she spoke, addressing her words to Isabella, who was staring intently at the two bodies, not trying to turn away again.

"When an underling fails, the responsibility lies with those directly over him. The two men I shot, my love, should have come to me with this man's request for the money for his son's operation. A failure of leadership, because they feared I would've taken the fee out of their end. And I might well have done precisely that, but it shouldn't have mattered, because this man was a solid earner for us who'd made them far more than that over the years while asking for nothing beyond what was due him. He behaved honorably and was dishonored in return. Vittorio," she said to the man kneeling before her.

"*Gracias*, jefa," he managed, with tears streaming down his face. "*Gracias.*"

Delgado handed the big pistol to Isabella, who nearly crumpled under its weight. "Don't thank me yet. You see, Vittorio, my apology was sincere. I truly am sorry for the action you've forced upon me, for making an example of you. Because you will take over as leader now, and with that comes responsibility that brings with it no forgiveness. I hope that this is a task you will welcome, a task you will embrace. And then you will train your son in the ways of the *familia*, so he may be as strong and loyal a soldier as you have been. You understand there is no choice here, no option."

"*Entiendo*, jefa."

"Then rise and stand like a man."

Garcia did. Bowing, he took Delgado's hand and kissed the ring that had belonged to her husband, resized to fit the smaller hand now speckled with gun dust.

She nodded and looked back at Isabella. "And what have you learned from this, my love?"

"The gun is very heavy, Abuela."

"I know," Luna Diaz Delgado said, making no move to take it back from her.

Until the main gate crashed open behind a battering ram on a truck with POLICIA markings.

Federals, for sure, going through the motions as they did regularly. Luna quickly yanked the pistol out of Isabella's slackening grasp and tossed it aside. One of her men would make sure it was disposed of properly.

During those moments, four more SUVs followed the battering ram through the breached gates, armed men spilling out in all directions. Delgado's people knew exactly what to do in such a situation, which was nothing. Drop their weapons, put their hands in the air, and look subservient to the powers that be.

The last to exit the SUVs was a short, stout man wearing a colonel's uniform. He had a protruding chest and a stomach flattened by him sucking in his breath.

"Colonel Rojas," Luna said, her hands in the air. "What a surprise."

Rojas approached stiffly, flanked by a bevy of armed officers from Mexico's Policia Federal who were looking for something to shoot at. His eyes fell on the two bodies that circumstances had not afforded the time to remove.

"Friends of yours?"

"Who?"

"Them." Rojas pointed.

"Oh, si. Two of my department heads, pushed into early retirement. My men found their bodies dumped just outside the gate earlier this morning."

"Did they?"

Luna nodded. "As a matter of fact, I was just about to call the authorities— until your arrival spared me the bother."

Rojas's gaze fell again on the bodies, as he twirled his thick mustache. "We'll include them in the arrest report," he said, whipping the handcuffs from his belt. "Please show me your wrists."

"What is the charge this time, Colonel?"

"I haven't decided yet. Thought I might spin the wheel and see what crime it stops on."

His flippant remark didn't unnerve Luna, but the message behind him arresting her without a firm charge was definitely cause for concern. It suggested something else might be afoot here, something Luna feared might be connected to the gift the desert had revealed after so many years. That made her reflect on her initial meeting with Texas Ranger Jim Strong and all that had followed, including the last meeting before they parted forever.

"Your hands, jefa," Rojas resumed, addressing her respectfully despite the impatience in his voice.

"You know there's no point to this," Delgado said, as he slapped the cuffs over her wrists. "You know whatever made-up lie you charge me with will hold no water. I'll be free and the federales will be embarrassed again."

"I'm not so sure about that this time."

"Oh? What changed?"

"I don't know. This arrest, this show of force, wasn't my idea."

"Orders?"

Rojas nodded. "From higher-ups outside the Policia Federal, maybe even outside Mexico."

"The United States?" Delgado posited, surprised by the mere possibility, given her relationship with the right American authorities.

"Your guess is as good as mine, jefa." Rojas shrugged. "But if I were you I wouldn't sleep too soundly until your lawyers secure your release."

38

NEW BRAUNFELS, TEXAS

"That's her," Enrico Molinari said to the two men with him in the back of the van. "The Texas Ranger who killed our men in Dallas."

Molinari's vast size made the confines uncomfortable, even if he'd been alone back there. He did his best to shift aside, so the other men could better regard the three monitor screens, all currently displaying the Texas Ranger standing outside the headquarters of Bane Sturgess in the company of a man Molinari didn't recognize and couldn't identify. The man had arrived here ahead of her, first on the scene, meaning they must be connected, allies likely, although he wore no cinco pesos badge identifying him as a Ranger as well.

"I isolated him in close-up off the monitor," Molinari explained. "We should have a better idea of his identity soon."

The specially equipped van was parked just down the street from Bane Sturgess. The video screens built into a console in the cramped rear compartment were attached to a trio of cameras offering views of the street beyond.

Molinari moved closer to the monitors, catching his own reflection thanks to the light spill refracting off the screen. That perspective allowed for a distorted view of his features. The angle captured his frame like a fun house mirror, his gray-toned face and light-shaded eyes looking preternaturally large, as if he might be able to see the future.

But right now he was concerned about the present, because someone had somehow gotten to Bane Sturgess ahead of him, someone who must have had their own stake in the contents of those stone boxes.

Years before, on his last trip to Texas, another Texas Ranger had been responsible for burying what had now gone missing yet again, as if the contents of those boxes were to remain forever elusive to Molinari. Incredibly, according to what Molinari had been able to learn, the female Ranger across the street was that man's daughter.

Talk about fate, talk about an epic cosmic convergence only God Himself could be behind.

"Kill them," he ordered the two men in the back of the van with him. "Kill them both."

39

New Braunfels, Texas

Caitlin had found Cort Wesley Masters waiting for her at the offices of a company called Bane Sturgess, which, from the outside anyway, looked more like a real estate firm that papered its exterior windows with its latest listings.

"The cavalry's not too far behind me," she told him.

"Good thing."

"What'd you find in there, Cort Wesley?"

"It's better you see for yourself," he said. When Caitlin steered for the entrance, he continued, "Last thing you want to do is go inside, Ranger, trust me. Check the window."

Caitlin did, and saw four bodies lying on the floor.

Cort Wesley laid it out for her while they waited for reinforcements to arrive, from his meeting with Jones in Marble Falls to Tom Baer to surplus arms and the outfit to which Baer had managed to trace them.

"You're telling me Bane Sturgess was behind the guns used in Dallas?"

"They were behind the shipment. Arranging transfer of the submachine guns and pistols from where they were warehoused as surplus to their buyers. Finding the identity of those buyers is what brought me here. But Bane Sturgess is also pretty heavy in the mercenary world and they aren't above taking on a job themselves, if the money's right."

"Toy soldiers?"

"The worst kind, Ranger."

"Somebody's covering their tracks here, Cort Wesley."

Something drew Caitlin's gaze across the road to a pair of men who'd stopped suddenly, as if aware they'd been seen. On second glance, the men seemed to be engaged in an ordinary conversation, and she passed her suspicions off to nerves about the bodies she'd glimpsed through the window.

He frowned. "You see any blood around any of those bodies inside?"

"Nope."

"Neither did I. That's why I stayed outside and why we're still outside now."

"Cort Wesley Masters exercising discretion?"

"I guess you're finally rubbing off on me, Ranger."

"You plan on telling me what the doctor said about your arm?"

"Maybe I haven't gone yet."

"Yes, you have. It's written all over your face."

"What's it say?"

"Nothing good, Cort Wesley. So . . ."

Cort Wesley tried not to show any concern. "I'm on blood thinners."

"That's your answer?"

"Do the math."

"Shit," Caitlin said, expression sinking.

"That was my thought."

"You're telling me it was a *stroke*?"

"One of those warning kinds people get."

"So what are you planning to do about it?"

"I told you I'm on blood thinners."

"Besides that."

"I'm going to see a neurologist."

"I'm coming with you."

"No, you're not."

"I'm coming with you if I have to shoot you, Cort Wesley."

"Well, everybody's gotta die of something."

Then they heard the first of the sirens screaming their way. Caitlin looked up the road for the appearance of their flashing lights, noticing that the two men she'd glimpsed a few moments before were gone.

PART FIVE

It was said that [Captain Bill] McDonald would "charge hell with a bucket of water," but that was also said of Captain Leander McNelly, who headed the Special Force during the 1870s. McDonald's personal motto later evolved into the Ranger's creed: "No man in the wrong can stand up against a fellow that's in the right and keeps on a-comin'."

Perhaps less known is McDonald's statement to a large mob that confronted him as he left a jail with two prisoners in custody. "Damn your sorry souls!" growled McDonald as the men surged forward, intent on hanging the prisoners in his custody. "March out of here and get away from this jail, every one of you, or I'll fill this yard with dead men." The mob quickly dispersed.

—"Lone on the Range:
Texas Lawmen" by Jesse Sublett, *Texas Monthly*, December 31, 1969

40

Doc Whatley emerged ahead of the other crime scene techs, all of them dressed in yellow biohazard suits with internal respirators. Caitlin watched as Whatley yanked off his mask and laid his hands on his knees, gasping for breath.

"I have trouble breathing in these things," he wheezed, still doubled over.

"What can you tell us, Doc?"

"According to every reading on those fancy machines Homeland taught my people how to use, the air's clear as a bell. No toxins, contaminants, contagions, or anything else present, subject to further testing," he said, glancing back toward the building entrance, which had been secured with thick precaution-ary plastic tubing, forming an anteroom to ensure that nothing from inside Bane Sturgess escaped. "But something killed those men, and, from my initial examination, I can say one thing and only one thing for sure: I've seen the very same thing before."

"The bodies from that train car, twenty-five years ago ..."

"Right as rain." Whatley nodded. "Maybe I can succeed now where I failed then. Maybe I can figure out what the hell it was that killed them this time. Where's Captain Tepper?"

Caitlin realized he must have strayed off, figured he was having a smoke, until she spotted him heading toward her from the direction of a pair of New Braunfels uniforms who'd been directing traffic across the street.

"Something you need to see, Ranger," Tepper said to her. "Follow me."

41

New Braunfels, Texas

Where were his men?

Enrico Molinari no longer believed himself capable of feeling fear or trepidation. His return to Texas on such a holy mission had seemed right in every way.

Until now.

The men he'd dispatched to right that wrong were nowhere to be seen and weren't answering his calls, filling Molinari with a cold, dread fear that history was repeating itself. That one Texas Ranger had beaten him a generation before, and another had risen in that one's stead to do the same, father and daughter to boot. Molinari couldn't let that happen, couldn't allow it.

They are coming from a far country, from the farthest horizons, the Lord and His instruments of indignation, to destroy the whole land.

The prophet Isaiah's words formed his greatest dream, of seeing that land perish in the very flames that had sought to consume him. And thanks to the true purpose of the mission that had brought him back to Texas, the means to achieve that were tantalizingly within his grasp. Little had he known originally—little had the Order itself known—that God had served up those means to be utilized in service to His cause.

The one who sins is the one who will die. The child will not share the guilt of the parent, nor will the parent share the guilt of the child. The righteousness of the righteous will be credited to them, and the wickedness of the wicked will be charged against them.

The prophet Ezekiel's words rang in Molinari's ears, carrying both forbearance and hope. For what if a lack of righteousness had caused his failure the last time, and what if he was no worthier a man now than he was then?

The mere possibility set Molinari trembling, threatened his entire view of himself that came from the mirror of his soul. The root of his failure the last time he came here may well have lain with the true nature of the mission he had undertaken, the pursuit of one thing leading the Order to the pursuit of something entirely different, something that could fuel their efforts for centuries and ages to come. No more displays like the one in Nigeria needed, because He had delivered a means to vanquish His enemies. Molinari had not been worthy enough to find it in 1994, and his return marked his being granted a second chance, rewarded for his service with the ultimate token of being the one to deliver that weapon unto the army of God.

If the two men he had dispatched had fallen to the enemy, let that be a lesson to him of the stakes involved and the steps he needed to take to address them. One army falling to another. But the war would continue, and Molinari needed a bigger army with which to fight it.

Amid the cramped confines of the van's rear, he rolled his chair back and typed a message to the Order's leader in the United States, based here in Texas: I NEED MORE MEN.

42

NEW BRAUNFELS, TEXAS

Tepper led Caitlin across the street to a darkened walkway between a pair of buildings, where a trio of Dumpsters sat.

"One of the uniforms spotted a leg protruding from the side of the front Dumpster. You can see for yourself what he found."

A pair of bodies sat side by side, as if they'd been posed that way, especially given that they sported identical bullet holes centered in their foreheads. Caitlin also spotted matching nine-millimeter machine pistols, same as the ones used in Dallas, lying nearby.

"I noticed these men before," she said, picturing the two figures who had seemed to be coming her way when her stare froze and then had been gone the next time she looked. "Just a few minutes before the cavalry arrived, D.W."

Tepper looked down at the pistols. "My guess, they weren't from the Welcome Wagon of New Braunfels. Give me your assessment of what went down here, the short version."

Caitlin studied the bodies anew. "Well, whoever did it was a pretty damn good shot. No powder burns, no scoring. If I had to guess, I'd say soft twenty-two-caliber rounds fired from ten feet at minimum." She looked toward the back side of the alley. "From there, maybe."

"Notice anything else?"

"Not off the top of my head, Captain."

"How about that, from the naked eye, it looks like those bullets took these boys in the same exact spot. Not close; exact. I'm guessing that would be hard even for you at fifteen feet, Ranger."

"Instinct in a gunfight hardly ever leads to that kind of precision," Caitlin agreed, "unless a robot was doing the shooting. That means we've got a shooter who's as close to a machine as it gets. Someone who's grown up around guns and was firing the real thing when other kids were playing cowboys and Indians."

"You're describing yourself," Tepper noted.

"It takes one to know one, I guess."

"You're a lot of things, Ranger, but an assassin isn't one of them. Let me show you something else."

Tepper took from his pocket his first real smartphone, a birthday present from his grandchildren, as Caitlin recalled, and jogged it to the photo icon.

"You know how to use that thing, D.W.?"

"Grandkids taught me, Ranger. Plenty simpler than I thought it'd be, too." Tepper worked the picture on the screen and zoomed in on the bullet wound centered over the victim's brow. "Here," he said, holding the phone so she could see the screen. "What's that look like to you?"

"A starburst, like cartoon drawings of the sun."

"Here's a shot of the second victim."

"Another starburst. Tells me the pattern's not random, that the shooter went through great pains carving striations into the inside of his gun barrel—fine lines normally produced by tiny chips of steel pushed against the barrel's inner surface."

"I know what striations are, Ranger."

"And I've got a sense you've seen these particular striations before, D.W. You want to tell me what this all means?"

Tepper snapped his gaze on her. "It means here we go again, Hurricane Caitlin's winds are picking up to gale force."

"The only thing I had to do with this was show up."

"Let's get back into the sunlight, Ranger."

"I'm about to tell you something you don't already know for a change," Tepper told her, the sun burning into his worn-looking eyes. "Those star-shaped bullet holes? I've seen them before. In classified reports pertaining to intelligence on the cartels, distributed to all Ranger companies."

"And you didn't think to share this with me before?"

"What did I just say about it being classified, Ranger? Need-to-know basis only, and you certainly need to know now. I'm going to assume the name el Barquero means nothing to you."

"The Ferryman?" Caitlin said, translating from the Spanish.

"As in Charon, the mythological figure who ferried the dead across the River Styx. Or, in this case, a legendary Mexican assassin. A hall of fame hitter working for the cartels to eliminate their common enemies in government, the courts, and law enforcement. A spook story that just happens to be real."

Caitlin ran all that through her mind. "Last time I checked, D.W., we were still in Texas, and the bodies of those gunmen in the alley don't fit the criteria of el Barquero's typical victims."

"Well, we know one thing for sure, don't we? If el Barquero did the deed, it was somebody in Mexico, somebody in the cartels, who gave the order."

"Maybe somebody by the name of Luna Diaz Delgado, Captain?"

"That thought had crossed my mind, Ranger, and I've changed my mind about telling you the tale of what happened after your dad and me ran into her in that train station."

43

San Antonio, Texas; 1994

Jim Strong didn't say a word on the drive back to Texas, leaving D. W. Tepper to do all the talking in the truck. Jim seemed to be someplace else altogether, snapping alert to respond to a question Tepper had already asked him three previous times.

"So you figure this is all on Delgado?"

"I'm of a mind to take the lady at her word, D.W.," Jim said, as if realizing for the first time that he was in the passenger seat.

"How's that?"

"Her cargo ended up inside a supposedly empty freight car at an unscheduled stop along the route that terminated in Chihuahua, with a pair of guards packing pearl-handled forty-fives."

"Okay." Tepper nodded. "I'm with you on that much. The train stops in Fort Stockton, her guards are executed along with the train crew by the Angel of Death, and something kills three men I make as coming from the professional mercenary category, before the cargo they came for gets stripped."

"By this Angel of Death, you figure? Could be he didn't come alone," Jim said, picking up on Tepper's thinking.

"I think he came with the mercs, gave them a job to do, and they dropped dead before completing it, leaving him to finish things himself. A job for somebody who should be setting Olympic strength records instead. That doesn't tell us what killed the mercs, though."

"Well, something in those crates for sure, as I see it, Ranger Tepper."

"As in the mercs being exposed to something that somehow spared the Angel of Death."

"And there's only one person who can tell us what that was, and we just left her down in Mexico."

"You wanna turn this truck around, Ranger Strong, I'm game. But just don't expect the Red Widow to greet us with open arms this time."

"Those open arms were holding Thompsons this morning. So unless we're gonna have to face off against tanks next time, I'm not concerned."

When Jim Strong and D. W. Tepper arrived back at Company F headquarters in San Antonio, they found a sharply dressed man waiting for them in their captain's vacated office, standing at the wall, reviewing an assortment of commendations the company had received. He wore Italian loafers and a suit so perfectly fitted that it showed the edges of his narrow, bony shoulders, and he had the soft, tanned complexion of someone who'd never spent a day working outside in his life.

"Name's Maurice Scoggins, special assistant to the governor," he greeted them, shaking each of their hands. "I imagine you're Rangers Tepper and Strong, but I don't know which is which. Call me Mo."

"I'm Strong, he's Tepper," Jim said. "So what brings the special assistant to the governor all the way from Austin?"

"It involves your latest case," he said, both his voice and expression struggling to remain casual. "It's been referred out to federal jurisdiction."

Jim Strong and D. W. Tepper exchanged a taut glance. They tended to view the presence of any politician with suspicion, but that was especially so whenever the term "governor" was employed, given Ann Richards's thinly disguised distaste for the Rangers in general. Almost invariably, whatever followed wasn't good, and today turned out to be no exception.

"And you needed to come all the way from Austin to tell us that?"

"Consider it a professional courtesy, gentlemen, one I'm hoping you'll return in kind."

"And how might we do that, Mr. Special Assistant?" Tepper quizzed.

"Austin is aware of the trip you made down to Chihuahua, Mexico. For starters, could you tell me on whose authority that was?"

"Our own," Jim answered him, stealing a glance at Tepper that basically said *What the hell?* "Who else's authority did we need?"

"We have information that you met there with Luna Diaz Delgado, subject of several federal probes being conducted in cooperation with Mexican authorities."

"We didn't know we'd be meeting with her until she showed up at the Chihuahua train depot," Jim explained, "obviously alerted to our presence and our interest in the contents of a certain train car. And if you don't mind me asking, sir, how was it exactly you found out we were down there?"

"That's none of your concern."

"Because," Jim rolled right on, ignoring him, "it occurs to me that, for you to have driven all the way here, you must've left around the same time we left Chihuahua. Have I got that right?"

Scoggins looked like somebody who got caught pinching a five from a cash register. "Let's just say that your presence south of the border raised some flags almost immediately."

"Did whoever was raising them express any concern over the ten bodies recovered from the Fort Stockton train station last night?" Jim asked him.

Scoggins settled himself with a deep breath, tried to hold both men in his stare. "I think we got off on the wrong foot here."

"One of us did, anyway," Tepper said.

"I'm here because the federal authorities asked me to intervene before any damage is done to the case they're trying to build against Delgado, in conjunction with their Mexican counterparts."

"You kind of said that already," Jim noted. "And it doesn't change the fact that five of the victims from Fort Stockton, the entire train crew, are Texas residents, and three were born and raised here. I'm going to go out on a limb and say that doesn't cut any mustard with you."

"This isn't about me or you, Rangers," Scoggins told him. "It involves a jurisdictional matter that is more or less typical."

"I'm going with 'less,'" said Jim, "given I don't know how Washington, or Austin, even found out we were in Mexico."

"You might consider that there's a mole planted inside Delgado's organization. His call set many a Department of Justice ass on fire, I shit you not. The DOJ is concerned that your continued involvement could set their investigation back significantly."

Tepper sneered at that. "Ten men died last night, Mr. Scoggins. That's the source of our continued involvement."

"Seven of whom were clearly murdered," Jim Strong added, "the other three victims from entirely different circumstances."

"This would be three bodies recovered from the train car," Scoggins interjected.

"That's right," Tepper affirmed.

"I'm afraid I can't comment any further on that particular subject."

"The subject of the ten dead," Jim wondered, "or only the three?"

"I can't comment on that, either. Look, Rangers," Scoggins said, starting to take a step closer to Strong and Tepper before thinking better of it, "I came down here to pay you the courtesy of hearing the governor's instructions in person."

"You see the governor anywhere about, Ranger Tepper?"

"No, I do not, Ranger Strong."

Jim looked back at Scoggins. "Then I guess we're hearing those instructions from you, not her, aren't we?"

"I'm ordering you boys to stand down," Scoggins said, with the voice of a man who'd already lost his patience. "I'm going to ask you to unsee whatever it was you saw last night. I'm going to ask you to forget all about whatever wasn't in that freight car or the three bodies that were. You won't see nothing about any of this in the papers or on the television, and the governor feels that it's imperative to keep it that way. We must ensure that nothing is done to jeopardize the case we're building with the Mexican authorities against Delgado."

Tepper rolled his head from side to side, considering those words. "So, even though the Red Widow is our best lead, we're supposed to just make believe five Texas families didn't lose their dads last night."

"I believe I've made myself clear, Ranger."

"You didn't answer my question," Tepper persisted.

"I wasn't aware you asked me one."

"Let me try it this way, sir," Jim Strong interjected. "We believe Luna Diaz Delgado has information extremely relevant to the murders we're investigating. She's the only one who call tell us what went missing from that freight car and why what went missing from the train car is directly responsible for five dead Texas residents."

"Priorities," Scoggins told them both, his skin so processed, smooth, and tight that it looked more like a doll's.

"And those priorities don't include catching the killer of five Texans. Can you believe that, Ranger Strong?"

"I cannot believe it, Ranger Tepper."

"It doesn't matter what you believe or what you don't believe, *Rangers*," Scoggins said, his use of the word this time sounding caustic instead of laudatory. "All that matters is what Austin believes."

"You forget about Washington, Mr. Special Assistant?" Tepper chided.

"Same thing, in this case. Your chief, head of the whole Texas Rangers, has been briefed on this as well. He's aware of my coming here and supports the governor's efforts one hundred percent."

"Funny how we haven't heard from him directly," Jim noted.

"Again, Rangers, it comes down to a jurisdictional matter."

"Rangers never paid much attention to such matters."

"And look how well that worked out for you, what with Governor Richards calling for the whole organization's reduction or even dissolution. What she, and I, know is that the gunfighter and lone gunman days are long gone. Civil rights, Miranda rights, equal opportunity rights, finished them once and for all."

"Oh, Ranger Tepper and I believe in equal opportunity rights, don't we, D.W.? As in equal rights to die for anybody who spills the kind of blood in Texas that got spilled last night."

Scoggins nodded, as if weighing the implications of Jim's words. "I hear told you're known to frequent the funerals of those whose killings you're investigating, Ranger Strong."

"I do indeed, sir. Partly as a comfort to the family, but mostly as a way to make me remember who I'm bringing justice for."

"Well, that won't be necessary in this case, Ranger, will it?"

"It sure won't, Mr. Scoggins. And please give the governor our best."

Through a window across the hall from their captain's office, Jim Strong and D. W. Tepper spied Mo Scoggins climb into the backseat of a black livery car with state government plates. They watched it head up the road until it disappeared around a corner up the street.

"We're not giving up this case at all, are we, Ranger Strong?"

"I'm not, Ranger Tepper, but you are."

"Come again?"

"No sense I can see in risking two careers."

"Well..."

"And there's something else."

"What?"

"If something happens to me," Jim Strong told him, "there'll be somebody to fry the grits of whoever did it."

44

NEW BRAUNFELS, TEXAS

"Why did Scoggins, and the governor, call you off the case?" Caitlin asked, once Tepper had finished. "Somebody got to them, right? But who? Who calls off the Texas Rangers?"

Tepper stamped out a cigarette she hadn't even recorded him lighting. "I never found out."

"That's hard to believe, Captain."

"How many times have you disobeyed my orders?"

"What's your point?"

Tepper popped a fresh Marlboro into his mouth and flicked his lighter to life, looking bewildered over Caitlin doing nothing to stop him. "That it runs in the goddamn family—that's my point. Jim didn't care about risking his own career, but he wasn't about to let me ruin mine. So not even an hour after the assistant to Governor Richards, or whatever the hell he was, ordered us to stand down, Jim was back on the case."

"You know how they say kids follow in their parents' footsteps, D.W.?"

"I don't like where this is headed, Ranger."

"Well, I know where I'm headed."

Tepper's expression tightened, taking on the contours of a dried-out tea bag. "You're not authorized to travel south of the border, Ranger."

Caitlin swiped a shirtsleeve across her brow to clean off some of the sweat that had started to bead up. "There you go, putting ideas in my head, Captain." She turned her gaze back on the alley, where forensic techs had begun working the scene around the dead bodies. "How long does el Barquero go back?"

"A century at least."

"It was a serious question, D.W."

"So was my answer, because that's how far the legend dates back."

"Around the time Mexico became the drug-dealing capital of the universe," Caitlin reflected. "Look, D.W., I've seen just about everything, but a hundred-year-old assassin? That's pushing things, even for me."

"You asked a historical question and I answered it," Tepper said tersely. "I wasn't making a case for anything beyond that. Near as I can figure, el Barquero has clearly worn plenty of faces. Stand-ins for the original. Or maybe there never was an original. Maybe the whole myth was perpetrated just so folks like us would waste our time chasing our tails. We're best off forgetting about what happened a hundred years ago and thinking about two hours back instead, because that's when el Barquero took out those two gunmen in the alley."

"The better question being, Who the hell were they? Same guns as Dallas suggests they're all part of the same group. And it's clear as day they had Cort Wesley and me in their sights."

"Until el Barquero showed up and stopped them in their tracks." Tepper scratched at his scalp again. "Boy oh boy, Ranger, it's getting to the point where your friends are worse than your enemies."

"If el Barquero saved my life, he must've had his reasons or his orders. Any guess as to where those orders may have originated?"

"Don't go there, Ranger," Tepper said, waving a finger in the air.

"All this goes back to 1994, Captain," Caitlin told him. "Since I don't have a time machine, I think I'll just jump in my truck and settle for the next best thing. I could use some personal time, and Mexico's beautiful this time of year."

"I suppose, if you like hundred-and-twenty-degree temperatures." Tepper scratched at his scalp, coming away with some flaky residue of Brylcreem under his nails. "Ordinarily I'd tell you not to bother, that you got as much chance of talking to Luna Delgado as I've got of fathering another child. But it turns out this might be your lucky day."

Caitlin looked back across the street, thinking of the four bodies inside Bane Sturgess who, according to Doc Whatley, appeared to have perished the same way as the three her father had found in a freight train car twenty-five years ago.

"It just so happens," Tepper continued, "the Red Widow was arrested this morning and is currently in the custody of Mexico's Policía Federal."

"My lucky day indeed. You mind paving the way for me, Captain?"

"No problem, Ranger," Tepper said, shaking his head. "No problem at all, given that you're about as popular down there as cancer."

"You once told me I've killed more people than cancer, D.W."

"And I was only talking about last month."

45

New Braunfels, Texas

Jones emerged from the plastic antechamber, which remained in place despite the preliminary finding that it hadn't been something in the air that had killed the three men inside Bane Sturgess. "Here's what we got, cowboy."

"'We'?"

"You wouldn't want out of this, even if I let you. Not after learning somebody sent two hitters your way."

Cort Wesley didn't bother arguing the point. "So what have *we* got?"

"The four dead bodies belong to the four principal partners of Bane Sturgess. That old ME's initial assessment puts time of death around dawn, a half hour either way, maybe while it was still dark."

"Strange time for a partners' meeting."

"Given all the business the company maintains in Europe, late nights and early mornings would've been SOP."

"Standard operating procedure," Cort Wesley translated.

"What did I just say?"

"Why do government types use acronyms so much?"

"Because we don't want to waste any time on unnecessary syllables, not when career life expectancies are so short in Washington these days."

"You're in Texas, Jones."

"Washington's not a place, cowboy, so much as a state of mind."

"Speaking of which, you should also know that the recently departed partners of Bane Sturgess had their fingers dipped in the mercenary world and liked to play soldier themselves. Beyond that, we should be focusing on the fact that the bodies Caitlin Strong's father found in that train car died of what must've been the same cause."

"Acute respiratory failure." Jones nodded. "The old ME already confirmed that, too. We've got a preliminary time of death and cause of death. What we don't have is any security camera footage to get us any closer than that, and the whole computer system is toast."

"There's always the Cloud," Cort Wesley reminded him, wondering what Jones would make of his sudden technological expertise.

"Not in this case. The company's Cloud connection has been severed. All their data is still backed up there, but good luck finding it."

"Well, that's a good thing, since the only clouds I know my way around drop rain and have silver linings."

"Not this one," Jones noted, "unless that Ranger rock star with the long hair can find a miracle in there."

"Young Roger," said Cort Wesley.

"Who?"

"The rock star Ranger with all the hair."

"I must've forgotten."

"I won't hold it against you, Jones."

Cort Wesley smelled talcum powder and figured Leroy Epps must be close by, found himself craving a root beer.

"Where you figure we go from here, cowboy?"

"Usually it's me asking the questions."

"Call it role reversal. I'm taking a lot of heat for Dallas. Since Communications Technology Providers was on my payroll, the fingers are already pointing, and Washington's looking for a scapegoat."

"This would be the Washington that's a state of mind?"

"Yuk it up at my expense, go ahead."

"Mr. Jones!" Young Roger called out, jogging their way from the parking area of a bank across the street.

Jones glanced back toward the building occupied by Bane Sturgess, as if he expected Young Roger to be coming from that direction. "I thought you were inside."

"I was. Figured I'd look elsewhere, when the security cameras and computers came up blank."

Cort Wesley glanced at the bank. "Need to use the ATM machine, Rog?"

"Nope, I wanted to see if the bank had an external security cam. Turned out it was built into that ATM machine and, if we get lucky, it just might show us something."

46

"So this is the daughter of the Texas Ranger Jim Strong, a Texas Ranger her-self," Luna Diaz Delgado said, after her Mexican police escorts had closed the door behind her. "It's a pleasure to finally meet you, Tejano."

Caitlin rose to greet Delgado, finding her handshake surprisingly firm. "That's what you called my father."

"A term worthy of the respect you deserve."

"Not the reception I'm used to getting in Mexico."

"That's because not all Mexicans share the kind of relationship I shared with the Texas Rangers, especially your father."

"Rather unusual, ma'am. Unconventional, to say the least."

Policia Federal headquarters in Chihuahua was located in Villa Ahumada, a location meant to show strength to the cartels perpetually at war with the nation as a whole. The Policia Federal, long known as the federales, had claimed it as their own in the wake of the 2008 attack on the facility by the Sinaloa Cartel, which had killed the police chief, two officers, and three civilians who'd been involved in a traffic accident.

The incident helped intensify the efforts of Coordinated Operation Chihuahua, a joint Mexican Army and Policia Federal effort. Colonel Enrique Rojas had distinguished himself prominently in that effort aimed at wresting control of Ciudad Juarez from the cartels. Caitlin knew the task force of which Rojas was a part had adopted an acceptance of ruthlessness and violence that mirrored that of the cartels, the unofficial motto of the operation being "*Combater el fuego con fuego.*"

Fight fire with fire.

The Rangers had joined forces with Rojas on any number of joint strikes. She didn't know him well, but Captain Tepper knew him well enough to get her in, on an unofficial basis, to see Luna Diaz Delgado while she was in custody.

They confiscated Caitlin's gun and kept her waiting in a sweltering interview room for nearly a half hour before Delgado was escorted into the room, absent of restraints and looking none the worse for wear.

Delgado smiled as she approached the table, more like a long-lost friend. "I make no secret of my business interests and the means by which I pursue them. I would not insult your intelligence by insisting otherwise."

"My father spoke to you about some cargo headed for Chihuahua that was stolen off a freight train in 1994. He had reason to believe it belonged to you."

"That reasoning was flawed. And I know no more about that cargo today than I did twenty-five years ago."

"I see."

"You don't have children, do you, Ranger?"

"You haven't earned the right to speak in such a familiar tone to me, señora."

"Consider it a word of advice. You're the last of your kind, Ranger, last in a line that will go extinct if there's no one to carry on the Strong name. It would be like the Strongs never existed, five generations of Texas Rangers forgotten, with no one to uphold the legacy. Even your infamous exploits will become a footnote to history."

"And what will the history books say about you, señora?"

"I've never cared much for that."

"Something we have in common, because I don't either."

"But I do care about my family's legacy."

"Your husband was murdered, and you stepped in to take his place."

"It was my duty."

"I'm sure it was. I heard your first act was to consolidate your power by executing the heads of the other three primary cartels as revenge for your husband's murder. A bold act, especially when undertaken by someone merely fulfilling their duty."

"I'm a fast learner, Ranger," Delgado said, interlacing her fingers on the table.

"So it seems. But I've heard other versions from a few who claim to be in the know. About how you'd tired of your husband's increasing devotion to religion, his decision to surrender control of his cartel to others so he might serve God better. He woke up one morning, found religion, and then found himself machine-gunned to death at a traffic stop."

"Weakness killed my husband, Tejano, not bullets."

"But you couldn't go after weakness, señora, so you went after the men behind the bullets instead. I'm surprised you didn't just send el Barquero."

Caitlin was hoping to get a rise out of Delgado by raising the mythical assassin's name. But she'd already determined that the Red Widow didn't spook easily.

"El Barquero." Delgado grinned, shaking her head. "You'll have to do better than that."

"He doesn't work for you?"

"I don't employ men who don't exist. I have enough trouble finding good ones who do."

"That's funny," Caitlin told her, "because earlier today a pair of bodies was found, killed by bullets with stars carved into their tips."

"You don't say."

"I just did."

Delgado nodded. "You know my father's true family business, the father I watched murdered on his wedding day?"

"Can't say that I do, señora."

"Cattle. His father operated a number of slaughterhouses throughout Mexico. The Meat King, they called him."

"*El Rey de la Carne,*" Caitlin translated.

Delgado's eyes widened. "Your Spanish is excellent."

"As you said, it's kind of in my blood."

"Blood is what I remember most from the few visits I made to those rendering plants. The smell," Delgado said, leaving it there.

"I've been around my share of blood, too, señora."

"So I've heard. I'm sure your father would've been proud," Delgado said, not bothering to hide the irony in her voice.

"That's why I'm here."

"Your father?"

"Particularly what brought him to you twenty-five years ago—the contents of that train car that went missing. My captain worked the case with my dad, and my captain believes that whatever was stolen from that train car ended up buried in the desert near Sonora, Texas, for safekeeping."

"Does he have a basis for such a conclusion?"

"Only that whatever it was got pulled out of the ground a few days back."

Delgado looked toward the door. "You should leave, Tejano."

"Why?"

"I'm doing this for your father."

"That doesn't answer my question."

"To save your life," Delgado continued, as if Caitlin had said nothing at all. "They'll be coming."

"Who?"

Delgado shook her head. "I'm disappointed."

"I seem to have that effect on people."

"You really have no idea what's going on here, the stakes involved. The lengths that people will go to."

"To do what, ma'am? Why don't you enlighten me? What's in those crates that's led to so many deaths?"

"Their contents are only the beginning," the Red Widow told her. "Believe me."

47

CHIHUAHUA, MEXICO

"Why should I believe you?"

Delgado fixed her gaze on the door. "They'll be coming. You should leave while there's still time."

"*Who's* coming, señora? And what do they have to do with the contents of those crates?"

"Your father was a fool, Tejano. Apparently, it runs in the family."

"I'm more concerned about the families of four men who were found dead this morning in New Braunfels. Preliminary indication is the cause of death was the same as the three men my father found in that empty freight car."

"Is that a scientific conclusion?"

"Near as any, I suppose, except for the lack of specifics."

"So you don't know what killed these men, either the ones from this morning or the ones from twenty-five years ago."

"No, señora, not yet. But I will," Caitlin added, with a confidence that defied reason.

"No, Tejano, you won't, because doctors and scientists will scour the knowledge of the world for something that doesn't exist. Because science had nothing to do with the deaths of those men or numerous others throughout history."

"Then what killed them?"

"A curse," Luna Diaz Delgado told Caitlin.

"Did you say a *curse?*"

Delgado nodded. "The Spanish word is *maldición*."

"I know what the Spanish word is; I'm just trying to make sense of how the supernatural fits in here."

"You should ask the crew of the Turkish freighter *Dolunay* that ran aground at the Port of Ordu in 1959 with all of its crew members dead."

"Carrying the same crates that went missing from a train car back in my dad's day now have gone missing again from where he likely buried them twenty-five years ago."

Delgado's stare bore into Caitlin's, lingering in expectation of Caitlin breaking it. When Caitlin didn't, she resumed. "What do you know about the red widow spider?"

"You mean besides the fact I'm staring at her right now?"

"Red widow spiders are a little-known species. They're difficult to study, due to the fact that they hide their places of dwelling. They even conceal their funnel-shaped webs in palmetto shrubs, specifically the opened leaves, rendering them invisible to the world. A mystery."

"And you think that describes you?"

"I'm a woman. People in my world have always tended to underestimate me, to look at me and see someone they'd never believe capable of what I've done and how I've done it. When you're a woman, a smile can often get you a lot farther than a bullet."

"Not in my experience," Caitlin told her.

Delgado leaned back and crossed her arms. "You're so much like your father."

"You ever tell him it was a curse that killed the three men in that train car? Because their bodies ended up at the Centers for Disease Control in Atlanta, same place the bodies we found this morning are likely headed. Normally, the CDC doesn't involve itself in curses," Caitlin said, not bothering to hide the bite in her voice.

"What do you want from me, Tejano?"

"I want to know who pulled the crates that went missing from that train car twenty-five years ago out of the Texas desert two nights back."

The Red Widow shook her thick shock of hair, smoothing it back out with her hands. In the process, a locket on a simple chain, hardly befitting a woman of Delgado's station, slipped out from inside her blouse. The locket dangled briefly, just below her neck, before she quickly tucked it back inside as if she'd just gotten away with something.

"You look a lot like your father," Delgado interjected suddenly. "The eyes mostly. You have the same eyes. I've always believed the eyes truly are the window to the soul. You agree?"

Caitlin was still thinking of the locket, a simple gold heart, noting the thin contours of its outline through the fabric of the Red Widow's blouse. A memory toyed with the edge of her consciousness, like an itch she couldn't quite scratch.

"To a point," Caitlin responded, trying not to be distracted by whatever the locket had triggered. "But I'm more interested in what killed those three men in that train car and what was inside those shipping crates that went missing."

The room's door jerked open. A man whose name tag read "Rojas" entered, followed by a trio of Policia Federal officers.

"You are being transferred, jefa," he said.

Delgado rose stiffly from her chair. "To where?"

Rojas's gaze fell briefly, dismissively, on Caitlin. "I am not at liberty to say. It is routine in these matters involving high-level suspects."

"But I'm not a suspect, am I, Enrique? Someone has already judged me, haven't they?"

"I'm sorry, jefa."

"It's not your fault." Delgado looked toward Caitlin. "The Ranger was just leaving anyway."

Caitlin joined Delgado on her feet, her attention turned to Rojas. "We're filing a request for extradition with your government. Why don't we just sit still here for a little while?"

The Policia Federal colonel shook his head. "I have my orders. And you have no jurisdiction or authority here."

Caitlin thrust a finger at Luna Diaz Delgado, the gesture just harsh enough. "This woman is guilty of crimes that have taken place on United States soil, specifically Texas. Details are being worked out to avoid another El Chapo debacle. We're saving the cell next to the one he's in now for her."

"I invite your people to take this matter up with my superiors, *el Rinche*," Rojas snapped, using the derogatory slang term Texas Rangers had been called in Mexico since the time of Steeldust Jack and William Ray Strong. "Any intervention will have to come from them. Until my orders are changed, I must see them through."

"Where is Señora Delgado being transferred to?" Caitlin asked, as Rojas's men fastened the Red Widow's wrist and leg irons back into place.

"I'm not at liberty to say."

"Why don't you tell her the truth, Colonel?" Delgado spat suddenly. "Why don't you tell her you plan to deliver me to the killers who've been after the same thing I have for the past twenty-five years, but for totally different reasons? Why don't you tell her how much they're paying you to do this?"

Rojas stiffened his spine, but otherwise showed no reaction. "Your transport is waiting, jefa." Then, to Caitlin, he said, "Two more of my men are stationed outside this room to escort you back to your vehicle. Your firearm will be returned to you at that time."

Luna Diaz Delgado felt for the locket beneath her blouse, as if to reassure herself that it was still there. "Your father was a fine man, Tejano," she said to Caitlin, a touch of genuine sadness and regret creeping into her voice. "You should feel proud that you take after him."

"We must go, jefa," Rojas said, as his men started to lead the Red Widow toward the door, her leg irons clanking against the grimy tile floor. "I'm sorry this action has become necessary."

"Just as I'm sorry that you're going to hell, Enrique. *Estaré esperando cuando llegues allí,*" Delgado said, as Caitlin looked on. *I'll be waiting when you get there.*

48

SAN ANTONIO, TEXAS

"Okay," started Young Roger, after syncing his computer to the wall-mounted flat screen in the conference room of company headquarters, "here we go."

Cort Wesley sat with Jones on one side of the table, Captain Tepper sat alone on the other.

"We got lucky with that camera built into that ATM outside the bank across the street from Bane Sturgess," Young Roger resumed, bringing up the camera's view from that morning. "It's aimed directly at a window, as you can see here."

The perspective projected on the flat screen barely showed the window at all. Even the building occupied by Bane Sturgess was so small they could only barely make out any of its features.

"What the hell good does this do us, kid?" Jones asked.

"Wait."

Young Roger began tapping a key, slowly and repeatedly, the building, seen from the camera's perspective, getting bigger and bigger. Then he activated the computer enhancement and extrapolation software, into which he'd already loaded the picture, and hit the Enter key.

"Voilà," Roger proclaimed.

"Holy shit," Tepper said, rising up from his chair. "Is this real?"

"You're looking at the scene inside Bane Sturgess just minutes before whatever happened ... happened."

"You're telling me you can advance the frame?" Jones challenged, standing up from his chair too, leaving Cort Wesley seated adjacent to the kid, little older than Dylan, who was playing the computer like a piano. "You're telling me the ATM camera was focused on that window the entire time this was going on?"

"Based on the lighting, this transpired just after dawn," Young Roger explained. "In the still shots that follow, you'll note a gradual brightening. Obviously, the bank hadn't opened yet, and traffic was virtually nonexistent, meaning there was nothing to block the camera's view until someone made a withdrawal, eighteen minutes into this recording. But by then it was over."

"You mean they were dead?" said Jones.

"It's better if you see for yourself."

"What's that on the table?" Tepper wondered.

"Looks more like a desk," Cort Wesley noted, changing his mind about letting everyone else do the talking.

"Okay, what's that on the desk?"

Young Roger was already zooming in on the camera's view, the picture first blurring and then sharpening, once the software got hold of the revised shot.

"All of this for a goddamn box," Tepper groused, shaking his head.

Jones slid closer to the flat screen. "More like a chest. Made of resin, maybe stone."

"Stone," said Young Roger. "Likely white or cream-colored when it was made, but now weathered, faded, and more gray-toned. The chest takes up about two-thirds of the desk, making it approximately three by four feet and three feet or so high."

"So we're going under the assumption that those dead Bane Sturgess boys are the ones who dug those chests, boxes, or whatever you want to call them out of the desert night before last," concluded Captain Tepper, scratching repeatedly at his scalp for want of a cigarette. "Working, almost surely, for the same folks behind those gunmen Caitlin plugged in Dallas. Means just because we can't see the other two boxes in these pictures, doesn't mean they didn't get lifted from that office too. How can you be sure the box is made of stone from a picture, by the way?"

"Because, Captain, it's an ossuary."

Tepper felt for his Marlboros, only to stop in mid-effort. "And what's that?"

"Like a coffin, a final resting place for the bones of the deceased in ancient times."

"Hold on," Jones broke in. "You're telling me all this is about *bones?*"

"No, sir, I'm telling you that chest is clearly an ancient ossuary associated with human skeletal remains. Since we can't see inside, I can't definitively say that's what this particular one contains."

"And how can you be sure how ancient it really is?"

Young Roger closed in further and froze the screen on a scrawl of hand-carved, curving letters that fit within the raised outline of a rectangle on the side of the chest facing the window.

"Because that language you see there is Aramaic, associated mostly with Jewish and Roman scribes from several thousand years ago."

"Aramaic," Jones repeated, as if he'd never heard the word before.

"What happens next?" Tepper prompted eagerly. "Advance the frame, son. Do that tapping thing with your finger again."

Young Roger obliged, the result reminding Cort Wesley of those old books that create the semblance of a moving picture when you flip through the pages. He followed the changing action on the flat screen as best he could, his mind extrapolating motion in between the still shots:

Four figures now in frame around the chest . . .

One of those figures stretching his hands outward . . .

The thick chest top gradually surrendering its position, to the point where the chest was opened halfway . . .

All four men peering inside . . .

The men looking at each other, engaged in conversation . . .

Then they were gone, only the half-open box remaining in frame.

"Shit on a shingle," Tepper muttered. "They dropped, didn't they? Dropped dead just where we ended up finding them."

Jones piped in before Young Roger could answer. "How long's the lag between those four talking among themselves and dropping out of frame?"

"I'd say twenty-six seconds. Add that to the roughly forty they were talking, and you've got just over a minute."

"Just over a minute between the time they opened that chest and fell dead to the floor."

Young Roger nodded.

"Bring us up to the point where somebody came in and took that chest they opened off the desk," Cort Wesley heard himself say.

"You're going to be disappointed." Young Roger shrugged, preparing them for what they'd see next: the vague shape of a hand snapping the wooden blinds closed.

"Must've come in through the back door," Tepper hypothecized. "Picked up that crate, and the two others, and off they go on their way, out of sight and mind."

"How much would an ossuary like that weigh?" Cort Wesley asked Young Roger.

"Educated guess: anywhere between a hundred and fifty and two hundred pounds."

"No easy lift," Jones noted. "And I assume you'll check the feeds of the security cameras angled on the back door, see what they might have seen."

"I wouldn't waste your time," Cort Wesley countered.

"And why's that, cowboy?"

"Because, Jones, whoever clipped those crates from Bane Sturgess clearly knew about that security camera from the get-go."

"So you're the resident tech expert now?"

"Stick with me and maybe you'll learn something. You mind rewinding the footage?" Cort Wesley asked Young Roger.

He brought the tape back to the point where one of the principals of Bane Sturgess slid the top of the stone chest off, exposing its contents. A time lag followed before all four principals of the company dropped out of the frame.

"Now, could you zoom in on that lettering," Cort Wesley asked him, "that Aramaic?"

"Got an eye for ancient languages all of a sudden, cowboy?" Jones asked him.

"No, but I know somebody who does."

49

Caitlin's two Mexican Policia Federal escorts led her in the opposite direction from those transporting Luna Diaz Delgado. There seemed little doubt that the Red Widow was about to disappear forever, not so much thanks to the Mexican government, with whom she was in league, as to the same mysterious entity responsible for the hit squad Caitlin had gunned down in Dallas. She'd seemed almost resigned to her fate, and Caitlin was not quite sure what to make of a person this ruthless and powerful going quietly into the night.

Luna Diaz Delgado might have accepted that, but Caitlin couldn't. Halfway down the hall, alone with the two federales, Caitlin pretended to stumble on a slick patch of tile. One of the officers reached out to grab her, and she quickly righted herself and yanked the semiautomatic pistol from his holster. She slammed the pistol butt into his nose and then, through the explosive flow of blood that followed, hammered it down on the soft part of his skull.

The second officer had almost gotten the assault rifle from his shoulder, when Caitlin jammed the other man's pistol under his chin.

"How this plays out from here is your call," she told him.

Caitlin made him slap the other officer's cuffs into place on the unconscious man's wrists. Then, having shouldered his M16 assault rifle, she did likewise to him, before supervising the process of him dragging his compadre into the interview room. Holding a Heckler and Koch USP pistol, standard issue for Mexico's Policia Federal, on him, she smashed both their walkie-talkies against the wall, grabbed hold of the keys clasped to his belt, then exited and locked the door behind her.

She'd just started to rush down the hall in the direction Colonel Rojas had escorted Luna Diaz Delgado, when gunfire rang out.

50

CHIHUAHUA, MEXICO

Caitlin couldn't be sure of its precise origins, because of the initial burst's echo. But the return fire placed it firmly at the main entrance to the building. It was more of a stockade, a fortress, than a building, with a high wall, topped by barbed wire, that enclosed the entire complex, complete with guard towers.

Boom! Boom! Boom!

The blasts came just as she'd formed that thought. Caitlin pictured rocket-propelled grenades taking out the guard towers.

She picked up her pace, bringing the assault rifle around to the front. Rojas and his men had clearly walked into a trap. The entire Policia Federal complex was under siege to make sure Luna Diaz Delgado never got the chance to tell anyone everything she knew.

Caitlin neared the front of the building to find all the forces the station could muster rushing up to defend it. Her boots crunched over glass from shattered windows, screams and shouts sounding from outside the breached front entrance. She knelt down when she spotted something shiny on the floor, retrieving what she recognized as the Red Widow's locket. Pocketing it, she neared a heavy steel door that had been blown right off its hinges and found a slew of bodies, both wounded and dead, fallen to what was clearly an elaborately staged ambush and deftly coordinated attack.

She guessed Colonel Rojas, leading candidate for the betrayal, would be nowhere about. Or, if he was, he'd likely also been betrayed, by the very forces that had contracted him to turn Delgado over to them.

The courtyard beyond, meanwhile, was a sea of gunfire. With the high ground surrendered, thanks to the flaming remains of the guard towers, the federales were outgunned and outmatched. Likely looking for a way to flee rather than to fight. Some of the vehicles that had been parked in rows were now askew, due to men trying to escape or to small-explosives blasts that had uprooted them from their positions.

Black-garbed, masked commandos continued to besiege the compound. Caitlin searched for Luna Diaz Delgado amid the carnage, the bursts of smoke and flame, and the fallen bodies. One especially thick pocket of smoke cleared to reveal the Red Widow pinned against the massive tire of an armored vehicle Caitlin recognized as the type Homeland Security supplied to foreign crime fighters to help win the elusive war on drugs.

Caitlin had trained with an M16 numerous times, but that was hardly the same as a combat situation, when forces of this caliber would be firing back on her. But she had to reach the Red Widow, had to find a way to spirit her to safety, and not only because Delgado was the key to finding the link between the dead bodies from both her father's time and her own.

It was because of something she'd now remembered, realized, a connection both inexplicable and impossible.

Caitlin thumbed off the assault rifle's safety, racked back the slide, and tested her finger on the cold steel trigger. The weapon was heavier than film and television made it seem, especially when being toted in fast, desperate motion.

She had sprinted out into the courtyard before consciously deciding to, letting go with a burst toward the blown gates, which a trio of trucks toting heavy machine guns had just poured through. Those guns opened up on the building entrance where Caitlin had just been, literally tearing it apart and scattering the last line of the federales' defense.

Still making her way toward Delgado's position, Caitlin continued to clack off individual shots from the M16, no longer trusting her prowess on full auto and keenly aware that she had no replacement magazines with which to reload. A pair of the black-garbed commandos, who might as well have been twins, were rushing toward the Red Widow. Caitlin was unable to tell whether the intent was to kill or to capture. Unable to accept the risk of either, she clacked off one shot after another, head shots all, given the likelihood that the men were wearing body armor.

The two commandos went down like somebody had yanked the world out from under them, clearing her path to Luna Diaz Delgado.

"Not our lucky day, eh, Tejano?" Delgado managed, her clothes soiled and torn, face streaked with grime and smoke-stained hair pasted to one side of her face.

"I'm getting you out of here, ma'am," Caitlin said, unclasping the Red Window's wrist and leg irons with the keys she'd clipped from the officer inside the barracks.

"Always the hero," Delgado managed to muse, "just like your father."

"That's why I'm doing this—for him," Caitlin said, leaving it there, as the gunfire intensified around them.

Delgado shed her wrist irons and pushed herself tighter against the big tire, going to work on the shackles binding her legs. "One riot, one Ranger," she said, repeating the Texas Ranger motto. "But this is a lot more than a riot."

Caitlin squeezed off a few more shots, the magazine just about expended, and, from her stance over Delgado, reached up for the passenger door latch of the armored RV. She had to stand all the way up to work the door, but the latch gave and the door opened.

"Like I said, we're getting out of here," she told the Red Widow. "Get in!"

51

CHIHUAHUA, MEXICO

Delgado had shed her elegant shoes and was barefoot when she slammed the armored vehicle's passenger door behind her, as Caitlin slid across the slippery fabric to claim the driver's seat. She still had the guard's Heckler and Koch pistol but had shed the nearly empty M16 to help the Red Widow and to climb into the vehicle herself.

Behind the cab was a flat space with jump-style seating for commandos. Slots for a variety of weapons, too, all of which were regrettably empty. But it had a push-button starter that required no key and an engine that sounded like a 737's when she got it revving.

The sound must have drawn the focus of the attacking commando force, because small arms fire began to rain down on the vehicle. Thanks to its armored skin, each hit resulted in no more than a *ping*, while more rounds carved tiny divots out of the windshield's bulletproof glass.

"Get down!" Caitlin ordered Delgado.

"Give me the gun!"

Caitlin handed over the pistol. She had no reason to really trust this woman, beyond the fact that they were under fire together, but there was no way she could drive this thing and shoot, anyway.

As the vehicle barreled for the blown gate, currently blocked by a pair of the attacking force's own heavy vehicles parked nose to nose, Delgado slid the passenger side window down just enough to allow her to poke the Heckler and Koch's barrel outside. She fired with the calm and dexterity of a truly practiced hand, holding off the enemy just enough to keep them from launching an attack from that side.

The bulletproof windshield burst into a dozen separate spiderweb patterns as fire was directed at Caitlin's vehicle from unidentified origins, leaving barely any of it clear and whole. But she could see well enough to aim the heavy thing straight toward the blocked gates.

Impact against the trucks in her path shook Caitlin wildly and sent her teeth crashing together. But she moved the trucks just enough to surge between them onto the street near central Chihuahua, where pedestrians and drivers alike were racing to flee. Stalled traffic forced many to abandon their vehicles and join the flight on foot, the armored vehicle plowing through everything in its path.

Caitlin worked the gas pedal and transmission, trying to gather the momentum needed to forge an opening, a chasm through the clutter. The scent of scorched rubber added to the chaos, which was further fed by those desperately fleeing and a chorus of blaring horns that gave no signs of stopping.

She wasn't getting anywhere. Sitting ducks right here, and even more so if she risked trying to flee with Delgado in tow, here and now, on foot.

A familiar *whop-whop-whop* touched the edge of her hearing, the sound rising above all others as a helicopter gunship soared overhead. Caitlin clung to the hope that it was Mexican Army or Policia Federal, but it had no markings of any kind, which made it more likely that it belonged to the commandos who'd attacked the federal police station.

The armored vehicle's rear camera, which Delgado had switched on, displayed a dozen, maybe fifteen or more of those masked fighters charging through the carnage of the street. They sprayed fire forward, oblivious to anyone or anything that might have strayed into the way, as much to keep their quarries pinned down and on the defensive as anything. And what chance did Caitlin and the Red Widow have, anyway, with a gunship backing up their efforts from the front?

Then the gunship opened fire, not at the armored vehicle but over it. Firing on the masked fighters, obliterating everything in the street with a relentless rage of 7.62-millimeter fire from a mini gun mounted on the chopper's underside. It swirled, dipped, and then darted directly overhead, letting loose with Hellfire rockets that launched abandoned vehicles airborne. These crashed back down to create a flame-rich blockade, behind which the attacking fighters were now effectively trapped. And the gunship, barely fifty feet over the street, just to the driver's side of the armored vehicle, continued to rain a blistering wave of fire down from its mini gun.

Caitlin glimpsed none other than Guillermo Paz in the cockpit.

"Angel de la Guarda..."

Delgado rasped the words out in shock. She obviously knew of the colonel's past exploits in Juarez, where her bullying minions had likely been among those with whom Paz had waged war and ultimately won.

"I wasn't sure he was real," Delgado continued.

"Oh, he's real, all right."

Paz smiled, waved. Caitlin waved back, and the colonel soared away to finish off the remaining fighters and cut off any possible pursuit of the armored vehicle.

"I owe you my life, Tejano," the Red Widow told her.

"And you can pay your debt by telling me the truth about what was in those shipping crates. But, first, I think you dropped this," Caitlin added, easing the gold locket from the pocket of her jeans.

"Gracias," Delgado said, closing her fist around it. "It means a lot to me."

"To me too, ma'am. Because it belonged to my mother."

Part Six

In his career in law enforcement, Manual T. "Lone Wolf" Gonzaullas became one of the "Big Four" in the Ranger service in the early to mid-1990s. The others were Francis A. "Frank" Hamer, Thomas R. "Tom" Hickman, and William L. "Will" Wright. They guarded the border; they tamed oil-boom towns; they chased outlaws and killers. Hamer will be forever remembered for taking part in the gunning down of Bonnie and Clyde. Gonzaullas belonged to another group also. He combined his faith—Presbyterianism—and his law enforcement work to become one of the leading Christian Rangers.

—*Tracking the Texas Ranger: The Twentieth Century*,
edited by Bruce A. Glasrud and Harold J. Weiss, Jr.,
University of North Texas Press, 2013

52

"I understand," Enrico Molinari said into the cell phone that automatically encrypted all incoming and outgoing calls.

He listened some more to the Order's leader in America, dual failures in Texas and Mexico stoking his ire.

"It is difficult to accept God's will in this case," Molinari responded calmly. "He may work in mysterious ways, but it's difficult to imagine those ways conspiring so much against our noble cause...."

"Of course, Your Eminence, as soon as I have something additional to report...."

"Yes, I believe I know what must be done. I am following the Lord's directive. I won't burden you with the details. If I succeed, you will have my report. If I don't, you'll know I've been called to Him."

"There is no place in His kingdom for failure, Captain," the head of the Order in America warned, referring to Molinari by his former rank in the carabinieri. "The reinforcements you requested are en route. The prefect has seen to it himself."

The phone call done, Molinari moved through the sliding glass door that led out to his room's balcony and gazed down at the cluttered Riverwalk, a veritable sea of the worthless and aimless, those without purpose and direction, among whom he couldn't even imagine mixing.

Molinari couldn't bear to be seen, especially in the daytime, because his appearance, that patchwork face resembling a scarecrow's, inspired revulsion. Gazes jerked away, his visage burned into their psyches forever.

There is no place in His kingdom for failure, Captain.

The report from Mexico had turned the day even darker than it had started. First there was the fiasco in New Braunfels, when the two fighters he'd dispatched to eliminate the Texas Ranger had turned up dead in an alley. And now the assault meant to capture or kill Luna Diaz Delgado had ended horribly and inexplicably, with dozens of his fighters killed or wounded. The wounded would never talk, regardless of whatever steps the Mexican authorities took to make them. They'd die before they'd talk, just as he would.

Then, just before his call, word reached him that Mexico had gone wrong, yet again, because of that same Texas Ranger—daughter of the very Ranger who had waylaid his efforts here a quarter century before, as it turned out.

God worked in mysterious ways.

Indeed.

For two years after all his surgeries and grafts, the hulking Molinari had worn a form-fitting nylon mask that held his face together and prevented infection. The mask covered his entire head and neck and was the one hope he had of keeping the new face the Order had given him. And when that mask finally came off, the results were considered a miracle, though not to Molinari. He looked into the mirror and a monster looked back.

The burn damage had also affected his nerves; this was damage that even the surgeons who'd sewed him a new face were ill-suited to repair. As a result, Molinari's face knew only a single, unchanging expression, never looking happy or sad, never smiling. His bald pate, perpetually colored a sunburned red, still showed the scars of his burning, above where the mask he had worn for two years had rested. Molinari still had that mask, keeping it as a reminder of his transformation and of finding himself in service to a God he had bitterly disappointed today.

Molinari moved back inside the room and fished from his travel bag the thick pouch in which he kept the mask. It had folded up on itself and he carefully smoothed the contours, holding it up before him and seeing the man he had been during the course of his transformation. He carried it as a testament to that time that marked the beginning of his transformation, while never donning it again.

Perhaps the mask's work hadn't been finished. Perhaps his becoming remained incomplete.

In that moment, on a whim Molinari started to squeeze the mask back down over his face. The fit was impossibly tight, the elastic fabric having returned to its original contours. Still he squeezed, pulled, tucked, and rolled it downward from his scalp, not caring if he peeled off his patchwork face in the process. The thing smelled rancid, of old skin, blood, and sweat mixed with antiseptic cream and liniment that had dried into the nylon fabric.

Instantly, Molinari's mind began to clear. The world looked so different to him through the slots molded into the mask to fit his eyes. He moved through the sliding door, back out into the balcony's blistering heat, which made him think this must have been what hell felt like.

In that moment, Molinari heard what could only be the voice of God through the fabric that covered his ears.

She must die. A pause followed, then, *Kill her.*

Her.

The Texas Ranger.

Follow God's word and His becoming would be complete, the Order's work done. Follow God's word and the contents of that long-missing ossuary would be his, the Lord's miracle delivered unto man in order to better do His work.

Once he killed Caitlin Strong.

53

Shavano Park, Texas

"I need your help with something," Dylan heard his father say through the cell phone braced against his ear, as Selina Escalante worked the buttons of Dylan's jeans.

He tried to push her away, but she wasn't having it. "My help?" Dylan said to his father. "Did you dial the right number?"

"All those ancient language classes you took at Brown as part of your archaeology thing..."

"It's a major, Dad, and, yeah, I'm just a whiz with dead things."

"How about we put that knowledge to good use? I'm on my way home now. I'd like you to try your hand at translating something for me."

"Sure," Dylan said, unable to hold Selina off. "I'll be here."

She'd showed up out of nowhere while he was playing a video game. His dad's call reminded him, yet again, that he needed to look into which classes to register for, once he was officially readmitted to Brown.

"How'd you get in?" Dylan had asked Selina.

"Door was open."

"I locked it."

"You thought you did."

She was dressed to slaughter, not just kill, leaving Dylan envious of whoever had been on the other end of her pharmaceutical sales calls earlier in the day. He gave up pretending to still be interested in killing the monsters on his flat screen and watched Selina yank open his closet door.

"What are you doing?"

"Changing. Just need to borrow a pair of jeans," she said, flipping through his hanging assortment before settling on one of the skinny pairs his dad hated.

"Those'll never fit you."

"No? You ever see a girl put a pair of these on?"

Dylan shook his head, embarrassed for some reason.

"Watch and learn, boy. Maybe you can help me squeeze in the last part of the way."

In the end, Selina managed the effort all on her own, wearing Gap Raw Selvedge like a second skin she'd have to peel off like the skin off a grape. She smoothed them out with her palms, down to the knees, clearly pleased with the result.

"I think I might keep these."

"That would make my dad happy."

"How about I buy you dinner in exchange?"

"My dad needs my help with something. He's on his way home now."

Selina checked herself in the mirror that had been perched on Dylan's bureau since he was a kid. Then she smoothed out the jeans some more.

"Want to do something until he gets here?"

54

Chihuahua, Mexico

"Gracias. It means a lot to me."

"To me too, ma'am. Because it belonged to my mother."

Caitlin's own words echoed in her mind, but there weren't many more spoken between her and Luna Diaz Delgado after they'd sped away from the fortress that held the headquarters of the Policia Federal in Chihuahua.

"There's a place we can go, one of my places," Delgado told her, breaking the silence that had settled in the big armored vehicle's cab. "Close by, but on its own pretty much. You can drop me there."

"It's safe?"

"At least until my soldiers arrive. I have several refuges where I can hide out in the event of a situation like this."

"You got bigger problems than that, señora. Those commandos raided a federal police barracks. They must want you dead awful bad, and if you think your own people can keep you safe with those odds, then be my guest."

"Do you have a better idea, Tejano?"

"I was thinking we dump this tank and get ourselves over the border into Texas."

The Red Widow snickered. "And you think you can keep me alive up there?"

"I think you already know who can keep you safe up there."

"Angel de la Guarda." Delgado nodded. "Your giant."

"The colonel isn't mine. He works for Homeland Security."

"They must have a serious staff shortage."

"Actually, it's the country's enemies who've been experiencing a shortage, since Paz signed on."

Delgado settled all the way back in the passenger seat of the cab. "I'll take my chances down here, if you don't mind."

"Not at all, señora, so long as you don't mind me sticking around for a time."

"And how long a time might that be?"

"Long enough for you to tell me how it is my father came to give you my mother's locket, and what exactly happened after the Rangers tried to pull Jim Strong off the case."

Delgado cast a sidelong glance at Caitlin. "You're just like him, and neither one of you are much for following orders, are you?"

"That depends on the point of those orders. In my father's case, back in 1994, he wasn't about to walk away from something that had gotten a whole bunch of men killed. The killing all started with the contents of that train car. Now those contents have resurfaced and the killing has started up again, even more than the first time."

"You can't win this one, Ranger, any more than your father could in his day. You're dealing with something you can't possibly comprehend."

Caitlin squeezed the thick steering wheel tighter, glad they were on a back road where there were far fewer eyes to regard the vehicle. Standing out now was clearly not in their best interest.

"How far away is this place you were speaking about, señora?"

"You know where the old freight depot is where I met your father for the first time?"

"Roughly."

"That's where it is."

The station in question had closed years before. Today it was no more than a boarded-up relic, replaced by a multirail depot several miles away that was far better capable of handling the big increase in trade that had sprouted in the wake of the signing of the North American Free Trade Agreement. A small cantina sat in the depot's shadow; it likely had been a bustling hotbed of activity before the depot moved to its new location.

From a distance, the cantina looked closed as well, waiting to be swallowed up by the encroaching desert just as the rail lines were overgrown with scrub and practically buried by the stones and gravel washed in by storms. Drawing closer, though, Caitlin caught lights flickering through the windows caked with grime.

"It's a safe house of sorts," Delgado explained. "One of numerous locations throughout Mexico my men can retreat to in the event they need to hide out."

"Bet you never expected that to be you, did you?"

Delgado stared at the cantina through the windshield, seeming to will it closer. "I'm worried about my grandchildren."

"You must have people you can trust taking care of them."

"After what happened today, I'm not of a mind to trust anyone. You don't need to convince me how dangerous this enemy I'm facing is. I've faced them before."

"Then I imagine you've got a pretty good idea who they are," Caitlin said, recalling the gunfight in Dallas where she'd gunned down four men who, by all indications, likely were part of the same force as the one that had just attacked the Policia Federal barracks.

"It's not that simple."

"Seems like it is to me, ma'am."

"To understand the *who*, Tejano, you have to understand the *why* and the *what*."

"By 'what,' you mean whatever was inside those three crates that just went missing for the second time."

The Red Widow didn't respond, her gaze remaining fixed on the approaching cantina. "Pull around the back, out of sight," she told Caitlin. "We can finish this discussion inside."

55

Chihuahua, Mexico

Besides two burly men wearing *bandeleros*, behind the bar, they were the only people inside, seated at a table positioned so both could watch, through the cantina's grime-encrusted windows, the open space between this building and the crumbling freight depot. Caitlin kept her eyes on the Red Widow, who took a satellite phone from behind the bar and made several calls.

"My people will be here in thirty minutes," she reported, sitting back down. "I don't think you want to be here when they arrive. A few have bad histories with the Texas Rangers."

"I'll take my chances." Caitlin paused. "You call your son, father of your granddaughter, Isabella, your chosen successor?"

"That's not something a lot of people know, Tejano."

"I did some research on you."

"Enough to tell you I wouldn't trust my oldest son with the lives of his own children?"

"Actually, it was you who told me that. You mentioned your granddaughter, Isabella, and daughter, Nola, by name but had nothing to say at all about any of your sons."

"That's because Isabella and Nola are ruthless." The Red Widow stopped, then started again immediately. "Like you."

"You think I'm ruthless?"

"I don't believe anyone could have survived all you've done if they weren't."

"Seems like you've done some research of your own."

"I like to be prepared."

"The difference being, ma'am, that I knew I was going to be seeing you, while the reverse wasn't true."

Delgado's eyes darted about again, anxious, the way she'd been for a time in the interview room. "You should walk away from this now, this very minute. You can't shoot what you're up against this time."

"I don't believe in curses, señora."

"There's a lot more involved here than just a curse, more than you've ever confronted before."

"Maybe you didn't do as much research into me as I thought."

"You're as stupid as your father. He didn't know enough to walk away, either—at least not when he should have. He paid a terrible price for that, one that haunted the rest of his days forever."

Caitlin stared across the cantina table at the impression of her mother's locket beneath Delgado's blouse. "That locket was a Christmas present from my father to my mother. The last time I saw it was the day she died, murdered by drug mules a decade before he met you. I'd like to know how he came to give it to you. I'd like to know why."

"Would you like something to drink?" Delgado asked, instead of responding.

"Anything cold."

"Beer?"

"Soda."

The Red Widow signaled to the men behind the bar, one of whom brought over a pair of Cokes in old-fashioned green bottles, the ice they'd been lifted from leaving a residue of frost across the glass. The man popped off the caps with an opener and then returned to his post behind the bar.

Caitlin took a hefty chug, the sugar seeming to stick to her throat on the way down. She'd never enjoyed a better-tasting Coca-Cola in her life.

"You were saying, señora?"

"I wasn't saying anything."

"I asked you about my father, about that locket."

"My men will be here soon, Tejano. We don't have time for the whole long story."

"A part of it, then," Caitlin said, leaning forward and laying her hands on the table, with the green bottle cradled between them. "There's nowhere else I need to be right now."

56

Buster Plugg looked pretty much like his name. Short and stout with a steel-belted radial for a stomach and a bald head that resembled a bowling ball. But it was his baby-soft face, flushed red by the sudden exertion of charging out of his house with a shotgun, that stuck out the most in Jim Strong's mind.

"Something I can help you with there, friend?"

"Man oh man, this is some truck," Jim said, whistling his admiration at the black Chevy with oversize tires gleaming in his driveway. "I'd call it my dream vehicle, except I can't afford to even dream that big. See," he continued, peeling back his jacket to reveal his badge, "Texas Rangers don't earn a big enough salary."

Buster Plugg's eyes widened at the sight of the badge, and he slowly lowered the shotgun to waist level. "I apologize, Ranger. You just never know these days."

"No, sir, you don't. You living all the way out here on your daddy's old ranch, so isolated and such, I can't say I blame you."

Plugg tightened his grasp on the twelve-gauge just a bit. "Did you know my daddy?"

"No, sir, never met the man, unless you count through you."

"Through me?" Plugg asked, the cheeks of his baby-soft face getting more flushed by the second.

"I did some checking before I came out here," Jim said, hitching back his jacket to make sure the man shaped like a fire hydrant could see his .45. "Figured I'd get acquainted with your past to better understand your present."

"My present?"

"As a dispatcher at the Fort Stockton train depot. I imagine you heard about the trouble there a couple nights back."

"Station just reopened this morning."

"You called in sick."

Buster Plugg half nodded.

"You don't look sick."

"I got a touch of the gout."

"I'm sorry to hear that, Buster, I truly am," Jim said, stepping out from the shadow of the gleaming truck and facing Plugg head-on. "What I'm wondering is how a man with so much debt he had to leverage his own nut sack could afford a vehicle like this."

"It's a lease."

"Hard to fathom, with your credit. You hit the lottery or something, play your birthday numbers and claim your prize anonymously?"

Plugg stood in the sun, the flushing starting to spread beyond his cheeks.

"I think you gave somebody the word a certain shipment was coming through Fort Stockton the other night. I think they came to you and made you aware of that shipment and put you on the lookout. And when you learned it was on its way, you made a call, and then you altered the manifest to make it look as if the shipment in question didn't exist, that the freight car where I found three dead bodies the other night was empty."

Jim Strong waited for a reaction from Buster Plugg, any reaction, but the man just stood there like a bulbous statue bleeding sweat in the hot sun.

"Of course, Buster, you couldn't have known about that, any more than you could know that whoever you placed that call to was going to murder the entire train crew. That makes you an accessory to capital murder. That's the death penalty, the electric chair. That worth the price of this road rocket here?"

"I got no idea what you're talking about."

Jim moved a few steps closer, daring the man to do something with his shotgun, but he knew Plugg wasn't about to do anything of the kind.

"Yes, you do, Buster. But let me tell you something you don't know. The two dead Mexicans carrying pearl-handled forty-fives? They worked for a woman named Luna Diaz Delgado, pretty much the most powerful crime boss in Mexico. And that electric chair frying your brains is nothing compared to what she'll do if she learns you had a hand in stealing her cargo."

"I didn't steal nothing, Ranger!"

"Do I need to tell you the meaning of the word 'accessory' here?"

"The bank is foreclosing on my daddy's ranch. I bought the truck because there's no point in bothering with those payments anymore. What do you want me to say?"

Jim took another two steps toward him. "How about who paid you to make that call and how can I find them."

"I'm telling you—"

"I know what you're telling me, just like I know you're lying. You're not much of a liar, Buster."

"Look—"

"Way I see it," Jim resumed, rolling right over Plugg's words, "you've got three choices. Smartest one is to own up to what you did and come clean. The dumbest is to stand there and keep lying to my face. Somewhere in the middle is to do something with that shotgun, besides holding it like your limp dick, and let me put you out of your misery."

Plugg stooped down and laid the shotgun across the superheated driveway pavement. "You wanna shoot an unarmed man, Ranger, go right ahead. But I can't tell you what I don't know, and I'm of a mind to report this harassment to the local sheriff."

"Sheriff Dabs Dabney's the one who filled in some of the blanks for me. I get the feeling he doesn't think much of you."

Plugg's lower lip trembled. "That don't change the fact I can't tell you something I don't know, or confess to something I didn't do. You want to shoot me, fire away. You want to arrest me, just slap on the cuffs. Meanwhile, I'm going back inside to keep on with my packing. By week's end I'll be trading these five hundred acres for a two-hundred-square-foot motel room."

Jim moved back up to the Chevy and tapped its gleaming hood, which must have been two hundred degrees. "Well, Buster, at least you got yourself a nice truck."

Buster Plugg tore out of the driveway an hour later, allowing for what he thought was a safe interim to make sure Jim wasn't still about. Jim had parked his truck an eighth of a mile down the main road outside Plugg's property, the only road he could use to get anywhere at all. He'd chosen that spot for the thick nest of brush he could park behind and still watch the road.

Sitting in his Ford, Jim suddenly realized how worn and faded the upholstery was. It had even developed a musty kind of smell, which was worse in the sun. This in contrast to the spanking new Chevy that Buster Plugg was driving, thanks to the man's ill-gotten gains. It was only in times like these that Jim bemoaned his civil servant salary, still high by law enforcement standards but not by much else. His dad, Earl, not just a fellow Ranger but also a legend who'd mixed it up with the likes of Al Capone and J. Edgar Hoover, had left his total net worth to Jim after passing. A lifetime savings that, coupled with a life insurance policy he'd partially cashed in, amounted to just over twenty-five thousand dollars.

Not a lot to show for ninety years of living, at least not in the monetary sense. Sure, there were a lot of things plenty more important than money, but try telling that to your thirteen-year-old daughter who needs braces and new shoes. Good thing Caitlin didn't care about clothes and the like as much as just about every other teenage girl—her wish list for guns dwarfed her shopping list for new dresses or fancy jeans.

Thanks, Dad, Jim mused as, an eighth of a mile ahead of him, Buster Plugg sped down the main road.

Plugg drove sixteen miles to a small strip mall where several occupants had already closed up shop and others were offering going-out-of-business sales. A pay phone had a spot to itself before a concrete seating area in front of a shuttered frozen yogurt store.

Jim had followed Plugg at a safe distance, as much as a half mile away, once they reached the interstate, and as little as a quarter mile after that. When Plugg's route spilled off onto the access road where the strip mall was located, Jim continued to hold back. A general fix on what he was up to was all Jim needed at this point, whether that was a meeting or, more likely, the pay phone he was currently standing near.

Jim pulled into a gas station with a decent enough view of that pay phone, ruminating again, in the course of Plugg's three-and-a-half-minute phone call, on Caitlin playing with toy guns when other little girls were playing with dolls. The only dolls she ever did play with actually had guns of their own, thanks to his father's skills with plastic and wood. Jim recalled Caitlin's Barbie and Ken dolls dressed up as updated versions of Bonnie and Clyde, only it was Barbie holding the tiny Thompson submachine gun, not Ken. Earl Strong had encouraged his granddaughter's every whim when it came to firearms. She could hit the target well enough with a Colt by the time she was seven and was damn good with a Springfield Model 1911 .45 before she was twelve. When most girls her age were headed to the soccer field, Caitlin was off to the gun range, biking there on her own and coming home smelling of sulfur and gun oil.

Once Buster Plugg finished his call and drove off, Jim waited for the fancy new truck to pass the gas station before he headed to the strip mall and fed a quarter into the same pay phone, which had a sticker saying it was owned by some phone company Jim had never heard of.

"Yeah, this is Jim Strong of the Texas Rangers," he said, once he finally got the right person on the line. "I need the last number dialed from this phone exchange."

Jim asked a man at the phone company for whom he'd once done a favor to get him the address that matched the number in question. That address turned out to belong to one of those economy chain hotels, maybe the one that always left the lights on for you. It was clean, simple, and offered free breakfast, HBO, and telephone. Jim entered the office and strode straight up to the reception desk, making sure the clerk could see his badge.

"Don't suppose you can tell me which of your guests completed a three-and-a-half-minute phone call just over an hour ago?"

The man, whose name tag identified him as Donnie, shook his head. "Sorry, Ranger. The calls are routed through the phone company."

"Then tell me this, son. Did you notice any of your guests leaving around that same time, an hour or so ago?"

Jim could tell by the look in Donnie's eyes that the answer was yes, even before he spoke. "He checked out early. I was glad to see him go. He was a big guy. I mean real big. But it wasn't that."

"What was it?"

"Ranger, I know this is gonna sound crazy, but he didn't have a face. It's like it was somebody else's face and he was wearing it," the man continued. "Like he sewed it on in strips. He wore a hat tilted low over his brow to disguise it as best he could. But when he was checking out, the light hit him just right and I thought maybe Halloween came early."

"Did you see what he was driving?"

"A van, Ranger."

"Cargo?"

"Yeah."

"Didn't get a look inside, by any chance, did you?"

Donnie shook his head. "No, sir. I ain't no snoop."

"How big was he, exactly?"

"I got a kink in my neck from looking up at him."

"So the maid hasn't gotten to his room yet."

"Like I said, Ranger, he only checked out maybe—"

"How about we go have a look?" Jim interrupted.

• • •

"We're gonna charge his credit card for this damage, I can tell you that much," Donnie snarled, seeing the condition in which the big man who'd checked in as "Fred Church" had left his room.

Checking out so fast likely meant the man suspected that Buster Plugg had blown his cover. He was somebody, then, who hadn't been born yesterday when it came to such things.

When it came to the way he'd left his room . . . well, that was something else again.

"Who does something like that?" Donnie said, shaking his head. "How did he even do it?"

The whole of the bathroom mirror had been removed from the wall, along with a vertical one that had been fastened outside the bathroom door. Donnie had found both mirrors fully intact, inside the closet, while Jim Strong found a bathroom wastebasket full of strips of gauze soaked with some kind of medicated cream or liniment. He'd put on plastic gloves before examining them and then had fit the whole contents of the tiny wastebasket into a large plastic pouch.

"Donnie, I'm gonna need to ask you not to rent this room out until the Rangers can go through it with a fine-tooth comb."

"I couldn't rent it in this condition anyway."

"And I'm going to need you to *leave* it in this condition, too. Shouldn't take more than a day or so."

Donnie didn't protest. He took out a notepad to catalog all the damage, while Jim moved to the nightstand. He pictured the big man with no face sitting on the bed while talking to Buster Plugg, retrieved the thin motel memo pad from the nightstand, and saw a jagged edge where the top page had been removed. Jim took out the number two pencil he always carried and used it the way his dad had shown him, to reveal at least a semblance of the message on the torn page. Looked like the man used a hotel ballpoint, which he'd likely later pocketed because it contained his fingerprints.

Jim watched the page come to life as he continued his magic with the pencil, revealing an address.

In Mexico.

"I'll be a son of a bitch," Jim muttered.

57

Chihuahua, Mexico

"It was your address, wasn't it?" Caitlin asked Luna Diaz Delgado, when she stopped the story only Jim Strong could have told her. "And the only way you could've known all this was if my father had told you. So tell me," she said, leaning across the cantina table, "what else did the two of you talk about? What happened when my father rode down to Mexico to save you from this man with no face?"

Delgado remained expressionless. On the side, Caitlin pictured the Red Widow's emotions churning like gale force winds. She could hear it in the undercurrents of Delgado's words as she related the circumstances of what had ultimately brought Jim Strong back to Mexico on the trail of the very same thing Caitlin was after now.

"Ma'am?" she prodded. "Señora?"

The cantina looked different from when Delgado had picked up the story, pretty much where Captain Tepper had left off in New Braunfels. Smaller and darker mostly, likely the result of the changed position of the sun, which had stopped pushing big amber rays through the building's windows.

"Yes, your father found my address in the faceless man's motel room," Delgado said finally. "Not where I live now, but my former home, where I had shared a life with my husband, Hector. I never should have returned there after that day he was assassinated by the cartels."

"And did this man with no face show up too, maybe around the same time as my father?"

"I never saw him, I never saw any of them. But there were many, an endless stream of them it seemed, just like what just happened at the Policia Federal compound. All of them, both then and now, beholden to forces with power beyond comprehension, Tejano."

"Even yours?"

"A different kind of power than mine, the kind that brings nations and governments to their knees."

Something toyed with the edge of Caitlin's consciousness, a sensation she'd come to recognize when the waters she'd waded into proved deeper than expected, which was pretty much all the time. She wondered if Guillermo Paz was starting to rub off on her, if she had somehow gained a crude form of second sight through osmosis. She recalled the part of the story about Mo Scoggins, special assistant to the governor, trying to close the case against Jim Strong's wishes, which suggested the fix was in—something that would take a whole lot of power to do with the Texas Rangers.

A different kind of power than mine, the kind that brings nations and governments to their knees.

The colonel had speculated that Texas was the moral epicenter of the planet, where great battles came to be fought. Caitlin couldn't say to what degree she believed that, but it had been proven true often enough these past few years.

"Care to share with me who we're talking about, exactly?" she asked Delgado.

"*We're* not talking about them; *I* am."

"But we are talking about more than just those three shipping crates stolen from you twenty-five years ago and dug out of the Texas desert a few nights back, aren't we?"

"After that Turkish freighter crashed in 1959, they went missing for a very long time. Fate brought me to them in 1994 and then again today, because I am meant to reveal the secret they contain."

"With all due respect, señora, you seem a lot more comfortable holding a gun than a secret."

Delgado's gaze grew elusive, the dimmer lighting in the bar making it impossible for Caitlin to see her eyes, almost as if they'd vanished. "When my men arrive, I'll provide you with a vehicle to get you home. Unless you'd prefer to drive the policia's armored truck back to Texas."

"I don't think that would sit too well with the Border Patrol, señora, and I'm grateful for the gesture. But you told me you wanted me gone before your men arrived."

The Red Widow's gaze finally found Caitlin again. "I've changed my mind. Out of respect for your father."

"Because he saved your life?"

"Yes." Delgado nodded.

"What else?"

"That's not reason enough?"

"It would be if it were true, señora, but you answered my question too easily. That tells me there's more to the story you don't want to talk about."

"I don't want to lie to you."

"I appreciate that."

"So I'm going to say nothing, other than it's for your own good."

"I believe I'm in a better position to know what's best for me, wouldn't you say?"

"No, Tejano, in this case I wouldn't. Some things are better left unsaid, and other things are better left unknown. Sometimes they are the very same thing."

Caitlin tried to gauge the meaning of Delgado's words from her expression, but the light wouldn't allow her.

"You never had children of your own," Delgado said suddenly.

"No," Caitlin told her.

"But I've heard told you treat the sons of this outlaw you once put in jail, and have now taken up with, as your own."

"You mentioned the red widow spider before, señora, but you left something out. Specifically, that it kills the male after mating. Maybe she eats him, too, but I'm not sure."

"Is there a point that I'm missing?"

"This is the second time you haven't held the upper hand," Caitlin told the Red Widow. "The first was back when you and my dad crossed paths."

Caitlin heard the rumble of big engines, followed by the crunching of gravel outside, and caught the flash of motion beyond the windows. She rose from her chair, making sure her empty holster was in evidence to anyone who entered the cantina.

"You joined forces with one Texas Ranger twenty-five years ago. Now you've joined forces with another."

Delgado regarded her in a way people do when they have something to say but can't push the words into place. So Caitlin remained silent, hoping that, if she waited just a few seconds more, that would change.

"I've said enough, Ranger," the Red Widow told her, as if reading Caitlin's thoughts, "and if I say anything more it'll be too much."

At that, the door burst open and a phalanx of her men flooded the cantina. Caitlin already had her hands in the air.

"I'll be in touch, señora."

58

Chihuahua, Mexico

Caitlin sat in the big truck the Red Widow had loaned her, the interior smelling of perspiration and gun oil, overheated, as if the occupants had ridden here without using the air-conditioning. She held her cell phone in her grasp the whole time, having forgotten she still had it. She'd taken it from her pocket to call Captain Tepper, then figured reporting that she'd lost both her vehicle and her gun south of the border was probably not news best shared over the phone.

So she sat in the big truck, trying to make sense of what she knew now that she hadn't known before, and how that fit into the bigger picture that was slowly falling together. She wished she'd made a tape of her conversation with Luna Diaz Delgado inside the cantina, not so much to replay her words as to listen for the meaning beneath them—the inflection, the way the Red Widow had let certain thoughts dangle, and the pain Caitlin detected as an undertone at times.

But it wasn't just the subtext behind her words that Caitlin found herself pondering, but some of those words themselves.

After that Turkish freighter crashed in 1959, they went missing for a very long time. Fate brought me to them in 1994 and then again today, because I am meant to reveal the secret they contain.

She pressed JONES on her contacts list and drew the phone to her ear.

"How long have you known?" she snapped, before he'd even gotten his greeting out.

"Known what?"

"The origin of those missing crates: a Turkish freighter that crashed in 1959."

"It must've had a bad crew."

"The crew was dead and you know that too. Killed the same way as those men my father found on that train car in 1994 and we found at Bane Sturgess this morning. I've heard it told a curse was to blame, but that wouldn't explain your interest, because you can't weaponize a curse."

"I'm hanging up now," Jones told her.

"I'll remember that next time you call," Caitlin said, beating him to it.

She settled back in the seat that was baking her skin through her clothes, lost in her thinking until she realized her cell phone was ringing.

"You coming back to headquarters anytime soon?" Young Roger asked, after Caitlin answered.

"Just about to make my way there now. Why?"

"Because Christmas came early, Ranger. I've got more news on that credit card receipt you found in the desert."

59

Shavano Park, Texas

"You're still here," Cort Wesley said to Selina Escalante, who nuzzled against Dylan on the living room couch.

The two of them were watching a movie, which Dylan paused as he eased her off of him.

"I came back after work," she said, rising and stretching a pair of arms that looked as toned as Caitlin's. "Sold enough pills today to addict a small country to painkillers."

"A lofty achievement."

"It's a job. How about you, Mr. Masters? How'd your day go?"

"Well, it wasn't boring," Cort Wesley said, meaning it.

He watched the girl strut her way into the kitchen.

"Those jeans look familiar," he said to Dylan, when she was gone.

"It's the pair you hate. I gave them to her. They don't fit me anymore."

"They never did, son."

"I'm talking about since I hit the weight room again to get ready for football."

Cort Wesley nodded, recalling that he'd added Dylan to his gym membership but wasn't sure he'd actually been using it. Boy's shoulders did look broader, though it was tough to tell with all that hair swimming around.

"So you need my help."

"What's with the smirk?"

"I don't ever remember you asking for it before, that's all."

Cort Wesley took out his phone. "You check your email lately?"

"No. Why?"

"Because I sent you something I need you to look at, some still shots lifted off a security camera feed."

Dylan sat straight up on the couch. "Whatever you need translated, right?"

Cort Wesley nodded.

"Sounds mysterious."

"I'll tell you what's mysterious," Selina Escolante said, returning to the living room with three beers, one for each of them. "Finding a bottle opener."

"Here," Cort Wesley offered. "Let me."

He took the bottles in hand one at a time and thumbed off the caps.

"Wow," Selina said. "Now I'm impressed."

"It's nothing. There's a trick to it. My dad showed me."

"I'll bet you were all of twelve or thirteen at the time, Mr. Masters."

"I believe I was."

Cort Wesley handed Dylan one of the locally brewed Back Pew Blue Testament American Pilsners and started with him for the stairs.

"If you don't mind, Dylan and I have something we need to do," he said. "Shouldn't take too long."

"He told me you needed his help with something."

Cort Wesley pushed his son playfully, just short of the stairs. "Sometimes he talks too much."

"So when do I get to meet the other member of the family?" Selina asked him, something about her voice sounding different.

"My younger son, Luke, is in Europe."

"I was talking about Caitlin Strong."

Cort Wesley stiffened, unsure where this was going, until Selina pointed to a framed picture of the four of them on one of the room's end tables. "I recognized her from the photo."

"She gets that a lot these days."

"Amazing she can still do her job."

"People shooting pictures aren't normally the same ones shooting guns."

"Yeah," Selina nodded, "all those gunfights. What about you?"

"What about me?"

"Dylan didn't say what you did."

"You didn't ask me," Dylan piped in.

"Anyway," Cort Wesley picked up, addressing Selina, "Caitlin's working a case. Might be back in ten minutes or ten days."

"If you want to wait," Dylan started, and let his thought hang there.

"I'll just gather up my things and get going," Selina said, her gaze rotating between the two of them but lingering on Cort Wesley in a way that left him uncomfortable for some reason. "Just realized there's something I need to take care of too. Sorry."

Cort Wesley watched his son's shoulders slump, always the clearest tell that he was disappointed. "What about dinner?"

She jiggled an imaginary phone near her ear. "Call me." Then, with a grin flashed Dylan's way, "And I like your dad, boy. I can see where you get your looks."

60

SHAVANO PARK, TEXAS

"What was that about?" Cort Wesley asked, while Dylan got settled behind his laptop computer, after Selina had gathered up her things and left.

"What?"

"Your girlfriend."

Dylan blew the hair from his face, what would pass for a snicker from anybody else. "She's not my girlfriend."

"You gave her your jeans."

"She kind of took them. And it wasn't like I bought them for her. That's relationship shit. It's not like I gave her a ring, either. Nothing like that."

"Felt a little creepy downstairs, that's all."

"What?" Dylan asked again.

"I'm not sure," Cort Wesley said, wishing he hadn't even raised the issue. "You got your email opened yet?"

Dylan turned sideways in his chair to better meet his gaze. "Takes too long, doesn't it? I told you I needed a new computer to take to school. And I need to ask you a question, too."

"Can we get this done first?"

"No," Dylan said, gesturing toward the right hand that Cort Wesley had tucked into his pocket. "Your hand's fucked up."

"Do you have to put it that way?"

"What way would you like me to put it?"

"It's not my hand," Cort Wesley said, not wanting to lie to his son, "it's my arm."

"You get shot or something?" the boy asked, suddenly tentative.

"Something."

"What?"

"I thought it was a cramp. When it didn't get better, I had it checked out. Good news is it wasn't serious and is getting better. Bad news is it was one of those mini strokes."

Dylan swallowed hard, looking in that moment like a boy again, instead of a man, wishing he could lose himself in the nest of hair that kept straying onto his face. "A TIA..."

"Don't ask me to tell you what that stands for."

"I know what it stands for." Dylan blew the hair from his face with his breath. "How is it I didn't notice this before?"

"Either 'cause you didn't look or you were too hungover to notice. It just happened, down in Venezuela."

"But you're okay?"

Cort Wesley nodded. "Call me one of the lucky ones."

"For getting this warning."

"And for having a son who knows his way around ancient languages."

Dylan sighed deeply and then opened his Gmail and scrolled down in search of the one sent a while back from Ranger headquarters. Cort Wesley stood over his son's shoulder, pretending not to look but glad to see the glut of incoming messages that came from various incarnations of the email address *@brown.edu*. As much as he'd kind of enjoyed having his oldest boy around these past few months, he was relieved beyond even his own expectations by Dylan's decision to return to Brown with only three semesters left to go. None of his relatives had gone to college, except for a distant cousin or two who'd graduated from one of various branches of the University of Texas across the state. There might have been one who went to TCU or Texas Tech, something like that, too. Cort Wesley hadn't been paying much attention, because it didn't matter to him, just didn't hit his radar.

Well, it did now.

He wasn't totally sold on Dylan's desire to play football, especially given the reality that he'd likely never see anything but the practice field. Then again, it would reunite him with his friends and help make his return to campus less jarring, given all he'd been through since he'd left. All fathers, secretly or not, want their kids to be like them, and Dylan had paid a very real price for possessing the same character traits that had nearly gotten both father and son killed on numerous occasions. How often Cort Wesley had complained to Caitlin, and even to Leroy Epps, that the son wouldn't learn his lesson, just as the father had never learned his.

Yup, Dylan was the apple of his eye, all right.

"Must be this one, if you sent it from the Ranger building," Dylan said, and he clicked on the message that had come from a URL that included *dps.texas.gov.*

"Somebody else sent it," Cort Wesley told him, peering over his son's shoulder, "but that's where it came from."

"Then let's see what we've got here...."

Dylan downloaded the attachments, which were large because they amounted to a bunch of high-resolution photos.

"Where'd you meet Selina?" Cort Wesley asked him, while they waited for the pictures to take form on the screen.

"Antone's, the other night."

"She approach you or did you approach her?"

"What's the difference?"

"Could you just answer the question?"

"It's a stupid question, Dad."

"Is it? Given your track record with girls? Do I need to recite the list for you?"

Cort Wesley watched his son's shoulders slump. "No. Thanks for making me feel better about it, by the way, given that two of them are dead."

"I know, son."

"Yeah, a cozy shoulder to cry on," Dylan mocked. "Oh, that's right, you couldn't lend me your shoulder because you had an assault rifle slung from it."

"She approached you, didn't she?" Cort Wesley asked, trying not to sound as accusing as he ended up sounding.

"Come on, can you blame her?" Dylan grinned, threading a hand through his long hair.

"She told you she's a pharmaceutical rep."

"Why?"

"Selina Escolante—that's her full name, right?"

"Why?" Dylan repeated, his voice firmer.

"Because I think we should have Caitlin check her out."

Cort Wesley watched his son shake his head derisively. "You want me to find something with her fingerprints on it?"

"Son, I've got a feeling it'd be tough to lift prints off what she's been touching."

The computer chimed, signaling that the download was complete.

"Here we go," Dylan continued, leaning forward and clicking on the attached file to open it. "Let's see what we've got here...."

61

Shavano Park, Texas

"Wow," Dylan said, working the machine's trackpad to scroll through the various still shots Young Roger had lifted off the ATM video assemblage. "This looks like the real deal, for sure."

"You mean a real ossuary?" Cort Wesley asked him.

"How much you know about such things?"

"What I learned earlier today."

"Then I'll assume nothing," his son told him. "An ossuary is generally a chest or box, just like this one, that serves as a final resting place for human skeletal remains. Lots smaller than a coffin, because it only holds bones, which is the point."

"Point of what?"

"In ancient times, bodies were first buried in temporary graves. After however many years it took for there to be nothing left other than bones, those bones would be removed and placed in a chest just like this one," Dylan explained, pointing at the weathered, boxlike, gray stone thing sitting on a table, or desk, at Bane Sturgess, just minutes before four men died.

"Using ossuaries that way means plenty less space taken up by each deceased, which means plenty more dead bodies can be laid to rest, permanently, in a single tomb. Coffins would take four or five times the space, even more in some cases."

Dylan enlarged the chiseled inscription to better regard its contents.

"So," Cort Wesley responded, "the bodies end up getting buried twice even though, last time I checked, they only died once."

"Not necessarily, Dad."

"How's that?"

"Plenty, maybe most of the time, ossuaries were stored in caves. They were carved out of stone, known for being able to resist the elements and capable of lasting forever—or until somebody wants to steal the bones contained inside, whichever comes first."

"Did that actually happen?"

"It did and it still does. These are ancient artifacts, virtual one-of-a-kinds, that are among the best-preserved relics from as much as three thousand years ago."

"Long time," Cort Wesley told him, because he felt he had to say something.

"This happens to be your lucky day, Dad, because my last semester at Brown, one of my classes covered Aramaic. A lot like Hebrew, and the dominant language of the time."

"What time?"

"Oh, roughly one thousand BCE, but dating back even farther, according to some experts."

"What's BCE stand for?"

"'Before the Common Era.' Used to be BC, for 'Before Christ.'"

How could I not know that? Cort Wesley asked himself.

"Getting back to these ossuaries... Some of them have intricate geometrical patterns and inscriptions identifying the deceased. Something like 'Simon the Temple Builder,' or 'Elisheba, wife of Tarfon.' This one probably says something like that," Dylan added, pointing to the screen. "But..."

"There's always a 'but.'"

"There are a whole bunch of Aramaic dialects, and each one has its own patterns to decipher. Easy work, way back when, but a pain in the ass today."

"Are you telling me you can't translate what that says?" Cort Wesley asked, regarding the close-up of the inscription on the ossuary that had disappeared from Bane Sturgess.

"Did I say that? No, I didn't say that, because I'm not sure yet. In addition to the different dialects, there's the problem of confusing Old Syriac Aramaic with the more traditional, spoken language. Cultures overlapped, and so did ages. Twenty miles was like two thousand today, and as long as the residents of one village could decipher the language, it didn't matter whether that village twenty miles away could or not. This inscription, all those squiggly lines, seems to resemble what Aramaic looked like in the first century. So, if I keep at it, I think I'll be able to give you at least a rough translation."

"Then keep at it."

Dylan nodded, his expression sobering. "I get the feeling a lot of people have died for the contents of this box."

"True enough."

"So how much you paying me for this again?"

"Your tuition for the next three semesters."

"Sounds fair." Dylan nodded. "You mind throwing in dinner, too?"

"Deal."

"For four, Dad?"

"Four?"

"Tonight, somewhere nice, on the Riverwalk," Dylan told him. "You heard her downstairs—Selina wants to meet Caitlin."

PART SEVEN

In April of 1997 the Republic of Texas standoff began when a couple of residents near Fort David, Texas, were taken hostage by members of the Republic of Texas (ROT), a group whose members professed the belief that Texas had been illegally annexed to the United States in 1845. The group claimed that Texas was not a state but an independent nation. Barry Caver was the Midland-based captain of Company E of the Texas Rangers and was responsible for the Fort David region. The ROT leader in Fort Davis, Richard McLaren, held out with his supporters for tension-filled days but ultimately, due in large measure to the patience and leadership of Caver, the episode ended peacefully with McLaren's surrender. Dramatic violence was averted. Would the Waco episode have ended as peacefully if the Rangers had been allowed to accept the surrender of the Branch Davidians?

—Bruce A. Glasrud and Harold J. Weiss Jr., eds.,
Tracking the Texas Rangers: The Twentieth Century
University of North Texas Press, 2013

62

San Antonio, Texas

D. W. Tepper had two glasses on his desk when Caitlin walked in. "One of these is poison," he said, "the other's Alka-Seltzer. The Alka-Seltzer's for the acid you love kicking up in my stomach. The poison's in case the Alka-Seltzer don't work, given this particular mess."

"Maybe I should be the one drinking it, Captain."

"I think it would be too scared to kill you, Ranger." He reached for the still-fizzy antacid. "Better get this down before the bubbles go away...."

And Tepper did so, leaving just a little at the bottom of the glass.

"Ahh, now that hit the spot. I'm guessing the Mexican Policia Federal have drunk more than their share today, too. They called me, they called the chief in Austin, they called the governor, and there's rumors they got a call in to the ghost of John Wayne. Apparently they're trying to work the story that the attack on their compound was your fault."

"How's that exactly?"

"You being the target, instead of Delgado."

"That's ridiculous."

Tepper drained the rest of his Alka-Seltzer. "It's called saving face. And to save further face, they're holding your gun and vehicle hostage. You try picking either up, expect to be in Mexico for an extended period. You can draw a replacement weapon, but it'll be billed against your salary. You own the SUV, so we can handle up to seven days' reimbursement for a rental."

"Maybe I'll ask Colonel Paz to get them back for me."

"That's another problem we've got. Your own personal King Kong's not exactly well liked south of the border, and his association with you is kind of an established fact. His involvement is why they're trying to lay this whole thing at your feet. Some Mexican cabinet minister told the governor of Texas to expect a bill for the damages."

"They got as much chance of seeing the money as we do of having them pay for a border wall."

"Didn't you hear, Ranger? Mexican government changed their mind, because they figured it might be the only way to keep you out."

Caitlin snatched an open box of Marlboro Reds from Tepper's desk and sat down in the chair set before it. "It was worth the trip, Captain."

"You solve the great mystery of those crates that have gone missing a second time?"

"Cort Wesley's working a lead."

"Yeah, through his son, translating that Aramaic to tell us something about the bones inside."

Caitlin nodded. "The Red Widow didn't tell me everything she knows about those funeral boxes, or whatever they're called, but she had plenty to say about my dad."

"Is that a fact?"

"Except the story stopped before the real fun began, with Jim Strong paying a visit to the Delgado hacienda back in ninety-four." Caitlin settled back in her chair. "I was hoping you could pick up the story there, D.W."

"Sorry to disappoint you, Ranger. I've got an inkling as to the bits and pieces, but I can't tell you what your dad never told me."

"He told you everything."

"Not this. This was different, on par with the murder of your mother. I know for a fact that he tracked down the three drug mules who did the deed, based on a combination of speculation and conjecture. Call it circumstantial evidence if you want, but the result was enough to drop him in the bottle for a time, until your grandfather knocked some sense into him."

"Old Earl knew plenty about loss, firsthand."

Tepper opened up his drawer and fished out a fresh pack of Marlboros. "Joke's on you this time, Caitlin. That box you swiped from my desk? I packed it with those candy cigarettes you're so fond of replacing my real ones with. Turnabout being fair play and all."

"I buy those candy cigarettes by the case lot now, D.W."

She watched Tepper tap the fresh pack hard on the desk to pop one of the Reds out—but ending up showering his plastic blotter with sugar dust.

"That's just not fair," he groused, dropping the whole pack in the trash.

"Turnabout being fair play and all."

"Where's this go from here, Ranger?" Tepper asked her.

"We figure out why those crates have disappeared again, Captain, and we figure out what's inside them in the first place. That means going back to 1994 and how they ended up buried in the desert. I know my dad had a hand in that, and the bodies that went with them, even if you don't want to fill in the details."

"I told you—"

"I know what you told me, just like I know it's not the whole story, starting with how those funeral boxes came into his possession or why they were so important to Luna Diaz Delgado."

"Well, Ranger, one thing I hope we can agree on is that I've got no idea who stole them yet again, this time from the offices of Bane Sturgess."

Caitlin nodded, conceding that much. "If we assume those two dead bodies in that alley across the street from Bane Sturgess, along with those gunmen in Dallas and the shooters who attacked that police barracks in Chihuahua, were part of the same force my dad went up against, it's safe to assume it wasn't them who dug the crates out of the desert. And it wasn't the Red Widow, either. Who's that leave us with, exactly?"

"You raise that in your discussion with Delgado?"

"She didn't have much to say on the subject."

"You ask her about the Ferryman?"

"El Barquero came up briefly."

"That's all?"

"That's a lot when it comes to the Red Widow, Captain."

Tepper plucked the box of candy cigarettes out of the trash and stuck one in his mouth, letting it dangle from one side. "Hey, these aren't altogether bad."

"Beats the real thing, as far as your lungs are concerned."

"My lungs aren't the problem. Thanks to you, it's my stomach now, remember?"

Caitlin's phone beeped with an incoming text before she could respond. She saw ROGER on the sender line, in bold print, above the simple message: I'M DOWNSTAIRS. CONFERENCE ROOM.

63

"You wanna tell me what all this means?" Young Roger said, closing the conference room door after Caitlin had entered. "Why somebody was watching that site in the desert after whatever was buried there went missing?"

Caitlin shrugged. "To see who showed up, would be my guess."

"Same party behind those dead gunmen in New Braunfels we can't get IDs on? What the hell is going on here?"

"All the cases we've worked, Rog, I've never known you to sound scared."

"Just answer my question, please."

"Which question? You asked me two."

"Take your pick."

"I don't know what the hell is going on here. I'm hoping that credit card receipt can fill in some of the blanks for me. Speaking of which, since that's why you called me down here..."

"It came from a card machine, not a cash register," Young Roger told her. "All card machines print out a merchant ID number on each receipt; in the case of this particular machine, it's located right near the top as a sequence of eight numbers, the last two of which had been burned off. Took me some time, but I compared those first six numbers to all the merchant IDs for a fifty-mile radius and found only a single potential match: a gas station and convenience store on an old access road just off Route 190, on the way to Fort McKavett. Ever heard of it?"

"Historical site where they give tours," Caitlin recalled. "I seem to remember going there once with both my dad and my grandfather. It stands out because the three of us didn't do a lot together. That whole area's pretty much a historical site in itself, thanks to the interstates and the oil wells going dry. It's also ten, maybe twelve miles from Sonora and the spot in the desert where those bodies were found."

"That's what I was thinking, too." Young Roger nodded. "I thought every business in those parts had closed its doors years ago. But the store that generated the receipt you found must still be open for business."

"Well," said Caitlin, "we know they've got at least one customer."

Her phone rang and she stepped into the hallway to answer it. She recognized the Bexar County Medical Examiner's Office exchange.

"What do you have for me, Doc?" she asked, figuring it was Whatley on the other end of the line.

"Nothing you're likely to want to hear, Ranger."

"Try me."

"Ballistics report came back on those four skeletons your captain dug out of the desert. The bullets came from your dad's forty-five, all right."

64

SAN ANTONIO, TEXAS

Caitlin and Cort Wesley sat at an outdoor table under an umbrella that looked like the Texas state flag, on the second floor of the Lone Star Café, overlooking the Riverwalk and all its congestion.

"What's bothering you, Ranger?" he asked her.

"Something I can't quite figure out."

"Nothing new, then."

She turned to look at him in the seat next to her. "Bullets from my dad's forty-five were a match for the ones that put those four bodies in the ground."

"I thought you were expecting that."

"Considering the possibility isn't the same as expecting, Cort Wesley."

"And what does it tell you?"

"Nothing I can make any sense of. If Jim Strong buried those bodies, it figures he must've buried the shipping crates containing those ossuaries too. What am I missing here?"

"Dylan and Selina Escolante, right now," Cort Wesley said, to change the subject as well as the mood.

"Why not tell me about your visit to the neurologist, instead, while we wait for them?" Caitlin asked, sliding her chair closer to him.

"I haven't gone yet, but I've got an appointment."

"When?"

"I forgot. Memory loss is another of my symptoms."

Caitlin shook her head, tightening her gaze on Cort Wesley. "Get back to Selina. What's she like?"

"This is Dylan we're talking about. What do you think?"

"Gorgeous and troubled."

"One out of two ain't bad, Ranger."

"I'm guessing gorgeous."

"'Troubled' is the last thing that comes to mind when it comes to this one."

"He never wanted us to meet the others, Cort Wesley. What's different?"

"I asked myself the same question. The fact that she's older than him—maybe that's got him wanting to do something that resembles an adult."

"Doesn't sound like Dylan. And how much older are we talking about?"

"Well, if I had to guess, I'd say three or four years."

"Not much."

Cort Wesley sipped his water. "Seems like more, the girl being in the real world and all, a career professional. That's a first, unless you count that porn star he met at school."

"I don't count her, no," Caitlin said, thinking back to circumstances she'd rather forget. "They met at a bar, you say?"

"Better than online, I guess."

"Not by much, Cort Wesley. Speaking of Dylan, how's the translation of the inscription on that ossuary coming?"

"He says he's working on it. Should have something for me tomorrow."

"His words or yours?"

"You know, I'm not really sure."

"Memory loss again?"

"I forgot."

Caitlin rolled her eyes. "You end up a vegetable, don't expect me to take care of you."

"I become a vegetable, just pull the plug."

"I'm going with you to the neurologist, Cort Wesley."

"Only if I remember to tell you when my appointment is, Ranger. Just do me one favor."

"What's that?"

"Don't say you'll be there for me, give me a shoulder to cry on, all that sort of shit."

"I was thinking more along the lines of changing your diaper and reminding you to take all your pills."

"I had a stroke, a warning stroke anyway, okay? And I'm taking meds and seeing doctors and doing all the things I never thought of doing before so I can stay alive."

"What about physical therapy?"

"What about it, Ranger?" Cort Wesley asked tensely.

She forced herself not to look toward his right arm and hand. "It might help."

He flexed his hand for her, as if he were a magician performing a trick. "See, it's already getting plenty better on its own."

"Physical therapy could speed the process."

Cort Wesley's expression changed, his eyes tightening on the point at which the stairs spilled out onto the restaurant's second floor. "Hey, looks like the rest of the party's here."

65

San Antonio, Texas

Caitlin followed his gaze to Dylan, who was heading their way arm in arm with a ravishing, dark-haired beauty who walked with a casualness that belied her red carpet looks. Caitlin couldn't help noticing more stares than she could count turning Selina Escalante's way, from women as well as men.

"He combed his hair," Caitlin said to Cort Wesley, as the two of them stood up.

"How can you tell?"

"I can see both his eyes at the same time."

Dylan reached the table a step ahead of the beautiful young woman who pushed up even with him, attention focused on Cort Wesley.

"Nice to see you again, Mr. Masters," Selina greeted him, kissing him lightly on the cheek before turning to Caitlin. "Dylan's told me a whole lot about you, Ranger."

"Call me Caitlin."

"Selina," she said, extending her hand.

Caitlin took it, felt her own firm grasp matched equally.

Selena broke the grasp first. "The rest I found after I Googled you."

"I can only imagine what that yielded."

Dylan and Selina took the two empty seats, leaving her seated next to Caitlin.

"You've never done it?" Selina said, pushing her chair in.

"Googled myself? No. So much written about me is made up, I'm afraid if I read too much of it, I'd start to believe it myself."

"Well, if half of what's out there is true…"

Selina's voice trailed off. Caitlin didn't wait for her to resume. "I hope it's the good half."

"You killing a whole lot of bad guys—more than any lawman, or *woman*, in modern times."

"It said that?"

"Uh-huh." Selina nodded. "But in a nice way. Title of the article was 'Strong as Steel.'"

Caitlin cringed. "Ugh…"

"It's not true?"

"That I'm strong as steel or that I've killed a whole lot of bad guys?"

"Take your pick."

Caitlin opened the menu. "I'm thinking the T-bone."

"Bison burger for me," Dylan said, closing his. "Will the two of you stop looking at each other that way?"

But Caitlin and Selina remained locked in a stare that was even tighter than their handshake. It was finally broken when Selina turned her eyes on the menu before her.

"I'm thinking salmon," she said, without opening it.

"Do they even serve that?" Dylan asked her, scanning his.

"Everybody serves salmon."

"Selina wanted to meet you, Caitlin," Dylan piped in.

Caitlin pretended to be regarding her menu again, so as not to meet the young woman's eyes. "Well, I hope she won't be disappointed. I've never actually met a pharmaceutical rep before, but I hear it's a great job to have in this day and age."

"It is," Selina acknowledged. "So far, so good, anyway."

"So which one do you work for?" Caitlin asked her. "Pharmaceutical company, I mean."

"Dylan didn't tell you?"

"I didn't ask him."

"Well, I'm kind of freelance, working for a consortium of smaller pharmaceutical companies that aren't budgeted for a dedicated national sales team."

"Sounds challenging."

"Until you figure that some of the most groundbreaking drugs ever were developed by companies nobody ever heard of until those drugs reached the market. Sure, there are challenges, not the least of which is the fact that only about ten percent of clinical trials result in regulatory approval. Imagine the same ratio when it comes to bullets."

"Except it only takes one hit to do the job," Caitlin noted.

"Same thing in my business. Small biopharmaceutical companies are becoming increasingly important as drivers of innovation in the development of cutting-edge drugs, to the point that the majority of drugs currently in development are in the hands of small biopharmaceutical companies. They range in size from virtual companies with no commercial products and no revenue to those with only a few commercial programs but a sharp eye on growth."

Dylan leaned in toward his father. "I told you she was smart, Dad."

"I'd hire you in a heartbeat, Selina," Cort Wesley agreed.

"To do what?"

"You could sell a car to an Amish couple."

Selina reached onto the table and squeezed Dylan's hand. "Anyway, small companies use a variety of approaches to address the challenges, including the use of new technical platforms, new formulations or technologies that enhance the actions of known drugs, and the use of trial designs that take advantage of the specific market they hope to enter. Some of the companies I rep for develop products that are spun off from or licensed from large companies, and others end up partnering with larger companies to add resources and experience. I don't like when that happens," she continued, aiming her words at Dylan, "because it means I might be out of a job."

"That's not good," said Caitlin.

"Well, the food here sure is," interjected Cort Wesley. "What do you say we order?"

"Just keep a clear head, son," Cort Wesley said to Dylan, after their server slid away from the table. "You got some work to finish for me, remember?"

Dylan rolled his eyes, started to blow the long hair from his face before remembering it was combed reasonably in place. "It's one margarita, Dad. I think I can handle it. Give it a rest," he said, tapping his father's shoulder playfully.

"Wanna make a stop in the ladies' room, Ranger?" Selina asked.

Caitlin looked toward Cort Wesley before responding. "Sure. Why not? First time for everything, I suppose," she added, pushing her chair out.

"You've never been to the ladies' room before?" Selina asked wryly.

"Not as a pair, no."

Selina grinned. "Like you said, there's a first time for everything."

66

SAN ANTONIO, TEXAS

They had the restroom to themselves, as it turned out.

"See?" Selina Escolante said, emerging from the stall. "Nothing to be scared of."

Caitlin feigned gazing about the polished tile floor and walls. "Looks different when you're in here with someone else. Guess I haven't had a lot of opportunities to do it before."

"Being that you're living in a male-dominated profession."

"True enough, Selina, since male Rangers aren't prone to inviting me to the bathroom with them."

Selina turned on the water and waited for it to warm up. "I'm lucky that way, given that the pharmaceutical industry is an equal opportunity employer— sometimes too much so."

"What's that mean?"

Selina realized the water wasn't going to get any warmer and pressed some fancy soap onto her hands from a nearby dispenser. "Well, let's just say some accounts expect certain fringe benefits to close a big deal."

Caitlin's gaze narrowed. "That's hard to believe, in this day and age."

"Hey, nobody ever asked me to do anything I wasn't comfortable with. And, to tell you the truth, all this political correctness can be bad for business. You use what you've got, right?" Selina grinned, rubbing her hands beneath the automated hand dryer. "Especially the first few years on the job. You know what one of the women who trained me in the field said? 'Sometimes you've got to give head to get ahead.'"

"I was sexually assaulted as a college student," Caitlin told her. "That didn't put me too far ahead."

Selina Escalante swallowed hard. "I'm sorry."

"No need, unless it was one of the companies you rep that manufactured the drug I got dosed with."

"Depends if it was Rohypnol, GHB, which is actually gamma-hydroxy-butyrate, or ketamine, aka Special K," Selina noted without flinching.

"They never did identify it."

"What about the man who dosed you?"

Caitlin washed her hands, just to have something to do. "Long story," she said.

Selina drew closer. "You've become, like, Dylan's mother, haven't you?"

Caitlin looked at her in the mirror. "He tell you the story of what happened to his real mom?"

"Along with how you saved his life." Selina nodded. "You've done that a lot, saved people's lives."

"I'm a Texas Ranger, Selina."

"But it's not just a job for you, not like pushing the latest wonder drug on unsuspecting doctors and medical practice reps."

Caitlin eased her hands under the dryer. "Law enforcement's all I've ever done, so I've never really compared it to anything else," she said, over the machine's voluminous rattle. "But am I like Dylan's mother? I suppose I am. We've been in shoot-outs together. Some might say it doesn't get any more maternal than that."

"At least in Texas."

Caitlin faced the young woman, standing between her and the door. "Dylan's been through a lot."

"I get that impression."

"He's gotten hurt."

"I got that impression, too."

"And here we are, celebrating, what, the anniversary of your third night together?"

Selina nodded stiffly. "Something like that."

"I believe you get my point."

They started for the door together, but stopped.

"I think he's looking for a woman like you," Selina said. "Someone strong as steel, who can't get hurt the way his mother did. Who can stand up for herself, take no prisoners, and take no shit. Go toe to toe with him, no matter what."

"We talking about me or you, Selina?"

"Both. At least, that's what I'm hoping."

Caitlin grabbed the handle but didn't open the door. "He's going back to college soon."

"He told me."

"By my definition, that makes him still a kid. Something a woman your age should keep in mind."

"My age?"

"You told Dylan you were twenty-eight."

"Twenty-six."

"I think you're younger than that, by a couple years anyway."

Selina smiled casually. "Comes with the job, Ranger."

Caitlin finally yanked open the door. "It's Caitlin, ma'am."

"So how was it?" Selina asked, when they were on their way back to the table.

"How was what?"

"Your first visit to the ladies' room with another lady?"

Caitlin showed her palms. "Well, my hands are clean."

Selina held her hands up before saying, "Don't worry, Ranger, mine are too."

67

SHAVANO PARK, TEXAS

Cort Wesley felt like going out for breakfast, not comfortable being home when Dylan and Selina started stirring. This was the first time he'd brought a girl home while Cort Wesley had been around. Her presence had the same effect on Caitlin, who opted against spending the night.

There hadn't been an opportunity for them to talk about whatever was bothering her about Selina Escolante. And the truth was, he was glad Caitlin had something else to focus on, since it kept her from noticing the difficulty he had working a fork with his right hand. Cort Wesley suspected her reaction to Selina was rooted in the same overprotective attitude he was prone to when it came to Dylan. One of the things that made him most happy about his son's decision to return to Brown University was the fact that it would get him out of Texas. To say the time he'd taken off from school had been bloody would be an understatement. Dylan had almost gotten himself killed twice, once saved only by him gunning down another kid just about his age, although age didn't figure into the M16 that kid was hoisting.

Yup, next week couldn't come fast enough, and Cort Wesley found himself hoping Dylan would lose Selina Escolante's phone number before departing.

He ended up at the nearest Magnolia Pancake Haus restaurant, a mainstay in the area since he was a boy. The place held a special association for him, given that his father and he had several times eaten breakfast here on the day of a job when it was called something else. Boone Masters had enlisted his son in his criminal efforts from the time Cort Wesley was twelve, and he had worked his way up from lookout to member of his father's gang, which specialized in boosting large warehouse-style establishments, ridding them of excess major appliances, many still crated up. They were inside jobs, mostly, that came with lots of heavy lifting and not a lot of danger or anything even remotely approaching gunplay. Violence, when it did happen, almost exclusively involved fellow members of Boone Masters's crew squabbling over respective shares or who sold out whom. Cort Wesley never sold out anybody, and his father figured that, as a family member, he didn't deserve a share.

The hostess brought him to a table for two, where he ordered coffee.

"Anything else for starters?"

"You have root beer?"

"Yes."

"The real kind?"

His question clearly confused her. "I'm not sure about real, but it's good."

"I'll take a large."

"*Thanks, bubba,*" Leroy Epps said, when she was gone.

Cort Wesley placed his phone on the table, pretending to work the keypad to make it look like he was texting.

"*Now, how about ordering me up one of those waffles with the whipped cream on top?*"

"Last time I checked, ghosts don't eat."

Leroy's red-streaked eyes glanced down at his root beer. "*We're not supposed to drink, neither, but that hasn't been stopping you.*" Leroy's eyes sought him out across the table. "*Your arm's better, bubba.*"

"Not much."

"*Sometimes a little is a lot.*"

"I couldn't work an M16 right now, champ."

Leroy's gaze narrowed on him. *"Guns being the ultimate determining factor."*

"I was just making a point."

"Most folks in your shoes would be happy if they could lift up their submarine sandwich with all the insides not falling out."

"Well, I'm not most people."

Leroy shook his head. *"And you wanna know where that boy of yours gets his sauce from.... He's a hoot, lemme tell you."*

"Hopefully his girlfriend gets an early start this morning so he can get back to that job I gave him."

"He known her how long and she's already his girlfriend?"

"Kids today, right, champ?" Cort Wesley mused.

"So what's got you scratching your ass over it?"

"I'm not sure."

"You ask the Ranger? Takes one woman to know another, right?"

"I think it's the fact that Dylan's going back to Brown next week."

"A good thing, right?"

"For sure, champ, but I guess maybe I wanted Caitlin and me to be what he missed the most."

"I see that being still a fact."

"Let me put it this way: I guess I don't like sharing him."

"On account of it means he's growing up, bubba?"

"He's been grown up since he watched his mother get gunned down at the front door. Maybe I made the wrong decision by keeping us in that house, not moving on."

"As I recall, that was a matter of teaching your boys not to run from nothing."

Cort Wesley noticed maybe a quarter of the frosted glass of root beer had been drained, or maybe the foam had just settled. "You know what they say about the road to hell."

Leroy looked at him wryly. *"Actually, I don't. I be somewhere else altogether different, thank the Lord."*

"Seen Him lately?"

"No, sir. But I hear told He's a root beer man too. Order up another and He just might make an appearance."

"Maybe next time, champ."

"And stop fretting on your boy."

"You get a look at the latest girl in his life?"

"All the more reason to stop fretting on him, bubba. She's a looker, all right."

"No doubt about that. But, I don't know, something seems, well, a little off."

"*Off?*" the ghost repeated. "*What's that mean exactly?*"

"Caitlin kept eyes on her all night, from the time they got back from the ladies' room. I've seen that look on her face before, usually when she's expecting someone to draw on her."

"*Then why you asking me? Ask her.*"

"I think I'll do that, champ."

"*After breakfast. Here come our waffles.*"

Cort Wesley turned around and, sure enough, his server was carrying a pair of matching plates, whipped cream and strawberries piled high atop a waffle as big as a tire.

"*Eat up fast, bubba,*" Leroy told him. "*You gotta get back on home to see what your boy came up with.*"

68

SHAVANO PARK, TEXAS

"Did we discuss my fee for this?" Dylan asked Cort Wesley, angling the laptop so his father could follow his explanation of what he'd found. "I forgot."

"No, you didn't."

"Can't blame me for trying." Dylan regarded him differently, his gaze fixing on Cort Wesley's right arm. "The arm looks a little better."

"Feels better, too."

"Not a hundred percent, though."

"No."

The boy blew the hair from his face, only to have it drift back into place. "You afraid it'll never come all the way back?"

"Sure, just like I'm afraid I'll get hit by a bus. There's plenty that scares me. This is just the latest in a long line. Like I never used to think anything of the phone ringing late at night."

"What changed?"

"You and your brother. Having a bum arm is nothing compared to the two of you," Cort Wesley said, hoping that would get Dylan back to the subject at hand. "Tell me you found something, son."

"I found something, Dad, in the form of the translation you were looking for. Mostly."

"Mostly?"

"Let's not get ahead of ourselves," Dylan said, turning back to the screen that displayed the inscription. "Aramaic is a difficult language to work with, because nobody's spoken or written it in like eighteen hundred years. The good thing about that is it means that the language has kind of been frozen in time. The bad thing is it's a difficult language to translate because there are so many dialects that possess only subtle differences but that can still change the entire meaning of a word or phrase."

"You learn all that at Brown?"

"I didn't know I had a knack for languages until I got there."

Cort Wesley closed his eyes briefly and shook his head in amazement. "Spanish and English are about my limit."

"You learned some Arabic back in Desert Storm."

"All forgotten now."

"Well," Dylan said, pushing his chair in closer to his Mac, "you won't be forgetting what I've got to tell you anytime soon. I'm pretty sure about this first part on these top two lines," he continued. "Almost positive it says something to the effect of 'He who died for his crimes and suffers in death.'" Dylan worked the keyboard, and that sentence appeared superimposed over the original Aramaic letters. "Of course, the translation reads left to right, while the actual letters run right to left, like Hebrew. You knew that, right?"

"That it's like Hebrew? Yeah, I did."

"That brings us to the final line, which, based on other, similar inscriptions I took a look at from the time, must be the date."

"Like a tombstone," Cort Wesley surmised.

"Except ossuaries like this one were normally stored aboveground, in crypts, mausoleums, or even caves, like I mentioned before. That was the whole point of salvaging the bones of the desiccated, because these burial boxes weren't even a third the size of a coffin."

"Get back to the date, son."

"Here's where dates get a little confusing, because the only calendar ninety percent of the world knows is the Gregorian, which is your basic three hundred and sixty-five days. Three hundred and sixty-six in a leap year."

"That much I know."

"What you don't know, what pretty much nobody knows, is what came before it. Remember, there were no millenniums back then, no BC and AD, or BCE and ACE. That didn't come about until the sixteenth century, when the term 'solar year' became the standard. You following this, Dad?"

"Just keep talking."

"Okay, back to the date, here on this third line," Dylan said, pointing to the last of the squiggly, shapeless letters stenciled in a long-forgotten language. "When 'He who died for his crimes and suffers in death' actually died."

"The tricky part," Cort Wesley recalled.

"Because of the Jewish calendar, the prevailing one of the time. This date on the final line has to be referenced with that perspective in mind. The date itself was easy, because it's just a number: fifteen. And the month, this string of Aramaic letters here," Dylan said, tracing his finger over them on his laptop screen, "translates as *Nisan*."

"Like the car brand?"

Dylan nodded. "But pronounced like 'nigh.' Nisan was the seventh month of the Hebrew calendar. So whoever's bones are in that ossuary died on the fifteenth day of the seventh month of the year 3970—that's this string of figures here."

"What's that tell us?"

"Will you let me finish?" Dylan said, shaking his head. "The seventh month in the Hebrew calendar is actually the fourth month of the Gregorian one we use today."

"April."

"Boy, Dad, you're really getting the hang of this shit," Dylan mocked, blowing the hair from his face with a burst of breath, only to have it tumble back into place yet again. "Anyway, the day, the fifteenth, remains the same because even back then this calendar was solar-based, three hundred and sixty-five days, just like now. The same intercalary cycle we use today." Dylan hesitated, waiting for a reaction that didn't come. "You see where I'm going with this?"

"I have no idea what 'intercalary' means."

Dylan seemed to ignore his statement. "Okay, let me spell something else out for you. That year, 3970 in the Hebrew calendar, translates into the year thirty-three in ours. Thirty-three AD."

Dylan worked the keyboard again, adding the translation he'd just provided, of the third and final line, to the first two. Cort Wesley eased closer to the screen to view the final product. His right arm, the one that had gone bad on him, started itching, and he stretched his left hand over to scratch it.

"You okay, Dad?"

"Just an itch. I can't see the screen."

Dylan rocked his frame backward so Cort Wesley could see the three lines in the middle of his laptop's screen:

He who died for his crimes
and suffers in death
15 Nisan 3970

"Oh my God," Cort Wesley managed, feeling like somebody had smacked him with a brick.

"Exactly, pretty much." Dylan grinned.

69

Sonora, Texas

Looking for something to pass the time over the course of the drive back toward Sonora and the off-the-beaten-path gas station/convenience store that Young Roger had found, Caitlin placed a call to Mo Scoggins. The former special assistant to Governor Ann Richards had tried to call her father off the case in 1994, something that had stuck in Caitlin's mind since she'd heard that part of the story. Scoggins had parlayed his former position in pursuit of his own political interests, which led to his becoming Texas's current lieutenant governor. He maintained thinly disguised ambitions for the governor's mansion and beyond.

"To what do I owe the pleasure, Ranger?" Scoggins greeted her, taking her call immediately.

"I'll get right to the point, sir," Caitlin said. "I'm working a case that goes back to my dad's time, and I think it's something you might be familiar with."

"Well, I lose my car keys at least once a day and I can't tell you what I had for breakfast this morning, but I'm willing to give it my best."

"Consider this off the record, sir. You recall a run-in you had with my father, Jim Strong, back in 1994?"

Scoggins hesitated before responding. "Well, I wouldn't call it a run-in, but I do remember the circumstances, yes. The run-in should've happened afterward, once I learned he ignored everything I told him. Not that I was surprised. He had his job to do, just like I had mine. Your dad crossed more lines than a drunken driver, and his efforts blew up an active federal investigation into the affairs of Luna Diaz Delgado that could have put a substantial dent in the Mexican drug trade at the time."

"That's what I'm calling about, sir. I know my father paid a visit to Delgado after learning that her life was in danger. I'm blank about what happened after that."

"My advice, Ranger," said Maurice Scoggins gruffly, "is to leave things there."

"I'm afraid I can't do that any more than my dad could, sir. It's just not the Ranger way."

Caitlin could hear Scoggins breathing noisily on the other end of the line. "It would seem you're making the case for both Governor Richards's and my own initial inclinations regarding the Rangers."

"I know the governor's mansion hasn't always held our greatest allies, but Rangers are just trying to do what's best for the state of Texas here."

"As are we in Austin, Ranger."

"I didn't mean it as an either/or, sir," Caitlin said, in as conciliatory a tone as she could manage.

"And what is it you'd like to know? If it's not classified, I'll do my best to fill in the blanks, if for no other reason than to dissuade you from your current pursuits."

"Since, according to you, my father destroyed the case against Delgado twenty-five years ago, it doesn't seem like I can do much additional damage."

"Your reputation would lead me to believe otherwise, Ranger."

Caitlin didn't argue the point. "Sir, I'd just like to know what exactly my father did that got you and the governor so upset. This is only about background for the current case I'm investigating," she lied. "I'm not looking to jam anybody up over it."

Dead air filled the line, broken only by the sound of Scoggins breathing noisily again.

"Can we speak off the record?" he said finally.

"As far as I'm concerned."

"Good, because what you're about to hear didn't come from me."

70

"Thank you for seeing me, Señora Delgado," Jim told the woman, while they sat on the veranda waiting for the iced tea the Red Widow had told one of her subordinates to fetch.

"I pride myself on having respect for the law, Tejano."

The spray of the sun's light made her face look even more vibrant and beautiful than it had in the Chihuahua railroad station, during their initial meeting. She dressed like a woman who fell into her clothes with the ease with which most folks fall into bed. Everything just rode her right and, truth be told, Jim Strong was glad for the opportunity to see her again, even under tense circumstances.

"I'm glad to hear that, señora, I truly am."

"Does your visit pertain to that missing cargo?"

Jim nodded, as another of the Red Widow's men brought their iced teas on a silver tray. "I'm here to see if you have a big man, a real big man, in your employ, who has a kind of patchwork face."

"Did you say 'patchwork face'?"

Jim nodded. "That's the way the motel clerk described him."

Delgado shook her head. "Doesn't sound like the kind of man I'd easily forget, if I ever had occasion to meet him."

"I'll take that as a no, señora. Problem being, he knows you. He had the address of your hacienda here in his motel room, and that can't be a good thing."

"I should say not, Tejano, most certainly not." She set her tea down on a table to the side of her chair and crossed her legs, seeming to shrink the distance between them. "If I'm in such danger, why didn't you just call to alert me?"

"I don't have your number."

"You're a Texas Ranger. I'm sure you could have gotten it."

"No way I could be sure you'd come to the phone."

"But I came to the door, didn't I?"

"I guess I wanted to see you again," Jim said, the honest answer surprising him.

Luna Diaz Delgado let her gaze linger on him. "I was thinking the same thing about you. I might have had you killed in the train station otherwise."

"You did bring a lot of guns with you."

"None about now, though, are there?"

"Guess we can call that progress," Jim followed, surprised by the ease of their conversation.

"I've lost a husband, you've lost a wife," she said, appearing to be even closer to him. "That's a lot to have in common with someone. Raising kids alone—something no one pays much attention to, for those in our respective positions."

"You speak like a very educated woman, señora."

"After my parents were murdered, I was raised in poverty. I saw education as the best means to lift me out of that."

"Sounds like a worthy endeavor."

"And then some, Ranger. It provided the foundation for my life as a businesswoman. You have a problem with me calling myself that?"

"Not at all, except that a big part of your success, the biggest part of all, involved bullets, not brains."

"And that poses a problem for you?"

"It's a crime, señora."

The Red Widow looked genuinely confused. "It's just that I thought I was talking to a gunfighter."

"My father was the gunfighter," Jim scoffed. "I'm just a lawman."

"I've heard different." Delgado eased her chair closer to his, the motion graceful, like everything else she did. "So, Tejano, did you come down here to rescue me from this big man with no face? Do you think my men aren't enough to do the job?"

"That depends what's got that big man's attention, señora. Comes down to the contents of those three crates I believe he has in his possession. If I had a better notion of what those contents are, I might be able to help you out here in that regard."

"Do you love your daughter, Tejano?"

"What kind of question is that?"

"Because if you love her you won't give those crates another thought, not if you want to see her grow up."

"We've come too far for that."

Delgado sat back in her chair. "I've also heard this isn't even a Ranger case anymore."

"True enough," Jim said, not bothering to ask how she'd learned that.

"So you shouldn't even be involved anymore. Why come all the way down here anyway?"

"To find out why it's not a Ranger case anymore."

And that's when the shooting started.

"How many men you have here?"

"Not enough, not against this."

Jim Strong palmed his .45. "Well, you've got me. However many it is, Rangers have held off more."

Glass shattered behind the distinctive clacking of automatic weapons fire, joined soon by a series of explosions that rattled the wrought iron table and spilled the remnants of Jim's iced tea.

"Not against assault rifles, grenades, and RPG, Tejano."

The Red Widow took Jim by the hand and jerked both of them away from the table as the echo of ratcheting fire echoed closer, the invaders having penetrated her hacienda by now.

"My husband taught me to prepare for this day," she continued, leading Jim Strong onward.

"You mean, besides praying to God to make the bad men go away."

"You seem to know an awful lot about my Hector."

"Just like I know it was really you who killed him, señora."

Jim felt Delgado squeeze his hand tighter, squeezing until he was ripe with an agony he wasn't about to show with a grimace. She finally let go when they reached the pool house.

Inside, she yanked back a throw rug, revealing a trapdoor sectioned out of the tile floor. Jim yanked the hatch up to reveal a ladder descending into what looked like a sewer tunnel.

"Escape route?"

"My husband was a man who believed heavily in preparing for anything, above all else."

"Before you killed him, you mean," Jim said, beginning his descent.

The Red Widow grabbed a thick flashlight from a cutout in the flattened earth wall, switched it on, and closed the hatch. Much to Jim's surprise, she didn't argue the point or avoid it. Instead, she seemed to embrace the truth Jim had gleaned from instinct as opposed to evidence. This woman hadn't earned the nickname the Red Widow, la Viuda Roja, for nothing.

"If I hadn't, the cartels would've come for me and our sons, too. If you want to judge me, feel free, but we both live in worlds where showing any weakness at all is a recipe for death."

Jim watched the beam bounce about as she clambered down the ladder.

"How'd you figure it out?" Delgado resumed, when he remained silent.

"I didn't. I guessed. But I remember when your husband was assassinated, none of the cartels claimed credit. I seem to recall them distancing themselves, instead, and it never sat right with me that they wouldn't have killed you at the same time."

"This way," Delgado said, taking the lead down the winding tunnel, which had been constructed to veer around the heavy limestone and shale deposits. "My husband, Hector, was a fool. He believed that God was his partner, that so long as he went to church and was kind to the poor, his power would multiply. I used to go to church with him." She stopped and swung back toward Jim, her face silhouetted by the glow of her flashlight. "Do you have any idea how hard that was for me, Tejano?"

"I do, señora, on account of you losing your parents the way you did."

The Red Widow started on again, one hand sliding along an earthen wall to brace herself. "You've done your research."

"It's my job. There's fact, there's assumption, and there's outright guessing," Jim Strong told her. "And I'm going to take a guess at something here. Whatever was in those crates that were headed down here on that freight train has something to do with your husband, with God, with the Church—things you hate the most in the world."

"I didn't hate my husband, Tejano."

"No, you just killed him."

Luna Diaz Delgado stopped and swung all the way around toward him, so the flashlight was suspended between them. The light caught both of their faces equally, but the combination of anger and sadness that filled Delgado's face rode her features so well that Jim thought she was the most beautiful woman he'd ever seen. At the age of thirty-one, she had also become the most powerful criminal force in Mexico because she knew the alternative was to watch her sons die, unless the cartels took her first.

"You used his death," Jim resumed, before Delgado could dispute his point, "as an excuse to wipe out the other cartel leaders and their families. Sounds to me like you became what you hated and feared the most. You turned yourself into a victim, a martyr, some kind of twisted avenger that made you a folk hero. Until now. Thanks to whatever's inside those crates, you took too big a bite, and now the monster is biting back."

An explosion rumbled the ground above them, as if to illustrate Jim's point. In the spray of his flashlight, he could see that the color had washed out of Luna Diaz Delgado's face.

"Who are they, Tejano?"

"I have no idea."

"Not even a guess, an assumption?"

"Why don't you tell me what was in those crates, so I can come up with one?"

She smiled thinly, sadly, in a way that made Jim's insides turn to mush. "You've already figured it out. You pretty much said it yourself—you just don't realize it."

"Realize what?"

"I wanted the Church to pay for all the pain it's brought me," the Red Widow said, her voice cracking a bit. "I wanted the world to relinquish the false hopes the Church breeds. I wanted the true believers, the millions and millions of them like my husband, to know that they've been party to the greatest lie ever perpetrated on mankind. I won't tell you what procuring those crates cost me, or how important it is that I get them back. But I will say that I'll be performing a service by revealing the truth to the world that believes what it wants to believe, what it's told to believe, Tejano. I had to purchase all three, even though the contents of only one contains what I needed to find the solace I've been after since my parents were killed."

The glow of the flashlight revealed her big, dark eyes moistening. But she didn't dry them with a swipe of her sleeve because, Jim knew, that would have shown weakness, something she could never let anyone see in her.

"I was the ring bearer at their wedding and, when they found me in the church, I was still clutching the ring. I've kept it all these years as a reminder. It gave me the strength I needed to kill my husband, gave me the resolve to keep looking until I found what I was truly searching for, until I found what I needed, what the world needs."

Jim took a step closer to Luna Diaz Delgado, swallowing the light that had illuminated the swath between them. "What's in those crates, señora? What was stolen from that freight car?"

"Call me Luna, please."

"What's in those crates . . . Luna?" Jim repeated, her name nearly catching in his throat.

"Ossuaries."

"I don't know what that is."

"Burial boxes from times long past. Not for the bodies, just for the bones."

Suddenly, Jim could see those big, dark eyes again, no longer moist but filled with the same resolve that must've been there when the Red Widow had killed Hector Delgado, must've been there when she massacred the heads of all four cartels and their immediate families.

"The bones of Jesus Christ," Luna finished.

71

SONORA, TEXAS

"Look," Lieutenant Governor Maurice Scoggins interjected, bringing the story to an abrupt halt, "I've gotta get to a meeting now. You can make of this whatever you want."

"Do you believe it was true?" Caitlin asked, needing to clear her throat in the middle of her words.

"I was paying more attention to the fact that your father disobeyed a direct order from Governor Richards. Show me a man foolish enough to poke a hornets' nest with a stick and I'll show you a man who's no stranger to being stung."

"You referring to my father?"

"His story had no credibility, and there were some who believed he made it up to increase his own self-importance."

Caitlin felt a pressure building behind her eyes. "I'm going to guess you only met Jim Strong that one time."

"That's true."

"Then you never got the opportunity to call him a liar to his face. That makes you a lucky man."

Caitlin thought she heard Scoggins try to muster a laugh. "Of course, that's what made him Jim Strong, just like it makes you his daughter. You Strongs are aberrations, leftovers from the world that time forgot. You don't belong in law enforcement, you belong on display in a museum. You, your father, and your grandfather were never content just to catch catfish; you had to go after great white sharks."

"It's the sharks that keep finding us, Mr. Lieutenant Governor. I don't have an explanation as to why."

"But there you are, saving the Red Widow's life yesterday, just like your father did back in 1994."

His knowledge of what had transpired the day before caught Caitlin off guard. "You heard about that."

"Word travels fast for those of us who know how to listen. So what would you call that, exactly, Ranger? Fate, fortune, dumb luck, fill in the blank?"

"I'd go with none of the above, sir. And let's fill in that blank later, after I've done some more digging. There's lots happening here that makes 1994 seem like yesterday, but I haven't got it all sorted yet."

"You will," Scoggins told her. "It's what you do. People are always spouting off about Caitlin Strong the gunfighter, last of a breed, a throwback to the days of Wyatt Earp and Bat Masterson. But that diverts attention from all the collateral damage you leave in your wake, like not caring if the whole basis of human history goes to shit. Does the phrase 'bigger picture' even enter into your vocabulary?"

"Depends on if that bigger picture includes whoever's behind the gunmen my father went up against," Caitlin said, thinking again of those four skeletons pulled from the desert with bullet holes that matched her father's .45. "The same force behind them appears to be back, in case you haven't noticed."

And that set her thinking about the still-unidentified bodies that had been found in the alley across the street from Bane Sturgess in New Braunfels. Killed by an assassin that legend had it was a century old. Hell, maybe el Barquero really was the Ferryman.

"But I've got another question for you, sir. Back in 1994, did you ever hear any mention of a man with no face?"

"Come again?"

"You heard me. He was big, too, the kind of man who needs to duck under doorways."

"No, and I have to get to my meeting."

"Just one last thing. When you tried to call Jim Strong off, in 1994, who was pulling the strings? I'm guessing it's someone with a foreign zip code, and I don't mean Canada. Which government we talking about?"

"You're so smart and you haven't figured out it wasn't a government at all."

Caitlin felt something hit her like a hammer to the back of the head. "The Vatican," she realized. "It was the Vatican that made you call my dad off, wasn't it, trying to protect the secret they couldn't let out for the world to know?"

"There's no calling the Strongs off," Scoggins said, the way a snake might if it could talk. "I have no idea where you are, where you're going, or what you're going to find when you get there. All I know is I don't want to hear about it."

"Just answer me this, sir. Was it you who sent that team to retrieve the computers the Rangers confiscated from Communications Technology Providers as evidence?"

"I have no idea what you're talking about."

"They showed up with Criminal Investigations Division badges dangling from their necks. Trouble is, CID had no idea of their existence, and no record of taking possession of those computers, when I asked them."

"So why are you asking me, Ranger?"

"Because it would take somebody with a lot of power to set up a ruse like that. And since you insinuated about the Vatican, I'm figuring maybe it was forces there that wanted to make sure their tracks were covered again."

Caitlin heard what sounded like a low growl from Scoggins on the other end of the line. "I have no idea what you're talking about," he said, in something like a hiss, "and I've had my fill of the whole Strong family, Ranger. I'd like to live out my days and never hear that name again, but somehow I know I will."

"So long as it's not on the obituary page, sir."

72

SHAVANO PARK, TEXAS

"Of course, it could be the bones of somebody else, who died the same day," Dylan continued, after giving his revelation time to sink in.

"It's not," Cort Wesley said, recalling the bloody path that box of bones had blazed since it reached Texas soil in 1994.

"Before you get too excited, I need to point something else out."

"There's more?"

"Can you just listen to me for once? This shit surprised the hell out of me too, so I looked up a whole bunch of other ossuaries and compared the inscriptions to this one," Dylan said, laying the original version alongside the one with the superimposed translation. "And I found a few things you should know. First thing I can tell you is that the construction is pretty much a perfect match, so you can bet carbon dating will confirm the general time period. It's something else that's bothering me."

"What?"

"Could be nothing. Why ruin the party?"

"*What?*"

Dylan swung back toward his laptop, Cort Wesley no longer able to read his eyes. "I've got some more work I need to do first."

"You told me it was something I should know."

"But I'm not ready to tell you yet."

Cort Wesley's phone rang as he formed that thought, JONES lighting up in the ID box. Cort Wesley didn't slip out of Dylan's room to take the call, figuring there was no need to.

"Saddle up, cowboy," Jones greeted, when he answered. "We're going on a road trip. I'm on my way to pick you up now."

"How do you even know where I am?"

"I always know where you are," Jones told him. "Shit's hitting the fan and we gotta hope the whole world is downwind when it comes."

"Where we headed, Jones?"

"Atlanta, cowboy. The Centers for Disease Control."

73

BOERNE, TEXAS

Guillermo Paz sat at his priest's bedside at the Menger Springs Senior Living Community. The side rail had been lowered so he could feed the man his dinner, consisting of watered-down oatmeal the texture of drilling mud to make it easier for him to swallow. Paz was the only one who could get him to eat anything at all, which convinced the colonel that Father Boylston could still grasp the meaning of his words, even if he could no longer respond to them. Strange that he hadn't even known the priest's name until Father Boylston had been brought here after suffering his stroke.

"I had to come see you today, Padre," Paz said, as the old man worked his mouth feebly and then managed a swallow, "because what I have to say, I can't share with anyone else. Not even with my Texas Ranger or the outlaw; they wouldn't understand. Even they don't know what it's like to face the devil and live to tell it. I know my new enemy, my latest test to continue my transformation, is just a man. But in my vision I saw a man without a face. And a man without a soul," he added, as an afterthought.

Paz had been hoping, just this once, for a reaction, as if mention of the devil himself might spur his priest back for a few brief moments of lucidness. That finally being enlisted on the right side in the epic battle between good and evil might stir something down deep in Father Boylston's core and bring it to the surface. A nod, a look, a flash of the eyes or squeeze of his hand. It didn't have to be much. Paz would take anything.

And he needed *something*.

But nothing came, and he dabbed the spoon into the bowl of soupy oatmeal and eased it forward. His priest opened his mouth a crack and sucked up the meager contents with a slurping sound.

"I know you can't talk to me anymore, Padre, but you can still listen, and I wanted you to know that all the time you put into me has paid off. Bet you never thought I'd be facing off against the devil himself, but here we are."

The old priest finished working that spoonful down his throat and opened his mouth for the next. His once bright eyes were dull and lifeless, his thinning white hair flattened to his scalp in some places and sticking up askew in others. The room was laced with deodorizing spray to hide the stale scents of bodily waste and dried, scaly skin racked by bedsores. Paz detested injustice of all kinds, but this seemed like the ultimate one, for a man who'd given his life to others to have his own snatched from him this way.

"I know whatever's still inside you, whatever's listening to me now, accepts the existence of evil in the world. I think I've brought you along to believing that evil is as much a force of nature as wind and rain, and just as unstoppable, if the right people don't get in the way. You from the pulpit, me from where I'm at. I think that's what makes us true kindred spirits. Your job is to make people think prayers can keep them safe from that evil, and I'm the answer to those prayers."

Paz watched his priest swallow the latest spoonful. He realized Father Boylston's lips were trembling in anticipation of more oatmeal, and he quickly readied the next spoonful, scooping up too much for the old man to manage and needing to shake some of it back into the bowl.

"I only just realized that, Padre. And I also realize now why you gave me that book about Mother Teresa. I remembered this quote, something like, 'Be faithful in small things because it is in them that your strength lies.' What she doesn't say is that small things lead to bigger ones, and there's no limit to how strong a man can become if he retains his faith. I learned that from you, and I wanted you to know that. I wanted you to know that if it wasn't for you, I'd still be on the wrong side of things, thwarting prayers instead of answering them on your behalf. And if you never have the chance to help anyone again, you'll always know how much you helped me along this new path you helped me chart.

"You know Kierkegaard is one of my favorite philosophers, and it was him who said, 'The function of prayer is not to influence God, but rather to change the nature of the one who prays.' But here's the thing: people pray in different ways. I'm not necessarily one to kneel and recite the prayers. I've got more of a conversational thing going with God, and even though he doesn't talk back, I know he's listening."

Paz waited for a response, then continued when none came.

"It was Buddha himself, I think, who said, 'Doubt everything. Find your own light.' Well, I wanted you to know that you've been that light for me, that when I kill the devil I felt today, it'll be my gift to you—to God, sure, but mostly for you."

Paz stowed the empty bowl back on the tray that rested by his priest's bedside. Then he rose, squeezed Father Boylston's hand, and kissed him lightly on the forehead.

He thought he felt something in that moment, and he looked down to see his priest squeezing his hand back. A flicker of life flashed briefly in his eyes, then quickly faded, just as his grip let go.

"Thank you, Padre," Paz said, smoothing Father Boylston's hair. "Thank you."

PART EIGHT

You know, we look back now at the Rangers in the late 1800's as having old-fashioned firearms, but then, the Colt was cutting-edge technology. In fact, the Walker Colt is named for a Ranger, Samuel Walker, who helped develop it. The Rangers saw a need for a reliable, well-designed, heavy-duty revolver that they could take out on remote patrols. The firearms that were available back then weren't as fast or as easy to load, so the Colt was a pretty revolutionary firearm. Until then, you had to hand-load every round, and if you carried one revolving pistol, you only had six rounds. We are always looking for new technology to make us better, and the Rangers were doing the same thing back then.

—Texas Ranger Frank Malinak as quoted in
Tracking the Texas Rangers: The Twentieth Century,
edited by Bruce A. Glasrud and Harold J. Weiss Jr.,
University of North Texas Press, 2013

74

"You're not going to believe this, Ranger," Cort Wesley's voice blared over the Bluetooth, as Caitlin drew closer to the combination gas station and convenience store from where the credit card receipt had originated.

"I was just pressing your number. You're not going to believe what I've got to tell you, either."

"I'll go first," he said.

Driving through the emptiness of space like this was something Caitlin had never gotten used to. The mostly barren road was like a black ribbon cutting the world in half. The convenience store that Young Roger had identified by using the receipt she'd plucked from the smoldering ruins of that small fire was located in the town of Spinnaker Falls. It was a town in name only, no more than a way station for people on their way to tour Fort McKavett or somewhere else, many of whom had strayed off the interstate that had rendered Spinnaker Falls obsolete.

"I got a tentative translation on that ossuary, Ranger," Cort Wesley continued. "Hope you're sitting down for this . . ."

"I'm driving, Cort Wesley."

"Because the bones inside might well belong to—"

"Jesus Christ," Caitlin completed for him.

Dead air filled the line, to the point where Caitlin thought maybe the call had been dropped.

"How'd you figure it out?" Cort Wesley asked finally, breaking the silence.

"How did *you*?"

Cort Wesley explained the content of Dylan's translation, finishing with "Okay. Your turn."

"I got the story from the current lieutenant governor of the state himself, Mo Scoggins, who tried to call my father off the case in 1994. Turns out Jim Strong had a hand in saving Luna Diaz Delgado's life, too."

"Like father, like daughter."

"According to the story, the Red Widow was after those bones to discredit the Church, a particular obsession of hers, given her background."

"I don't believe it," Cort Wesley muttered.

"The story or the fact that we came by it at the same time?"

"Take your pick, Ranger."

"Where are you, by the way?" Caitlin asked him. "The background sounds funny."

"I'm in a plane, flying to Atlanta with Jones."

"Atlanta?"

"The CDC," Cort Wesley told her.

"About those bodies found in that freight car twenty-five years ago?" Caitlin asked, recalling that they had ended up in the Centers for Disease Control and Prevention's possession.

"That's all I can tell you, because it's all Jones has told me."

"Word from the past is it was a curse that killed those men on the train car," Caitlin said, recalling the story Luna Diaz Delgado had told her father. "What happens when somebody opens something they're not supposed to?"

"Well, since we're headed to the CDC, it's safe to say maybe it was something that got out, instead."

Caitlin's hands tightened on the wheel, a black patch of air in the narrowing distance suddenly entering her field of vision.

"Uh-oh."

"What is it, Ranger?"

"A fire, Cort Wesley. I think the place I'm headed to might be burning."

75

The source of thick, black, billowing smoke was something else entirely.

The effects were akin to an oil fire, in this case fueled by natural gas, the kind of job hellfighters like Red Adair would have relished battling. The heavy, soot-rich smoke drifted over a slew of irregularly placed pump jacks that had long ago stopped pumping, as if the oil had abandoned these parts along with the people.

Drawing close enough to smell the noxious smoke, even with the air-conditioning on, helped Caitlin recall that she'd had actually heard of this site, at least anecdotally. Fire wasn't spewing from an oil well per se so much as from a trench. What had transpired here was akin to a similar incident that had taken place in the Karakum Desert, located in the country of Turkmenistan, wherever that was exactly. It was called the Darvaza gas crater, more affectionately known as the Door to Hell.

In 1971, Caitlin recalled, when the republic was still part of the Soviet Union, a group of Soviet geologists had gone to the Karakum in search of oil fields. They found what they thought to be a substantial oil field and began drilling. Unfortunately, it turned out they were drilling on top of a cavernous pocket of natural gas, which couldn't support the weight of their equipment. The site collapsed, taking their equipment along with it, and the event triggered the sedimentary rock of the desert to collapse in other places, too, creating a domino effect that, by the time all was said and done, resulted in several open craters.

Reportedly, no one was injured in the collapse, but the scientists soon had another problem on their hands: the natural gas escaping from the crater. Natural gas is composed mostly of methane, which the scientists determined must be eradicated, or at least controlled, at all costs. So they decided to light the crater on fire, hoping that all the dangerous natural gas would burn away in a few weeks' time.

Problem was, the scientists in Turkmenistan weren't dealing with a measured amount of natural gas, so a burn that was supposed to last days or weeks at most was still burning a half century later.

Caitlin had heard that Texas was dotted with wells beset by a comparable calamity, although she couldn't say exactly when this burn had started or how much it had actually contributed to the abandonment of Spinnaker Falls. Nor did she have any idea of where the town had gotten its name, given that there were no falls anywhere to be seen when she pulled into the lot fronting the convenience store. The gas pumps out front looked as old as any she had seen in years, the place likely owing its survival to the fact that this was the only gas for fifty miles in every direction. That was the thing about Texas. Only about five percent of its land was actually settled; the rest remained pretty much as it had always been, dating all the way back to when her great-great-grandfather, Steeldust Jack Strong, had been a Ranger.

Between the burning oil trench and the convenience store and gas station stood a ramshackle Spanish mission that looked a lot like the Alamo in its original form. The walls were still whole, and Caitlin thought she glimpsed cannon mounts from which the most potent weapons of the time had likely fired on marauding Mexican bandits or soldiers, way back before Texas gained statehood.

There was something about seeing structures like this in their original form, as opposed to rebuilt, that made her appreciate her heritage even more, as well as the part the Rangers had played in the formation of modern Texas. The number of their deadly exploits was nothing compared to how many encounters were likely preempted merely by their reputation, keeping plenty of the bad guys of the time at bay.

The convenience store and gas station shared a parking lot with an old-fashioned diner. Its windows were covered in plywood now and probably had been since the opening of the interstate, which could be glimpsed in the distance. Caitlin had her choice of empty parking spaces, picturing a time in the past when the lot would have been teeming with eighteen-wheelers and sedans owned by salesmen on their way from one call to the next.

She entered to the sound of jangling bells, a few seconds passing before a door set behind the still well-stocked counter opened and an overweight man wearing denim overalls emerged, mustard staining the top of his lip and both sides of his mouth.

He seemed to notice Caitlin's exposed badge before he noticed anything else. "A real Texas Ranger in my store? If that don't beat all. Whatever you want, ma'am, it's on the house."

"How about some information?"

"Glad to help any way I can, Ranger," the man said, laying a pair of beefy hands on the counter. "Name's Wyatt Bass, by the way."

Caitlin shook one of his big hands and felt it swallow hers. "Any relation to the outlaw Sam Bass?"

"Distant cousin maybe, on my father's side, but I've never seen any firm proof on the subject. So if your visit somehow involves Sam Bass, I'm afraid I can't help you none."

Caitlin took off her hat and rustled a hand through her hair. "Sign outside says you're open six to six, seven days a week."

Wyatt Bass nodded. "Except for the days I oversleep or the help is too drunk to show up on time or make it through the day."

"Six o'clock in the morning to six o'clock in the evening?"

"That's right."

Caitlin eased a printout of the credit card receipt fragment Young Roger had managed to decipher. "Then would you mind telling me, sir, how it was that, this past Tuesday night, this receipt says seven thirteen p.m.?"

76

SPINNAKER FALLS, TEXAS

Bass chuckled, sounding like a department store Santa Claus. "You called me *sir*. A Texas Ranger called me *sir*."

"You have an answer for me, to earn the salutation?"

"Could be a calibration problem, I suppose. We do maybe three to five credit card transactions on average per day, that's all. For some stretch of time, the machine wasn't even working right and we never got the funds properly credited. Not that it would've made too much of a difference, of course, 'least not these days."

"How is it you can make ends meet after that diner failed?"

Bass took off a baseball cap that was greasy and sweat-stained along the brim and scratched at his hair, showering white flecks of dandruff into the air. "My grandpa founded this place, and for a long stretch of years my grandma ran that diner. When business went bust with the opening of the interstate, the diner was the first to go. And we'd be gone, too, if not for the stipend we get from the state highway department because of some unofficial law about making sure there's at least one gas station every hundred miles. I could get by with three fuel deliveries a year, four or five at most. But, hey, I'm still standing here, and if you need to fuel up 'fore you go on your way, that's free too."

Caitlin spotted the credit card machine, connected by a twisted collection of wires to both the wall and the cash register, perched just to the side of the bigger machine. "I appreciate that, Mr. Bass, but right now I'd settle for you checking to see if the machine's calibrated or not."

Wyatt Bass pressed a few keys with fingers too big to work them agilely. Nothing happened, so he tried again, and this time the machine printed out a receipt, still with those telltale pinkish-red marks running up the side.

"It seems to be working just fine, Ranger."

"Were you here on Tuesday night, sir?"

"I think so. If I wasn't, my wife was. It's just the two of us these days, splitting the shifts. We don't see a lot of each other, which some might say is why we're still together. And we both tend to stay as long as there's customers. Tuesday was a pretty busy day for us, and, now that I think of it, I looked at my watch and realized I'd kept the place open almost two hours past closing."

"Did you pay yourself some overtime?"

"Truth be told," Bass said, lowering his voice dramatically, "I'll likely put in for it with the highway department. As long as you're okay with that, Ranger."

"We never even discussed the issue. So, do you remember somebody paying with a credit card for something on Tuesday evening, just past seven o'clock?"

"Not off the top of my head, but let me check something."

The cash register jangled open and Bass removed a thin pile of receipts comparable in size and shape to the fragment she'd plucked from that wood ash earlier in the week.

"Here we go," he said, after sorting through about half of them. "Seven thirteen p.m. in the amount of twenty-two dollars and seventy-five cents."

"Remember what the person bought?"

"I remember it was a man."

"That's the first thing you've sounded so sure about, Mr. Bass."

"Process of elimination, Ranger. We didn't have a single female customer all day. That's another reason why I was so glad to see you."

"I don't suppose you remember who this particular credit card receipt belonged to?"

Bass shook his head, jowls seeming to vibrate. "Probably somebody I'd never seen before and would have no reason to remember."

"I suppose. Do you have any security camera footage that might refresh your memory?"

"I've got cameras but no footage, on account of the cameras being broke since before nine-eleven. Replacing them didn't seem worth the expense, given that we could perform a comparable task with a Polaroid and a single box of that instant film that develops in front of your eyes. I understand they're popular again."

"I hadn't heard."

"Except they're not made by Polaroid anymore. That company, big as it once was, is good and gone. Plenty of unhappy lessons to learn from that, and we would've gone the same way if not for that stipend. Long as we sell gas, and the money don't get cut from the state budget, we'll be in business."

Caitlin nodded, leaning just enough over the counter to get Bass's attention. "When you opened that register, I noticed plenty more cash than could be explained by eight customers."

"The nearest bank's a hundred miles away, and no robber in his right mind would come this far out of the way to pretend he's Baby Face Nelson."

"I'd say that money came courtesy of sales from today alone, sir. Otherwise, you would've put it in the safe you've got under the counter."

Caitlin caught him looking down, confirming her suspicions.

"That cash has nothing to do with what you came here about, Ranger," Bass told her.

"I don't suppose it does, but if you can't tell me anything about the man from Tuesday night, maybe one of your regular customers knows something that can help me."

Bass remained silent.

"You're talking to a Texas Ranger here, sir, not an ICE agent," Caitlin assured him. "You live nearby, sir?"

Bass nodded. "Close enough to smell the gas bled off by that fire when the wind's right."

"Because the Dumpster outside is full of the kind of stuff you'd be dumping inside it, if you lived closer, in addition to broken up storage boxes and the like. So who's using it, if not you?"

Bass looked down, then back up at Caitlin. "You notice that old abandoned mission out back?"

"I did. Why?"

"Because it's not really abandoned."

77

"That bad arm bothering you, cowboy?" Jones asked, as the Homeland Security private jet settled into its descent.

Cort Wesley flexed life back into his fingers, the steady improvement he'd been experiencing having slowed considerably. "Must've fallen asleep on the flight. And I'm going to hazard a guess here," he continued, changing the subject. "What you told Caitlin about your involvement with that private intelligence firm, how it was nothing more than zero-footprint operations, that was a lie, a great big frigging lie."

Jones didn't bristle. He didn't grimace, flinch, or scowl. His squarish head, topped by a quasi-military, high and tight hairstyle, didn't even move.

"You know your way around a zero-footprint operation, don't you, cowboy, dating all the way back to Desert Storm?"

"Is that your way of answering my question or avoiding it?"

"I'm just making a point here about how business gets done. You do what you have to."

"Can I take that as a yes?" Cort Wesley asked him, trying not to sound as caustic as he felt.

Jones looked away, out the jet's window, toward the growing shape of downtown Atlanta. "I'm about to lose my parking privileges."

"What's that mean?"

"Figure of speech." He turned back to Cort Wesley, his gaze uncertain and his jawline missing the sharp ridges that looked like they could cut flesh. "I've enjoyed free rein for as long as I have because things happened and I responded. That's all Washington cares about, cowboy. What they don't care about is the middle, what happens in between. Because if they know the middle, it's because you fucked up along the way. That's what I meant about losing my parking privileges. It's like showing up for work to find somebody else's name on your space. It's how you know you're either down, out, or both."

"You're telling me you fucked up. That's what the killings at Communications Technology Providers ended up revealing," Cort Wesley said.

"What they were doing, what they ended up finding, was at my direction.

I gave them a job I thought was impossible, because nobody had ever succeeded before, and people have been trying for twenty-five years, believe me."

"You're talking about that site in the desert around Sonora, the place where Caitlin figures the same crates—ossuaries, we know now—went missing for a second time after they were buried by Caitlin's father."

"To say the contents of one of them has the power to change the world would be an understatement."

Cort Wesley nodded, trying not to appear too smug. "Like I already told you, I've learned that much for myself, thanks to my son being a whiz with ancient languages."

"This crap about the bones of Jesus Christ."

"It's not crap. You want the very definition of world changing, there it is."

Jones's expression remained dismissive. "Let's put that aside for a minute, okay? I don't give a shit about Jesus Christ, or Pontius Pilate, King Herod, Moses, or even Charlton Heston. Those bones might change the world, but they can't end it." Jones had the look of a man confessing his sins to a priest. "I was looking for something that could end it."

"You're talking about a weapon."

"I am."

"You're talking about whatever killed those men in the offices of Bane Sturgess a few days back, and the men in that train car twenty-five years ago."

"Right as rain," Jones said flatly, his voice bled of any emotion.

"And since we're headed for the Centers for Disease Control . . ."

"The things that excite me the most, cowboy, are the same things that scare the living shit out of me. Because if we can't control it, if we can't own it, that means somebody else will. Possession may not really be nine-tenths of the law, but it's a hell of a lot more than that when it comes to survival. If something like this ended up in the hands of the Russians, the North Koreans, the Chinese, ISIS, al-Qaeda, the worldwide nationalist movements, or Wile E. Coyote, you think for a minute they wouldn't use it to push the world off a cliff?"

Cort Wesley didn't bother responding.

"Exactly," Jones picked up, taking his lack of an answer for a yes. "So when a report of this mysterious case worked by none other than Caitlin Strong's father reached my desk, you can bet I took notice."

"You had reason to believe it was Jim Strong who buried this shit, even before Caitlin pretty much confirmed it," Cort Wesley concluded.

"But I didn't know where, and I won't bore you with how much area is covered by all the possibilities."

"I have an idea how big Texas is, Jones."

"I think we should break the state up and sell off parcels to the other forty-nine. Or better yet, how about slicing it off from the continental United States and making it an island all unto itself? Or, hell, just deed Texas back to Mexico, given that half the crazy shit in the world seems to happen there."

"Texas also leads the nation in gun ownership, Jones. I don't think the residents would take too kindly to becoming part of Mexico again."

"You get the idea, cowboy."

"Not really."

Jones eased himself into the aisle from the window seat, so he'd be closer to Cort Wesley. "Then let me put it this way. Communications Technology Providers was looking for those bone boxes on my direction. Whoever was behind those gunmen in Dallas bought my intelligence and then murdered the people who'd provided it to them to hide their tracks."

"Which you must have suspected was going on. Hence having Caitlin serve the warrant on behalf of the Criminal Investigations Division."

"I figured that warrant would be enough to get CTP to give up whoever was after the same thing I was, cowboy." Jones suddenly looked impatient. "How long we going to keep rehashing this?"

"You want to change the subject, tell me it was CTP who came up with that site in the desert."

"Consider yourself told, cowboy."

"And since Bane Sturgess ended up with the ossuaries in their possession, it's a safe bet they were contracted to dig them up."

"Amateur hour, cowboy, because they must've done the same dumb thing the dead men from twenty-five years ago did."

"They opened one of the bone boxes," Cort Wesley picked up, "the one thought to contain the last remains of Jesus Christ."

"And whatever climbed out has the capacity to kill within seconds, no ifs, ands, or buts. You get exposed to whatever it is and you die."

"Respiratory and heart failure," Cort Wesley recalled from Doc Whatley's preliminary reports, both in 1994 and today.

"The original three bodies from back in ninety-four were transferred to the CDC, where they've remained in stasis ever since."

Cort Wesley felt like the student in the room yet again, only with Jones as the teacher instead of Dylan. "What's that mean, exactly?"

"That the bodies were preserved as much as possible, because the CDC hasn't been able to identify the exact biological culprit behind their deaths."

"After twenty-five years?"

"You heard me, cowboy. Whatever killed them is there, until it isn't. It kills without leaving a trace, it kills everyone the same way, and it kills everyone it comes into contact with, period. We're talking about the thermonuclear bomb of the biochemical world."

"I guess we can throw the proverbial curse out the window," Cort Wesley noted.

"Oh, it's a curse, all right, just one that's got nothing to do with the supernatural or divine inspiration. And it's not man-made, either."

"How can you be so sure?"

"Because man could never come up with something this perfect."

"Hold on while I clean out my ears, because I think you just called whatever's inside that ossuary 'perfect.'"

"From a weapons standpoint, that's what it is. We're talking a hundred percent mortality rate in, what, maybe thirty seconds, tops. And then it goes away, like it was never there."

"So why are we going to Atlanta, if the CDC hasn't been able to figure out much more than that?"

"Because they've developed some notions, theories. Have ruled things out and narrowed the options down to some general parameters. Until four days ago, that information was above even my security clearance, and mine is about equal to the president's."

"Dallas changed things."

"For me it did," Jones affirmed. "But it was those four bodies at Bane Sturgess that altered the dynamics of this for the whole damn country."

"History repeating itself the other day in New Braunfels." Cort Wesley nodded. "Okay, so we know you don't have these bone boxes."

"Obviously."

"And we know whoever sent those gunmen to Communications Technology Providers to cover their tracks doesn't have them either. So, Jones, here's my question," Cort Wesley continued. "If the good guys don't have these ossuaries, and the bad guys don't have them, who does?"

78

"I'd join you if I could, Ranger," Wyatt Bass continued, "but that would leave the place untended."

"I think I can handle this myself," Caitlin told him.

"You speak Spanish?"

"I do. Might be helpful if you made the intro, just to smooth the waters, so they don't take off running."

"They won't," Bass said stiffly, no sense of doubt whatsoever in his voice. "Because if you're there, they'll know it's because I sent you."

"There" was the crumbling Spanish mission, bathed in the vapors and coarse smoke from the burning trench, which had thinned somewhat as the winds died down. Approaching the mission, though, still felt like stepping into the effects of nuclear winter.

In addition to the stilled pump jacks, Caitlin also noticed a horizon dotted with similarly frozen wind turbines, evidence of another failed attempt to breathe life into this moribund area. Drawing closer in her rented SUV, she realized that the mission itself was bigger than it had looked from the convenience store parking lot, and with portions in much better condition than even her initial impression had indicated. The walls looked sturdy enough to again support the manning of the ramparts in battle, structurally sound to the point that they could hold the requisite cannons. The courtyard beyond was dominated by the bell tower attached to a Spanish mosaic chapel built by the original Spanish settlers of this frontier, who, in search of a better life, ended up facing all manner of bandit and Indian. Stephen Austin had founded the Texas Rangers to "range" the land and provide law and order, setting the tone for all who came after them to serve justice on those who harmed the innocent.

She supposed things hadn't really progressed all that much.

Caitlin emerged from the SUV, certain she was being watched, and walked with both her gun and badge plainly in view but with her hands in the air to alert whomever that she came in peace. Hell, if she'd had a white kerchief, she might be waving it now.

Drawing within a stone's throw of the mission, she watched the big wooden double doors open to the inside, the warped wood dragging against the ground. A Caucasian figure emerged at the head of a small group of Latinos. He signaled them to stop and then continued outside the mission's walls to approach Caitlin alone.

"I'm going to guess this isn't a social call, Ranger."

Caitlin lowered her hands but kept them in view as she stopped. "But I'm not here to roust the people here, either. As far as the rest of the world knows, I was never here and neither were you."

"Then, by all means, step inside."

Caitlin started walking again, coughing out the chalky residue that had settled in her lungs from the trench fire burning a quarter mile to the south. Passing through the open gate, she saw the inside of the mission to be thriving, taking on the aspect of what it must have looked like two centuries before. The courtyard was as well landscaped as the desert conditions would allow, wiped clean of scrub brush and dried gravel. Rows of plantings that somehow thrived in the desert climate sat amid a combination of wood and stone benches and a circular seating area that she took for an outdoor classroom. The chapel and its spiraling bell tower dominated the rest of the courtyard, obscuring most of the single-story structures that clearly had been rebuilt. An old truck packing a pair of tanks labeled "Propane," which must have supplied the mission's power, was parked parallel to the church, the tanks' silvery finishes blinding in the sunlight.

The man who'd invited her in was tall and lean, mustachioed and wearing a red plaid kerchief around his neck for easy drawing up over his mouth to ward off the trench fire fumes and residue, which was already clinging to her clothes and skin like glue. He had the look of a movie cowboy whose name doesn't make the end credits, except that his rawboned look and tanned, leathery flesh was real and not the product of makeup.

"I'm Daniel Aidman, Ranger," he said extending his hand. "Wyatt Bass called ahead to tell us you were coming."

"Explains why those men you got poised on that wall didn't shoot me," Caitlin said back, taking Aidman's hand. "Aidman's not a Spanish name, last time I checked."

"My mother was Mexican, as are all those who reside within these walls."

Caitlin glanced at the gunmen wielding .30-06s, stationed on the wall and positioned to be invisible from the outside. "They were already up there before I made my way over, Mr. Aidman. Care to tell me what they're guarding against?"

"Intrusion," Aidman said, and left it there. "This is our home."

Caitlin could tell there was something else but didn't press the issue, with other priorities in mind.

"You ACLU, something like that?" she asked Aidman.

"I *was* ACLU, *then* something like that."

"What happened?"

"I was considered too obstinate and none too good at following the rules."

"I can relate to that, sir." Caitlin looked around at the people who continued to spill out into the courtyard from wherever they'd been hiding. "Don't suppose any of these folks have credit cards, Mr. Aidman, but I'm guessing you do."

Aidman remained silent, swallowing hard as Caitlin extracted the copy Young Roger had made for her of the piece of the credit card receipt she'd extracted from the ash.

"I'm guessing the numbers we were able to salvage from this," she resumed, handing it to Aidman, "match one of your cards. I'm guessing you purchased some sundries before you made your way out into the desert outside of Sonora, where, from that mesa, you had a front row seat for all the excitement."

Aidman continued regarding the piece of paper, avoiding Caitlin's gaze.

"Could you tell me if I have that right, sir?"

He finally looked up and handed the piece of paper back to Caitlin, after folding it back into quarters for her.

"I'd like to show you the chapel, Ranger. We can talk inside there, get out of the heat."

"It was a simple question, sir."

"But the answer is considerably less so. Goes back a whole lot of years."

"How many?"

Aidman grabbed Caitlin's stare and held it, his eyes saying more than his words. "1994."

"Let's check out that chapel, Mr. Aidman."

79

"I want the whole world to know what I've known my entire life, Tejano," Luna Diaz Delgado continued, addressing a visibly shocked Jim Strong. "That there is no God."

"Well," he managed, collecting his thoughts as he coughed out the chalky residue that had collected in his lungs while following the winding path of the Red Widow's escape tunnel, "that explains your claims about it having been a curse that killed those three men we couldn't identify. But it wasn't a curse that just attacked your hacienda, señora; it was an army. And, given a choice, I think I'd rather take on a curse."

"Who are they?" Delgado asked him.

Jim hesitated, caught in the grip of ruminating on his own faith, or lack of it. He hadn't been to church even once in the near decade since the murder of his wife, the last and only woman he'd ever loved. He despised not so much God as religion in general, with a fervor that approached his feelings toward drug gangs and wife beaters. There'd been a time in his life, after his daughter was born, when he'd gravitated toward the Church to do the right thing. It was to please his wife, sure, but he took comfort in the notion that the mere act was bringing him closer to God, something that could definitely prove advantageous in his particular line of work.

A devout Catholic, his wife had gone to church far more often. And then Mexican druggers had gunned her down inside his own home with four-year-old Caitlin hiding just steps away. She bore no memory of that night, but Jim remembered speeding home when word reached him, seeing her in the company of local cops and D. W. Tepper, with a blanket wrapped around her shoulders.

Jim's weakness as a man, and what had ultimately dropped him into the bottle for a stretch, was the need to always have an enemy. The spare room in their modest home was papered with wanted posters and police reports covering the most heinous of crimes committed by the most brutal criminals who'd escaped the clutches of the local police. Each of them became his quarry, as if Jim was determined to stamp out every bit of evil from one side of Texas to the other. A mandate he'd taken on because, clearly, God couldn't be relied on to do His job.

What kind of God lets an innocent woman be murdered under witness of her own daughter?

The question might have been a cliché, just as it was a cliché that Luna Diaz Delgado was one of the few survivors of the massacre that had ended the wedding of her parents and made her an orphan. So here he was, in a tunnel with a woman who'd murdered her own husband and then blamed the cartels, which gave her the excuse she needed to wipe out their jefes, along with the families of the jefes, as a warning to anyone who might otherwise have taken up arms against her. Delgado had learned long ago, in a painful and bloody manner, that the number one rule of pursuing power of any kind really was to be more ruthless than your opponent. Being willing to do the unthinkable, to go beyond what those opponents were capable of acting upon or even considering.

"We should get going, señora," Jim said to the Red Widow.

"You haven't answered my question yet, Tejano. Who are these people that are doing this? What are they after?"

"Seems pretty obvious to me that they're doing everything they can to protect this secret you're so determined to release to the world."

"The truth is the truth," Delgado said stiffly.

"Not in the minds of most folks, on this topic. Their faith won't let them think differently on the subject." Jim stopped there, but another thought occurred to him. "There's a difference, señora, between struggling with your faith and losing it altogether."

"You believe that's the case with me," the Red Widow said, as the end of the tunnel appeared, "and you're right. But, tell me, where does your faith come from?"

Jim tapped his holster. "The twenty-five hundred feet per second my bullets travel."

"You've got *who* with you just short of the border?" D. W. Tepper said, through a mouth that had dropped almost to the floor.

"You heard me."

"I need to hear it again, to make sure my hearing's not even worse than I thought it was."

"The Red Widow."

"Luna Diaz Delgado?"

"Is there another Red Widow in these parts? We're just south of the border and I don't want to cross until there's somebody friendly on the other side."

"I'm not sure that describes me, in this particular case, Ranger Strong."

"Maybe you didn't hear what I said about more gunmen than fought in the Battle of the Bulge attacking her home today, Ranger Tepper."

"Maybe you should've joined them."

"How fast can you get down here?"

Jim Strong checked Luna Diaz Delgado into the very same roadside motel where the man with no face had taken the mirrors off the walls of his room. Not only did he figure that this was the last place the same man would look for her, but also it was the kind of place that didn't ask a lot of questions. The clerk who checked him in, while the Red Widow remained in D. W. Tepper's truck, also seemed to be ecstatic over serving the needs of the Texas Rangers.

"Let's keep this between us," Jim said, shaking the man's hand.

"Does this make me a deputy or something?"

"Close enough."

Back in the truck, parked out of sight from the clerk's view, Jim could sense the tension that had settled between Tepper in the front seat and la Viuda Roja in the back. He knew he should come clean to Tepper about what Delgado claimed was inside one of those shipping crates that had gone missing, but he still could see no sense in risking the destruction of two careers as opposed to one.

"You know what they say about in for a penny, in for a pound," Tepper noted, after Jim had escorted her into the motel room. "When I picked the two of you up, your baggage came along for the ride."

"The woman and I travel light."

"You, maybe. She's lugging around more weight than Marley's ghost."

"Leave it be, D.W.," Jim said, his gaze straying to the motel room door across the lot from where Tepper had parked in the shade. "At least for now."

"Only if you give me a notion as to where this is headed next. Back to Buster Plugg, maybe?"

Jim shook his head. "There's nothing more to get out of him than what he inadvertently gave up already. This man with no face paid cash, so we got no credit card number to run. And there's no sense in pulling the prints from that room where he took down the mirrors, because we won't get a match on them anyway."

"So, like I said, where is this headed, where are *you* headed next, Ranger Strong?"

Right then, Jim hadn't thought that far ahead. Since Delgado had no more of a notion of who was behind the gunmen who'd attacked her home than he did, there wasn't much more she could do to help him, but she was still all he had.

"I've involved you enough in this, Ranger Tepper," Jim said.

"I'd say 'Anything else you need,' but I'm guessing that's a call you won't be making."

"Actually, D.W., until I can figure out how to get mine back, I could use your truck."

"How long you think you'll have to keep me stashed here?" Luna Diaz Delgado asked him.

"You know what's waiting for you back home, señora. What about your kids?"

"As soon as word about what happened reaches those responsible for their safety, they'll disappear until I say different."

"Then we've got some time," said Jim Strong, "and I'm going to need your help figuring where to go with this next. Bullets have been flying on both sides of the border and it's a safe bet plenty more'll follow unless we figure out who we're dealing with."

Delgado sat on the edge of the bed, the television muted before her. Jim could see her spine stiffen as she regarded him.

"Those crates are my property. I want them back."

"We can cover that issue down the line, señora, assuming we survive this."

She looked toward the room phone. "One phone call and I can have fifty men here to serve our efforts."

"You had that many down at your hacienda and we still ended up in an escape tunnel."

"You haven't exactly posed another alternative."

"Choosing no alternative's better than choosing one that requires an unacceptable risk."

The Red Widow rose from the bed. "You think someone inside my organization is talking," she stated, in what had started as a question. "You think my organization is compromised."

"Tell me more about the crate in question."

"The ossuary containing the bones of Christ was found in a cave outside of Jerusalem, in 1959, by archaeologists and historians who thought they'd found the Holy Grail," Delgado related. "By the time their ship returned to Turkey, they were all dead, and according to the story that's been passed down, someone at the port knew the cause to be a curse, from reading the burial inscription."

"Sounds awfully convenient that the whole crew was dead and somebody just happened to be in the vicinity who knew how to read ancient languages."

"That's what happened, Tejano."

"No, that's the *story*. We don't know what really happened, because it may well have been embellished or exaggerated over the years."

Delgado nodded, conceding his point. "I don't know how many times those ossuaries changed hands since 1959, only that the dealer I purchased them from swore to the authenticity of that one in particular."

"What made you trust him?"

"The fact that he knew what would happen to him if he was lying. I could track him down again, if you think he could be useful."

Jim pondered that for a moment. "He's dead, señora, almost for sure. Killed by the same force behind the attack on your hacienda, because he sold you out."

"You don't know that."

"Only option I can see, and that tells me he feared this other party even more than he feared you. And who else could have told them about your connection, so they'd know where to look?"

"That doesn't leave us with a lot, Ranger."

"I do have one idea," Jim told her.

"My truck wasn't enough?" D. W. Tepper said, picking up his phone on the first ring.

"I decided to take you up on your offer."

"Thought you didn't want to ruin two careers."

"Just make sure nobody notices you digging up some information I need."

"Concerning?"

"Airports, Ranger Tepper, specifically international flights on private jets."

"Good notion, Ranger Strong. On account of the puppet master pulling all these strings would never send armed commandos on a commercial flight."

"There are eight airports within a hundred-mile area around here that fit the bill, D.W."

"Give me until morning."

"You don't have to stay," Luna Diaz Delgado said, joining Jim Strong on the covered walkway outside her room.

"Get back inside please, señora."

"You worried about me running off?"

"I'm worried about the man with no face coming back."

"You said this was a safe place to hide."

Jim Strong turned toward her, grasping the twelve-gauge he'd propped against the flimsy chair, to make sure it didn't fall. "I said it was as safe as could be expected, under the circumstances."

Thunder rumbled in the distance, the already stiff wind picking up with a big storm's portent riding it. Jim Strong could almost smell the ozone in the air as the wind whipped the first big drops into his face.

"You can keep watch as easily from inside the room, Tejano."

"Not really."

He felt Luna Diaz Delgado close her hand warmly around one of his and tug lightly. "Please."

Jim got her meaning right away, even though it had been a long time since he'd felt such a grasp. He saw it in her eyes, too, a combination of longing and loneliness, combined with the inability to ever let her guard down. Jim wondered if he'd let his guard down for a single moment since his wife was murdered. Always worrying, always fretting, always seeing the men who'd killed her in every lowlife he hunted or came across. He'd killed so many men because of what those druggers had done, and he would be killing plenty more as long as he was strong enough to hold his pistol.

As the Red Widow led him back inside the motel room and locked the door behind him, Jim realized she was the first woman who'd made him feel this way in the whole decade since his wife's death. He worshipped women for any number of reasons, but he could never understand why not a single one had ever led him to doing what he was about to do tonight.

Jim realized, in that moment, that it wasn't beauty or personality or vulnerability; it was nothing like any of those.

It was strength, power.

Jim Strong imagined that, had he been in Delgado's shoes through the series of violent encounters that had come to define her, he would've acted just as she had, every time. He realized that the last thing he wanted was a woman who needed him, and la Viuda Roja needed no one at all. She had been effectively alone since the murder of her parents on the day of their wedding. Though Jim had been alone for a lot fewer years, that experience was magnified by raising his daughter, Caitlin, and intensified by the bloodlust that had followed his wife's murder.

Falling into bed with Luna Diaz Delgado was like slipping off a dock into the water. The impact was hard, but not crushing, and then it gave way to the whole dark world receding, with him sinking into it.

In those moments, the bones of Jesus Christ didn't matter, the man with no face didn't matter, the powerful forces above him didn't matter, whatever had really killed the men in that train car didn't matter. Even his wife's killers didn't matter.

All that mattered was the woman tangled in knots with him, whose beauty was enhanced by a power no one had given her, power she had seized even though it was never supposed to be hers to take. A woman who lived in the moment yet had a high regard and respect for the bigger picture of time.

They would do this in the thin spill of light from the muted television, they would do it and need never speak of it again. A dream more than a memory, which would fade, as all dreams did, with time.

It was already fading, with Luna Diaz Delgado still wrapped in his arms and the motel phone ringing, as dawn pushed the first of the sun through the flimsy drawn curtains.

"I think I found your private jet for you, Ranger Strong," greeted D. W. Tepper, "but you're gonna have to hurry."

80

Spinnaker Falls, Texas

"My father told me that story," Aidman finished. "He was the one who was involved with your father, twenty-five years ago. I've got a pretty good notion of how the story ends, but that's as much as I know for certain."

"Including how those bone boxes ended up ultimately buried in the ground fifteen miles from here in the Sonora desert. Are you suggesting your father played a role in that?"

Aidman shook his head. "If he did, he never told me."

Caitlin gazed about the chapel, trying to fill in the blanks of the story, things Aidman had left out or hadn't gotten to. All the pews were long gone—whether stolen or rotted, Caitlin couldn't say. In their place, the floor was dotted with makeshift seating formed of whatever the Mexicans squatting in the mission could salvage and covered with floral linens that, she guessed, either Wyatt Bass or Aidman himself had donated. She sat on the creaky remnants of a pew the squatters had managed to reconstruct. All the makeshift seating had been arranged to face the reconstructed, raised altar, where pristine white sheets covered coffin-size tables upon which candelabras and the tools of the blessed sacrament rested. It seemed odd that so much effort had been paid to a holy cause, given this mission's involvement in potential proof that the son of God was just a man like everybody else.

Which brought her back to Daniel Aidman's father, whom he'd clearly succeeded as an activist lawyer fighting for the undocumented. How long ago had they claimed this mission for their own? Could it be that they'd occupied it back in 1994 and had remained here, unmolested by authorities, ever since?

"I've told you everything I can," Aidman said defensively, his shoulders looking board-stiff and his expression set in a way that made it look permanently molded on his face.

"But not everything you know, sir, starting with what role, exactly, your father played back in 1994 and what role these people you're protecting have been playing ever since." The words spilled out as fast as Caitlin could form her thoughts, the realizations piling atop one another. "I don't think they remained here by accident, and I don't think this location was chosen at random. Tell me, Mr. Aidman, if I pulled your dad's bank records, would I find a whole bunch of withdrawals to support whatever cause he committed the people he was protecting to? And if I pulled yours, would I find similar evidence that you're still enlisting these people in the same cause that began in 1994?"

"I don't think you need me to answer that question, Ranger," Aidman said, sounding far away.

"As a lawyer or a man?"

He looked down, then up again. "Interesting, isn't it? Both of us following in our fathers' footsteps. Even if you don't believe in God, you have to believe in fate, Ranger."

"Many would say they're the same thing, sir."

"What about you?"

"I've learned not to dwell on such things," Caitlin told him.

But she couldn't help thinking of Colonel Guillermo Paz's many rumina-
tions on the subject. Paz believed that God was part of everything, and his
search for a relationship, at least an understanding, with Him had led him to
all manner of pursuits to prove himself worthy. Even Paz, though, acknowledged that true worthiness began with what you saw in yourself, what looked
back at you from the mirror instead of from on high.

"I told you I don't have all the details of what followed in 1994."

Aidman's words lifted Caitlin from the trance into which she'd slipped.

"My father and I," he continued, "didn't always get along, and I didn't realize how much I loved him until he passed. It was the least I could do to pick
up the cause he felt he'd been entrusted with. I don't know how much he remained in contact with Jim Strong after the crates, and bodies, were buried."

"Any idea who belongs to those four skeletons, sir?"

Aidman started to shake his head, then stopped. "I imagine they were part
of the same force behind the murder of that train crew and the theft of those
crates to begin with."

"Your father say anything else about this man with no face?"

"Never; not a word. I wish I could tell you more, but the rest of the story's
been buried in the family plot with my father for a decade now."

"What was his name?"

"Francis, but he went by Frank. It was brain cancer that got him, and those
last few days he thought it was 1994 again. He talked a lot about your father.
He didn't even know who I was at the time, but he knew Jim Strong."

Caitlin's throat grew heavy at that, and she let the sweep of her gaze take
in the chapel's reconstructed interior yet again. "Somebody had to pay for
making this place inhabitable, and defensible, again. First your father, then
you. Feel free to stop me if I'm wrong, but I think the people squatting here
are directly connected to our fathers, dating all the way back to 1994. I think
they helped Jim Strong then and, ever since, have been guardians of the ossuaries and bodies my dad must've dumped into that hole in the desert. And I'm
betting that means somebody here must've seen something on the night last
week when those bone boxes were dug out of the ground by some hired guns
working for the same force as the man with no face."

"That's quite a mouthful."

"I just want to talk to whoever was out there that night, Mr. Aidman. Since
you know me, just like your dad knew my dad, you know they've got nothing

to fear from my end. In fact, maybe there's something the Rangers can do to help them out. We do carry some weight in these parts."

"They're long gone, Ranger," Aidman said, "disappeared just like the ones who helped your father twenty-five years ago."

"Back to Mexico, no doubt," Caitlin reflected. "That explains how Luna Diaz Delgado learned those crates had been recovered from the desert. Whoever those men were, they must have done some talking when they got back home. That's how word reached her. You might as well have taken out an ad in the newspaper."

Aidman looked put off by her comment. "I've spent a good portion of my life safeguarding this secret, Ranger, as..."

Aidman's voice trailed off, Caitlin not about to let that go. "As what, Mr. Aidman?"

"As God is my witness," he said softly.

"Guess we'll see about that, won't we?"

81

SPINNAKER FALLS, TEXAS

Caitlin reached Cort Wesley just as he was landing in Atlanta with Jones. She filled him in on the additional information provided by Daniel Aidman, keeping it as brief as possible. Then she stopped off at Wyatt Bass's convenience store. She wanted to thank the man for his help, as well as prod him a bit on the story Daniel Aidman hadn't quite finished, specifically the role played through the years by the people squatting in that mission. It would be easy to pass them off as nothing more than frightened immigrants hiding out from the authorities in the middle of nowhere, but that was the problem.

Why settle here when there was no work for them anywhere close by?

Unless the source of that work was defined by the old mission and whatever had transpired there in 1994. She didn't believe for a moment they'd just happened to be watching that site in the Sonora desert the night somebody had come for the long-missing crates. Caitlin was starting to think that it was a ritual, a duty, a job in return for which the people here received housing and protection, at the bequest of Frank Aidman, first, and now of his son, Daniel. And she was hoping Wyatt Bass could shed some light on all that.

She'd never attempted a count of the cases she'd worked as a Texas Ranger, so many of them black pits lined with despair. The light of the wronged, the hurt, the killed, and the innocents they left behind had long provided the only illumination she needed. But this particular case was more like a black hole that nothing could light. The more she searched for answers, the deeper into the darkness she sank. Kind of like swimming underwater and running out of air before you can make it back to the surface.

The bells jangled again as she pushed her way through the entrance to the convenience store, assaulted instantly by the dual scents of blood and gun smoke. She saw Wyatt Bass first, his upper body resting on the countertop, his head hanging straight down, his arms splayed to the sides as if someone had crucified him on the shattered, blood-streaked glass. Shards lay on the floor, and Bass's sightless eyes were angled as if to look at them.

Caitlin spotted his killers next. The two of them were sitting side by side on the floor, posed just as the bodies in the New Braunfels alley had been, looking like they'd passed out drunk.

Except for the neat bullet holes carved into the center of their foreheads, bullet holes shaped like stars.

PART NINE

When they started talking about giving us computers, you know, I was a street officer. I didn't have any use for a computer. I didn't think a Ranger should be tied down to an office. Anyway, they issued all of us laptops and sent us to a weeklong computer school so we would know what a cursor was and where the power button was. When I got back to Laredo, I used mine as a doorstop.

—Texas Ranger Doyle Holdridge as quoted in
"Law of the Land," by Pamela Colloff, *Texas Monthly*, April 2007

82

"Right this way, gentlemen," one of the guards in the building's lobby said to Cort Wesley and Jones, leading them down a short hallway toward what looked like a service elevator.

The sprawling steel and glass headquarters of the Centers for Disease Control and Prevention was located in Druid Hills, Georgia, near the campus of Emory University. It was a relatively easy drive from the Hartsfield–Jackson Atlanta International Airport, especially when an SUV was waiting on the tarmac for the two of them after the private jet completed its taxi.

At the elevator, the guard pressed a code into a keypad. The door opened and he leaned in enough to insert a strange-looking key into a slot tailored for it and turned, activating the cab. Cort Wesley noticed there were no floors listed or bulbs to light up; nothing other than that single key slot.

"Where we're going doesn't exist, even for the vast majority of people who work in the building," Jones explained, ignoring the guard's presence as the cab sped downward

"Sounds ominous," Cort Wesley noted.

"Let me put it this way. You could destroy the world a million times over with what's stored where we're headed, where we'll find the leftovers from 1994."

"Good idea to keep that from the world."

The elevator door slid open and they spotted a man with a powder-blue lab coat and horn-rimmed glasses waiting for them in this subterranean level of the CDC.

"Just remember, this is off the books," he said, by way of greeting, leading them forward. "You were never here, and I never saw you."

"Be hard for you to see us if we were never here, Doc. We can address you as 'Doctor,' right?"

He stopped and looked back at them, focusing almost entirely on Jones. "As long as you forget you ever saw me. When the likes of you show up here, it's never good. Usually means we're about to add some new residents to the Crypt."

He used that word casually, and Cort Wesley could tell Jones knew exactly what he was referring to. After passing through four additional layers of security, they found themselves inside an atrium-style structure contained behind cinderblock-thick glass, leaving them standing beneath it all, enclosed in what was effectively a glass bubble or dome.

The Crypt.

"How much do you know about this place?" the man whom Jones had addressed as Doc asked.

"My first visit."

"Well, let me give you the short version of what you're looking at. Take a look around," Doc continued, doing just that through his thick glasses, "and picture an atmospherically preserved corpse behind each of those doors about us."

"Standing room only," Jones noted.

"They're not all occupied. I couldn't tell you how many are, even if I wanted to. Nobody touches these bodies. Everything is handled robotically to mitigate risk and eliminate the possibility of contamination."

"We're still listening, Doc," said Jones.

"I wanted to give you the opportunity to take it all in."

"We've already taken enough in back in Texas. That's why we're here."

"1994, right? The bodies originally recovered at Fort Stockton?"

Jones nodded. "Those would be the ones, on top of four new ones who've likely just arrived on the premises in the very same condition, separated by twenty-five years."

Doc turned more of his attention on Cort Wesley. "When we get a body killed by an infection we can't positively identify or even find, that body is preserved here in stasis."

"It looks like some medical version of a library," Cort Wesley said.

"With all manner of death contained in the card catalogs," Doc said. "The earliest residents of this place are actually mummies that ended up here after their sarcophagi somehow led to the deaths of the archaeologists who discovered them. We also have remains lifted from graveyards the world over, but behind most of the doors you see around you are bodies dating back over seventy years, since the time the CDC was established, in 1946."

"Talk to me about 1994," Jones said.

Doc gazed upward. "Those three bodies are somewhere up there, truly one of our most baffling unresolved cases. And the potential risk factor is off the charts—a seventeen on our own particular scale, truly rarified air."

"No pun intended," Jones smirked.

Doc didn't smile, and had the look of a man who never did. "In this case, the ranking was due primarily both to the swiftness of death and the unidentified nature of the causative factors."

"What killed them, in other words," Cort Wesley interjected.

"To this day we've never positively isolated the agent in question. We have a notion as to what it is, but it's one elusive son of a bitch."

Cort Wesley exchanged a glance with Jones, triggered by the potential ancient origins of the ossuaries in question, not to mention the bones contained in at least one of them.

"How about we fill in some blanks for you, Doc?" Jones asked. For instance, we have every reason to believe that whatever killed those men you've got tucked away here was living inside some ancient ossuaries from around the time of the Roman Empire. How does that jibe with the notion you've developed?"

"You say these ossuaries date back approximately to the time of Caesar?"

"A fair estimate," Jones said, not elaborating further.

"Then I'm afraid we have an anomaly."

"How's that, Doc?" Jones asked him.

"Let's jump ahead a bit, shall we?" He circled his gaze around the whole of the neat swirl of iron doorways that opened to all manner of death and potential to wreak true havoc on mankind. "Every one of these is occupied by a corpse who died of some element, infection, pathogen, germ, microbe, virus, or bacteria that we can't positively identify. We keep them here, frozen, in the hope that newer technological tools that don't exist yet will help us toward that end." Doc turned his gaze back upon Cort Wesley and Jones. "In the case of the three bodies from that train car in 1994, we were able to identify the cause of death but not the mutation responsible for one of the deadliest pathogens ever encountered evolving into something potentially even more dangerous."

"What pathogen is that?" Cort Wesley asked, before Jones had a chance to.

"The bubonic plague, also known as the Black Death."

83

SAN ANTONIO, TEXAS

Enrico Molinari hadn't felt this way in a very long time. Not since his last trip to Texas.

He'd sent the three men to the train car, their task simply to secure the ossuaries for transport. This after he had first killed the two men assigned to guard the boxes and then wiped out the entire train crew, dumping all seven bodies out of sight on the far side of the train.

Molinari knew something was wrong when he returned to the car to find the door still open but none of his men in evidence. He shined his flashlight inside the car and spotted all three men dead, fallen to what he genuinely believed was the curse that had protected the contents of one of the bone boxes for two thousand years. His man who'd opened that box, unable to resist the temptation, must've had second thoughts and resealed the top. Too late, though, to prevent the release of what had killed all three of his men almost instantly, which explained why the shipping crate itself was still open.

He'd hammered the top back into place with a rock and then set about loading all three crates himself. The bone boxes inside weren't as heavy or as large as he'd been expecting, enabling him to hoist them up and load them into the cargo van that had been arranged for him. He'd been expecting something the size and heft of coffins, felt somber at the thought that the sum total of a man's person could end up in a space so small, nothing but bones. Then again, the true measure, true weight, of a man lay in his soul, not in his skin.

The mission that had brought him back to Texas was about more than preserving a secret the world could never know. In a miraculous act of blessed fortune, the Lord Himself had used that very secret to deliver a weapon of His own making to the Order so that the group might be able to protect His word and vanquish the enemies who would besmirch His kingdom. In that respect, this was an even holier mission, putting within reach the means to eradicate those who would challenge, refute, or blaspheme the word of God. A means lifted from a simple limestone bone box, which could secure the Order's holy mission for time eternal.

At night, in his dreams, he often saw himself lugging the box thought to contain the bones of the son of God from the train car into the back of the cargo van. In the dream, lightning struck him on the way and God appeared to Molinari as he had come to Moses. A strong but gentle hand laid on his shoulder made Molinari feel as if he were literally melting, dissolving back into the ether from which he'd come, until he heard the voice speak.

"My son."

The apparition's mouth didn't move as he spoke those simple words. Molinari lived every day of his life hoping to lift that feeling from dream to reality, hoping that if he delivered His gift unto the Order, God would come to Molinari to thank him for his service to a higher calling.

God had taken his face to prepare him for what was coming, a great final epic battle that would end with him having the limestone box in his grasp once more. In his dreams, having no face mattered not at all, as would be the case in the new reality he was helping to forge. There were times when Molinari even let himself fantasize that God would restore his face in return. That which He'd taken to serve one purpose restored so that Molinari might better serve another. During his first trip here, Molinari had removed all the mirrors from the motel room's walls because he did not need a mirror to see inside, to see himself as God saw him.

Which was the great overriding point.

"Have you located the ossuaries?" Molinari heard the American leader of the Order ask through the phone at his ear, even though he had no memory of grasping or dialing it.

"No," Molinari replied, "but I know how to find them now. The Lord has shown me the way."

84

"You can see the source of the anomaly I mentioned," Doc continued. "The Black Death ravaged Europe between 1346 and 1353, not during the time of Christ. It killed over fifty million people, which, at the time, was sixty percent of Europe's whole population. If a mutated form of it, that could kill its victims literally within seconds, struck the world today, the death toll would be somewhere between four and five billion."

Cort Wesley and Jones exchanged a glance, trying to figure out how this fit with what they'd assumed from Dylan's translation.

"Maybe your son was wrong, cowboy," Jones said, as if Doc weren't even there. "He is a fuckup, after all."

"Keep talking, Jones, and it won't be the Black Death that puts you in one of those steel chambers up there behind all that glass."

"Ahem," Doc said. "If you want to take this outside, go right ahead. Otherwise, you might be interested in what else I have to say."

"You said you were jumping ahead a bit," Jones noted.

"And now let's jump back a bit. It's the prevailing opinion of CDC scientists who work on this level that all seven bodies, both the four from today and the three back in 1994, died of a mutated form of the Black Death. Now, based on the information you've provided, identifying the source of their deaths as the contents of one or more ossuaries, we can assume with a reasonable degree of certainty that the bones in question belonged to one or more victims of the Black Plague. That places the time line squarely in the fourteenth century, not the time of Caesar."

"You said 'mutated form,'" said Cort Wesley. "What's that mean, exactly?"

Doc nodded, squarely in his element now, almost seeming to enjoy himself. "The Black Death was an epidemic of the bubonic plague caused by a bacterium called *Yersinia pestis*, common to wild rats."

"Is there another kind?" Jones smirked.

Doc ignored his question. "When wild rats collect in the kind of numbers and concentrations they did back in that age, they're a breeding ground for all manner of diseases dangerous to man. The bubonic plague was more or less typical in that regard, except for the close proximity of the dwellings of these rodents to the homes of the soon to be infected. Black rats, where the disease originated and incubated, are generally scavengers, meaning that, unlike other rat species, they build their nests as close to people as they can."

"A recipe for disaster, in other words," Jones noted.

"Especially since it likely took all of ten days to two weeks before all the infected rats would be dead. Do you have any idea how many humans they could spread the disease to in that time?"

"You already told us how many it ended up killing," Cort Wesley said.

"Once infected," Doc continued, "the infection in humans typically took three to five days to incubate and another three to five days to kill."

"As opposed to less than a minute," Jones reminded, "which is what we're facing today."

"Because of that mutation I noted earlier. The vast majority of plague victims were burned. But noblemen who perished to the pestilence, especially in the early stages, were given traditional burials, their bodies left to rot in the ground of a cemetery or within an aboveground tomb. More likely the latter."

"Why do you say that?" Cort Wesley asked this time.

"Because, based on what you're telling me, somebody stole the bones from some medieval mausoleum and placed them in this ossuary you've mistakenly identified as coming from the time of Caesar. What you've uncovered is a fabrication, a hoax, which would likely become abundantly clear if these ossuaries were given a closer examination."

"Except all we have are pictures of one, and not very good ones at that," Jones said.

"Get back to how the Black Death mutated into something even worse," said Cort Wesley.

"Okay," Doc resumed, "the bones of the plague victim get placed in this ossuary to create some kind of sham. Maybe over the years that ossuary ends up tucked away in some cave, likely in Israel, where the majority of them have been recovered. A cave would feature the ideal conditions for the disease that has been lying dormant in those bones to regenerate itself."

"Is that even possible?"

"From a scientific standpoint, I would have said no, until now. That said, we seem to be facing something we've never encountered before."

"Another anomaly," Cort Wesley noted, starting to hate the word.

"And how could this anomaly have occurred?" Jones asked.

"Theoretically?"

"Any way you want to describe it, Doc."

"You're not talking about an anomaly so much as a metamorphosis. The conditions in that cave brought strains of the bubonic plague that had settled in the bones of the interred victim back to life, and then those strains fed off the fetid air, heat, and humidity—conditions ideal to grow mold spores. And, in fact, what we could be looking at here is actually a spore bred of the bacterial chain we call the Black Death. In other words, the disease was dormant within those bones of this particular plague victim until the environmental conditions of that cave, or possibly crypt, brought it back to life as something different and far, far more dangerous, as difficult as that is to believe. An ultra-potent bacterial neurotoxin, derived directly from the pneumonic stage of the Black Death, that kills by short-circuiting the respiratory system.

"And that's not totally unprecedented at all, really," Doc continued. "There's valley fever—quite common among archaeologists, by the way—which takes the form of a fungus within soil but becomes dangerous only after environmental conditions, especially rain, transform it into a spore."

"But can a bacteria like the one responsible for the bubonic plague," Cort Wesley started, "transform into a spore, too, the way a fungus can?"

Doc grinned from ear to ear, as if, like a classroom teacher, that was exactly the question he was hoping for. "Some bacteria, perhaps the Black Death among them, can form spores when it finds itself in a hostile environment. The bacterium, through a process called sporulation, replicates its genetic material and then surrounds it with a thick coating. In spore form, the bacterium's water is released and metabolism ceases. It can survive temperature extremes, radiation, and lack of air, water, and nutrients for extended periods of time, to be revived when nutrients are abundant again. You see, gentlemen," he said, as if coming to the end of his lecture, "a spore's virtual indestructibility renders it the ideal biological weapons agent."

Jones and Cort Wesley looked at each other.

"Nature," Doc continued, before either one of them could say a word, "is the ultimate threat to mankind. What you're describing could never have originated in a lab." He seemed to be talking more to himself now. "Remember, in its advanced and most virulent pneumonic stage, the Black Death laid waste to the lungs, so it makes perfect sense, theoretically, that it would attack the respiratory system in its infinitely more dangerous form."

"Only seven victims, though," Jones pointed out. "Three in 1994 and four more today. That doesn't sound like the Black Death to me."

"Because a spore spreads differently than a bacteria. It's not an infection that can move from person to person. It comes with no assembly required, with this cell or that, inside the body, and in this case it kills with what we can only conclude is a one hundred percent mortality rate."

"So if somebody opened the ossuary in question and got exposed to what was inside…"

"That thirty- or forty-second clock, according to the investigative reports, would start ticking." Doc pointed at the rows of corpse storage on the levels circling above them. "I already mentioned that spores make the ideal biological warfare agents. That's because, if placed in an explosive device and detonated, they could potentially be as effective a weapon of mass destruction as a nuclear bomb. Maybe even more so, given that you wouldn't have to worry about the lingering effects of radiation or the impact of physical destruction. It would kill only those who breathed in the released spores, and once its victims were dead, the spores would be trapped inside them."

"In short," said Cort Wesley, "you're talking about the perfect weapon."

"Oh," Doc nodded, "to say the least."

85

SPINNAKER FALLS, TEXAS

"El Barquero must've walked in on these boys after they clipped the owner," D. W. Tepper said, leaning over the bodies with stars drilled into the center of their foreheads.

"His name was Wyatt Bass, no relation to Sam."

Tepper stood all the way back up and checked the area where the local medical examiner was still examining Bass's body, splayed over the counter glass. "You wanna tell me what you got out of him?"

"You already know about the remnants of that credit card receipt."

"But that's not what you came to discuss with the late Mr. Bass, though, is it?"

"You're always seeing conspiracies with me."

"Because most of the time they're there. And it's obvious something had brought you back here, before you made that call about finding three more bodies to add to your ever-growing collection." Tepper glanced down at the corpses propped up near his feet. "Something else is obvious, too: These two boys came gunning for you."

"So now you're using your sixth sense à la Guillermo Paz?"

"And tomorrow I'll wake up to find I'm seven feet tall." He mopped his brow. "The way it plays from my end is that Bass told you something that sent you someplace else, and you were making a stop to see him again from wherever that was. The shooters showed up in the meantime, likely killed him when he refused to say where you were at. Do I have that about right, Ranger?"

Caitlin turned toward Wyatt Bass's corpse so Tepper wouldn't see the affirmation of his conclusions in her gaze. She tried to make her expression as empty as possible when she looked back at him.

"Whoever's behind these shooters must've been behind the ones we found in that New Braunfels alley across from Bane Sturgess, too, Captain," she said, eager to change the subject.

Tepper scratched at his scalp, showering the air with dandruff and flecks of hardened Brylcreem. "You wanna tell me how it is you've inherited a protector who isn't seven feet tall, why it is that the legendary Ferryman himself keeps coming to your rescue?"

"Luna Diaz Delgado would be my guess, given that we're on the same side now."

Something in her words made Tepper swallow hard, his gaze turning evasive. "That's what your dad thought, too."

"Did he prove to be wrong on that front? Maybe you should come clean to me about her ossuaries ending up buried in the desert."

"I already told you—"

"That Jim Strong kept you out of the loop. I remember. Except we both know that was a lie, since he called you about helping him track the man with no face to a private airport. I know you've got your reasons, and I'm sure they're damn good, but that doesn't change the fact that you know what happened from the night my dad and the Red Widow spent together at that motel, and I'd appreciate it if you didn't lie to me about it again."

"Likewise," Tepper said tersely.

"When did I lie to you?"

"A lie of omission, not telling me where it was you went after your conversation with the late Mr. Bass and what you found when you got there."

"This confession time, D.W.?"

"Only if you go first."

"Later."

"Sounds fine to me. But there's things I'll tell you that can't be untold, Ranger."

"When?"

Tepper fanned the air with his Stetson, as if to brush away the dandruff and Brylcreem. "Jeez, Caitlin, can't you take yes for an answer?"

86

ATLANTA, GEORGIA

"Hope you brought a credit card," Jones told Cort Wesley when they emerged from the CDC, "because our return flight home's been canceled."

"How's that?"

"Comes with the fact that I've been canceled, too. I told you, free rein to do anything I wanted so long as I didn't fuck up. What happened in Dallas, at Communications Technology Providers, proved to be that fuckup."

"You knew what you were after when you hired CTP to find it, didn't you?"

"You give me too much credit, cowboy. I had an inkling, sure, as soon as I came across manually typed reports that nobody had read for years. But I had no clue, no conception, not even the shadow of a notion that I was after a mutated version of the Black Death that comes complete with a one hundred percent mortality rate. I'm not easy to scare when it comes to new methods of taking out our enemies in a big way, only this shit gives victory a bad name. I should've known to stay away when the Strong name came up."

"As in Caitlin's father."

"My career's as dead as him," Jones said, the words sounding like he had to push them past the icicles forming in his mouth. "You can take the car back to the airport. Hope you find a nonstop flight for your trouble."

"After what we just learned, you're dropping this, Jones?"

"You're not listening to me. I'm not dropping this; I got dropped. Big bad Washington dropped me. They only recognize two things: assets and liabilities. You get carte blanche to operate as an asset, and you don't exist anymore as a liability."

"What happens to you now?"

"I survive and live to fight another day. Memories are short in Washington. It's the city of goldfish, where the world begins again every thirty seconds."

"About the same time it would take to kill the whole world, if this stuff ever gets loose, Jones."

Cort Wesley was in the terminal, waiting for his flight to be called, when his phone buzzed with a call from Dylan.

"How's the girlfriend?"

"Oh, man, I think she might be the one."

"Listen, son—"

"Give it a rest, Dad. I'm kidding. Selina's off in Los Angeles pushing painkillers or something."

"Certain to return sometime soon?"

"She's got my number."

"And you've got hers."

"I texted her last night. No response."

"What's that mean in millennial etiquette?"

"Am I a millennial?"

"Assume so for now."

"I think she's blowing me off, Dad. I feel used."

"Is that you kidding again?"

"Only a little, actually."

"Let me tell you something I've learned the hard way. When you feel used, it's often because you were using somebody else, too."

"Depends on your perspective. Do you think Caitlin liked her?"

"Hard to tell, son. But I've seen Caitlin watch people like that before— most of them she'd either made as suspects or were about to draw down on her."

"Where does Selina fit into that picture?"

"I don't know," Cort Wesley said. "Probably nowhere. She was probably just being protective. You know Caitlin."

"I wonder what they talked about in the ladies' room."

"Really?"

"No."

"Selina ever return your jeans?"

"The ones you like so much? No."

"Good. You call me with more news on that bone box?"

"I found some . . . anomalies. You know what that word means?"

"How about a father who's got an asshole for a son?" Cort Wesley retorted, thinking back to how Doc had used that same word up in the CDC's Crypt.

"I'll take that as a yes. Anyway, I compared that inscription I translated to others from the period and found a few things that don't add up."

"Like what?"

"You know what a patina is?" Dylan asked.

"No."

"It's the residue that collects on the surface of an ossuary, kind of like moss, only not moss."

"Okay," said Cort Wesley.

"I think the box itself is authentic, dating back all of those couple thousand years. The problem is the Aramaic description I translated. When I enlarged and enhanced the pictures, it was clear the patina inside the letters of the inscription is completely different than on the structure of the ossuary itself."

"So you're telling me the box was made two thousand years ago but the inscription wasn't."

"Even from the pictures, you can tell it's off by a bunch. A thousand years or more."

Cort Wesley tried to make sense of that. "All this for something a college kid can tell was a fake from *pictures*?"

"Thanks for the vote of confidence, Dad, and you're missing the point."

"Which point is that?"

"When was the ossuary uncovered, originally?"

Cort Wesley tried to remember what Caitlin had told him. "Stolen from a Jerusalem cave and brought to Turkey in 1959, I think."

"They may not have noticed the difference in patinas that long ago, or maybe they didn't care. Beyond that, there's plenty of scholars who'd say what I just told you was bullshit, that patinas age differently in the body of the box as opposed to the lettering. Something to do with variances in structural integrity, from what I was able to learn."

Cort Wesley hesitated. "Is there any way somebody could have traced the trail of this learning you did, find you through what you dug up?"

"I was doing Google searches, Dad, not hacking government websites."

"Good thing, because whatever's going on here is heating up in a hurry. Maybe you should go join your brother in Europe."

"He's coming back Saturday, day before I leave."

"Then be careful."

"Just don't send Paz. I can take care of myself. I don't need him watching my back."

"Believe me," Cort Wesley told his oldest son, thinking of what he'd learned at the CDC, "you need him."

87

ATLANTA, GEORGIA

"Can we get on with this?" Dylan asked him. "I was all excited. Did I ever tell you what a buzzkill you are?"

"It's kind of a father's job. So, what did you find?" Cort Wesley continued. "And please don't use the word 'anomaly.'"

"You need to pay attention and stop me if I lose you."

"You haven't lost me yet, son."

"Good, because I found something else, another *anomaly*," Dylan said, stretching the word out, "starting with the fact that whoever carved this inscription into that ossuary was as meticulous as they could be, which wasn't meticulous enough. If these bones really did belong to Jesus, the inscription would've been written strictly in Aramaic. But this, as it turns out, is classical Syriac."

Dylan had barely gotten started and Cort Wesley found himself already confused. "I thought the language was Aramaic."

"It is. Classical Syriac isn't a language, it's a dialect—the most popular Aramaic dialect not during Jesus' time but between roughly the fifth and eighth centuries. Issues with the syntax, punctuation, and lettering suggest this inscription was done by someone trying to imitate what he thought was the Aramaic of Jesus' era, but he ended up using characters that didn't exist until the fifth century at the earliest."

"Anomalies," Cort Wesley made himself repeat.

"The prefixes or curve of the letters don't match the language of the time. I could go into more detail but you'd be bored as hell and would need to be in front of a computer to follow the distinctions."

"I never heard you talk like this before, son. Always had your brother pegged as the smart one."

"I got pretty good grades at Brown, you know."

"For some reason, that didn't register with me. But I'll tell you what does register: you saying that the inscription on that ossuary is a forgery, which means it doesn't contain the bones of Christ, after all."

"That would be my conclusion, Dad, also because, under further review, the lines aren't totally straight and the angles of the letters don't match up. Could be whoever was behind this found a truly ancient ossuary and altered the existing inscription just enough to create the hoax. Way back then, they'd have no reason to suspect anyone would ever notice. Never could imagine the kind of technology we use today—or, really, any technology at all."

"You said between the fifth and eighth centuries," Cort Wesley noted. "Is it possible the bones actually came from much later? Say, the late fourteenth century?" he added casually, not wanting to be more specific or mention the bubonic plague.

"Of course, maybe even more likely, given that it better explains how the forger could have employed the wrong dialect of Aramaic. Fourteen hundred years removed, back in those days, how the hell could he have known? That time line would also explain the subtle differences in the patina, something else that wouldn't have been a consideration for a forger in the fourteenth century. But it makes perfect sense from a historical perspective, too."

"How's that?" Cort Wesley asked, still not believing this was Dylan he was talking to.

"Well," the boy said, "there was a thing called the Western Schism that went on from the late fourteenth century through the early fifteenth. I'll spare you the details, but it was basically an internal war in the Church that led to there being two popes at the same time. It isn't too much of a stretch to figure that one of the sides came up with this plan as a way of using the bones of Christ as leverage to serve their cause. We'll never know what happened from that point, but it's pretty clear the forged bone box went missing for a long time before somebody got their hands on it again."

Cort Wesley was left shaking his head, still amazed by the product of his son's efforts, how he'd managed to fit all the pieces together, this Western Schism happening at roughly the same time the Black Death was running rampant. "I am damn impressed, son. Thank you."

"Glad to be of service, Dad. Gotta go, the doorbell's ringing."

"Tell Paz I said hello," Cort Wesley finished, looking up to see Leroy Epps seated next to him.

"Believe we could both use a root beer right now, bubba."

• • •

Cort Wesley kept the phone at his ear so nobody would notice him talking to somebody who wasn't there. "I couldn't find one before, and our flight's about to board."

"*Our flight,*" Leroy repeated, flashing a toothy grin. "*Don't want to burst your bubble or anything, but I don't require an airplane to get me somewhere I want to be. Meanwhile, you're in one hell of a pickle this time.*"

"Never thought I'd miss Jones, champ."

"*Man makes his bed, so he can sleep in it. When he falls out, that's on him, too.*"

"We could've used his help on this, big-time, though."

"*He might still show.*"

"Not in time for it to matter, the way things are headed," Cort Wesley said, as much to himself as to the ghost. "A little direction here would be appreciated."

"*As it pertains to the road ahead, is what you're referring to.*"

Cort Wesley nodded.

"*Road ahead is a pickle too, bubba.*"

"That's the best you can do?"

"*We all have our limits,*" Leroy told him. "*Where I be now just imposes different ones. I've seen enough of the future in my time here to know it ain't set, not nearly at all. You see what's coming, but you can't be sure until it gets here.*"

"What's coming? Can you tell me that much?"

The ghost shrugged his narrow, bony shoulders. "*Can't tell you much more than you already know, aside from this: End's coming, one way or another.*"

"Thanks for the help, champ," Cort Wesley chided.

"*Your arm seems better,*" Leroy said, looking at it.

"Not enough. You heard what that walk-in clinic doctor said, that it might never come back all the way."

"*Just as likely that it will.*"

"Until the next one, champ. Can't you just heal me or something?"

"*I believe you have me confused for God. But I do have a question for you, too, bubba: What's an anom-a-ly?*"

Cort Wesley's phone rang and he saw it was Caitlin, finally calling him back, as he moved to take his place in the proper boarding line.

"It's bad, isn't it?" she said, hearing his voice crack when he answered.

"No, Ranger, it's worse."

88

It wasn't Colonel Guillermo Paz at the door at all.

"I didn't expect you back so soon," Dylan said, as Selina Escolante brushed past him through the door.

"Los Angeles sucked. I might as well have been valeting cars at the restaurants I picked up all the tabs at." She yanked off a thin, biker-style leather jacket. "What have you got to drink here? I need something hard."

"What's your poison?"

"The Rémy that costs two hundred and fifty bucks per glass, but I'd settle for bourbon."

"Maker's or Jack?"

Selina nodded, impressed. "Not such a little boy after all, are you?"

Dylan smirked. "Whoever said I was little?"

He went to fetch both bottles and met Selina in the kitchen, where she'd filled three-quarters of a tall glass with crushed ice from the refrigerator's dispenser.

"Got any mint leaves?"

"This isn't a bar."

"Don't feel bad, boy. Most of them don't have mint leaves, either."

"I wasn't feeling bad," Dylan said, handing Selina both of the bourbon bottles.

She chose the Maker's Mark and poured it over the ice, which crackled and shrank up under the spill. The glass was full by the time she finished, with the crushed ice reaching all the way to the top.

"Want to join me?" she asked Dylan, sounding a bit guilty about the oversight. "I could grab another glass."

"No, thanks. I'm working on something."

Selina sipped at her drink, the ice sloshing up against her lips. "You don't go back to school until next week."

"This isn't for school. It's that thing for my dad."

Selina frowned. "Based on what you've told me about your dad's 'work,' I don't see how you fit into the picture."

Dylan rolled his eyes. "Thanks. A lot."

"I meant it as a compliment, boy."

"Well, it didn't come out that way. And I guess I forgot to tell you I'm majoring in archaeology at Brown, which includes knowing my way around ancient languages."

"You mean the kind nobody ever speaks? Hey, you really are smarter than you look. And me thinking you were just a pretty face."

He drew closer to her. "Have you looked in the mirror lately?"

She laid her drink down and grabbed him around the waist, hands dipping lower through his jeans. "I forgot to bring your jeans back."

"Don't bother."

"Then how I could see you in them?"

"They look better on you anyway, believe me," Dylan said, feeling a dam break inside him as she pressed tighter against him.

"Won't know that until we do a comparison test, like a double-blind clinical trial."

"With jeans?"

Selina reached back with a single hand, flailing about the counter for her drink. "I'm game if you are."

"Game for what?"

"Can't find out if you don't play," she said, cupping her hands around his neck and easing him closer.

Dylan could hear the clink of the crushed ice shifting about, felt the glass's coldness against the back of his neck. "Do you even have another gear?"

Selina eased away from him and sipped at her drink. "Why don't you let me make you one of these and we'll find out?"

89

MARBLE FALLS, TEXAS

Caitlin was standing in the driveway, shrouded by the floating mist and feeling the flutter of drizzle against her clothes and hair, when the headlights poured down the dead end on which D. W. Tepper had lived for as long as she'd known him. She recognized the truck as his because one of the headlight fixtures was cracked and sliced through the darkness in the shape of a spiderweb on that side.

She stepped to the side to make room for the truck, catching Tepper's in-
credulous expression in the spill of the floodlight mounted over the garage
that he'd converted into an apartment for one of his grown kids. He stepped
out of the truck, not seeming to notice the mist or the drizzle any more than
Caitlin did.

"Why do I think this isn't a social call?"

The log house was simple but sprawling, thanks to a number of additions to
make room for his ever-expanding family. The detached garage was off to the
side, a world unto itself, and the additions made the log home look absurdly
pumped up, like a weight lifter on steroids.

Caitlin took a deep breath, hearing raindrops patter against her jacket. "You
notice that old Spanish mission out a ways from Wyatt Bass's convenience
store?"

"I caught a glimpse of it, along with the stench drifting from that oil
fire."

"It's a gas fire, D.W."

"Whatever. You were saying?"

"The late Mr. Bass steered me to it. Turns out a whole bunch of undocumented people are squatting there, same as they were in 1994. But you know
that already, don't you? You got pissed at me for not telling you something
this afternoon I believe you already knew."

Tepper didn't say anything one way or another. Caitlin waited him out,
determined to get a response.

"I hate you sometimes, Ranger," he relented finally. "I ever tell you that
before?"

"Nope. This is the first time."

"Then I guess I never told you why: on account of you remind me so much
of your damn father. And when I hate you it's because I miss him."

"You miss him now?"

"More than ever."

"Me too, Captain."

Tepper hitched up his jacket. "Let's go inside."

"Out here's just fine."

He looked up at the night sky. "It's raining."

"I met a man at the mission named Daniel Aidman, a lawyer just like the
father who preceded him, fighting the never-ending battle for migrants in
these parts. He told me about my dad showing up there, but not what followed.
He told me those people have been watching over that site in the desert ever

since the night my dad shot four men and buried them, along with the shipping crates containing those ossuaries. It's kind of a mission for them, and it explains what they were doing in Sonora the night the remains of those four men got pulled out of the ground. And they must've been there when the now dead principals of Bane Sturgess showed up a while before that, lugging a backhoe."

Tepper tightened his coat. "Anything else you want to tell me before I catch my death out here?"

"No, it's your turn. Your turn to tell me the rest of the story, starting with the night my dad spent with Luna Diaz Delgado in that motel room."

90

San Antonio, Texas; 1994

"I think I found your private jet for you, Ranger Strong," greeted D. W. Tepper, "but you're gonna have to hurry."

Jim Strong eased the receiver softly back onto its cradle, not wanting to disturb Luna Diaz Delgado, who was still sleeping. He leaned over from his seated position on the side of the bed and stroked her long black hair, trying to remember a time in the past decade when he'd been this happy. A few drunken escapades stood out, before he gave up the bottle cold turkey, along with watching Caitlin win a pistol-shooting contest as the youngest entry and only girl in the competition.

"You have to go, Tejano?" the Red Widow said, without opening her eyes.

Jim continued to stroke her hair. "*We* have to go."

"Can we pretend the phone didn't ring? Can we stay here a little longer? I don't want this to end."

"Everything ends. And we've got to go. That call came from a fellow Ranger with the information I asked him to dig up. Turns out there's a private jet leaving from Stinson Municipal Airport in two hours, according to the flight plan the pilot filed. We need to get a move on."

Luna opened her eyes and sat up. "Why that airport, that flight?"

"Because the flight's bound for Rome."

"You think this man with no face will be on board," she surmised. "You think he'll have the ossuaries with him."

She flung the sheet off her, and Jim Strong turned so as not to see her naked, to give her a measure of privacy while she dressed.

"That's not necessary. You saw everything there is to see last night...Jim."

He almost melted at Luna calling him that for the first time. She was the most beautiful woman he'd ever seen in his life, which made him feel guilty, because that included his late wife.

"It was dark, señora. And I had other things on my mind."

She came around the bed to where he couldn't avoid the sight of her, tucking her blouse into a pair of slacks they'd purchased at Costco the previous day. "You feel that guilty over sleeping with a criminal?"

"Not over what I did," Jim confessed, "but how good it felt."

Stinson Municipal was located seven miles south of downtown San Antonio and featured three runways, one of which was long enough to accommodate smaller Learjets and Gulfstreams, in addition to a grass runway for piston- and prop-based general aviation activities. The U-shaped terminal building was finished in mosaic stone and, from a distance, looked like a small prison, thanks in part to the control tower, which could easily have passed for a guard tower.

D. W. Tepper met them in his wife's tiny sedan, on a rise overlooking the airport, which Jim Strong was currently eyeballing through a pair of binoculars.

"I've got a fix on the jet in question, with a match to the tail designation you provided, D.W.," Jim said, handing the binoculars to Tepper. "But no sign of this man with no face or those shipping crates yet."

"Could be he's in the hangar or the waiting area inside that terminal building."

"A man who hates mirrors that much wouldn't be in the terminal building, where eyes could fix his way and linger."

"Okay, the hangar then."

"Let's get a move on."

Luna Diaz Delgado took a seat in the back of the truck that Jim Strong had borrowed from D. W. Tepper, the two men up front growing grimmer and more determined the closer they drew to the hangar. They'd ridden into gunfights before, in trucks instead of on horseback, and the feeling of trepidation, anxiety, and nervous energy was always the same.

"Rome," Tepper said, repeating the information he'd provided to Jim earlier that morning. "You're thinking it must be the Church, the goddamn Vatican, who sent all these gunmen this way, on account of what's inside those crates."

"There won't be much of a Church left if the bones of Jesus Christ really have been found. Are you really surprised they're pulling out all the stops?"

"They got more gunmen in town than extras in an old Western movie," Tepper noted. "But that Lear's only a six-passenger."

"My thoughts exactly. Gives us a shot to pull this thing off."

"There's no way they're just going to hand those crates over without a fight," Tepper said, as Jim pulled into the complex and parked well out of view of the mounted security cameras, "especially the head honcho, whose favorite holiday must be Halloween."

"I know."

"You wanna share your plan with me?"

"Be glad to, if I had one, Ranger Tepper."

Tepper seemed to sniff the air. "You hear that, Ranger Strong?"

"Hear what?"

"Sounds to me like that Learjet just fired up its engine. I'd drive straight onto the tarmac, if I were you."

And that's exactly what Jim did, easing Tepper's pickup behind the cover of the hangar adjacent to the tarmac. This after a flash of their badges led the guard to manually slide the gate open. He looked genuinely excited by the presence of two Texas Rangers on the premises, following them with adulation as Jim steered the truck for the hangar.

From the side of the hangar, they watched a massive figure emerge, wearing a floppy farmer's hat to keep the sun from his face and wheeling a luggage cart piled high with three shipping crates that matched the size of the ones that had once resided inside a freight train car in Fort Stockton.

"Holy shit," Tepper mumbled.

"The crates or the man?"

"How about both?"

Jim cocked his gaze back toward the truck to make sure Luna was heeding his orders to stay put. So far, so good.

"What now?" Tepper asked him.

Jim said nothing while the big man watched four hulking subordinates hoist the crates off the luggage cart and into the Learjet's cramped cargo hold. The hatch had barely closed on their bulk when the four strapping figures followed the one who nonetheless dwarfed them up the stairs and onto the plane.

Jim chose that moment to finally respond to Tepper's question. "Let's go."

He drove Tepper's truck right up to the Learjet, the move so innocuous and casual that nobody in sight paid them any heed. Anyone watching would think it was just more passengers about to board, Jim having parked at an angle that took advantage of the passengers' and cockpit's blind spot.

The cargo hatch had been closed but not locked. The engines were continuing to fire up while the pilots went through their preflight checks. Jim hoisted the cargo hatch open, Tepper ready at that point to help him hoist each of the shipping crates from the hold. They'd loaded two and were just lifting the third out when the Learjet's door opened and two of the big figures they'd glimpsed earlier leaned out, pistols flashing in their hands. No way Jim and D. W. Tepper could drop the crate and get their own guns out in time for it to matter.

An instant before the gunmen's first shots rang out, though, a blistering roar split the air and a divot the size of a softball appeared in the Learjet's suddenly pockmarked skin, just to the right of the open cabin door. Luna Diaz Delgado's second shot with Tepper's twelve-gauge carved a similar divot over the opening, but her next two were dead-on with the opening, chasing the hulking gunmen back inside and buying the Rangers the time they needed.

"Hurry!" she yelled, pulling herself up behind the wheel.

Jim Strong and D. W. Tepper lugged the final crate into the pickup's bed and joined her in the cab, the Red Widow tearing off before they even got the doors closed, an instant ahead of the back window exploding.

"Shit!" Tepper exclaimed.

"You running a damage report in your head, Ranger Tepper?"

They both had their pistols out, firing through the jagged gap where the rear window used to be.

"I'm sending you the goddamn bill, Ranger Strong!"

Luna crashed through a gate, much to Tepper's consternation, to reclaim the road. No pursuit was evident, at least for the first mile. They pulled over long enough for Jim Strong to take over behind the wheel.

"I hope you got a plan," Tepper said from the backseat, with Luna looking over her shoulder from the passenger seat.

"As a matter of fact," Jim Strong said, "I do."

• • •

That plan started with Jim Strong pulling over, a few miles down the road, once he was satisfied they weren't being followed. Tepper and Luna Diaz Delgado piled out of the truck in his wake.

"What gives, Ranger Strong?"

Jim glanced toward the Red Widow. "Make sure she stays safe, and get her back home, Ranger Tepper."

"Say that again?"

But Jim's attention remained fixed on Luna.

"Those crates belong to me, Tejano."

"And I'll get them back to you in short order. But you won't be able to stick the truth about the Almighty in people's faces, give the Church what you think it's got coming, if you're dead. Beyond that, you've got kids who already lost their father and can't afford to lose their mother too. We square on that much?"

She stiffened. "Running's never been my style."

"You're not the one running. I am. The man with no face will be coming, and I'm gonna find a place to have it out with him and whoever tags along for the ride."

"But—" Luna started.

That was as far as she got, when Jim kissed her hard on the lips.

"I owe you this much, señora," he said, holding her at arm's length. "For last night, for making me feel like a man again."

Luna swallowed hard, the rare vulnerability that flashed in her eyes putting her at a loss for words. "And to you," she said finally, "for making me feel like a woman."

Jim Strong reached up to his neck and unclasped a thin chain from which dangled a locket he'd given his wife and hadn't taken off since the day of her murder. He eased it gingerly into his grasp and handed it to the Red Widow.

"This is for you, for safekeeping until we get back together."

Delgado nodded, her expression one of resignation as if she knew that day would never come.

They left it there. No embrace, hug, last kiss—nothing. Just a tall, lanky man with focused but weary eyes, climbing up behind the wheel of the pickup and tipping his hat Luna's way, as she squeezed his wife's locket tight in her grasp. He met D. W. Tepper's stare one last time, more passing between them than any words could hold.

Of course, Jim Strong had no intention of ever delivering those shipping crates to the Red Widow, not with those three bodies he'd found in the freight car still at the forefront of his mind. It hadn't been a curse that killed them, and that was enough to tell him God did indeed work in mysterious, and often deadly, ways. Religious thoughts aside, there was something inside one of those crates that had killed three men in seconds, and there was no way Jim could risk that falling into the wrong hands.

So, after dropping D. W. Tepper and Luna Diaz Delgado off, he headed west, clinging to the less traveled roads. Jim had no firm plan in mind at that point, other than the knowledge that the desert held a lot of secrets beneath its sandy soil. There was a shovel in the truck's bed and, absent finding another suitable resting place for the three crates, he'd dig a hole as deep as he could, someplace their contents would never again see the light of day.

He drove with the intention of burying the crates in the first wasteland he came to, ending up on the road to the desert around Sonora, which fit the bill perfectly. He drove along old Route 190 and was just passing a convenience store and diner rest stop with no customers when he caught the sounds of a helicopter soaring overhead.

He'd noted several of them back at Stinson Airport, and he cursed himself for not anticipating that the man with no face might commandeer one to come after him. And he'd made that task all the easier by driving out here on a road where he was the only vehicle.

Should've given the truck to Tepper. Should've thought of another way to stash the crates.

Well, too late now, Jim thought, as twin sprays of automatic fire clanged against the truck, the windshield shattering under the dual burst and almost costing him control of the wheel.

Jim righted the truck as best he could and tried to speed on. But the hood was bleeding smoke from a shot-up radiator, and he felt the pop of a tire going out, which left him riding on the other three and one rim.

Sorry, D.W.

The rest stop could offer him no respite or cover from which to fight back.

His gaze swam about the horizon, locking on an old Spanish mission that looked ready to crumble into the desert, and he twisted the pickup that way.

The truck thumped and bumped across the rocky, gravel-strewn terrain, a front tire joining the rear one, blowing out under another fusillade from inside the chopper circling overhead. The abandoned mission's gate was cracked open and Jim slammed through it with the last the truck would give him, spinning to a grinding halt that coughed dust plumes into the air and almost obscured the audience that had gathered.

Because the mission wasn't abandoned at all.

He ended up right next to an old oil tanker that looked World War II vintage, a relic more grown out of the desert than parked atop it.

"You folks need to get out of here!" Jim ordered, dropping out of the truck and already slamming fresh rounds into the twelve-gauge Luna Diaz Delgado had used back at Stinson.

Then he repeated the words in Spanish to make sure his instruction was heard.

None of them moved. Undocumented, for sure, Jim thought, squatting here in this old mission that was as close to a home as they had.

As Jim was scrabbling for a ladder that led to the high ground offered by the mission wall, he saw the chopper drop into a descent that whipped the desert grounds into a tornado-like funnel cloud. He pictured it settling down on the desert floor, as he climbed the rungs with one hand and clutched the twelve-gauge with the other. Then he felt the ladder wobble. Someone else was joining him on the climb.

"Who the hell are you?" Jim asked, twisting to look at the man.

"Frank Aidman."

"Well, Frank Aidman, get your ass down and as far away from here as you can!"

"These are my people, Ranger. I'm responsible for them."

"Then get them as far away as you can, too!"

"How can we help?" Frank Aidman asked, determined grit stretched over his otherwise smooth complexion.

An office type, Jim figured. A man who worked with pencils instead of guns.

"It's my fight," he told Aidman, trying to sound firm. "Get lost."

But Aidman joined him at the wall a few seconds after Jim reached the ledge. The five figures he recognized from the airport were heading through the dust storm still being whipped around by the slowing rotor. One towered above the other four, and all five were armed like they were going to war.

Close enough, Jim reckoned.

"This is their home, Ranger," Aidman said to him. "They've got nowhere else to go."

"All right," Jim said to him, "maybe there's something they can do for me, after all...."

"This thing have any oil left in it?" Jim asked, tapping the old, weather-beaten rig's tanker as if to check.

"Not for thirty years maybe," Aidman told him. "We retrofitted it to carry water."

"Water?"

Aidman nodded. "A full load, as of this morning."

Jim pictured the five gunmen continuing to advance across the desert, getting an idea. "That'll do. But, first, I need your help hiding something for a time."

When the man with no face led the gunmen crashing through the mission gate, they found the ground damp and pooling with liquid that spread about them as they stood with their guns pointed at the tall figure standing near the truck that was the source of the flood.

Jim Strong held both hands overhead, one holding a lighter spouting a long, thin flame. "It's in your best interests to stay right where you are."

The three shipping crates had been removed from the bed of D. W. Tepper's pickup and rested side by side in the thickest puddling of liquid.

"It's kerosene," Jim told them, "explaining the lack of smell. But, man, will it go up if this flame hits it. I mean, *poof!*, and we're all yesterday's news."

He focused on the massive figure of the man whose face looked stitched together out of cardboard in patchwork fashion, almost like a jagged checkerboard. First time he'd actually laid eyes on the man and the fear of fire was plain in every visible feature.

"I'm guessing you've been there and done that already. You really want to visit that hell again?"

One of the other men crouched low enough to rake a hand over the darkened ground, touching a finger to his mouth. "Hey, this is—"

His words were ended by a rock slamming into his skull, ahead of the nonstop flurry raining down from the mission wall, flung by Frank Aidman and the people he was protecting here.

Jim had his pistol out in the next instant. He fired and kept firing at shape and motion, not particularly distinguishing between the two.

The rocks continued to rain down, as if spit out of the sky, frames pinwheeling from the impact of the big .45 slugs. Jim traded a spent magazine for a fresh one and heard the crackle of the errant rocks smacking gravel, and the more distinctive thud when they struck flesh and bone.

Gunfights were all different and all the same, dominated by the fog that covers a man's consciousness when he's shooting for his life. For Jim Strong, in the midst of those moments, there was the pistol, the trigger, the slight kick as the bullet blew out the barrel and tore through the air toward its target. Flesh and blood instead of cardboard.

Jim recorded four downed bodies by the time he ejected his third mag without even remembering slamming it home and racking a round into the .45's chamber. But then fresh fire erupted, sounding like a nonstop cacophony of firecrackers on the Fourth of July. The hail of rocks stopped as a few people dropped from the wall, victims of automatic fire.

Thirty shots from an M16 take little more than a breath's length to release, and Jim found the conscious thought he needed to sight in on the big man with no face who was trading his spent thirty-round mag for a fresh one. Jim let go all eight shots his way and was certain that at least one of them had hit, given the way the man's absurdly broad shoulders twisted and his first spray from the fresh magazine was sent skyward.

Then Jim was on the move, diving under the tanker that was still spewing water from its open spigots. He racked his final magazine home as he crawled to the other side, while fresh fire from the M16 kicked up gravel just short of his boots.

Jim Strong reached the other side of the truck and propped his shoulders against one of the tanker's dual tires, which could take a 5.56-millimeter round. But none came, and he popped up and curled around the tanker's rear—just as he heard the engine of D. W. Tepper's shot-up truck rev to life.

Did I leave the keys in the ignition?

Jim absurdly felt for the keys in his pocket, as Tepper's truck limped forward on a blown-out tire and busted rim. The hail of gravel it coughed in its wake joined the steam bleeding from its radiator. The truck tore on in a cloud of its own making, out of reasonable range of his .45, which didn't stop the Ranger from emptying his final magazine toward it.

When the slide locked open, Jim Strong turned his gaze on the four gunmen he'd shot dead. The bodies of five people who'd been shot off the mission wall were lying not far from the gunmen, in the mission courtyard. But he had to put that out of his mind and focus on the desperate task that awaited him before the man with no face made it back with more shooters.

"I'll make sure the wounded get tended to, no questions asked, sir," he said to Frank Aidman. "But first I'm gonna need to borrow your van."

91

MARBLE FALLS, TEXAS

"My truck was totaled," Tepper finished. "Jim Strong never made good on it, but insurance picked up the tab."

They'd adjourned to a storage room that Tepper had converted into a small, windowless study on the second floor of the log home. It smelled of the same cigarette smoke that had stained the wallpaper. They'd entered with their clothes dampened by the drizzle but had dried out over the course of his tale.

Caitlin let the story settle for a few moments. "From there, my dad buried the four men he shot, and those shipping crates, in the very spot where they were dug up last week."

Tepper nodded, looked like he was holding his breath. "Aidman sent a couple of the migrants with him to serve the cause. Helps explain why nobody ever found the spot."

"Until Jones hired Communications Technology Providers to find it," Caitlin noted. "Only he wasn't alone, and CTP ended up playing both sides against the middle. The dead principals of Bane Sturgess dug up the crates that, after they had the bad sense to open one of the ossuaries, were later clipped by the squatters who witnessed the whole thing. That all sound about right, D.W.?"

"Your dad happened upon my truck in a drainage ditch, with its engine and both axles blown. Totaled, like I told you."

"And the man with no face?"

"He was gone, never to be seen again."

"Until now."

"You think he's back?"

"Paz thinks he is. Surprised?"

"You getting a shot at the man who escaped your father?" Tepper said, awash in the cigarette smoke that had settled stubbornly in the air between them.

"Nah, not at all. Never know what the winds of Hurricane Caitlin are going to stir up."

"There's something I haven't told you, Captain. I heard from Cort Wesley. He's on his way back from Atlanta. Alone."

"Come again?"

"Never mind. He and Jones paid a visit to the CDC, where they learned what all this is really about. The story of that ossuary containing the remains of Christ was a hoax, passed on for centuries, meaning people have been dying for almost seven hundred years to protect a secret that isn't real. But those old bones, that's something else again. Turns out they had an entirely different story to tell," Caitlin said, filling Tepper in on what Cort Wesley had learned at the CDC.

He'd sunk into the study's one chair by the time she'd finished. "The bubonic plague? Did I hear you right on that?"

"A mutated version, some kind of spore, that brings with it a one hundred percent mortality rate."

"Your dad and me didn't know a damn thing about that. We knew it had to be something, with those bodies in the train car and all, but the Black Death?" Tepper groped about the table before him in his tiny man cave for his pack of Marlboro Reds, shooting a caustic stare Caitlin's way before he lit up. "This is my home, Ranger. And I'll smoke in it as much as I please."

Caitlin didn't bother protesting, watching him puff away, cigarette held in a trembling hand. He stopped long enough to open a small cabinet and take out a bottle of Jack Daniel's from inside, along with a single glass.

"You need to keep a clear head, D.W."

But he proceeded to fill the glass halfway. "Oh, this isn't for me, Ranger. It's for you."

"How's that?"

Tepper extended the glass toward her. "See, there's something else I need to tell you, too, one last part of the story about what happened between your dad and the Red Widow."

PART TEN

As silly as this sounds, I think one reason we don't have more females in the Rangers is because we wear Western clothes. Most females coming up through the ranks at DPS [Department of Public Safety] are from metropolitan areas, and they wouldn't feel comfortable wearing a cowboy hat. Personally, I love it. I mean, I get to wear this and you're going to pay me? That's awesome. If I had been told, "Okay, you're going to make Ranger, but you have to wear a dress and high heels every day," I would have said, "No thanks."

— Sergeant Marrie Aldridge as quoted in
"Law of the Land," by Pamela Colloff, *Texas Monthly*, April 2007

92

Caitlin spotted Guillermo Paz rocking on the front porch swing, M4 assault rifle laid across his lap, as soon as she climbed out of her rental.

"That's Cort Wesley's spot," she noted, climbing the stairs.

"The outlaw's on his way here from the airport now."

"He ask you to watch over Dylan?"

Paz kept rocking. "I almost got here too late. Boy's okay, but he's gonna be out for a while. Strange dreams, then a wicked headache when he gets up."

"What happened?" Caitlin asked, feeling her muscles tighten and flesh ripple, as something fluttered in her stomach.

The swing creaked as Paz lifted himself off it. "There's something you need to see inside."

Selina Escolante sat tied up on the floor, her limbs bound together by a collection of extension cords that Paz had likely yanked from the wall sockets. He had looped them around her throat for good measure, so if she tried to jerk herself free she'd end up strangling herself. She was wearing a tight-fitting black shirt and raw denim jeans tucked inside black boots. Caitlin wasn't sure whether it was the pair Dylan had lent her or not.

Paz leaned over and plucked the balled-up dishrag from Selina's mouth. "Tell my Ranger who you are."

"I know who she is," Caitlin said, her stare chilling the air between them.

The young woman coughed up a wad of spittle full of cloth fibers and smirked. "I heard your father only slept with two women in his entire life. Guess you figured out who the second is."

"You're my sister." Caitlin nodded.

"Half sister," Selina corrected, "but who's counting?"

"I should have known from the first time we met. I had figured you for twenty-four or so, but I didn't do the math."

Paz handed Caitlin a small bottle. She read the label, eyes widening.

"Why'd you knock Dylan out?"

"For his own good," Selina rasped, still coughing up fibers. "To keep him alive."

"Bullshit."

"Actually, it isn't."

"She told you who she was?" Caitlin asked Paz.

"She didn't have to, Ranger. I knew from the moment I first saw her."

"You're Nola Delgado," Caitlin said, "daughter of the Red Widow."

Nola Delgado bristled. "I hate when people call her that."

"Why? It's well earned, given the number of men she's killed. But I get the impression you're not too far behind."

Nola seemed to take that as a compliment. "Wanna compare notes?"

Caitlin shook her head. "I'm no match for el Barquero."

"He was a man."

"No," Caitlin said, looking Nola right in the eye, "he's a myth, which suits you just fine."

"Aren't you going to ask me how long I've known, Sis?"

Caitlin bristled. "I'm not sure I care."

"El Barquero saved your life twice. How about some thanks?"

"To you or your mother?"

"A combination. She sent me up here to pick up the trail of that bone box somebody dug out of the ground again. I improvised from there. You mind untying me?"

Caitlin flashed the small medical bottle containing fentanyl down at her. "What'd you mean about keeping Dylan alive?"

"That he won't be able to join us for the final battle, when I get that ossuary back for my mother. When you think about it, it's the reason I was born."

The irony of that had already struck Caitlin, but hearing it from Nola Delgado, aka el Barquero, made her shudder.

"I was thinking you'd have the endgame all figured out by now, where we can find my mother's crates."

"What makes you think I'll tell you where I'm headed? Why wouldn't I just leave you tied up right there on the floor?"

"Because you need my gun, Sis. You came back here to get your boyfriend and the big man. But it won't be enough, not against what you'll be going up against. You know that as well as I do."

Caitlin didn't bother refuting the point, not after Cort Wesley had told her about Jones being taken off the map. With him went the endless supply of gunmen Guillermo Paz usually had at his disposal. And they might well be going up against an army. She hadn't told Captain Tepper what she was thinking, because he would have either ordered her off or insisted she wait for the cavalry to arrive. But there was no time, not anymore, not with what Cort Wesley had uncovered about the real contents of that ossuary thought to contain the bones of Christ.

Caitlin leaned over and undid the rubbery bonds holding Nola in place.

"Thanks for trusting me, Sis," Nola said, shaking the blood back into her hands.

"There's a difference between trust and necessity."

"He took my guns," Nola said, gaze cocked toward Paz. "And you're right to trust me, because I'd never hurt you, the sister I'm meeting for the first time."

"You mean like your mother would never kill her husband, Hector?"

"Bullshit!"

"Is it?"

Caitlin could see Nola's eyes wavering, no longer fixed like a sniper rifle's scope.

"And here's something else for you to consider. The contents of those ossuaries your mother's been after for twenty-five years? Those bones are no more Christ's than the ones you picked out of your salmon the other night at dinner. So if you want to go home empty-handed, with your tail between your legs, to give her the bad news, be my guest."

"If it's all the same to you, I'll stick around. See if you're as good as I've heard."

A truck rumbled into the driveway. Caitlin recognized it, from the headlights pouring through the window, as Cort Wesley's. She looked back toward Guillermo Paz.

"Give her back her guns, Colonel."

• • •

"You okay to drive?" she asked Cort Wesley through the window.

"I drove here, didn't I? What you really want to know is if I'm up to handling a gun, if this comes down to shooting."

"The way it always does."

"In special ops training, we were taught to fire with a single arm—*either* arm."

"That was a long time ago."

"So was last week."

"Don't change the subject."

"The arm's better, Ranger. Not all the way back, but better. And, who knows, maybe we won't need to go to guns this time."

Caitlin nodded, regarded his right hand poised atop the steering wheel again. "I wouldn't count on it, Cort Wesley."

93

Spinnaker Falls, Texas

Dawn was just breaking when Cort Wesley's truck bounced over the uneven desert ground toward the old Spanish mission occupied by undocumented immigrants, the "illegals" who, first under Frank Aidman and then under his son, Daniel, had stood vigil over the spot where they'd helped Jim Strong bury four bodies and three crates twenty-five years before.

As they thumped across the rocky terrain, kicking up stray gravel in their wake, Caitlin couldn't help but think of a similar scene in 1994, of Jim Strong rattling along as best he could in D. W. Tepper's shot-up pickup truck.

"We've gotta hope they didn't beat us here," Cort Wesley noted.

"They didn't," said Caitlin.

"How can you know that?"

Instead of answering, Caitlin looked toward Paz in the front passenger seat of the cab.

"She's right, outlaw," he said, without turning around. "And the big man, the one with no face, is coming. I understand what I've been feeling now."

"I wish we had your men with us right now, Colonel."

Paz appeared not at all perturbed by their absence. "The great painter Vincent van Gogh once said, 'Great things are done by a series of small things brought together.' The same can hold true for people. As Plato believed, 'A hero is born among a hundred, a wise man is found among a thousand, but an accomplished one might not be found even among a hundred thousand men.'"

"Does he always talk like that, Sis?" Nola asked Caitlin.

"Don't call me that. And he's killed even more people than you have, a lot more, so he can talk any way he wants."

Paz still hadn't turned from the front seat. His gaze was fixed intently out the windshield, toward the mission. Caitlin caught Cort Wesley eyeballing her in the rearview mirror yet again, his shoulders and neck both held stiffly, as he continued trying to make sense of all she'd told him on the way, to reconcile it with the knowledge he'd gained firsthand at the CDC.

The trench fire that had been burning for years now had a peculiar beauty when, off in the distance, it was cast against the morning sun, the grayish-black smoke shaded amber at the edges. Caitlin could feel the strong breeze outside rattle Cort Wesley's truck, stoking flickers of life from the long-untended wind turbines.

"Looks like the Alamo," Cort Wesley said, as the mission sharpened in view.

"Here's hoping the metaphor stops there."

"Yeah," he groused, "good luck with that." He finally twisted his gaze toward her in the backseat, eyes brushing over Nola Delgado as if seeing her for the first time. "Tell me again why we're here?"

"The people in there have been watching that site ever since 1994, when my father first buried the missing ossuaries. Bane Sturgess dug those crates out of the desert, and those people must've followed them back to New Braunfels and stole the bone boxes, after the four men we found dead were stupid enough to open one of them."

"Releasing those plague spores again, which means…" Cort Wesley said, letting his thought dangle there for Caitlin to finish.

Caitlin joined him in gazing toward the mission. "Which means the crates must still be inside," she completed.

Cort Wesley nodded. "So a fanatical religious order is after a weapon that can kill anyone and everyone. What could go wrong?"

That left Nola shaking her head, stopping just short of a laugh. "You people should really listen to yourselves sometime."

"Welcome to our world," Caitlin told her.

"Just tell me when I can start shooting."

94

SPINNAKER FALLS, TEXAS

The mission gates jerked open as they approached, Daniel Aidman standing there to greet their arrival. Some of the people Caitlin recalled from the other day were already at work tending to the garden and harvesting what looked like tomatoes. A few men stood back a bit, suspicious of her presence, holding their ground with a confidence that suggested that the shirts flapping outside their belts in the stiff breeze concealed pistols.

"I got your message," Aidman said to Caitlin, when she stepped down out of the truck.

"Any sign of them?" she asked him, while Paz moved to the covered cargo bed to retrieve the duffel bag he had stowed there.

Aidman shook his head. "Not yet. Let me get this straight. You're saying these are the same people from my father's time, the same people behind the four men your father killed here in ninety-four?"

Caitlin nodded. "He let one get away, unfortunately."

Aidman's eyes bulged as Paz unzipped his duffel and began pulling out an assortment of weapons, which made Caitlin think of Santa's endless sack of gifts.

"Those crates you took from Bane Sturgess, they're in the mission chapel, aren't they?"

Aidman's response was to begin leading her in that direction. "Your father warned mine about the bodies he found in that train car. We took precautions. Hazmat suits and respirators."

"The box was open when you found it."

Aidman nodded. "We sealed and packed it up again, brought it here with the other two until we could figure out what to do next," he said, yanking open the rickety chapel door.

"And you neglected to mention that when I was here yesterday?"

Aidman shrugged. "When it comes to what we thought was inside those crates, nobody's hands were safe, including yours. I didn't know who I could trust."

Caitlin followed him up to the chapel altar, where he removed the sacraments from their resting place. Stripping the white sheets away revealed a trio of shipping crates, likely the original packaging in which Jim Strong had found them before he'd buried them in the desert.

"It's the one in the center," Aidman said, pointing down at the crate in question as if he were afraid to touch it.

Caitlin didn't blame him. "We need to get it out of here while there's still time," she said, as the first explosion sounded outside.

Caitlin charged out of the chapel, SIG Sauer in hand, just as a second explosion roared. She saw a plume of dirt coughed into the air, one squatter down and another rolling in pain, and figured the source to be a grenade tossed over the wall.

Then she saw the drones.

95

SPINNAKER FALLS, TEXAS

She knew the Rangers had a few drones of their own for surveillance, and she recognized these as facsimiles of the ones she'd glimpsed in advertisements and electronics store windows. Squat, oblong flying machines, maybe a yard in diameter.

A swarm of them, in this case.

The drones filled the air like giant wasps, the buzzing sound they made supporting the illusion, which she quickly shook from her head. More grenade blasts sounded; each of the drones was carrying at least one, and maybe more, of them. The drones were acting like miniature dive bombers, either being driven remotely or homing in on motion or heat signatures below to acquire their targets.

Caitlin opened up on the swarm randomly, draining her first magazine into a congestion of four of the flying machines, two of which fell and exploded on impact with the ground, downing another pair of squatters.

Rat-tat-tat . . . Rat-tat-tat . . . Rat-tat-tat . . .

Cort Wesley and Nola Delgado were firing bursts from their M4s skyward, rotating the barrels back and forth, trying to take drones out by the bushel. Guillermo Paz held matching M4s in both hands, firing upward to the left and right at the same time, blowing drone after drone out of the air.

Caitlin was into her third mag, unable to shake the sense that she was playing one of Dylan's or Luke's video games, the wave of attacking drones seemingly endless. She fired while dragging to cover people struck by shrapnel, brushing up against Daniel Aidman, who was desperately shepherding as many as he could gather through the chapel doors.

One of the drones, then another, and a third trailed him inside before he could get those doors closed. Caitlin lit out in a dead sprint, straight through the refuse coughed up by one of the explosive charges that forced her to angle sharply to the right. Then she veered back to the left to avoid the debris coughed up by a second charge.

She felt the sting of steel and stone piercing her clothes and pricking her flesh. Caitlin lurched through the door and dove to the floor beneath a flash that showered husks of the makeshift reconstituted pews into the air.

Wood splinters pierced her scalp and she felt the warm ooze of blood as she twisted onto her back and shot down one drone, and then another, emptying the rest of her mag into a third before two more soared through the door.

Cort Wesley swept his eyes over the mission courtyard, where pockets of mist, thickened by the constant stream of explosions, mixed with the ever-present wisps of black char smoke wafting in from the trench fire beyond. He fired on the move, resolved to remain a moving target to keep the machines' targeting mechanisms from getting a firm fix on him. He wielded his assault rifle in his left arm; his right arm was better, but not better enough to trust.

Before him, in the center of the courtyard, amid the thickest nest of farm plantings, Guillermo Paz moved like a giant gazelle, shooting, stopping to re-aim, and then shooting some more, as if following a choreographed routine, his motions lithe and dance-like, one with the air.

Nola Delgado, meanwhile, stood off to the right, feet rooted in place, not caring if the drones homed in on her, probably because she wanted them to. She fired burst after burst, grinning the whole time, maybe even laughing, though it was impossible for Cort Wesley to tell, given the cacophony of rival sounds that pushed a flutter through his ears.

He watched people scampering to and from cover, watched plumes of dark, manure-rich soil coughed into the air by drone blasts that left fallen bodies in their place.

Then he was shooting again, the M4 feeling like an extension of his hand, like flesh and blood instead of steel, as he eyed the chapel into which Caitlin Strong had just disappeared.

• • •

The pair of drones sped over Caitlin's supine form, speeding for the altar, where the bulk of the mission's residents, led by Aidman, had been forced to retreat.

The altar!

Caitlin tried not to picture the effects if a coming blast blew open the ossuary containing the bones infected with the Black Death. But she couldn't help but imagine those spores of the bubonic plague showering the air.

The squatters would die.

She would die.

They would all die.

She was sprinting down the center of the chapel, without memory of reclaiming her feet, draining the rest of this magazine and then starting in on a fresh one, her last. The feeling of a video game was strong with her again, except her breaths were coming in short, quick huffs that left her heaving. A pair of *booms* sounded, followed by flashes as, under her fire, the drones crashed through the windows on either side of the chapel.

Caitlin was still heaving for breath when she charged back outside to see Colonel Paz shooting out a final phalanx of the explosives-equipped drones as they dive-bombed him. Cort Wesley and Nola handled the ones that slipped through his line of fire, Nola from right out in the open and Cort Wesley from the cover of his truck. The hood and engine block were a charred mass of shrapnel, and he clutched his assault rifle in his left hand instead of his right.

The smoke residue continued to cloud the courtyard after the shooting had stopped, and the ground was an obstacle course of smoking remnants of the drones they'd shot out of the air.

Nola Delgado let the M4 dangle by her side. "Is that the best they can do?"

"*¡Allí afuera! ¡Allí afuera!*" *Out there! Out there!*

The cry, from a Mexican perched on the mission wall, seemed to come in answer to Nola's question. The squatter had climbed to that post with only a rake in his hand, to battle the drones by sweeping it through the air, and Caitlin thought she recalled him actually clipping one of them. She scrambled up the ladder, with Cort Wesley just behind her, as the man cried out again.

"*¡Prisa! ¡Prisa!*"

Hurrying, indeed, Caitlin mounted the wall and held the ladder still to ease the last of Cort Wesley's ascent, and then the two of them moved to the chest-high wall to see what the man had spotted.

"You gotta be frigging kidding me," Cort Wesley managed.

96

Men, as many as three dozen of them, rose from their camouflaged positions on the desert floor, led by a massive shape almost as big as Paz.

"The colonel was right," Caitlin muttered. "He's here." She swung to the side. "He was waiting for us, Cort Wesley. He knew we'd be coming. We walked straight into a trap."

"Son of a bitch had been here before, just like you said," Cort Wesley noted, clenching his teeth. A mixture of soot, grime, and blood streaked his face.

"My father beat him then, just like we're going to beat him now."

"Used up lots of our ammo on killing those drones, Ranger."

Caitlin moved for the ladder again. "And we'll kill those men with whatever we've got left."

"We can't let him get that bone box, Ranger," Paz said, when she reached the bottom.

"Any ideas, Colonel?"

He seemed to sniff the char on the air. "Just one."

Caitlin met his gaze, getting a notion of what he was thinking. "It's inside the chapel. Aidman will show you."

Paz disappeared and Caitlin swung around to find a grinning Nola Delgado by her side.

"You're crazy," Caitlin said to her. "You know that?"

"What, because I'd rather kill men than machines?"

"Because you like killing *anything*. You said we're the same, Nola, but that's where we differ. I do it when I have to. You do it whenever possible."

"I don't get the distinction, Sis."

Caitlin again bristled at Nola calling her that. "I'm sure you don't."

"Come on," Nola said, as she moved to Paz's duffel bag to get a fresh weapon. "You telling me you don't enjoy this kind of shit, even a little?"

"I enjoy staying alive," Caitlin said, reaching into the bag and grasping the first gun her hand closed around.

• • •

Enrico Molinari signaled his troops forward, their ratcheting gunfire instantly breaking the stillness of the morning. He'd donned the form-fitting mask again, to protect his patchwork face from the harshness of the sun as well as to remind himself of the transformation that had brought him to this place on the holiest of missions. It took all his strength to squeeze the mask over his jagged assemblage of flesh, and he wondered if he'd ever be able to peel it off, even as the stench of decay and the oily residue of his own face assaulted him.

No matter, because very soon the contents of the ossuary would be his, the Order's. A weapon in their possession to vanquish all the enemies of the Church, the worst of the unbelievers, once and for all.

With the weapon in the hands of the Order, all who failed to follow the true word of God could be made to perish in a hellfire of their own making. He realized that this moment was what his entire life up until this point had been about. The service, the dedication, the heroism, and, finally, the burning. All leading to now. The purpose of his life was about to be realized with this completed mission in the service of God.

In the hands of the Order, this weapon that had been delivered unto them from heaven itself would allow the Church to strike fear into those who rebelled with their words and deeds. The heathen swarm could be silenced from continent to continent. Those who blasphemed His word, those who worshipped false gods, those who did not kneel before the Almighty, would be punished for their sins in the most fitting way possible.

God really did work in mysterious ways.

Paz wrapped the box thought to contain the bones of Christ in the sheet that had been covering it. It weighed too much to conveniently strap it to his frame or to stuff it into something he could sling over his shoulder. But it wasn't as big as he was expecting, and it fit snugly under his arm.

He wished his priest were here so he could seek counsel on the ossuary's very existence, even though its purported contents were in all probability a hoax. Then he wondered if this was some holy mission he was meant to fulfill, one of the true cosmic reasons for his coming to Texas in the first place, all those years before.

That entire stretch flashed through his consciousness. Paz had been called to a great mission by the very higher power to whom he had been speaking in the hope of gaining a response. Maybe this was it, God entrusting him with a mission to erase forever the fallacy imprinted on the bones contained in this box. Destroy it and he would effectively be destroying doubt, the greatest enemy of faith. Destroy it and Paz would be providing the ultimate service to the Almighty he sought only to serve.

You'd be proud of me, Padre....

There was only one way to complete the task, only one way to be sure.

Cort Wesley couldn't remember the last time he'd had to *think* about firing a weapon. The process had become so ingrained, so instinctive, that the gun felt like an extension of himself, of the arms hoisting it. But now one of those arms had trouble managing the weight. The gun was heavy in his grasp and the barrel seemed to rotate in slow motion.

He fired from the ramparts at the hordes of men laying siege to the mission with all manner of weapon in hand. He was dialing everything back a notch, focusing more on aim and accuracy than on speed of fire. The young woman he knew as Selina Escolante, Nola Delgado, stood on the wall as well, across from him, on the other side of the structure's gate.

She fired nonstop, the lag between aiming and firing less than his, less than Caitlin's. A woman, then, well versed in the use of pretty much any firearm. She might be known in the darkness as a mythical assassin utilizing a signature .22-caliber pistol, but she was clearly much more than that.

El Barquero.

Cort Wesley pictured Nola's mother retaining special ops soldiers and maybe Navy SEALs to teach her daughter the ways of the gun. Train her how to be a killer, not just an assassin—the distinction as vast as between the sun and the moon. Train her to be able to hold her own in any form of gunplay, even under siege, as was the case today.

He wondered if they taught her how to enjoy it, too, since Cort Wesley had never encountered anyone who seemed to revel as much as she reveled in the simple majesty of working a gun to snuff out lives. Nola cradled the blazing assault rifle in her hand like a child's doll, lovingly and with purpose, the two of them joined both physically and in the subconscious. The weapon was a living thing in her grasp and her mind.

Was God trying to do him a favor here, weakening his arm so that he could no longer know the life that pulsed through him as death poured from the muzzle in a gas-fueled stream?

Cort Wesley's own bullet stream might not quite match the effectiveness of Nola's, but men were falling to his bullets as he stood on the wall, tempting the return fire that was closing in on him. As a boy, his favorite story had been of the brave and loyal defenders of the Alamo, and he'd never forget his first visit to the place that had dominated so much of his imagination.

Never in his thoughts, though, had he ever imagined he'd be fighting his own version of that epic battle, knowing what Lieutenant Colonel William Travis, Jim Bowie, and Davy Crockett must have been feeling in the midst of the final fight that would claim all their lives.

He felt the ladder leading to the top of the wall shift and wobble, glanced down amid the gunfire pouring in from both directions, and saw six of the Mexican men climbing up with the last of Paz's weapons dangling behind their backs.

Reinforcements, Cort Wesley thought, something the fighters at the Alamo had never received.

"Good luck, Colonel," Caitlin said to Paz, as Daniel Aidman finally got the rear doors of the mission open.

"You don't need luck when you have faith, Ranger. I was spared the noose in my home country for this moment. I can feel my mother smiling down on me even now."

Caitlin looked out toward the eternal flames spouting from the trench beyond, gray-black smoke dragged up to paint the air in its wake. "A quarter mile, or thereabouts, is still a long way to cover in the open."

"I have God to guide me," Paz assured her. "My priest told me so. He passed away as our battle was beginning, his ending at the same time. I felt it. So I have the ultimate backup, Ranger, to complete my mission and the journey that brought me to you."

She reached out and squeezed his arm. "The contents of that box, Colonel . . ."

"Never to be seen again after today."

Caitlin watched him speed into the sun, his motions impossibly quick and agile for a man his size. He was there and then he was gone, his shape shrinking farther into the distance, as she turned back to Aidman.

"That truck parked alongside the chapel," Caitlin said. "Don't tell me: Those tanks labeled 'Propane' contain water, just like back in 1994."

"Actually," Aidman told her, brightening, "no, they don't."

97

Molinari worked his way around the side of the mission, taking advantage of the battle raging in the front to seek an angle to better shoot down the enemy defending their ground from atop the wall. The incessant clacking of gunfire soothed his ears. The relentless onslaught waged by the best soldiers the Order had to offer was certain to weaken the resistance enough for him to finish it off in effortless fashion.

A lot of these soldiers had already perished in their holy mission to provide the Order with the weapon, a price worth paying to render God's army invincible in dealing with sinners. The search for one thing had led to another, and Molinari felt blessed to be chosen for a mission that had expanded into something far greater than its original mandate.

The true origin of the bones interred inside that ossuary no longer mattered; what mattered—*all* that mattered—was the great weapon those bones carried. To be received only by the worthy, one of faith.

Him.

The Order.

Molinari slid along the mission wall, just coming upon a jagged opening carved by time, when he spotted a huge figure dashing through the desert, heading straight for the flames burning out of a pit that might lead to hell itself. At first, he thought it was an illusion, an apparition.

Then he saw something covered in white clutched beneath the figure's arm, about the size of—

Molinari lit out into a dead sprint before even completing that thought, all his plans threatened, the great battle he thought himself to be on the verge of winning yet to be fought.

Paz felt a coldness slice through the blistering heat of the desert, an icicle jabbing at his neck and letting its chill leak downward. He knew pursuit was coming, coming fast, even before he felt the disturbance in the ground at his feet. It was a disruption he couldn't define or explain but likened to the feeling of trying to traverse a rope bridge only to have someone else step out upon it, behind him, and worsen the wobble.

He felt that pursuit closing, the bulk of the bone box and the awkwardness of carrying it making it impossible to gather any more speed. In his mind, he saw a man with no face, not even any eyes, nose, or mouth, coming fast in his wake. Saw him even as the gunshots began to ring out behind him.

Half the men who'd climbed the wall to add their guns to the battle, three of the six, had fallen to the onslaught. Two more, whom Cort Wesley hadn't noticed before, had joined Nola Delgado on the other side, one of them dropping to the torrent of fire as well. Nola glanced at him through the wafting char smoke, her face empty and devoid of any emotion or feeling.

Initially, they'd managed to hold the gunmen laying siege to the mission at bay, forcing them to advance only in fits and starts. In between, the high-ground fire kept them pinned, pushed them to the ground in the meager cover provided by stray rock formations, boulders, and arroyos carved out of the desert floor.

But now they were advancing, and advancing fast—faster, the closer they got. Coming within easy range of the—

The mission wall shook under the impact of the first rocket-propelled grenade, a huge plume of stone and mortar coughed into the air. The next RPG blew a hole straight through the wall on Nola Delgado's side, sending the last man lending his fire to hers plunging thirty feet. But Nola didn't so much as waver, never missing a beat as she exchanged a spent magazine for a fresh one.

For his part, Cort Wesley sighted in on a pair of figures firing the grenade launchers from prone positions on the desert floor. He could barely see them, and, without a scope, two hundred yards with an M4 might as well have been a mile. He'd wielded a sniper rifle plenty often in his time, most recently while leading the rescue of Guillermo Paz from the gallows in Venezuela. But nobody had been firing back at him then, giving him all the time he needed to sight, hold, and shoot.

Still, from two hundred yards he wouldn't have to worry about wind or air density or anything like that. Just sight, hold, and shoot.

Cort Wesley sighted on the figure holding the RPG launcher, who'd propped himself over a slight rise, torso angled over it.

Then he pawed the trigger.

Held.

Fired.

"Get your people out of here, Aidman!" Caitlin told the son of the man her father had met here twenty-five years ago. "Get them out of here now!"

Where her father had been forced to bluff his attackers with water, she had the benefit of two propane tanks that might actually help her prevail, or at least buy the time Guillermo Paz needed to rid the world of the deadly contents of that ossuary forever.

Molinari fired a burst into the sun, visualizing the bullets exploding from the barrel and moving on a direct course toward the huge figure running through the desert—dead on target, the superheated shells dancing in the air before tumbling in his wake.

The figure continued running, the limestone box cradled beneath his arm.

Molinari fired another burst, watched flecks of ground, stone, and gravel coughed into the air not just behind but also in front of the figure, as if his bullets were passing straight through.

What is this? What is happening?

Paz felt portions of the ground kicked up around him, capturing him briefly in the cloudbursts they created, fissures carved out of the air. He thought he may have felt a few ding his Kevlar body armor, like a *thump, thump, thump* that made his spine arch as he ran.

He didn't fear the bullets, nor the faceless figure firing them. The bullets couldn't hurt him and neither could the man.

Paz kept running, not just toward the sun but *into* it, the shroud of superheated cosmic gases protecting him from the bullets, melting them before they could find his flesh. Soft spits digging divots out of the earth all around him, their hushed ratcheting overcome by the pounding of footsteps in his wake.

It took eight single shots squeezed off one after the other, but misty fountains of blood erupted from the skulls of the men lying prone with rocket launchers angled upward. He saw them twitch, their hold on their weapons lost. Cort Wesley managed the task with his left arm just fine.

But the damage was already done, the mission's heavy gates breached, just like those at the Alamo nearly two centuries before.

Out of ammo, Cort Wesley grabbed a weapon from the grip of one of the dead squatters who'd fought on this wall for the semblance of the home he'd built here. Cort Wesley had aimed it downward, toward the first of the enemy gunmen to surge through the breached gate, when he spotted Nola Delgado, el Barquero, on ground level now, shooting them as they came.

In that moment she looked just like Caitlin, might have been Caitlin, standing in a shooter's stance square in the open, impervious to the desperate hail of bullets whizzing past her. It was like watching a crazed dance routine, both horrific and beautiful at the same time, Cort Wesley thought, as he opened up from the wall, adding his fire to hers.

98

SPINNAKER FALLS, TEXAS

Amid the gunfire raging just beyond in the courtyard, Caitlin used the butt of her SIG to knock the spigots off the dual propane tanks loaded in the truck bed. She could see partially buried hoses running from the tanks outward, supplying a modicum of power that had helped make this old mission into a livable place, where many were now dying.

A pair of those hoses dangled free, Caitlin's nostrils assaulted by the powerful odor of propane. A drone had crashed nearby, its explosive charge intact. The device, modeled after a traditional grenade except oblong in shape, looked like a black Easter egg. Nothing fancy, just detonation on impact once triggered.

Caitlin could feel the flow of the gas wafting over the courtyard as her half sister stood like a living statue in the center of it all, shooting nonstop.

Paz could feel the faceless man gaining, closer on his heels now. The coarse smoke rising from the trench fire was thicker and darker here, making it hurt to breathe and filling his lungs with acrid heat.

Paz was fifteen feet from the edge of the pit when he stopped and twisted in the same impossible motion, as if he'd gone straight from A to F, skipping all the letters in between. The bone box was in his grasp, and then it wasn't. Instead, it was speeding through the air, straight toward the faceless man, who froze and dropped the weapon he'd been about to open up with again.

He tried to catch the ossuary but only managed a meager deflection, enough to create a slight cushioning of its fall, so it teetered only slightly when it landed, before seeming to right itself.

Paz pounced, before the faceless man could make another move. He was not used to an adversary of nearly equal size and strength. The two giants slammed into each other like a pair of eighteen-wheelers in a head-on freeway crash, whipsawing about with hands as their only weapons. Twisting, flailing, groping in a blurred dervish of motion that left neither with the advantage.

Paz felt himself stumble in a spot where the ground fell off, the scorched land angling lower as it got closer to the flames spouting from the trench as if they were angry with the world. Those flames illuminated the big figure before him, revealing what looked like an ACE bandage wrapped around his face, exposing only his eyes, his nostrils, and a slit from the mouth, smelling of rot and mold and dead skin, darkened in splotches by sweat over the cheeks.

Paz tried to keep sight of his hands, but the figure kept them whirling in a blur, Paz struck repeatedly by blows he never even glimpsed. He felt the world go soft and cushiony beneath his feet, the desert floor seeming to sink under his and his attacker's vast weight. He managed to deflect one blow and countered with one to the face beneath the mask, feeling bone crunch and recede on impact.

Paz's next glimpse of the man revealed what looked like a dent in his mask, a depression left by whatever bones he'd shattered in the man's face, enough to down any other man he'd ever encountered. His own face was numb from the beating he'd taken, and Paz feinted next with his right hand and tried to sweep the masked figure's feet out with a sweep of his right leg. Paz felt one leg waver and the other buckle, but the masked figure never went down, never even lost his balance. He unleashed a furious flurry of blows in response, staggering Paz and forcing him backward toward the lip of the burning hole in the ground.

Paz wondered if their dual destiny was to tumble over into the fires of hell itself, if his priest's death had somehow been a harbinger of this very moment. Father Boylston going up while he went down. He was searching for something to tip those scales, to keep him from the darkness so that he might remain in the light, when he thought he heard his priest speak to him in his mind.

"So do not fear, for I am with you; do not be dismayed, for I am your God."

Cort Wesley leaped the final ten feet from the ladder to the ground, one assault rifle in hand and the last one he'd been able to salvage slung behind him. He added his fire to Nola Delgado's, the two of them engaged in a bizarre pirouette on the courtyard grounds riddled with bodies and debris.

There were no forms, no textures, no shapes—just blurs of motion to fire toward. The wave had at last ceased pouring through the jagged remnants of the mission gate, when he thought he heard his own name splinter the ratcheting gunfire.

"Cort Wesley!" Caitlin cried out again, getting his attention this time.

She flashed the oblong-shaped explosive she'd plucked from one of the downed drones, hoped he'd see it gleam through the swirling clouds of dust and muck from the trench fire blowing downwind.

She could tell, from one brief look, that he recognized what she was holding, grasped the meaning and intent in her eyes. He seemed to sniff the air as, still firing, he moved for Nola.

Cort Wesley smelled the propane on the air, the stench almost overpowering, as he drew even with Nola and grabbed her by the arm. He dragged her away toward the chapel, toward Caitlin Strong, her Texas Ranger half sister. Opposite sides of the same sharp-edged coin.

Then Caitlin flung the explosive shaped like a big egg into the air.

"I will strengthen you and help you; I will uphold you with my righteous right hand."

Those words, spoken by his priest, from his favorite prophet, Isaiah, resounded in Paz's mind. Filled him not just with assurance but also with purpose.

And a plan. Father Boylston was serving it up to him, providing the wisdom for what he must do, from Proverbs.

"Whoever hates disguises himself with his lips and harbors deceit in his heart. Though his hatred be covered with deception, his wickedness will be exposed in the assembly."

Exposed....

Amid the battering he'd taken at the hands of the faceless man who matched his strength, amid the pain and rich taste of blood, Paz followed his priest's direction. He jerked his right hand upward as they grappled, grasping the moist, rancid fabric stretched over this demon's face, and pulled. Then he pulled again, with all his strength.

The shredded mask came away in his grasp, holding much of the man's face within it. The sight of the pulpy remains, exposed bone and gristle, stole Paz's breath, as the demon's scream split the black air that enveloped him like a shroud.

Paz felt the ossuary in his grasp in the next moment, not exactly sure how it had gotten there. Then it was airborne, hurtling through the air, deep into the thickest, blackest patch of smoke rising from the pit.

Toward the flames.

"AHHHHHHHHHHHHHH!"

Paz heard the man with no face scream even as his massive frame soared past him, airborne, launching himself through the air to catch the box before it dropped. And his grasp somehow did close on ancient limestone, capturing it in his hands the size of meat slabs in what had all the makings of a looming miracle.

But no miracle followed. The man with no face could no more float in the air than walk on the water, and Paz watched as he dragged the box with him down into the depths of hell itself.

The explosion sounded as Caitlin, Nola, and Cort Wesley clung to the side of the chapel, protected by its shroud, downwind from the blast that turned the courtyard into a fountain of flame.

Cort Wesley had closed his arms around both Caitlin and Nola, his own back bearing the brunt of the shock wave, his knees buckling. The wave of heat seared Caitlin's skin and clothes, made her feel she was on fire too, even as she glimpsed the still-standing skeletons of the enemy gunmen who'd been incinerated in the blast. Then she realized she was breathing freely, realized she was whole, even with her clothes and hair stinging to the touch.

Caitlin tried to speak and then realized she couldn't hear her own voice, hell itself having stopped just short of the mission chapel walls.

99

"This used to be the church where my parents were murdered," Luna Diaz Delgado told Caitlin, as workmen cleared the debris around them. "I burned it to the ground last week, but I can still smell the blood. Can you smell it too?"

Caitlin ignored the vulnerability, the plaintiveness in the Red Widow's voice. "No, ma'am, I can't. But I understand, because violence sticks to us like cooking onions to a wool sweater. You can't wash that smell out, no matter how much you try."

"I think I get the point."

"I wasn't really trying to make one."

"You saved my life. That's a debt I can never repay."

"Yes, you can," Caitlin told her. "I want to talk about my sister."

"*Half* sister," the Red Widow corrected.

"Still flesh and blood, ma'am."

"More mine than yours."

"She's my father's daughter, just like I am."

"You planning on celebrating Christmas with the legendary el Barquero or arresting her?"

"El Barquero isn't my sister."

"Are you capable of distinguishing between the two?"

Caitlin kicked at the ash and charred wood. For some reason, she hadn't been able to smell much since the explosion at the old Spanish mission two days before, but her hearing was almost all the way back, and that made for a fair trade.

"I'm not sure," she said.

Luna smiled sadly, picked up a blackened husk of wood, and snapped it in two. "You're both the same, exactly like your father. Speaking of which ..."

The Red Widow eased from her pocket the locket Jim Strong had given her.

"This belongs to you," she said, holding it out for Caitlin to take.

But Caitlin left it there. "My father wanted you to have it, señora."

Luna made no move to pull it back. "That doesn't seem right."

"It did to him at the time, and that's all that matters. He gave you the locket and you gave him a daughter he never knew he had."

"She saved your life, Tejano. Twice. You should leave things there."

"If you know her, and we really are the same, you know I can't do that."

Luna frowned. "I suppose I do."

"And she may have saved my life twice, but she took advantage of a boy who's as close as I've got to a son just to get close to me."

"What do you want, Ranger? Spell it out for me."

Caitlin looked at Luna Diaz Delgado, imagining her father doing the very same thing twenty-five years before. "Tell Nola I want to see her."

They met at the same cantina where Caitlin had fled with the Red Widow after the gun battle at the Policia Federal barracks. Looking at the younger woman coming through the door was like looking at herself when she'd just graduated college.

Instead of the business-casual outfit she'd worn when they'd had dinner on the Riverwalk, Nola wore brown leather pants that looked glued to her skin, their sheen dulled by a dry coating of dust, which she brushed off before taking the seat across from Caitlin.

"I never met our father," Nola said tersely, laying her gun on the table.

Caitlin laid her SIG next to it. "I've got no jurisdiction down here."

Nola looked as if she found that funny. "I know all about you, Caitlin Strong. Hope you don't expect that to make me feel safe."

"If you know so much about me, then you know you *should* feel safe, especially with your gun on the table."

"One of them anyway." She smirked. "I assume the same holds true for you."

Caitlin shook her head. "One's all I need."

"Back at that mission—"

"Save it, please."

"I was to going say you're even better than I'd heard."

"You, too, given that all I've heard said makes you out as an assassin. But you're a gunfighter too, a man killer, when someone just as ready is trying to do the same to you."

"Thank you, Ranger."

"I'm not sure I meant it as a compliment, Nola."

She nodded, her gaze going from flat to bittersweet. "Me either."

"We are what we are."

Nola settled back in her chair and laid her boots on the tabletop, just skirting the pistols resting there. "So, what's this about? We going to start celebrating each other's birthdays? You going to invite me for Thanksgiving dinner? Maybe we can watch the ball drop together on New Year's in Times Square."

"None of that. You need to speak to Dylan."

Nola huffed out some breath. "I don't care whether you believe me or not, but my feelings... well, I really liked him."

"You give fentanyl to everyone you like?"

"Only the ones I want to stay alive."

"One more milliliter and he would've been dead."

"I knew what I was doing."

"Because you've done it before, probably with that extra dosage."

"You want me to deny it?"

"Wouldn't matter if you did."

Nola pulled her boots off the table, eyed the pistols with their barrels resting against each other. "Our work isn't finished, Ranger. That man with no face worked for a group of religious whack-job zealots who call themselves the Order. He's still out there—*they're* still out there."

Caitlin shook her head. "Not interested."

"As in finishing what our father started?" Nola shot back, frustration lacing her voice. "Am I hearing this right? The great Caitlin Strong running from a fight?"

"We've already won."

Now Nola shook her head, her breathing edging up a notch, a kid on Christmas morning who didn't get the present she asked for. "So you just wanna have at it, go for the guns and see who's better?"

Caitlin smiled, then chuckled.

"What's so funny?" Nola said, snapping forward.

"That's something I would say. Actually, it's something I *have* said."

Nola settled back again. "You ever tell a man you'd shoot his balls off, if he had any?"

"Once or twice," Caitlin said, after a nod.

It was Nola's turn to nod. "We could go on like this for a while."

"We could."

"Comes with the blood, I guess. So maybe you're not the only one who's strong as steel; maybe we both are." Nola stopped, then started again, her thoughts veering. "I've got Dylan's cell number. I'll call him."

"To say good-bye. One gunfighter in his life is enough for any man or boy to handle."

Nola smiled. "I'm good with a lot more than guns."

"I'm sure you are."

Nola leaned forward and folded her arms on the table. "Is this where you tell me that you'll be coming if I step out of line?"

"No, because I know you won't. You're el Barquero, the Ferryman. Taking people to their death is what you do, and there's no shortage of passengers for your boat down here. I'm not going to try to talk you out of being who you are, or what you are, either. So long as that's what it is and not what the Red Widow made you."

Nola stiffened. "Don't call her that."

"Why not? She earned the title."

That struck a chord in Nola. "We really are the same, Ranger, aren't we?"

"What happened to 'Sis'?"

Nola shrugged. "I made my point."

"Here's mine: We're not the same. I may be a gunfighter, but you're a killer."

"Like I said, the same, only on different sides. If the fates were different and your Jim Strong had married Luna Diaz Delgado, she'd be your stepmother."

"But they weren't. And he didn't." Caitlin stood up, hovering over the table as she holstered her pistol. "We won't be seeing each other again, Nola."

"No? Even if the Order comes back?"

"They won't."

Nola scowled at her. "You can't be sure of that, Sis."

"Yes, I can," Caitlin told her, "because I still have one last card to play."

100

AUSTIN, TEXAS

The state capitol building in Austin was one of the most ornate in all of the country. Topped by the beautifully forged iron statue of the Goddess of Liberty, it was built way back in 1888, surrounded by twenty-two acres of parklike lands highlighted by statues and monuments to important people and moments in Texas history. These were not just for remembrance; they were also a testament to the bravery and traditions that persist to the modern day.

Caitlin stood in the back of the rotunda, listening to Lieutenant Governor Maurice Scoggins wrap up his speech to the delegates of the Texas House of Representatives, which had included a formal announcement of his intention to run for governor, earning him a standing ovation. Scoggins's security team escorted him from the chamber, but he was intercepted by Caitlin before he got more than ten feet.

"Do you have a minute, sir?" she asked Scoggins, as the pair of men on either side of him stiffened.

He made a show of checking his watch. "I'm already late for my next meeting, and I'm afraid I'm booked for the rest of the day. Can we do this tomorrow?"

"It's in your best interests to do it now, sir."

It was the look in her eyes, more than Caitlin's words, that led Scoggins to capitulate. He nodded to his security guards and moved off to the side, his back turned to the chamber so none of those exiting would notice him.

"Make it fast, Ranger, please."

"I wanted to thank you personally for your help."

"My pleasure, and I apologize if we got off on the wrong foot," he said dismissively. "Now, if you don't mind . . ."

"See, that's the problem, sir. I do mind; I mind very much. I mind you getting in my dad's way in 1994 and in my way last week. Turned out, those men who confiscated the Communications Technology Providers computers from our Ranger company office really were CID. Only their mission was off the books. Care to guess where their orders came from?" Caitlin stopped there, jostled by the increasingly crowded lobby confines. "Maybe we should finish this somewhere more private."

Scoggins posted his guards in front of the men's room door to make sure no one else entered. Caitlin waited until one final man exited, in the wake of a stall toilet flushing.

"Get in your way? I assure you, Ranger," Scoggins started, before she could resume, "I've done nothing of the kind. I have no idea what you're talking about."

"And I suppose you have no idea what the Order is, either."

The lieutenant governor just looked at her.

"Let me give you a hint, sir. It's an organization that fancies itself protectors of the Church and the pillars on which the Church was founded. Ring any bells?"

Scoggins remained silent.

"The Order is a remnant of the bad old days, of all the Church's conspiratorial, power-mad nonsense from centuries ago. You know what they say about the more things change.... So here we are. We traced a phone number, dialed by a man named Enrico Molinari, to you, sir. Molinari was the Order's top operative—or should I say assassin. But you already know that, don't you?"

"I'm afraid I don't," Scoggins said, trying to remain nonchalant, except for the sweat that had begun to bead up on his forehead. "And once I'm governor, I'm going to turn the Texas Rangers, relics that you are, into crossing guards."

"Oh, I'm actually not here for the Rangers today, sir. I'm here on behalf of Homeland Security."

That seemed to get Scoggins's attention.

"I've got a friend at Homeland," Caitlin continued, smiling inwardly at referring to Jones that way, "who's looking to reestablish his bona fides and who filled in a few holes for me about the Order's reach, purpose, and priorities. I'm guessing those changed a whole lot after they figured out they let the ultimate weapon slip through their hands a generation ago. Tell me, sir, how's it feel to watch it happen all over again, this time for good? You know what else is done for good? You."

"I've heard enough," Scoggins said, starting to reach for the door handle.

Caitlin slammed a hand against the door to prevent him from opening it.

Scoggins finally swiped the sweat from his forehead. "I'd think real hard about your next move, Ranger."

"I already have, sir. It's a shame, watching such a promising political career go down the drain, but it beats prison—so long as you give us the names to make your secret society not so secret anymore, especially the man at the top—the Prefect, or whatever it is you call him. I'm sure my friend at Homeland would really appreciate the gesture, maybe even enough to spare you from vacationing at Guantanamo for the next twenty years or so. The Order aren't the only ones who can make people disappear. How much did they have to do with your political career, exactly? Until today, you were about to walk into the governor's mansion. I'd fire them from your campaign if I were you."

"You're a real piece of work, Ranger."

"I want those names, sir. You have a pen or would you like to use mine?"

Scoggins shook his head in genuine disbelief. "All this because of a phone call?"

"A series of them, actually."

"And that's all you've got? That's your proof? I chair a committee on how unsecure cell phone technology today really is."

"Oh, sorry to have given you the wrong impression, sir. The phone calls I'm talking about weren't placed recently; they were placed twenty-five years ago." Caitlin held Scoggins's stare as she continued, "From a motel outside San Antonio."

His lower lip was trembling now.

"Turns out modern technology can work surprising wonders with old phone records, especially when the number called was a dummy exchange. Turns out the real number belonged to a cell phone back from the dinosaur days." Caitlin held his weakening stare again. "*Your* cell phone, sir."

Scoggins swallowed hard. His mouth started to open, then closed.

"Of course," Caitlin resumed, "the real giveaway was the number itself, that three-number prefix I figure you must've chosen yourself: four six three."

But she could tell, from the man's befuddled expression, that she had that part wrong.

"Check the keypad on your phone," she told Scoggins. "Four six three spells G-O-D."

EPILOGUE

In that rough rural terrain, no officer excelled like the Texas Ranger. He knew his prey and his territory, but tenacity was his greatest asset. Indeed, a Ranger's charge was to range the frontier: to cross city and county lines, to spend a week or a month or a year in pursuit of his quarry, to suppress lawlessness with any weapon at his disposal. It fell to other Texas officers to mingle with the public and wear starched uniforms. A Ranger was a Ranger because he was bred for the prairies and the backwoods. He personified the frontier and lived by its rough-hewn ethic. In the city he always seemed out of place. When Joaquin Jackson visited New York a few years back and toured the Harlem projects with the city vice squad, he believed he had stepped into Ranger hell. "I could never do what y'all do," Jackson told the city cops. A Ranger belonged in the wilderness. He was the earthiest of Texas lawmen, and yet there was always a little bit of the dreamer in every Ranger, for he lived the dream of the virtuous wanderer, slaying serpents in God's garden; every man who coveted Rangerhood sought his mythic place among the wanderers.

—"The Twilight of the Texas Rangers" by Robert Draper,
Texas Monthly, February 1994

"That wasn't so bad, was it?" Caitlin asked, rising from her chair in the waiting room when Cort Wesley returned.

"Not something I'd want to do every day," he said, scratching his arm where they had injected the contrast dye for the CT scan to read.

"Hey," she said, gaze tightening on him.

Cort Wesley looked down, realizing the ease with which he'd managed the simple motion. "I told you my arm was getting better. Just needed a good gunfight to wake it up again."

"Your father wasn't much older than you when he died, was he?"

"It was cancer that got him, Ranger, not a stroke."

"My point being that maybe it would have. I think you caught a break. We're talking genetics here."

"Something else I can blame my old man for."

They started walking toward the elevator, both eager to be gone from all the pain bouncing about the walls.

"When's your next appointment with the neurologist, Cort Wesley?"

"The office is supposed to call me when they get all the test results. But, like I told you, the doctor didn't seem to be too worried. He sees what I've got every day."

Caitlin nodded, looking away for a moment before fastening her gaze back on him. "It's okay to be scared."

He grinned. "Leroy said I should've told you about that."

"You didn't have to."

"I still can't hold a gun right, Ranger. I still can't make a fist tight enough to punch Jell-O."

"You think that's all you've got?"

"I think it's what I'm best at, and I don't know how much good I'd be to anybody else if I couldn't do it anymore. Hell, right now I can't even open a pickle jar."

"What did you tell Leroy?"

"That I was afraid of looking in the mirror and not recognizing the person who looks back."

Caitlin let him see her smile. "Every morning, when I do that, you know what I see? A woman who's got to overcome that fact every time she straps on a gun. I know it's not physical, not a stroke, but it's there, and it never goes away. And I find a way to get past it, because it's who I am." She tightened her gaze on him. "And when you look in the mirror, who you are is going to look back, even if your fist isn't as tight as it used to be."

Cort Wesley smiled too. "I told the doctor I want to live to be a hundred."

"What'd he say to that?"

"That if I beat this long enough, they could try a brain transplant."

"Come on," Caitlin scoffed.

"I'm serious. They're experimenting on rats."

"Glad I'm not a rat."

"Imagine waking up a different person, Ranger."

Caitlin smiled. "Seems like I do that every morning already. And by the way, Cort Wesley, I'd be glad to open that pickle jar for you."

The San Fernando Cathedral was packed for Father Boylston's funeral. Guillermo Paz had staked out a seat in the very last pew, one he had refinished himself a few years before, so as not to cause a stir for the other mourners. He was glad to see so many coming to pay their final respects to his priest, a fitting testament to a man who had been *their* priest, too. Until the stroke, Paz had spoken to Father Boylston only a few times outside the limits of the confessional, where he'd made his priest privy to his deepest, darkest secrets, which would have scared an ordinary man.

The organ music had just begun to play softly, when Caitlin Strong and Cort Wesley Masters took seats on either side of him. Paz exchanged glances with them both, his eyes saying all that needed to be said, as the priest presiding over the funeral mass took his place on the dais.

"*Many of those who sleep in the dust of the earth shall awake,*" he began, speaking into the microphone. "*Some shall live forever, others shall be an everlasting horror and disgrace.*"

"It's from Daniel," Paz whispered, over the soft, melodic hum of the organ. "One of my priest's favorites."

"*But the wise shall shine brightly like the splendor of the firmament,*" the priest continued, "*and those who lead the many to justice shall be like the stars forever.*"

"Well," Caitlin whispered back, reaching up to lay a hand on Paz's shoulder, "I think we can relate to that."

Author's Note

Well before I started *Strong as Steel*, I understandably had no idea what it was going to be about, but I knew it was going to be different than the last books in the Caitlin Strong series. That's because I'd gone from casting the Chinese as the bad guys (*Strong Darkness*) to the Russians (*Strong Light of Day*) to ISIS (*Strong Cold Dead*) to Nazis past and present (*Strong to the Bone*). Pretty tough to top all that, right?

I started thinking about casting Caitlin and company in a more traditional big-scale thriller, without having any idea what shape it was going to take. Then, lo and behold, I was Googling one thing, only to find something else—a headline—totally by accident:

BURIAL BOXES MARKED WITH JESUS' NAME REVEALED IN
JERUSALEM ARCHAEOLOGICAL WAREHOUSE

Sometimes, as they say, fortune really is the residue of design. I had found my McGuffin, as Alfred Hitchcock might call it, perfect fodder for a high-stakes thriller that centers on a secret unearthed somewhere in the Texas desert. Since this is the book's afterword, I'm not giving anything away when I say to you now where the whole concept of those ossuaries in *Strong as Steel*, and the bones allegedly contained in one of them, originated.

But I didn't want to do *The Da Vinci Code* again, nor did I want to suggest something as controversial as the bones of Jesus being found in the Texas desert. So, I asked myself, what might make the bones contained inside that particular ossuary just as dangerous to the world if discovered? And the answer brought me to the familiar ground of biotechnology—in this case, how the bubonic plague, aka the Black Death, could morph into something even deadlier than its original form, something that would make for a great weapon of mass destruction.

The first time I read *Strong as Steel* myself, as you just did, I found I couldn't put it down. It's been a long time since I opened a book with such an extended action scene, and I also liked the fact that Caitlin and Cort Wesley were pursuing the same thing along different tracks, as opposed to pursuing different things that happen to converge. The journey was different and, in this case, the destination also allowed me to have Caitlin and Cort Wesley (along with Guillermo Paz, of course) together in the end for a single climactic battle, instead of separating them amid multiple ones.

Did I pull all of that off? That's for you to judge. Writing a series that has now reached its tenth book reminds me of something Sam Goldwyn is purported to have said when he was asked what he was looking for in his next film: "Give me the same thing, only different."

Well, I try to give every Caitlin Strong book enough of the same thing, while making each one just different and distinct enough from all the others. Managing that task for ten books, though, only means I have to accomplish it again in the eleventh. I'm considering *Strong from the Heart* as a title. Same thing, only different.

ACKNOWLEDGMENTS

Stop me if you've heard this before, but let's start at the top with CEO Tom Doherty and Forge's publisher Linda Quinton, dear friends who publish books "the way they should be published," to quote my late agent, the legendary Toni Mendez. The great Bob Gleason, Karen Lovell, Elayne Becker, Patty Garcia, and especially Natalia Aponte are there for me at every turn. Natalia's a brilliant editor and friend who outdid herself in these pages, as always. Editing may be a lost art, but not here thanks to both Natalia and Bob Gleason, and I think you'll enjoy all of my books, including this one, much more as a result.

My friend Mike Blakely, a terrific writer and musician, taught me Texas firsthand and helped me think like a native of that great State. And Larry Thompson, a terrific writer in his own right, has joined the team as well to make sure I do justice to his home state, along with his son-in-law and soon-to-be Texas Ranger himself. And special acknowledgments to Bill Miller who helped me smooth out the geography of the Lone Star State, and "Steeldust" Jack Briggs for his expertise with all things firearm-related. Thanks, again, to Terry Ayers for making my scientific jargon sound at least somewhat credible, along with infectious disease expert Dr. Melanie Palmore, who I so miss seeing at Brown University football tailgates.

Check back at www.jonlandbooks.com for updates or to drop me a line, and please follow me on Twitter @jondland. I'd be remiss if I didn't thank all of you who've already written, Tweeted, or emailed me your thoughts on any or all of the first nine books in the Caitlin Strong series. You are truly the wind beneath this particular author's wings and I genuinely hope you enjoyed number ten as much as the others.